AND HELL
FOLLOWED
WITH HIM

ROBERT WISEHART

WOLFPACK
PUBLISHING
— EST 2013 —

And Hell Followed With Him

Paperback Edition
Copyright © 2021 (As Revised) Robert Wisehart

Wolfpack Publishing
5130 S. Fort Apache Road 215-380
Las Vegas, NV 89148

wolfpackpublishing.com

Paperback ISBN 978-1-64734-548-8
eBook ISBN 978-1-64734-570-9

AND HELL
FOLLOWED
WITH HIM

And I looked and behold a pale horse: and his name that sat on him was Death, and Hell followed with him.

-- Revelation 6:8

Prologue

I expect to die soon – any minute now is a strong possibility– but I have been saying that for at least ten years and here I still am.

No matter how you look at it, time is not on my side and I feel the strong need to get this down and finish the final task that I set before myself. The problem is that when you are ninety-three years of age and know that you must hurry you can't. On a good day I can write two or three pages before my hand starts to tremble so that I can't read the words I have written. On a bad day I sit here hour after hour and stare at nothing, overwhelmed by my own life.

My purpose is to bring justice to the best man I ever knew, but I fear that I have waited too long.

The attendants in this...place – that is another problem when you grow old; too often the right word will not come – all encourage me in this mission. Well, most of them.

I have it now. I am in a facility, or maybe an institution, in upstate New York. I forget exactly where, for the moment, and it doesn't really matter. It is one of those places where the world puts people who have lived too long and have no family to care for them.

It is not a bad place, all things considered, and I am happy enough. Fortunately, I have more than sufficient financial resources and was able to choose from among the possibilities. The facility is clean, the staff is kind, and the physicians seem competent.

The fact is that despite my age I am one of the healthy ones. My mind is sound, more or less, as are most of my teeth. I can still walk on my own and enjoy it, although a long stroll around the wooded grounds exhausts me. I see through spectacles, too, thick ones, although much of the world still is a cloudy place. I hear enough to get by and to hell with the rest of it.

I have fallen twice, and attendants came to rescue me once I was missed. I suspect that the day will come when I will not be missed in time. For my own safety, I have been advised not to stroll at all, but I will not take that advice. I would rather die outdoors than in bed.

Death does not frighten me. I lived so close to it for so long that it became a familiar neighborhood. Almost everyone I knew when I was young, and all who I loved are there now. Perhaps they are waiting for me. I would like that. But I have no answer to that great mystery. I will find out soon enough.

I suppose what got me started on all this was the death of Nelson Miles a few years back. Miles' story seems admirable, rising from lowly beginnings as a Boston crockery clerk before the Civil War to become commanding general of the United States Army some thirty years later. But I knew Miles as a man whose greatest talent was self-promotion, seizing credit he did not deserve, and climbing high on the backs of better men.

Mac and Miles were rivals, but more than that they detested each other. I am biased, but I believe that Miles mostly was at fault. A self-educated man who worked his way up the ranks, his background made him an outsider who resented the West Point officer class, consumed with ruthless determination to advance in what he saw as a hostile world. He could be an officer of daring and imagination. His peers wanted to like him. He made it impossible. It wasn't enough for Nelson Miles to rise, he had to bring down anyone he perceived as a rival.

Scandal and controversy dogged Miles but never damaged him. After the war, he was the commandant at Fort Monroe, where Confederate President Jefferson Davis was held while the government figured out what to do with him. Although Davis was eventually released, playing the lickspittle to powerful Congressmen who wanted him either shot or hanged, Miles treated his prisoner so badly it wouldn't be a stretch to call it abuse. During the Nez Perce War, Miles drove his troops across Montana to intercept the exhausted band of Indians trying to escape to Canada after General Oliver Howard pursued them for almost a thousand miles. Howard did the hard work, but Miles captured the headlines, arriving just in time for the kill and dismissing Howard's role as minor. Howard never spoke to Miles again. In Arizona, Miles was outfoxed by Geronimo's small band of marauders until Lieutenant Charles Gatewood and a handful of men hunted down Geronimo and negotiated preliminary terms so that the Apache finally surrendered. Miles claimed that Gatewood played a minor role and then had the lieutenant transferred to obscurity in Dakota Territory. Among the Apache exiled to Florida were friendly Apache who worked as army scouts. Once they served their purpose, Miles had no use for them.

He finally did the decent thing and died in 1925. As I recall, he was eight years younger than I am now. I wasn't trapped in this *facility* yet, a hostage to time. A year later, I paid to be transported from my comfortable townhouse on a fine shady street in New York City to Arlington National Cemetery, not far from that den of rascals known as Washington, DC. I asked to be left alone at Miles' grave, as if to pay homage to an old comrade. Instead, I spent my time gloating. There's a lot to be said for outliving people you don't like.

Miles' death brought forth all sorts of effusions from the newspapers, all of them nattering about his "epic" career in every conflict from the Civil War through the Indian Wars and the Spanish American War.

In 1917, the old fool even volunteered for service in Europe. The "war to end war" they called it. Fat chance. People will always find something to fight about, even if it makes no sense. President Wilson had the good judgment to turn him down, just as Miles knew he would. Miles was in his late 70s, for God's sake! It was a final attention seeking gesture by a man who couldn't stand being out of the spotlight, even as a toothless dotard.

Maybe the root of my dislike is that Miles got everything that should have gone to Mac. I can't help but compare the outpouring about Miles to the few words that marked Mac's death so long ago. The only mention I saw was in the New York Times, buried in the middle of a page with all the other anonymous obituaries. I kept a copy, although I don't know why. It enrages me every time I read it, all yellow and brittle with age.

MACKENZIE. At New Brighton, on the 19th of January, Brig.- Gen. RANALD SLIDELL MACKENZIE, United States Army, in the 48th year of his age

And that was it, damn them all to hell.

This is Mac's story, but it is my story, too. We were so closely linked for so long how could it be otherwise?

I will try to explain how it was, what we did, and why the name of Ranald MacKenzie is worth remembering.

Chapter One

Of course, I was nervous. How could I not be?

What did Ulysses S. Grant, who was now facing Robert E. Lee in what promised to be the last great bloody spasm of a bloody war, want with me, a newly minted captain of not quite twenty-four years of age?

Naturally, I expected the worst. What that might be I didn't know. It was one of many things I didn't know, including the terrible reality that the war still had a year to go, with astonishing slaughter on both sides yet to come.

They say it was necessary to forge the nation that we are today. Perhaps it was but tell that to the dead.

I approached the command tent. I identified myself and told the guard that I was ordered to report to General Grant. I was announced. I was told to enter. I did. I saluted like hell.

And there he sat; the great man himself.

I saw him many times before, but always on horseback and never this close: Scruffy brown beard, even scruffier uniform with the stars of a lieutenant general on his shoulders the only insignia of rank, and the usual cigar at the corner of his mouth, unlit, for the moment.

At that time, Grant was only the third lieutenant general in the country's history. The other two were George Washington and Winfield Scott. Good company.

Ulysses Grant was a smallish man who seemed content with it. Sitting on a camp stool behind a portable campaign desk covered with paper, he seemed even smaller. He didn't huff and puff to appear to be something that he wasn't or call attention to himself. When he put his mind to it, Georgie Custer probably displayed more gold on one uniform than Grant wore his entire life.

To most of us, it was significant that Grant's headquarters was in a simple tent devoid of fuss or pomp, smack in the middle of camp. He wasn't one of us, exactly. How could he be? But he was with us and we were proud of it. While George Meade officially commanded the Army of the Potomac, as his superior, Grant commanded every Union soldier in the country, and we knew who really gave the orders.

After being so badly led for so long, we all were pleased and proud to finally serve under a general who knew what the hell he was doing. Grant was a much-appreciated improvement over his predecessors. The parade of infamy and incompetence that came before him is firm in my memory even now.

Grant took the cigar out of his mouth and motioned with it. "Take a seat, Captain Stone."

I looked around and saw no place to do that unless the general expected me to sit on the ground. Apparently so did Grant, who nodded at someone behind me.

"John, do you mind?"

I realized that we were not alone. General John Rawlins, Grant's crony from Galena, Illinois, and fierce protector of the general's person, was behind me, sitting on one stool with his feet propped up on another, ankles crossed.

With a look making it clear that he barely tolerated my lowly presence, Rawlins hoisted his polished boots off the stool, hooked one foot beneath it, and flipped it in my direction. I put it on the ground and sat as directed.

As far as anyone could tell, John Rawlins' only mission was to tend to his old friend, see to his needs, and keep him from drinking, which, by reputation, Grant knew how to do. Serving in the northwest after the Mexican War in the late '40s, it was common knowledge that Grant was almost cashiered for drunkenness. In a rare show of good sense, the army allowed him to resign instead.

Getting back into service after the Rebs took Fort Sumter, if you believed the gossip, Grant tumbled off the wagon more than a few times while whipping the Rebs at Fort Donaldson, Shiloh, Vicksburg, and everywhere else he met them in the west. If Rawlins made a success of his assignment, and so far, he had, that alone might make him the most valuable man in the army.

"Cigar?" Grant asked.

It took a moment before I realized that the offer was to me.

"No, thank you, sir. I never acquired the habit."

Why did I say that? Ulysses Grant didn't give a damn about my habits, acquired or not. Curb your tongue, fool!

"I have habit enough for the both of us, I 'spose," Grant gazed at his stogie like he was puzzled to find it between his fingers. "Fifteen to twenty a day, most times. After Vicksburg, word got out that I was fond of cigars, and people sent me dozens of boxes, maybe hundreds. They still do. Got me hooked even more than I already was. They come in faster than I can give 'em away."

No one suspected that all those cigars would eventually kill the man. There was a lot we didn't know then.

Grant scratched a match into flame with his thumbnail, applied the flame to his cigar, and got it drawing to his satisfaction.

"Captain, I brought you here because I want to talk about another officer. I understand that he is a good friend of yours; Major Ranald MacKenzie."

Seeing the puzzled look on my face, Grant raised his hand, the one without the cigar.

"There is nothing ill-meant in this, I promise you," he said. "From what I have heard, MacKenzie is one of the most promising young officers in the army. I have something in mind for him, but I don't want my judgment to be misplaced, if you take my meaning. I want to find out everything I can about him, the kind of detail that dry reports and cautious comments from his superiors can't tell me. If MacKenzie is all that he is supposed to be, he will be one of those tending to this army of ours long after I am gone. I just want to be sure of myself. There is damn little else I can be sure of these days."

The general's speech didn't seem to require a response, so I didn't give one.

When I didn't, he poked me.

"You've known him a long time?"

"Since we were boys, sir, almost as far back as either one of us can remember. His folks more or less adopted me."

"How did that come about?"

I could not figure where this was going, but there was no choice but to answer.

"My Ma died in childbirth, my birth. My Pa was in, uh, business. He was on the way to New Orleans to see a, um, associate when his ship got caught in a hurricane and went down off the Florida coast. I was an only child, five years of age with no living family. Mac's folks – uh, Major MacKenzie's folks, I mean – took me into their home and treated me like a son."

I hesitated and stumbled the way I did because much of my background, while not exactly secret, was not well known either. I preferred to keep it that way.

When my penniless grandfather arrived in New York City from Austria his name was Gregor Stanislovsky. As happened with many immigrants, when he entered the country his name challenged the patience and spelling skills of an overworked government clerk who took it upon himself to change Gregor Stanislovsky to George Stein, take it or leave it and welcome to America.

A tailor in Austria, grandfather soon found work in the same line and made a go of it, a respected craftsman who eventually opened his own shop for high-class clientele to considerable success.

But his son, who was also my father, wanted nothing to do with the hum-drum life of a tailor. After several false starts, he went into business for himself, buying and selling anything he could anywhere he could before he started loaning money for short terms at high rates. He called himself a "financier", a new word at the time.

Early on, I never knew exactly when he changed his name to Stone. It was solid, he said, a name to be relied on, even if it wasn't his. Grandfather didn't mind. He always said that he never felt like a Stein, whatever than meant.

The other reason for the change was that prejudice against immigrants, especially Jews, was common then just as it is common now, in the army and everywhere else. I have never been a religious man and haven't gone to synagogue since I was a boy. People can worship what they want as long as they don't bother me with it. My birth name is Daniel David Stone, and there was no good reason why anyone else, even Ulysses Grant, should know the rest of the story.

"MacKenzie comes from a prominent family, I understand," Grant said, gently urging me along. He probably figured that at the rate I was going, the war would be over before I finished.

"Yes, sir, he does. There is a northern branch and a southern branch, both of them prominent, as you say. His uncle, John Slidell, was senator from Louisiana and then ambassador to Mexico during the Polk administration. Slidell, Louisiana, is named after him. It is part of family lore that he helped win the close election for Polk by giving him Plaquemines Parish, down near New Orleans, which was enough to give Polk the state."

I did not mention that, according to more family lore, Slidell accomplished the deed by putting a hundred or more voters and plenty of liquor on a river boat, then transporting both from one end of the parish to the other and back again, illegally casting ballots everywhere the boat stopped. If local authorities were inclined to protest, the dozen armed bully boys on board put a stop to it. As the gaggle of crooks at New York's Tammany Hall say, a sure way to win an election is to get your people to vote early and vote often.

"And now John Slidell is a high-ranking diplomat for the Confederacy, an important man among the traitors," interrupted Rawlins with a voice that sounded like gravel being ground underfoot. "Does that ever pose a problem for young MacKenzie?"

Feeling like I was taking fire from front and rear, I swiveled to face Rawlins.

"Not at all, sir. He barely knows his uncle and he is hardly the only one with a divided family in this war. I believe that his record speaks for itself."

Facing Grant again, I warmed to the subject.

"Another uncle was chief justice of the state Supreme Court in Louisiana and his grandfather was a prominent New York City banker. Mac's father – I'm sorry, sir, I mean Major MacKenzie's father – was a navy commodore, Alexander Slidell MacKenzie, at a time when commodore was the navy's highest rank. He was a well-known author, too. We were too young to know it then, but his book *A Year in Spain* was very popular. He also wrote biographies of Commodore Oliver Perry, Stephen Decatur, and John Paul Jones. I remember Washington Irving and Henry Longfellow coming to the house, though I was too young to know who they were."

Now I had gone from curbing my tongue to babbling like a fool. Get hold of yourself, Stone!

Grant blew a cloud of smoke into the air, where it hovered under the tent's low canvas ceiling.

"Feel free to call him Mac, if it makes you more comfortable," he said. "He *is* your friend after all." He nodded at Rawlins. "You should hear some of the things that man calls me."

"MacKenzie's father ran into a bit of trouble, didn't he?" Rawlins asked. "I particularly recall one incident where it seems that he didn't think things through before acting."

"I wouldn't put it that way, sir, although I think I know what you refer to," I said. "During the commodore's command of the *Somers,* in the Atlantic near West Africa a troublemaker tried to incite the rest of the crew to mutiny. As I understand it, he intended to take over the ship and turn pirate. The commodore ordered that man and two others arrested. The *Somers* was a small ship, too small to have a brig. They were far out at sea and not scheduled to return home for months. Drastic steps seemed necessary to keep the conspiracy from spreading, so he decided to hang all three of the plot leaders."

"Yes, I remember it well," Rawlins said. "It was rashly done, I'd say. The *troublemaker* you refer to was Philip Spencer, who just happened to be the Secretary of War's son. When he learned that his only son died dangling from the yardarm, or whatever they dangle from when the navy hangs a man without benefit of trial or hearing, John Spencer did everything within his power to get revenge, which included the commodore's head on a platter. All things considered, perhaps Commodore MacKenzie should have showed a bit more restraint?"

"A naval inquiry ruled otherwise, sir," I replied. "And you will remember that the commodore went on to serve with great distinction during the Mexican War."

"He was acquitted, yes, but still under a shadow," grumbled Rawlins, who would not be denied.

"I seem to remember that MacKenzie's father passed," Grant said, offering a merciful interruption.

"Yes, sir. He returned from the Mexican War in poor health, took medical leave and went back to New York to recuperate. The family was living on a farm near Tarrytown when he died. The commodore's daily routine included going on long rides by himself in the afternoon. He found it restorative. On the day he died, I remember opening the gate and watching him reach down to ruffle Mac's hair before he galloped away. When the horse returned alone a while later, a search party found him a couple of miles away. They said his heart gave out."

"How did MacKenzie take it?" Grant asked.

"How does any eight-year-old boy take it when the father he loves suddenly dies?"

"Tell me, Captain, how did you *both* get into the academy at the same time?" Grant asked, smiling around his cigar. "Do I sense some pulled strings by that influential family of his?"

Abrupt as it was, I appreciated the change of subject and gave a loud harrumph as I cleared my throat.

"As you say, sir, in those days Mac's family was influential in certain areas, although I am afraid that influence is somewhat diminished with the passing of time. He always wanted to go to West Point, and I go where Mac goes. As you know, only one academy nominee is allowed per congressional district, so my official residence had to be changed to keep us from residing in the same place. It wasn't difficult to work out the details. With no family or resources of my own, the free education was an inducement, too."

"Don't ever be ashamed of that, Captain," Grant said. "A free education was one of my own motivators. MacKenzie finished at the top of his class, didn't he?"

"Yes, sir."

"And you?"

"Fourth, sir."

Grant stared at me for what seemed like a half hour, though it could not have been more than a few seconds, smoke curling up from the cigar in his hand. It appeared that he was considering his next question, and I had the feeling I would not like it.

"Captain, there are rumors that MacKenzie fought a duel at the academy, where dueling is strictly forbidden and the penalty is expulsion," he said. "Risky behavior, I'd say. Would you happen to know anything about it?"

I knew everything about it. And I wasn't going to say a word, certainly not to Grant.

For no apparent reason, an oafish Indiana cadet named Abel Costigan took a dislike to Mac and started razzing him about his relationship with a young lady from a nearby village. We all rode each other, of course, sometimes a little too hard. What group of young men does not? But Costigan laid it on without mercy. The fool didn't know when to shut up.

Despite our friendship, I did not know if Mac really had such a relationship. I'm damned if I know how he would have pulled it off, although I'm sure he would have found a way. He could always keep a secret. I did know that he was not going to take Costigan's insults for very long.

Costigan had a reputation as one of the best swordsmen at the academy. While Mac was good with a cavalry saber on horseback, he was indifferent with a blade when his feet were on the ground. When Mac finally responded to the insufferable insults with a hard punch that bloodied Costigan's big nose, to the surprise of no one the Indiana cadet chose rapiers as their dueling weapon.

With the location up to Mac, you could have knocked his opponent, along with the rest of us, over with a hummingbird's breath when he picked a darkened room. The macabre setting was a clever choice because it negated Costigan's superior skill. Some of the cadets thought it too clever by half and less than honorable. I doubt that Mac cared. I certainly didn't.

We didn't want the duelists stumbling over furniture in the dark, so in the middle of the night we quietly moved all of the furniture out of my room and into the room next door. If we were lucky, the authorities would not discover what was going on and expel us all. Costigan's second anxiously waited outside the room with me while two other cadets kept watch downstairs.

Rapiers in hand, the two men entered the room, and the door was shut. After several minutes of agonizing silence, we heard Costigan scream, "Open the door! Open the door!" When we did, he burst out of the room into the hallway, red-faced and so overcome that he was practically weeping. The humiliated cadet threw his rapier to the floor and ran down the stairs to his room.

When Mac coolly emerged a moment later, we demanded to know what happened.

"Nothing," he said with a shrug.

We did not believe that for an instant and pushed him to tell what really went on.

"That's the truth," he said, handing the rapier to me to put away. I had filched the weapons from the armory, yet another infraction with expulsion as the penalty. It wasn't until that moment I noticed that Mac's hand was shaking.

"In the darkness, as fast as I could without making a sound, I felt my way to a corner and stayed there. I figured Costigan for a high-strung sort who is brave when he has the advantage but wouldn't like dueling in a dark room with an opponent he couldn't see. I wanted his nerves to work for me."

Mac offered a relieved grin. "Not that I was fond of it myself. It was pitch black in there. I couldn't see a thing.

"After a moment or two, though it seemed much longer, he began to slash this way and that. I heard his weapon flailing in the air. When he finally stopped, I heard him breathing, too, long sobbing breaths that told me my plan was working. The man was close to panic already. The next thing I knew, he was screaming for someone to open the door. We couldn't see it in the darkness."

It was a good thing the duel ended without bloodshed. Young blockheads that we were, we never considered how we would explain a rapier wound suffered by one of the duelists, or worse, a death.

Of course, I revealed none of this to General Grant.

"As you said, sir, dueling is strictly forbidden at the academy. If such a thing occurred, I am sure I would have known about it."

It was not a lie, exactly; such a thing did occur, and I did know about it.

The general's eyes narrowed. It was obvious that he did not believe me, and I feared what might come next, but he let the subject drop. Behind me, Rawlins erupted with a skeptical snort, but following Grant's lead, said nothing more.

"What did you mean when you said where he goes, you go?" Grant asked.

"Just that, sir. It's always been that way."

"That takes some work, Captain. It's a difficult thing to arrange in the army or anywhere else, for that matter," Rawlins said, launching another flank attack. "Living in another man's shadow can be a detriment to your own career, too. Doesn't that bother you?"

I thought that a strange comment coming from Rawlins, considering what he did for most of the past two or three years.

But maybe it was not so strange. If anyone understood, it might be him.

"I can only tell you that we have always managed it, sir. Besides, I don't think of it that way. I do well enough for myself. My record is not without merit."

"Don't be modest, Captain; your record is excellent, one of our best." Grant shuffled through some papers on the desk until he found the right one. "I see here that MacKenzie's been wounded several times."

"Five times, sir. He has seen a lot of action. We both have: Second Manassas, Fredericksburg, Chancellorsville, and Gettysburg, among other engagements."

"How serious?"

"Two of note, though I suppose they are all notable when it's you who gets shot. He was hit in the back by a sniper, his first wound just a few weeks after we joined the army. And he was struck in the right hand by a shell fragment and lost his first two fingers. There was a lot of scarring, too. Let me assure you that the wounds do *not* inhibit him in any way."

Although there were five wounds, three were major wounds, not two, as I told Grant. Mac was also shot through his lung. While he seemed fully recovered, I knew that it still bothered him. With too much exertion, his breath became labored, and it sapped his strength, although he hid it well and talked the doctor into reporting it as a minor chest wound with a complete recovery.

"Five times wounded? You only graduated from the academy in, what, '62? Is the man reckless, then?" Rawlins asked. "Is he the sort of officer who deliberately puts himself and his men in danger? I have known too many such glory-seeking fools. Bravery without purpose or reason is mere stupidity."

"Absolutely not...*sir.*"

If Rawlins was trying to get under my skin, he succeeded admirably. I deliberately inserted the pause and emphasis on "sir" to show the gimlet-eyed bastard that I had enough of his insulting my friend and his family. I would not take that, not even from a general. Mac would have advised me to ignore it, but I never possessed his self-control, and never really wanted it. It's better to let off a little steam occasionally.

"What Mac does is lead, as a good officer should. He won't *heroically* wave his sword from the rear while his men get bloodied. He will never say, 'You men take that hill.' He'll say, 'We will take that hill' and then he'll lead the charge."

Grant again. "You are both young men with all the pride of young men. You have not yet learned that sometimes an officer, especially a senior officer, can be more valuable if he does *not* lead in that way. It would have done our cause a world of good if Bobby Lee got himself killed foolishly leading his men into battle early in the war instead of figuring out how to whip practically every Union general set before him."

"Until now," Rawlins said.

"You're damn right until now!"

I could see Grant's jaw working as he clamped down on his already well-chewed cigar. Apparently, Rawlins struck a tender spot.

"It's about time Lee started worrying about what *we're* going to do instead of us always fretting about *his* next move. The way people talk, one of these days he's going to turn a double somersault and land at our rear and both of our flanks at the same time."

"I fully agree, sir," I said, as if I had a choice. "And I'm sure Mac will know when that time comes. As will I. After all, we are not generals, yet."

Grant grinned around his cigar again, showing stained teeth. "Not generals *yet*. I like that. I like that very much. It seems like a good note to end on."

Instead of dismissing me with a salute, to my surprise he rose from the camp stool to see me out with one hand on my shoulder.

"Thank you, Captain Stone. You have done much to form my thoughts. I am sure that no order I give would keep you from telling your friend about this conversation, and I would not want to put you in a position where you had to either disobey an order or lie to your friend. However, I would appreciate it if you would keep this between the two of you until certain action is taken. It won't be long."

I snapped off a salute to both generals and turned to leave, but Grant stopped me halfway out of the tent.

"And, Captain, Major MacKenzie is fortunate to have you as a friend. I hope he knows that."

Chapter Two

"Grant said *that?*"

Although he liked to appear otherwise, Ranald MacKenzie deeply cared about what people thought of him. He also possessed his share of vanity. I may have been the only one who knew how he constantly measured himself against others, including his long-dead father.

When I told him about my strange conversation with Grant and Rawlins, he looked half dazed.

"Danny, what do you think the old man's planning?"

"Exactly what he said," I replied as if I knew what I was talking about. "Grant doesn't strike me as a man who wastes anything, including words. He has something in mind for you and it won't be easy, or he wouldn't take so much care with it."

Another long day was done. It was late and we were ravenous, gobbling a meal by the flickering light of the small fire near the tent we shared. We rose before dawn, as usual, and our duties took us in separate directions. Neither of us had eaten since breakfast, and bad as it was, the army meal disappeared quickly.

"Do you ever wonder how much salt pork and hardtack we've eaten since we got out of the academy?" As usual, I chewed until my jaws ached in a vain effort to soften the hardtack. "Even after soaking it in coffee, it's like eating a pine board."

A smile flickered across Mac's face. In all the years I knew him, I don't think I ever saw him really cut loose with a laugh, even as a boy. For him, a quiet chuckle was practically the same as another man overcome by hilarity and rolling on the ground.

"It's still better than most anything they fed us back then." He speared a chunk of salt pork with his knife and contemplated it like Yorick's skull in *Macbeth*. "Practically everything is an improvement over life at the academy, except that nobody was trying to blow our heads off, at least not that we knew."

"You know, maybe that's what they intended all along, to make life there so wretched that *this*"—I waved my hand to take in the massive camp of more than a hundred thousand mostly sleeping men—"seems so much better."

"If that's true, then I'd say they did a fine job," Mac said.

* * *

I don't know if West Point is still that way. It has been more than seventy years since we graduated, and unlike most cadets I never went back, with the sad exception of one funeral. Since the place did everything to shape us into the men we became, perhaps I should tell you something of life there.

We entered the academy in 1858. Except for rare breaks of a few days, we did not leave it in four years. It was there that we learned the importance of institutional discipline combined with what I can only describe as selective disobedience. We also learned to regard fellow cadets – later fellow officers – as competitors in the race for promotion *and* as brethren.

In short, we were supposed to honor and sacrifice for each other and at the same time beat each other's brains out. To my surprise, it was not that difficult.

We also learned civil engineering, which never did me much good except for a few dull months building pontoon bridges early in the war. We learned, or at least studied, mathematics, which I grew to detest, a smattering of French and Spanish, a lot of technical jargon, which always impressed outsiders, a little about strategy, which came in handy, and almost nothing about tactics, which we learned in the field if we learned it at all, mostly that an officer must be adaptable because all grand plans go to hell in a hurry. There were bits and pieces of other subjects, too, a few of which I enjoyed.

Standards were brutally high. Less than half of those who entered West Point went on to graduate. Most of those who did not make it were casualties of demerits or academics. A few couldn't take the life, including one suicide in our class. We found him in bed after he cut his wrists open. His room was filled within twenty-four hours.

Yes, it was that cold blooded.

Any cadet who received more than one hundred demerits in a six-month period was automatically dismissed, and believe me, demerits were easy to come by. While Mac and I earned our share, we never came close to dismissal because we knew what we could get away with, at least most of the time. Too many of our peers never figured that out and went on to become by-the-book officers devoid of original thought. Mac and I were never the worst, but we were far from the best when it came to "proper" cadet decorum as the academy tried to forge us into some wretched ideal of a good Christian soldier, whatever that meant.

Grades were posted weekly to foster competition while, our daily lives were regulated in every way possible. Our rooms were freezing in winter and stifling in summer. The food was terrible and the clothes uncomfortable. Genuine intelligence was appreciated, but not necessary for success. Creativity was regarded as troublesome.

Our only time off was a few hours on Sunday afternoon, but there was nothing to do. Debating clubs were the only voluntary organizations and we were not allowed to debate political questions lest passions run too high. Cadets could subscribe to one periodical per month, but only after it was approved by the administration, which meant that it was not worth subscribing to. The boredom of routine was soul-crushing, but routine was almost all there was.

Somehow all this was supposed to instill the values of duty, loyalty, honor and courage. That it did to some degree still astounds me, although I have come to believe that what it really did was polish those qualities if you had them anyway, which may have been the goal all along.

Liquor was forbidden, as were playing cards, chess, gambling, tobacco, cooking utensils in the room, games of any sort, going off post, bathing in the Hudson River, and playing a musical instrument. We were allowed only a few personal items and each of those had to be in their assigned places at all times.

The rooms were available for inspection at any moment, night or day. The furniture consisted of an iron bedstead, a table, a straight-backed chair, a lamp, a mirror, a mattress, a blanket, a washstand, and a small armoire for our clothes. Unapproved items were confiscated and earned piles of demerits.

Even the West Point uniform was painful; the shoes were heavy and clumsy and the pantaloons too tight for comfort. The coat, with its three rows of eight yellow brass buttons, inspired a popular verse handed down from class to class: *"Your coat is made, you button it, give one spasmodic cough, and you do not draw another breath until you take it off."*

The academy even turned headwear into a trial. Every cadet wore a bell-crowned black leather cap – seven inches high with a polished leather visor and an eight-inch black plume. It weighed an astonishing five pounds and felt like an anvil on top of your head.

I remember Mac once lying full-length on the floor of his room to study – a time-honored way to keep the press in the uniform – and then receiving demerits for having a spec of dirt on his pantaloons, which was discovered by an upperclassman with a magnifying glass and a hostile attitude.

Demerits meant punishment tours, usually four hours of silent marching back and forth in full uniform while carrying a rifle. On Sunday there was more marching followed by another kind of punishment, this time in chapel where we sat ramrod straight on hard wooden benches and listened to a two-hour sermon from an ancient bag of gas who made me want to make a deal with the devil.

Even if we wanted to sin, and believe me, we all did, there was damn little opportunity. Not in that scholastic monastery.

Bad as it was, the food might have been the worst – four years of boiled potatoes, boiled meat or fish, boiled pudding, bread long past its prime, and coffee that could take the rust off a sword. Even now, I shiver to think about it. Since then, I have never been able to eat fish, no matter how it's prepared. I would rather go hungry.

Although we were young men in the prime of life, most of us dreamed more about food than women. We were so desperate for something decent to eat that we took absurd risks to get it.

After weeks of planning that rivaled a Napoleonic campaign in attention to detail, one moonless night I stole a rooster from the officers' chicken coop. I wrung its neck, plucked it, scattered the feathers so they could not be traced to me, and cooked it in the small fireplace in my room.

When a surprise inspection early the next morning discovered my cooking utensils, I received a bombardment of demerits and drill. Fortunately, I disposed of the chicken bones so that no one could prove that I had stolen, cooked and eaten anything, although everyone knew that I did. If I were discovered raiding the chicken coop, I would have been dismissed from the academy.

It was worth it. I never ate a finer meal.

We formed lifelong friendships and rivalries, often with the same people, and we were all treated the same, no matter our background. Our class included a Washington from Virginia, a Buchanan from Pennsylvania closely related to the fifteenth president, and a Du Pont from Delaware. We were paid thirty dollars a month but never saw a penny because every cent went to the commissary for razors, clothes, mirrors and other overpriced essentials. We were forbidden to receive money from home. Despite his family's wealth, Henry Du Pont did not leave the post for two years because he was in debt to the commissary the entire time.

According to the honor code, we could not lie, steal, or cheat, but if necessary, we did all three and did not hesitate for a second. I did not turn myself in when I cooked my chicken, although the honor code demanded it. That would have been idiocy, and everyone knew it. Although rumors abounded, as far as I knew no one said a word about Mac's bizarre duel. I never saw anyone turn himself in for anything. Although we heard of it, it was always in some other class long before us, lost in the realm of myth and legend.

Since those days, I have sometimes wondered if all that wasn't the academy's way of fostering original thinking: how to get around and over the obstacles placed before us. If so, it was excellent preparation for war.

When a cadet managed to sneak off to Benny Haven's, a local tavern that employed a few *available* young and not so young ladies along with brain-busting alcohol at a reasonable price, the other cadets admired his daring. Most of us did it at least once, some of us several times.

We learned to always cover for your friends, which was as valuable a lesson as I ever had.

That's what I call *esprit*.

Nearly all our learning was by rote. Imagination was like an unused muscle. You figured out what the instructors wanted and gave it to them. I once wrote a much-praised essay for ethics class titled "The Elements of Ideal Moral Perfection" without believing a word of such claptrap.

Probably because we were so isolated from the world and dependent on each other, cadets from north and south got along well, although almost to a man the southerners left for their homes when the war started, including several friends I did not see again until Appomattox more than four years later.

Before the fighting began, most of us, including the faculty, naively assumed that the war would consist of one huge battle, with the winner triumphantly marching to capture the opposing capital. When that did not happen, as the days and months passed, we feared that the war would end before we graduated and had a chance to become heroes. How little we knew.

Before the war, army promotion was so slow that after a few years, many of the best officers despaired of their future and left the service. Under ordinary circumstances, even with an excellent record an academy graduate could expect to be a second lieutenant for at least five years and first lieutenant for ten more. If he was lucky, he might make captain before he turned forty. If not, he probably ended his career as an aged lieutenant.

The war changed all that. After the Southerners left, a few of the Northern cadets resigned, too, and returned to their states. Thanks to their academy training, they became captains, majors or even lieutenant colonels in their state militia.

Most stayed on as Mac and I did. We graduated, received regular army commissions as second lieutenants and hoped for a combat assignment because that was where promotion came fastest as senior officers were killed, injured, or revealed to be incompetent, and those below promoted to replace them.

The war brought opportunity at every hand and we were all determined to take advantage of it, even at the risk of our ignorant young lives. I am not exaggerating when I say that every one of us possessed an unquenchable thirst for glory. Some were more obvious about it than others, but it was always there. Everyone caught the fever.

The old saying that "the paths of glory lead but to the grave" may be true, but those same paths also lead to promotion, medals, and the chance to make a reputation.

Yes, we were idealistic fools. But we were young, and that was expected. The army counted on it.

Chapter Three

Once I told Mac about my mysterious meeting with Grant and Rawlins, the only thing we could do was to wait and see what happened next.

The following day, it did. Mac received orders to report to Brigadier General Emery Upton, who commanded the Second Brigade of the First Division of Sixth Corps. Thanks to my warning, Mac was prepared as much as possible. He knew something was about to happen, even if he did not know what, and that all the signs were good.

He told me about it later. We told each other everything. Until the end.

* * *

"Take a seat, McKenzie."

Mac did and Upton explained his summons.

"I am pleased to inform you that you have been promoted." Upton rose to his feet and offered his hand. "May I be the first to offer congratulations, Colonel MacKenzie. I don't know of anyone in this army who deserves it more."

In case you are wondering, a jump of two ranks was unusual, but not unheard of, in those days. If the Rebs did not kill or maim you, camp sickness often did, regardless of rank. There were more openings to fill than good officers to fill them, one reason why the army had so many incompetent officers.

Returning to his camp stool in the spacious but stifling tent, Upton continued, "That was the good news. Now we come to the perhaps not so good. You are to command the 2nd Connecticut. I assume you know it?"

While Mac was not disappointed – promotion is never disappointing, especially a leap of two ranks – he was not thrilled either. The 2nd Connecticut was a well-known disaster, the worst regiment in the army.

"I know *of* it, sir," Mac said.

The 2nd Connecticut was a volunteer regiment, mostly used as a source of bodies shoveled toward the enemy guns in hopes of overwhelming by sheer numbers. Its first two commanding officers were killed in battle, although it was rumored that the second was a vicious martinet shot by his own men who hated the army and the officers who used them so badly. The attempt to name a third failed when the candidate resigned rather than accept the promotion.

"The regiment is out of control," Upton admitted. "Hard discipline and genuine leadership are what's needed to bring it in line if it isn't already too late. It's a symbol of everything that was wrong with this army before Grant took over."

"Instead of dispersing the men to other regiments, we believe that if we can turn it into an effective unit it will become a symbol of a better kind. The problem is that it will have to be done quickly. I doubt that you will have more than a few weeks before Grant finishes reorganizing and launches his offensive. If the regiment is not ready, I will have to break it up."

"And I will have failed at my first command, and my career, such as it is, will be all but over," Mac said.

A long stare from Upton: "Something like that. You can always refuse the assignment. I doubt that anyone of reasonable mind would hold it against you."

Mac could do no such thing and Upton knew it. He wouldn't even if he could. There wasn't anything he could say except what he said: "I understand, sir. And of course, I gratefully accept."

"You will need a capable second, a man you can trust without question. Any thoughts?"

That took Mac back a bit. It was army largesse on a greater scale than he ever experienced.

"I would like Captain Stone, if the appropriate promotion can be arranged."

Upton nodded. "I thought you might say that. I know how close you are. Some of the officers will grouse about *both* of you being promoted so high so quickly, but I'll take care of it."

And just like that, I became a lieutenant colonel; two jumps in rank for me, too.

"Anything else?"

When Mac didn't reply, Upton pushed harder.

"Dammit, man! Ask for something. You may never have this chance again. The worst that can happen is that I'll say no, or that it can't be done even if I want to do it. But I'll support you in any way I can."

Steepling his fingers, at least those he had left, in front of his chin, Mac considered the offer.

"As you know, sir, it's the sergeants who run this army," he said. "A good sergeant is the linchpin that holds everything together, just as a bad sergeant can ruin everything."

"That's true enough, though most generals I know wouldn't

admit it," Upton said. "We like to think we are more important than we really are."

"Well, sir, I would like at least two who I know and can count on. If I am to do this the way it needs to be done, I need the proper tools."

"I assume you have two in mind."

"Callahan and Gomez. You may be acquainted with them, sir."

"Indeed, I am," Upton said. "Their officers will squeal like stuck pigs if I take them away. They may be unorthodox, and Callahan too fond of the bottle, but they get the job done."

Upton drummed his fingers on his knee, thinking it over.

"All right, MacKenzie, you have them. What else?"

"There may be some requests regarding supply, depending on what I find when I assume command. But there is nothing else I can think of for the present, sir."

Upton rose to his feet and extended his hand again. "Very well, Colonel MacKenzie. I wish you luck. You'll need it."

Chapter Four

A meeting of senior officers was scheduled that afternoon, the first since Grant took command. To our surprise, Upton wanted us to accompany him.

As we rode three abreast to the meeting place in a small stand of trees, Upton explained, "I'm sure it would be all right if you two lingered close enough to hear what the general has to say. Considering what we're asking, I think you have every right to be there, even if you do look like a couple of choirboys. Just don't be too obvious about it and stand there with your ears flapping. Try to look like you have a purpose."

I am not sure why Upton liked us, but he did, despite the good-natured insults. As his conversation with Mac showed, many times he went out of his way for us, which some other officers resented. Maybe he sensed that we liked him? Sometimes that's all it takes. Or maybe he thought we really were as good as we thought we were? It might have been a matter of similar ages, too. He graduated from the academy only two years before we did.

I know that Mac admired Upton. Until he found his own way, he often imitated Upton, what he called the general's "high quiet courage" and his way of setting the best possible example without seeming to try.

Let me tell you, not seeming to try is hard work.

Using pews brought outside from a nearby church to form a rough circle, everyone was in place well before the set time. Even veterans who were Grant's superior in age if not rank were eager to make a good impression. While we weren't part of the inner group, we lingered within hearing as Upton suggested. As it turned out, no one noticed us. Every eye was on Grant.

Although these days I can't remember what I ate for breakfast, or even if I *had* breakfast, I vividly remember Grant's words that day. In print, they are not that striking, but there was something about the man that made us believe in him. It was as if he calmly explained how the future would unfold, not the usual platitudes to boost the spirits of an oft-beaten army. Grant was one of those rare men who have the ability to inspire. It comes naturally to some. Others have to learn, if ever they do. Mac had it when he chose to use it. But most don't, though many try.

The general didn't bother to stand when he addressed the assembled officers. There were no grand oratorical flourishes. He sat at the end of a wooden pew beneath the trees, leaned forward, put his elbows on his knees and calmly explained how we would win the war.

Meade was at his side, sitting with his legs crossed and looking cranky, as usual. In Grant's presence, he might as well have been a potted plant. I suspect that he knew it, too.

"Gentlemen, once we finish reorganizing, our strategy will be simple," he said, the ever-present cigar clutched in one hand. "I propose to seize Robert E. Lee in a bulldog grip and never let go. I intend to grind the enemy while we rob him of time and movement. Our warfare will be constant, and it will be bloody. Lee may be a master of maneuvers, but we will give him no room for it. He will always be on the defensive. If he is forced to give up Richmond – *when* he is forced to give up Richmond – we will follow him wherever he goes. I am sure you understand by now that taking the Confederate capital is not enough. Robert E. Lee *is* the Confederacy. He is the heart and the spirit. Where he goes, we will go."

Someone, I think it might have been General Winfield Hancock, the handsome hero of Gettysburg, where he was wounded and just recently returned to duty, reasonably pointed out that Grant announcing his intentions in such a public way guaranteed that the Rebs would know it within an hour or two.

"I *want* them to know," Grant replied. "They'd figure it out soon enough anyway. I want them to be crushed by the inevitability of it. I want them to know exactly what we're doing *and* to know they can't do anything about it."

Grant looked around at his officers while he let that sink in.

"What could be more demoralizing? Robert E. Lee may be a great general, but his day is done. It won't be easy. War is cruel, I have no doubt that casualties will be unspeakably high, and we will be criticized for it. The newspapers will fire their paper salvoes and politicians will bombard us with empty rhetoric. Ignore it, as best you can. I know I will. With this great army we have the perfect weapon at the perfect time in the perfect place. All we have to do is use it properly and stay the course."

Someone, I did not know who, because our view was partially obstructed by the trees and I did not recognize the voice, asked about Lee getting reinforcements that would allow him to take the offensive. The gray fox performed such miracles so often before that we almost assumed it would happen.

"Tell me, from where will he get these reinforcements?" Grant asked, making it clear that he did not expect an answer.

"In the western theater, General Sherman will push Joe Johnston so that eventually Johnston's backside will rub up against Atlanta. I commanded the men under Sherman and know what they can do. Johnson isn't strong enough to meet Sherman in battle and he's smart enough to know it. He will stall, retreat, probe for weakness and stall some more, giving up ground to gain time while waiting for Sherman to make a mistake. But Sherman will not make that mistake."

Grant took a deep drag on his cigar and blew the smoke down around his boots.

"At the last minute, when there is no more ground left to give, I have no doubt that Jefferson Davis, who has the mistaken notion that he is a great military mind, will replace Johnston with another general, fearing that Atlanta will fall without a fight if he doesn't."

Grant surveyed our faces again. Every man there felt that the general was looking at him and taking his measure.

"Who will that unfortunate man be? I have no idea. When Davis forces that poor soul into battle, Sherman will destroy him. At the same time, we will keep relentless pressure on Richmond and everywhere else from the Carolinas to the Shenandoah Valley. Lee will get no significant reinforcements because the South won't have the men."

After a few more questions, Grant straightened up in the pew, dropped his stub of a cigar, and ground it under one boot.

"How long will this take? I am not fool enough to make a prediction. But I can promise you that as long as we hold our resolve, the end is in sight."

With that, he rose to his feet, nodded at the assembled officers, and walked away.

No one walked with him. He did not bother to bring staff to the meeting, not even Rawlins. He did not need help. Some generals keep what seems like a battalion of staff with them at all times because it makes them feel important. Grant didn't need that. He was important and he knew it.

At that moment, I think Mac and I would have stormed an erupting volcano for the man.

As it turned out, we did everything but.

Chapter Five

It began to rain after the officers' meeting, not hard, but with no break in the dismal gray sky we knew that it would be wet for the rest of the day.

"Danny, I think this might be a good time to take a look at our new command," Mac announced.

We weren't scheduled to join the regiment for a few days while the paperwork of our promotions made its way through the ponderous bureaucracy, but with no pressing duties until then we were eager to see what we faced.

"If we wear slickers over our uniforms no one will know we're officers, especially if we find a couple of slouch hats somewhere," I said. "We can wander around at will. It'll be the next best thing to being invisible."

"Exactly," Mac agreed.

Something in the way he said it made me realize that was what he had in mind from the start.

"Don't gloat," I said. "You know I hate it when you gloat."

"Me? Never!" he gloated.

If we sometimes sounded more like boys than men, it was because at not even twenty-four years of age, sometimes we were just that. Despite all the fighting we had seen, the horror of war had not yet scarred our souls, though the time would come soon enough.

Despite our best efforts, we looked as young as we were, too. I grew a thick black beard to appear older and it did help, but not that much. While I was two inches over six feet and powerful at two hundred pounds, I knew there was something about me that seemed young and there was nothing I could do about it.

It's ironic that most people spend their youth wanting to look older and the rest of their lives wishing they looked younger.

The sandy-haired Mac was three or four inches shorter and much slimmer, which made him seem taller than he was. He recently grew what people were calling sideburns, after Ambrose Burnside's flamboyant facial extravaganza. Other than getting badly whipped at Fredericksburg, growing exceptionable facial hair is the only memorable thing Burnside ever did. Mac's version was much simpler, side whiskers running down to his jaw. In those days, I am not sure he could grow anything else. Attempting at a mustache would have been tragedy.

To be as unobtrusive as possible, we decided to walk instead of ride to the 2nd Connecticut's camp, which was removed from the rest of the army by at least two hundred yards, as if the regiment was a pariah and no one wanted it close.

We smelled it before we saw it. It was no wonder that the rest of the army didn't want the regiment close. The stench was overpowering. It resembled more of a dump than a camp. Maybe it was a dump; a human dump.

The lack of organization and pride was obvious at a glance. There was no regimental flag or headquarters. The camp seemed strewn haphazardly over the ground without purpose or reason.

In a generally well-supplied army, the men were so badly clothed it was hard to believe – rags more than uniforms. Several of the men appeared drunk. Equipment, much of it broken or worn beyond use, was strewn everywhere. The tents were in such tatters that a rain like today's probably soaked everything inside. It didn't look or smell as if anyone bothered to dig latrines and if they did, no one cared.

"You lucky bastard," I murmured. "Do you think we could get a transfer even before we get here?"

Judging by the size of the camp, the regiment was badly undermanned, too. Officially a regiment was a thousand men divided into ten companies, each with its own captain. But with casualties, sickness and desertion, I didn't know of a regiment that was at full strength.

"What do you think, Danny?" Mac asked as we walked through the awful camp. "Maybe five hundred, or so?"

"A few more, I think," I replied doubtfully. "The numbers don't worry me as much as the quality. I've seen livelier men in a mortuary."

We stopped our seemingly aimless stroll to watch a brute of a sergeant berate a half-dozen cowering men. There seemed to be no point to the bullying other than the sergeant's foul mood as he knocked one man to the ground and kicked him hard in the ribs.

When he saw us watching from a distance, he marched toward us, glowering as he sloshed through the mud.

"What are you turds starin' at?"

He was even more unpleasant up close, all rotting teeth, foul breath and bulging muscles.

"Not a thing, Sergeant," mildly replied Mac with a tip of his hat. "We're just passing through."

"Well see that you keep passin' or I'll help you along with the toe a' my boot," he bellowed, spitting a giant yellow gob at our feet. "I don't like meddlers."

He couldn't tell that we were officers. His arrogance was so profound that I'm not sure it would have mattered. I wanted to knock the ill-mannered oaf clear to Vermont, but Mac put a restraining hand on my forearm and led me away.

"Time enough for that, Danny," he whispered. "Remember, we're here to get the feel of things, that's all. Let's keep moving."

We got the feel of it, all right, and it didn't feel good.

"What we need is to put the fear of God into 'em, starting with that man," Mac said. "I can't wait to get started."

Chapter Six

Taking command two days later, we met with the regiment's senior captain, Franklin Dandridge, a middle-aged officer who looked twenty years older than he was.

There should have been at least one major, but the regiment had been without one for months. With no colonel and no majors, for all practical purposes there was no one in charge while the men languished.

We arranged to meet Dandridge in some piney woods a good distance away from camp so that we could speak freely without anyone around to see or listen.

Dandridge rode up, dismounted, snapped off a crisp salute and immediately began talking, as if he wanted to get something unpleasant out of the way before he lost his nerve.

"Sirs, I offer my congratulations on your promotions along with my condolences that you are now in command of the second," he said. "Please don't take it personally, but I am resigning from the army and intend to be away from here as soon as the paperwork is completed."

As the senior officer, Mac spoke first. "Captain, why not stay a while and see what we can do? You can always resign later. I promise that I will not stand in your way."

There was something in the way that Dandridge took off his hat and ran his fingers through his thinning gray hair that turned it into a gesture of unspeakable weariness.

"With all respect, sir, I want no more of this damn war," he said. "No power on earth can stop me from going home."

"I might as well say it because you'll see it for yourself soon enough. The second isn't a regiment; it's a home for derelicts, soft brains, ne'er do wells, and the mutinous. I feel like I've aged more in the last year than the previous twenty, but at least I survived. Believe me, I'll die a happy man if I never see another uniform."

It took only a glance between Mac and me to agree that we would not try to persuade Dandridge to stay. A worn-out officer desperate to get out is no good to anyone. Better to start over with people of our own choosing.

With nothing at stake, Dandridge was candid about the regiment's problems.

"Without a doubt, the worst canker is Gunderson. He's only a sergeant but he rules the regiment with an iron hand and practically turned it into his personal fiefdom. Most of the enlisted men are cowed by him and his gang, and the officers are either afraid or just don't care anymore. Most of 'em are as eager to get out as I am."

"Really? All that trouble from one man?" I asked. "That's a little hard to believe."

"He has twenty-five or thirty hardcore followers, I guess," Dandridge continued. "He's a brute, but a cunning brute. He's careful about picking his spots, and anyone with the courage to defy him gets the life beaten out of 'em some dark night when no one's around to see it. He's grown more blatant with time, too. I'm sure he's skimming everything from supplies to payroll, and I wouldn't be surprised if he had a hand in the killing of our colonel, who was the last officer to stand up to him, though nobody much liked him either."

"Is Gunderson a big man with a lot of muscles and bad teeth?" I asked. "Bellows like a wounded bear?"

"That's him, all right." Dandridge nodded. "You've noticed him already?"

"Oh, yes, we *noticed* him all right." Mac said, a hard gleam in his eyes, "And it won't be long before he notices us."

* * *

Our second act was to arrange new outfitting for the reg-iment, including uniforms, weapons, tents and other equipment. Upton promised to support us in any way he could, and we took advantage of it. The first step toward acting like a soldier is to look like one.

We outfitted the regiment one company at a time, with new uniforms, belts, suspenders, shoes, socks, under garments, and hats handed out from the back of supply wagons pulled into camp one by one, which made it easier for us to watch.

Instead of helping to supervise the distribution like a good sergeant should, the same big man we ran into earlier – Gunderson, we now knew – shoved his way to the front of the line. He forced the rest of the men to wait while he took his sweet time picking out exactly what he wanted for himself and his gang, a great deal more than their allotment. What he didn't take he threw on the ground.

While we looked on from a distance near Mac's tent, I muttered, "Why the hell don't they fight back?"

"Because they know their officers won't back 'em up," Mac

replied. "At least not 'til now. Sergeant Callahan!"

The sergeant seemed to materialize out of nowhere, which might have been alarming if we weren't used to Callahan's peculiar ways. As always, his faced was flushed with liquor. No one knew where he got it or where he kept it, but it never kept Callahan from performing his duties better than any sergeant I'd ever seen.

"Yes, Colonel darlin'. At your beck and call, I am."

It was all I could do to keep from laughing. From the moment we met, Callahan called us both that, varying only according to our rank at the time. For reasons he never explained, he took us under his wing shortly after we joined the Army of the Potomac, fresh out of the academy like newly baked bread. We picked up more practical knowledge from him in a month than in four years at the academy.

"Callahan, I told you not to call me that...oh, the hell with it," Mac said, smiling despite himself.

He lifted his chin toward the supply wagon. "You see that big brute of a sergeant over there pushing the other men around?"

"I do, indeed, Colonel darlin'," Callahan said. "Noticed the noisy clod right away."

"Bring him to us. If he resists...persuade him."

"I'll have the boyo to ye right proper, Colonel darl...sir!"

I wanted to watch, but our dignity as officers demanded that we not stand there and gape like schoolboys watching a fight at recess. The two sergeants were about the same size and seemed well matched. I am a big man myself, but they both outweighed me by at least twenty-five pounds. Callahan probably was ten years older than Gunderson, pushing forty, and gnarled like an old oak tree. Although Gunderson was a formidable creature, Callahan was a veteran of a hundred such scrapes. I had no doubt of the outcome.

Inside the tent, Mac coolly sat on his camp stool while I anxiously perched on his cot.

"Kill the head and the body dies," Mac said. "We deal with Gunderson and I'm betting the rest will fall in line."

"I don't think we can kill him," I said, getting another smile out of Mac. "I have heard there are rules against it."

We heard a surprised yelp in the distance. Within a few seconds, Gunderson stumbled into the tent as if propelled by an invisible force.

"Goddamn it! What the hell...?"

Entering right behind, Callahan used his forearm to club Gunderson between his shoulders, knocking the big man to his knees. With a muttered, "Beggin' your pardon, sirs," to us, he grabbed a handful of hair, jerked Gunderson back to his feet and forced him to face us. "Time you learned some respect fer yer betters, boyo."

Gunderson seemed more confused than beaten. It had probably been so long since he was challenged that he genuinely didn't know what to do.

"Sergeant Gunderson, I'm busting you back to private, effective immediately, and I wanted to say it to your ugly face," Mac announced, rising to his feet. "Consider yourself lucky that I don't throw you in the guardhouse, though there may come a time when you'll wish I did. Still, I figure every man deserves a second chance, even a repugnant swine like you."

Mac paused to give the ex-sergeant a chance to say something in his own defense, though neither one of us could imagine what that might possibly be.

Apparently neither could Gunderson. When the stunned man remained silent, his mouth hanging open, Mac continued, "Sergeant Gomez went through your kit while you were, ah, otherwise engaged. I think you might be hard pressed to explain where you got all the money he found, especially on a sergeant's pay. Lieutenant Colonel Stone, exactly how much was it?"

"One thousand, four hundred and fifteen dollars in gold and greenbacks."

Gunderson suddenly discovered the power of speech. "By God, you can't do..."

"I can and I did," Mac interrupted. "It's really too bad you don't approve of banks. Oh, well, it's your loss. Sergeant Callahan, remove his stripes."

Callahan pulled a folding knife from his pocket. With a few expert flicks of the blade, he cut most of the threads that attached the sergeant's stripes to Gunderson's blue sleeve. When he cut enough, he ripped the stripes off and handed them to me.

"One more thing, Gunderson," Mac said. "I saw how eager you were to get at the new uniforms. We don't want to get your new outfit dirty, do we? Take off your pants."

"What?"

Of all the things Gunderson probably expected, that wasn't one of them. Astonishment showed all over his beefy face.

"Take 'em off," Mac repeated. "Leave your shoes on. You'll need 'em."

After a wild look around, as if he hoped to find an ally in the crowded tent, the sullen ex-sergeant sat on the ground and tugged off his pants, revealing muscular but pale legs and underpants than looked like they hadn't been changed in a month.

"Sergeant Callahan, has Sergeant Gomez assembled the men as ordered?" Mac asked.

"Underway as we speak, sir."

"You know what to do," Mac said. "Drill 'em, you and Gomez. Drill 'em so hard their tongues hit the ground and then drill 'em some more, dawn to dusk. And take Private Gunderson with you. He will be drilled along with the rest of 'em."

"Without, ah, full uniform, sir?"

"Exactly as he is."

Callahan and Gomez weren't the only sergeants in the regiment, but they were the only sergeants we knew we could trust. We would see about the rest in time.

When Callahan and the bare legged Gunderson left, I raised my eyebrows at Mac.

"His pants?"

Mac stepped to the tent entrance and looked outside. Gomez had the men assembled and waiting while Callahan booted the surly Gunderson into line. In the bright sun, his pale legs seemed to glow.

"A bully like Gunderson understands force," Mac said. "He can deal with punishment because he's familiar with it. He probably takes pride in his ability to withstand it, and I doubt it would ever break him. The men respect that. They fear it, too. It makes him even more formidable in their eyes. Humiliation will break him faster than anything and the example will resonate with the rest of the regiment. That's why I didn't put him in the guardhouse. He'd only come out nastier than he went in. By the way, I wouldn't be surprised if he makes a run for it."

"Desertion?" I asked.

"Sooner rather than later, I think."

His energy bubbling over, Mac began pacing back and forth in the tent. There wasn't much room. Three steps forward, turn, three steps back.

"Danny, we have to find a way to turn these men into something close to professionals in the short time we have. I want them trained and fully confident. I want them *eager*. We must help them find discipline, pride in excellence, and, most important, pride in each other. Without it they're doomed."

Mac stopped pacing and faced me dead on. We weren't more than three feet apart.

"From what I've seen, I'm convinced that most of the men want to be good soldiers. But so far, the army hasn't done anything but let them down or ignore them. It's our job to show that things have changed for the better."

And so, it began.

Chapter Seven

We drilled the men until they hated us and then we drilled them some more. If an inspection revealed a violation by anyone the entire regiment was drilled for extra two hours. The men had to learn that they were in it together. If one failed, they all failed. Gomez and Callahan dealt out their own rough discipline, too. The sergeants did not hold back.

We discovered that most of the men were ashamed of the regiment's sorry reputation and wanted to be good soldiers. As pride returned, so did some early signs of *esprit*.

Our first desertions came after four days. We were not surprised that Gunderson was among them.

Mac was out with the men when Sergeant Gomez brought the news to me.

"What happened?" I asked.

"Looks like he got away around midnight with two other men," Gomez replied. "They took three good horses, clothes, weapons, and enough food for a week. I doubt it was a notion that suddenly came to 'em by the light of the moon. They planned it probably from the day command changed."

"Any idea which way they went?"

"South."

I was surprised. "South? Really? To the Rebs?"

"That's what they want us to think," Gomez explained. "But why desert one army and run straight to another? Short-handed like they are, the Rebs'd probably just put 'em in the front line where they'd get killed anyhow. No, I'm thinkin' they'll go south a bit to throw us off, then cut west and head for the mountains. Most of the farms and settlements out that way are pretty isolated and it'd be easy to plunder their way from one small farm to the next. At least that'd be the smart thing to do, though nobody accused Gunderson of bein' smart."

"Clever, though, in his way," I said. "Think you can find 'em and bring 'em back?"

Gomez smiled, revealing even white teeth beneath a thick black mustache.

"Be my pleasure."

"Want some help, Sergeant?" I asked. "There *are* three of 'em."

Gomez did not seem offended by the offer, but I knew he would not accept it, just as he knew I did not mean it as an insult. He took it for what it was, something I was obligated to ask.

"If it's all the same to you, sir, I'll move faster on my own, especially if I run into any Reb patrols," he said. "They've got a head start but I don't see a problem makin' up the time."

"If that's the way you want it," I said. "Bring 'em back in as close to one piece as you can, especially Gunderson."

Before Gomez could leave, I held up my hand. "You don't have a horse of your own, do you?"

We were, after all, an infantry regiment. Gomez explained what I already knew: He intended to draw a mount out of the regiment's small herd of twenty-five head for the officers, couriers, and transport for our artillery battery.

I suggested that he take my second horse, a black named Gregor. He was named for my grandfather, though no one knew it except Mac. If anyone asked about the peculiar name, I said the horse was named after a friend from the academy who was killed early in the war. My lead horse was named Commodore, for Mac's father.

"He's not the fastest," I told Gomez, "but you won't find a better mount for endurance. You can use my spare saddle, too."

The sergeant nodded his thanks. I scribbled two orders. One authorized him to take my horse and saddle. The other ordered him to find the deserters, which he would need if he were stopped by one of our patrols, though I doubted that patrols from either side would know he was passing through.

After his usual sloppy salute, Gomez left the tent, eager to get started. I had no doubt that he would be successful, despite the deserters' head start and the three-to-one odds.

Gomez was a Texan, though he called himself a "*tejano*". His father was born in Mexico, his mother in Tennessee. Although Gomez looked Mexican, he spoke with the accent of the deep South, no doubt his mother's influence. The year before he was born, his father fought with Sam Houston against the Mexican army at San Jacinto, where Texas won its independence.

After the revolution, like many of his people, Gomez's family was abused by ignorant newcomers who did not understand why the new republic was full of the hated Mexicans. It never occurred to those deep thinkers that the people they hated so much were there first and helped win the revolution. I knew enough history to know that without the help of the *tejanos* Texas might still belong to Mexico.

Gomez never talked about it that I knew of, but a story made the rounds that when he was only twelve, his father, mother, and young Juan were attacked by a gang of border trash who intended to rob and pillage the *rancho* after murdering everyone who lived there and probably raping the woman.

After a twenty-four-hour siege, with a third of their number dead or wounded, the gang decided that the price was too high and broke off, but only after Gomez's mother was cut down by an unlucky shot as they galloped away.

The boy quietly left his grief-stricken father sobbing over his wife's corpse and followed the gang on his own. Experienced beyond his years, silent as a ghost, he snuck into the gang's camp at night and killed three men, including the man who fired the fatal shot, slitting their throats while they slept.

He scalped all three and hanged the bloody scalps from a tree as a warning.

No longer the boy he was just a few days earlier, he returned home and helped bury his mother. His heartbroken father died a year later, leaving his young son alone on a *rancho* he never wanted.

Years later, when Fort Sumter was attacked and war broke out, Gomez wanted nothing to do with fighting for the South. He sold the *rancho* for much less than it was worth and made his way north to enlist with the Union, a lonely trek that took him from just north of the Rio Grande to Illinois.

Much shorter than Callahan – with his massive shoulders, Gomez appeared almost square – he was the best tracker I have ever seen. It was as if he possessed a sixth sense, like he could read a fly's trail through the air. Once he caught his man, he was ruthless, unless he had specific orders to bring him back alive, Gomez usually didn't bother.

I would not want him chasing me.

Chapter Eight

It took five days.

A growing crowd of men followed Gomez as he wound his way through the camp to our tent, his three prisoners trailing along behind. First Gunderson, wobbling bareback on a boney old mule that looked like it might collapse with every step. The two other deserters, dimwitted slackers named Osgood and McCarty who followed Gunderson because he told them to, brought up the rear, sharing a horse also with no saddle.

When they drew closer, I saw that Gunderson was wounded above the knee. Someone, presumably Gomez, applied a rough tourniquet, but his pants were caked with dried blood. Despite an injury that kept him from running even if he was inclined to try, Gunderson's hands were tied behind his back. Osgood and McCarty looked like they were near done in from pain or exhaustion, probably both. I did not know how far they had come, but if a man weren't used to riding bareback it turned his butt and the inside of his thighs into raw meat. Like Gunderson, their hands were bound behind their backs.

The quartet stopped at our tent. Mac was inside pretending to be the busy regiment commander. He was as aware as I was of Gomez's return, but didn't want to show it. I was so eager to hear what happened that it was all I could do to keep from hopping up and down.

Still, if Mac wanted to play it formal, I was obligated to follow his lead.

"Colonel MacKenzie," I announced, "Sergeant Gomez has returned with the deserters."

Mac emerged from the tent and looked at the prisoners the way a vulture regards carrion. While Osgood and McCarty resembled whipped dogs, Gunderson radiated the defiance of a man with nothing to lose who intended to make a last stand.

The attitude didn't last long.

"Sergeant, I don't want to look up at him."

With the ease of the natural horseman he was, Gomez backed his horse (my horse, Gregor, I suddenly remembered) until he was beside Gunderson and towered over the old mule. He kicked the prisoner hard in the side with the flat of his foot, just below the ribs.

With a wounded leg, and hands tied behind his back, Gunderson couldn't keep his balance and toppled over. Unable to protect himself with his hands and arms, he screamed in pain as his shoulder took the brunt of the fall. His defiance disappeared like morning dew on a hot day.

Despite the awkward way their hands were tied, Osgood and McCarty dismounted almost instantly, scrambling down the horse's side practically on top of each other, pathetically eager to avoid Gunderson's fate.

"Tell me about it, Sergeant," Mac said.

"Like I figured, they went south a ways and then cut west. They were hidin' out at a little farmhouse about forty miles southwest of here," Gomez explained. "They surprised the old man who owned the place, but he still put up a good fight and shot two of their horses with his old Kentucky rifle before they took him while he was reloadin'. They tied him to a chair so they could cuff him at their leisure. Killed the old man's dog too, just for the hell of it."

That brought a growl from the men gathered around us. It always surprises me how few people care if a man is badly treated but let anyone harm an animal and he's a candidate for lynching.

"'Course I didn't know any of this when I came up on the farmhouse," Gomez continued. "When I saw tracks goin' in but not goin' out, I waited till the middle of the night before makin' my move. I busted through the door, figurin' they'd be asleep. Too damn dumb to post a watch, I figured. Gunderson tried to wiggle out of a window but a shot through his leg was persuasion to stop. It would have been a pleasure to kill him, but the lieutenant colonel ordered me to bring him back in one piece. After seein' what happened to Gunderson and hearin' him yowl, the other two couldn't give up fast enough."

"Boys, that ain't even close to how it was!"

Still on the ground, Gunderson had propped himself up on his elbows, hoping for sympathy when defiance didn't work.

"That greaser's a damn liar. Truth is I gave up first thing. By then I was sorry as hell that I took off and left you boys, but you saw how they were treatin' me. Had my hands in the air and everythin' when that son of a bitch shot me in the leg! Probably crippled me for life! You better watch out! They'll do the same to you if..."

"Sergeant, shut him up!"

With a happy smile, Gomez slipped of his horse, casually stepped around the mule and kicked Gunderson hard in the face, splitting his lips, probably breaking his nose, and putting an end to the man's caterwauling.

"How's the old man?" Mac asked.

"Scuffed up some, but he's fine," Gomez replied. "The tough old boot misses his dog more'n anythin'. Once I cut him loose from the chair it was all I could do to keep him from killin' all three of 'em. I believe he mentioned cuttin' out their gizzards with a spoon. The farm's poor place and I left him two of the saddles so he could sell 'em or trade 'em. Seemed the least I could do for the trouble they caused him. Hope you don't mind, sir."

"You did just fine, as usual," Mac said. "Lieutenant Colonel Stone, do we still have the money – what was it, fourteen hundred dollars, or so – that Gunderson stole?"

"We do, indeed, sir. It's safe in the regiment strong box."

I was careful not to say where the regiment strong box was located, which was under my cot.

"Assign a courier to take that money and deliver it to the old man, compliments of the Second Connecticut. That's probably more than he makes out of his farm in a couple of years. Tell the courier to make sure he gets a receipt if the old boy can write. Have him make his mark if he can't. He can get directions from the sergeant. Tell the courier that if he's not back in three days I'll send Gomez after him. That should light a fire under his backside."

Chapter Nine

The order to move out finally came. It was the direction that surprised us.

Despite Grant's promise to fight it out this line if it took all summer, after taking heavy casualties with no progress to show for it he decided to try something new – a move on Richmond from the south through Petersburg, a little town that also happened to be Richmond's railroad hub.

Searching for a breakthrough, Grant concluded that Petersburg might be the key to forcing Lee out in the open. If we took Petersburg, Lee couldn't supply his army by railroad and couldn't remain where he was no matter how strong his entrenchments. If nothing else, defending the railroad hub would extend the already thin Confederate line.

We marched on June 12, along with the rest of the corps, moving out three hours before dawn so the Rebs' scouts and spies couldn't see what we were up to.

For all it mattered, we might as well have marched at high noon with a brass band leading the way.

After only two miles, we got tangled up at a crossroads with the Second Corps, and both sides were too stubborn to give way. The wretched mess in the dark led to a chorus of yelling and cursing from officers who should have known better, including Mac and me. Our bellowing only added to the chaos. If Grant came along, he might have cashiered the lot of us.

After hours of failing to bring order out of confusion as even more troops piled up at the crossroads, with daylight we could finally see what we were doing. It took a while, but the two corps finally untangled. Pointed in the right direction, we marched all day in the blistering sun.

After six days of eating dust while we marched in a long half-circle around the Confederate capital, we finally arrived at the Petersburg entrenchments, a line already more than thirty miles long. As miserable as it was,9 the march would be the highlight of our campaign.

No one seemed to know what to do with us while we contemplated the Virginia dirt and dodged the most accurate sniper fire I have ever seen. The Rebs' weapons may have been old and worn after years of war, but those boys knew how to use them. Anyone who stuck his nose above the trenches stood a good chance of getting it blown off, along with the rest of his head.

After five miserable days, seven casualties, two of them fatalities, and no chance to return effective fire, we were relieved to escape the trenches with orders to support a frontal assault, where casualties promised to be heavy.

Looking back, I marvel that we were all so eager to die.

We geared up our courage and then did more nothing. The assault never took place. We were ready and eager and still we waited.

Four days after the aborted assault, we were ordered to join two corps in an advance against a Rebel position held by one of Lee's best, James Longstreet, a master of defensive warfare. Nobody in their right mind looked forward to attacking Longstreet. After crossing the Chickahominy River, we camped for the night near the James River before crossing it the next day.

Before we settled in, we received an order to advance against the Rebel trenches, an order that was countermanded within a few minutes, although we did come under brisk fire for a short time and suffered a handful of casualties.

We later learned that it was only a bluff designed to test the Confederate strength, information already well known by every officer and trooper on the line, except that no one bothered to ask.

While our men held their nerve under fire, they did not like taking casualties for no good reason. Mac and I did not blame them. Something as simple as, say, a reconnaissance in force might look reasonable on a map, or suggested at an officers' meeting, but it always means that men die. Maybe something valuable is learned, and maybe it isn't, but men die anyway.

And so, we returned to our miserable life in the trenches. It rained hard most afternoons and turned the ground into gooey yellow bog that seeped into our weapons, our food, and every crack and crevice in our bodies. I felt like I would never be clean again. Every dream I had involved a hot bath. When it didn't rain, and sometimes when it did, the Virginia heat was brutal. It baked your brains to mush while it sapped your spirit and turned us all into lethargic lumps of humanity.

But what I remember most about those days is the stink. Living with it all day every day you might think that I'd get used to it. Maybe some men did, but I was never one of them.

After so long, I still remember it exactly. I have never smelled anything like it, a putrid combination of unwashed men, general rot, fast-growing mold, fetid earth, foul human odors astonishing in their variety, uncollected garbage and the copper scent of blood from wounded men. All of it made worse by the heat that seemed to bake our brains and rain that turned everything around us into a merciless sea of ooze while the Confederate snipers popped away.

And fear. Yes, fear has a smell. Do you find that hard to believe? You shouldn't. I've smelled it often enough to know.

The only good thing to come out of our first experience with trench warfare was the promise Mac and I made to each other that if we ever got independent command, we would not waste the lives of our men in such a profligate way.

Maybe it all served some higher purpose, but damned if we could figure out what it was.

And then we were on the march again.

Chapter Ten

Here is all you need to know about Winchester, Virginia: During four years of war, it changed hands more than seventy times, including thirteen times in one day.

You don't believe me? I was there for some of it.

The little town in the northwest corner of Virginia was a key position throughout the war, especially during Stonewall Jackson's Shenandoah Valley campaigns when that lunatic made everyone we sent against him look like fools. One of Jackson's raids closed down the critical Baltimore & Ohio Railroad for ten long months.

Given how they virtually owned the valley for most of the war, Winchester was an ideal base for a Confederate push into Maryland, Pennsylvania, and even toward Washington itself. Of course, we knew that and tried to take it from them. Often, we did. And they took it back from us just as often.

After Jackson's own men did us a favor and accidentally killed that bloodthirsty bastard at Chancellorsville, Jubal Early assumed command of the Confederate forces in the valley. Early was no

Stonewall, but he was good enough. He terrified Washington by launching an offensive at a time when no one thought he had the men to do it. Before they were stopped, the Rebs were so close to the capital they could hear church bells ring. If it hadn't been for his crippling lack of numbers, he might have taken the place, which, in my opinion, wouldn't have been much of a loss.

Finally, Grant had enough. The Rebs were on the defensive everywhere but the Shenandoah Valley. It was time to put them on their heels there, too.

He found the right general in Phil Sheridan, a tough-talking character who was assigned to command and reorganize the Army of the Shenandoah. Grant's orders were simple: "Give the enemy no rest... Do all the damage to railroads and crops you can...if the war is to last another year, we want the Shenandoah Valley to remain a barren waste."

The task was straightforward. We were to engage Jubal Early and crush him, then march the width and breadth of the valley and destroy everything in our path with fire and sword, from apple trees and grain-stuffed barns to farm equipment and livestock. The Shenandoah Valley was a fertile land that helped feed the Confederacy ever since the war started. Grant wanted Sheridan to turn it into a desert. If the enemy can't eat, it can't fight.

All this grand strategy looked fine on paper, but the 2nd Connecticut was among the troops that actually had to do it. It would not be easy because nothing in that damn valley was ever easy.

* * *

The Rebs moved first.

By launching another offensive in the valley, Lee hoped that Grant might withdraw some of his forces from the Vicksburg-Petersburg line to protect Washington, opening the possibility that the siege of the Confederate capital could be broken.

But we had men to spare as long as Grant used them wisely. The 2nd Connecticut was part of two corps quickly transferred by rail to defend Washington. With the capital bristling with defenders, Early looked elsewhere to make trouble and sent two brigades of cavalry to Chambersburg, Pennsylvania. When the town failed to deliver a ransom to the cash-starved Confederacy, the Rebs burned it to the ground.

Sheridan responded, but cautiously. The canny Irishman was never as pugnacious as his carefully cultivated reputation made him seem. He was no fool, even if he looked like one of P. T. Barnum's sideshow freaks – a little man with a huge bullet head that seemed to sit directly on his torso without benefit of a neck. From the waist up, he could have been a strapping six-footer. Unfortunately, his short legs seemed to have come from another manufacturer, while his arms were so long that President Lincoln joked that he could scratch his ankles without stooping.

Like many small men, Sheridan made up for his lack of stature with noise. Given to intense rages, he was quick to censure, slow to forgive, and constantly demanding. At his best, he burst with energy and ideas, many of them absurd. But a few were brilliant. In the right circumstances, he could even be inspiring. At his worst, he toadied to those above, bullied those below, and found fault with everyone but himself.

It seems strange now, but in 1864 Lincoln's re-election was in jeopardy and the outcome of the war with it. While it was late in a war, the Rebs could no longer win, they didn't have to win and the wisest among them knew it. They just had to keep from losing for as long as possible and hope for terms from a war-weary North.

With Grant stalled on the Richmond-Petersburg line, Lincoln's Democratic opponent was none other than George Mc-Clellan, who for a time looked like a better candidate than general. He castigated Grant as a butcher who slaughtered his own men by the tens of thousands. It was time, McClellan declared, to let the South go its own way, conveniently ignoring that he played a large part in dragging the war out. It seemed possible that another defeat might swing the election McClellan's way.

With all that churning in the background, it was as important for Sheridan *not* to lose as it was for him to win. No wonder he was cautious.

For more than two months, the opposing armies marched back and forth, as if they were engaged in a massive game of chess, with each general trying for an advantage and unwilling to commit until he had it.

Finally, early in the morning of September 19, Sheridan made the first decisive move, sending his cavalry splashing across the shallow Opequan River to begin what became known to history as the Third Battle of Winchester.

Chapter Eleven

From the lowliest private to Mac himself, everyone in the 2nd Connecticut was nervous but eager. We were like hunting dogs straining at the leash.

As the armies felt out each other, we were held back with the reserves. Although we took fire in the trenches at Petersburg, we had yet to prove ourselves in battle. The truth is that we weren't fully trusted yet. To a man, we intended to change that at first opportunity.

While we waited, Mac took me aside.

"Danny, when we move out, I'll be riding in front," he said. "The men have heard me talk, now they need to see me *do*. But I don't want you with me. If something happens to me, the regiment can't lose both of us. Stay off your horse and advance with the men on foot. Is that clear?"

Distracted by my own thoughts about what could happen in the next few hours, I absently nodded in reply. The truth is that I wasn't really listening. I certainly did not know just how far in front Mac intended to be.

Following the cavalry probe across the Opequan River, Sheridan sent in three infantry divisions that met only token resistance.

Where were the Rebs?

Luring us into a trap.

They knew the country better than we did and used it to their advantage. The terrain was rough, checker-boarded by woods and open fields slashed with ravines concealed by thick brush. Our advance began to break up as it struggled over and through the natural obstacles. As our unit cohesion dissolved, the Rebs' counterattack not only stopped our boys, it pushed them back.

Watching through binoculars astride his big horse, Rienzi, Sheridan ordered in most of his reserves, two brigades that slowed the enemy advance without quite stopping it. The Rebs responded by sending in the last of their own men.

In a flash of insight, I saw Sheridan's plan. He was familiar with Jubal Early's aggressive reputation. In fact, he counted on it.

With the outnumbered Rebs fully committed, their heedless pursuit of our retreating troops passed a brigade hidden in the woods, commanded by General Upton and led by us, the lowly 2nd Connecticut. We hit them on the flank like Thor's hammer. Two murderous volleys, sheets of flame that cut down the Confederate ranks like corn stalks falling to the scythe, then a bayonet charge through the thick smoke of discharged powder from hundreds of weapons.

All the frustration built up over many months was in that charge. Mac led the way, riding far out in front with his hat raised high on the point of his sword so that even the men in the rear could see him galloping back and forth between the two armies. He was in as much danger from our own fire as he was from the enemy, a lone figure ignoring the shot and shell that fell so thick around him it seemed impossible that he still lived.

Despite what you read in novels or see in the moving pictures

I have grown fond of lately, anyone engaged in battle loses perspective in the first minutes. All you can see and all you care about is what's around you. Although our furious flank attack pushed the Rebs back with heavy losses, I had no idea if the rest of the army was winning or losing. All I knew is that I had to join Mac out in front, forgetting his order to remain on foot with the men. I could not hang back while he rode into danger. None of this was reasoned thought. I just knew where I had to be.

I had Commodore brought up, struggled to mount while he jittered in a nervous circle, and spurred him forward. Unlike Mac, I kept my hat firmly on my head and my sword in my scabbard while Confederate shot whizzed past me.

I felt a hard punch on my left side. Certain that I was shot, but puzzled by why I felt no pain, I looked down expecting to see my guts spilling out only to find that a ball struck the sword hilt at my hip, probably saving my life. In those days, a belly wound meant death. All I got out of it was a bad bruise.

Lightheaded with relief and grinning like an idiot, I galloped to Mac's side.

"You goddamn fool!" I shrieked. "Are you trying to get me killed?"

"Oh, shut up!" Mac laughed, waving his sword in the air while his mount half reared, his hat still stuck at the tip. "You're supposed to be with the men, you insubordinate jackass!"

When I told you that Mac never really laughed, I should have mentioned the lone exception: When he was in the middle of a fight his whole personality changed. I have never known another man who enjoyed being under fire, although I have known many who acted the part. I don't mean that as criticism.

Mac never admitted it – it's possible that he didn't even know it – but I truly believe that he loved it.

And me? I never told anyone, but although I'd been under fire before and would be many times again, that day was the worst. Maybe it was because I came so close to being shot in the guts, but I was terrified, aware of every rifle ball and round shot that passed by, threatening to take my head off. It was all I could do to keep from wetting myself.

Is it blasphemy to say that I didn't care if we won or lost? It was beyond my control anyway. I just wanted to keep from getting shot to pieces and cursed Mac with all the considerable language at my command for getting me in this mess.

I remember the nonsensical thought that if only I was the best friend to some nice boring farmer I would not be here.

The day was just beginning.

Chapter Twelve

After our bayonet charge, the battle developed a rhythm: fire a volley or two, push the Rebs back until our momentum slowed, then gather ourselves for another push. Over and over until it felt as if it would never end.

What I remember now are snatches of fighting happening faster than I can tell it:

* I saw Callahan kill with his bayonet like the deadly expert he was. After a feint that made a Reb over-commit with a hasty counter thrust, Callahan buried his bayonet deep in his opponent's belly. He planted his foot on the dead man's chest, pulled out the bloody bayonet, and looked for another man to kill, the light of battle shining in his eyes. Callahan could do that all day, drink a bottle of whiskey that night, and do it all over again the next day.

* A few steps away, Gomez used the butt of his rifle with deadly force. Like Callahan, he made his foe commit, then swept sideways with his rifle butt and turned the side of the Reb's face into pulp. As the Reb fell, Gomez disdainfully cracked him hard on the side of the head to make sure he stayed down.

* As the two sergeants fought side by side at the point of attack, I saw at least two hundred men fighting in their wake. The men instinctively knew that the best place on the field was with Callahan and Gomez. It was men like those two who won the war.

* I saw seven of our boys blown apart by a blast from Reb canister. One second, they were living men with sweethearts, wives, and children. The next second they ceased to exist, blown to bloody hell.

I favored a LeMat pistol in those days, a beautiful a nine-shot, forty-two caliber cap-and-ball revolver with a walnut grip and a blue steel finish. What made it unique was the additional under-slung barrel that fired sixteen-gauge buckshot. It gave me a lot of firepower without having to reload and the buckshot was brutal at close quarters. I kept it in a holster attached to my saddle until I lost it in the last of the fighting just before Appomattox.

I shot two men that day.

The first Reb infantryman tried to stab me in the guts with his bayonet. With most of his weapon broken off, the rifle barrel and bayonet were all he had left as he jabbed at me with one hand, like a sword. Commodore reared, throwing the Reb off balance, and I shot him point blank in his bearded face.

The second man grabbed my arm and tried to pull me out of the saddle before I emptied the sixteen-gauge into his skinny chest. I am sure that I that killed them both – two of the fourteen men I know that I killed during the war. Probably there were more, but fourteen are enough.

Mac was riding slightly ahead of me when, to my horror, he and his mount disappeared in a huge explosion of blood. Commodore shied in terror and I jerked the reins hard to keep him moving forward, afraid of what I'd find.

Mac's horse was blown to pieces by Reb grapeshot fired at

close range from concealed artillery. The blast drove Mac to the
ground, covered in gore. When I reached him, he was lying on
his back in his mount's oozing remains, dazed from the macabre
explosion and the hard fall. Strangely, the horse's head sat on the
ground a few paces away. Neat and unblemished, it looked like
a trophy on a wall.

I threw myself off Commodore and rushed to his side. He
raised one hand to wave me off, needing a moment to recover and
take stock of his injuries. He rolled to one side in the sticky mess
and began to rise. I seized his arm to help him up while concerned
men flocked around us, awed by how he survived such carnage.

Bloody from head to toe, Mac took a staggering step while he
regained his balance.

"Not much of a dismount was it?" he said.

"How's your leg?"

His boot was in shreds and he tentatively bent his leg at
the knee.

"It's cut up but not too bad, I think. Not as bad as it looks
anyhow. I can feel it everyplace I'm supposed to."

More men gathered around us. I saw it in their grimy faces;
they were desperately worried about the same man they detested
just a few weeks ago. I don't think anyone gave voice to it then or
later, but despite the merciless punishment, drilling and discipline,
they did not follow a flag or a cause. They followed him. There
were times when they hated him, but there was no doubt who led.

Mac seized my shoulder. "Danny, we've got to keep moving.
If we stop, we'll never get the momentum back. I need to find a
horse so the men can see I'm all right."

Commodore, bless him, was still at my side, his attack of
nerves forgotten. I grabbed the reins and shoved them at Mac.

"Here, take Commodore," I said. "I'll have Gregor brought
up for me."

Mac held the side of my face with one gloved hand. He knew what that horse meant to me.

"Thanks, Danny. I'll be as careful with him as I can."

"If anything happens to that horse, I'll shoot you myself."

Still not sure how badly Mac was hurt, I made a stirrup with my hands. He put his boot in it and I heaved him up, a spasm of pain crossing his face. Commodore remained rock steady despite the overpowering blood stink. Mac was drenched in it.

"I'll be along as soon as I can," I yelled. "Now go!"

I gave Commodore a smack on the haunch and Mac galloped away, waving his sword and shouting for the men to follow him.

I never did mount Gregor. There was no time to bring him up.

We fought all the rest of the day. We had the advantage in numbers, but the Rebs made us pay for every foot. I was lucky to survive. My uniform was pierced a dozen times by Confederate shot.

With less than two hours until sunset, thanks to Sheridan's unrelenting pressure on the flanks, the Confederate line was bent into an L shape. Someone with a better vantage point than ours saw that if we could split the Rebs at the angle formed by the two lines the whole thing might collapse.

During a lull in the fighting, Upton rode up, dismounted and waved us over. Using his sword in the dirt to draw a primitive map, he explained what Sheridan wanted.

"Tell me straight. Can you take that position?" he asked, pointing at the angle drawn on the ground.

We couldn't very well say, "Of course not, you fool!" Phrased more diplomatically, it would have been a reasonable reply. The men were exhausted, our casualties heavy, and our ammunition so low some of the men had none at all.

So naturally we nodded like idiots eager to take on the impossible.

"I'm sure we can, sir," Mac said, leaning against Commodore's side to give some relief to his injured leg. At least he'd wiped most of the blood off his face.

"How long do you need to get ready?" Upton asked.

Mac replied, "Give us fifteen minutes."

I thought that was an ambitious timetable to resupply the regiment with ammunition and water and organize for another charge, but I kept my mouth shut.

"Colonel MacKenzie, this time stay off that goddamned horse," Upton ordered. "Nobody's sure if you're brave or crazy. Have that mount sent to the rear where it belongs."

My sentiments exactly. I ordered a trooper with a shoulder wound to take Commodore to the rear. With one arm useless, he was headed that way anyway and happy for the ride once I helped hoist him into the saddle.

Certain that moronic young fire-eaters like us would never turn down the chance to lead a suicide charge, Upton ordered ammunition and water brought up for the desperately thirsty men before he talked to us. He knew we'd say yes because we never said no.

Fifteen minutes later the regiment was as ready as it would ever be.

On foot this time, Mac raised his sword and we moved forward over an open field toward the angle in the Reb line. Mac's boot was in shreds and he was limping so badly he looked like a cripple.

I never truly believed that we would make it over the open ground and was not surprised when we didn't. The fire was so heavy it drove some of our men back while the rest of us hit the ground to seek what little protection there was in the open field. I wanted to burrow deep into the earth like a gopher.

Mac and I lay side by side while the Rebel shot exploded

around us or flew over our heads. Between explosions, we could hear the screams of wounded and dying men on both sides.

"We can't stay here," I gasped. "We'll be shot to pieces."

Mac rolled over on his back and raised his head for a quick estimate of how many men we still had with us, then flopped back on his belly.

"Danny, crawl around and get as many men as you can to form a group around us. Pack 'em tight."

Seeing the protest on my face, he explained his plan. "I know we'll be a better target bunched up like that, but it won't last long. I want concentrated firepower right at that angle. Put everything we've got into a volley and then charge like hell while they're still stunned. They think they've got us pinned down and won't expect it. Tell the men what we're doing so they'll understand I'm not asking them to lay here and get shot. It's the only way out of this mess. We can't stay, and if we fall back, they'll cut us down."

I crawled around as best I could, making sure every rifle was loaded and the men ready. By the time I finished we were so tightly packed that a half-dozen well-placed canister would have killed half the men.

I slithered back to Mac's side. He was lying on his back reloading his pistol.

"We're ready and waiting for your order," I gasped.

"You'd better move over to the left a ways," Mac said, waving his pistol in that direction. "Get some separation between us so we can't be taken down at the same time."

As I crawled away, I tugged the LeMat from my belt, so nervous that my hands were shaking. Mac rose to one knee, making himself a prime target for the Rebs. With his sword in his right hand, he raised his left arm and held it there. There was a rustle all down the densely packed line as the men raised their weapons.

Mac dropped his arm and bellowed, "Fire!"

The earth shook as the shattering volley blew away my hearing. Through the dense smoke, I saw, but couldn't hear, Mac rise to his feet and yell, "Charge!"

And charge we did!

Partially hidden by the smoke from our volley, we were on the Rebs before they knew it. We weren't aware of it, but Sheridan ordered a simultaneous cavalry charge against the Confederate flank. With no reserves left, Early couldn't reinforce his center against our unexpected charge.

The Rebs fought all day just like we did, but they had lesser numbers and didn't have the strength to stop us as we poured over their breastworks like water. We felt them waver and break after doing all that brave men could do.

Exhausted ourselves, we couldn't pursue them, not even one step. But we won, by God! We won! Damned if we knew how.

We didn't learn until later how much it cost us. In one day's fighting, one officer was killed and seven wounded, including Mac. Sixteen enlisted men were killed and a hundred and one wounded, with fifty-three men missing and presumed dead, including two officers.

The 2nd Connecticut's losses that day were higher than any other regiment. Such is the madness of war that we were proud of it.

No one would ever doubt us again.

Chapter Thirteen

Jubal Early was not done with us yet.

Unfortunately, little Phil – a popular nickname Sheridan privately detested – had so little regard for Rebs' beaten army that he passed up the chance to destroy it.

Sure, that Early was a spent force, Sheridan contented himself with destroying the bounty of the Shenandoah Valley. We were plagued by raids by that hellacious partisan ranger John Mosby, the man they called "the Gray Ghost", and his band of rag-tag rascals, but even that was only an irritant. Mosby was good, but that late in the war his reputation exceeded his effectiveness.

We would pay dearly for Sheridan's overconfidence. Ignoring the Rebs not only gave them time to recover, but, unknown to us, Lee once again accomplished the impossible and cobbled together reinforcements for Early, who began looking for the opportunity to strike.

By now it was mid-October. The morning air was so crisp that it seemed a privilege to breathe it as the leaves turned brilliant colors. As we continued our plundering, the war seemed far away, as if we were on a fall lark.

Certain that Early posed no threat, Sheridan left for Washington and a conference with Secretary of War Edwin Stanton, the second most powerful man in the Lincoln administration, after only Lincoln himself. Mostly I think he went so he could be patted on the head and told what a great general he was. Everyone likes praise, but no one liked it more than Sheridan.

He left us camped between the small village of Middletown and a twisting stream named Cedar Creek, not far from where it flows into the north branch of the Shenandoah River. By then we'd heard rumors that Early received reinforcements, though no one took it seriously. Such a thing seemed impossible because it would weaken Lee's thin line along the Richmond-Petersburg front.

Once again, we underestimated Robert E. Lee.

We learned later that we did our job in the valley too well. Ironically, it was a shortage of provisions that led to the Confederate offensive. With his newly increased numbers, after our destruction Early couldn't feed his army. His men were near starving, and his choice was simple – attack or retreat. The pugnacious old general figured that he wasn't reinforced just to run away.

What happened next came dangerously close to a disaster that could have driven us out of the Shenandoah Valley and perhaps change the course of the war.

They hit us before dawn, and we couldn't have been more surprised if we wore ear plugs and blinders. John Gordon, Early's best general, led the assault across the river. Gordon's snarling offensive was coordinated with a second thrust across Cedar Creek. They were on us before we knew they were coming.

Even after the sun came up, the morning was enshrouded in such thick fog that most of us couldn't see anything. The Rebs couldn't see either, but all they had to do was attack. We had to defend, but defend where? With the way fog distorted sound, the firing seemed to come from everywhere at once. The men didn't know what to do or where to go. Orders were tentative and confusing when there were any orders at all.

In the first thirty minutes, the Rebs pushed so hard that half the army ran away in blind panic. It wasn't a retreat; it was a rout.

We were saved on that cool foggy morning by the bravery of our old classmate, Captain Henry Du Pont, the officer who, as a cadet, was so deeply in debt that he couldn't get even a few days leave despite his family's wealth. Du Pont's daring use of a few mobile artillery pieces slowed Early's advance just enough to give those of us who didn't run time to form a defensive line. A few minutes and it would have been too late.

When we heard the firing in the dark, Mac and I roused our men. Without waiting for orders, we drove the sleepy regiment toward the sound of the guns. Later we were praised for our initiative, but we were lucky. We camped on a knoll that night and the few feet of extra height gave us an advantage when it came to figuring out the right direction to move.

The fog was finally breaking as we formed a line, joined by a steady trickle of men from broken regiments who were drawn to us because in the chaos we looked like we knew what we were doing, maybe fifteen hundred men altogether. We didn't know what was happening anywhere else, but we knew it wasn't good. Without orders, we resolved to make a stand to slow down the Rebel advance and give the rest of the army time to reform.

The ground in front of our position sloped down to a small stream, then up to a patch of woods. We heard the Rebs but couldn't see them. We ordered the men to lie down and hold their fire until the enemy charged out of the woods as we knew they would.

I moved up and down the line, repeating the orders to make sure they were understood: "We have to keep them from crossing that creek when they come out of the woods. It's vital. The Rebs must *not* get across that creek."

Holding the creek didn't matter a tinker's damn, but men on the defensive fight better if they have something specific to defend.

Gordon's lean veterans burst out of the woods and we blasted volley after volley into their faces. We drove them back and they reformed to charge again, back and forth so many times I lost count. After more than an hour of hot work and heavy casualties, we held, but just barely.

Then I saw some of the troops around us begin to withdraw, though none from the 2nd Connecticut. Only a few at first, it quickly turned into a flood. In attack or retreat, men follow other men.

Hurrying over to see what was happening, I was told that the retreating men were out of ammunition and had no choice but to fall back.

When I informed Mac, he screamed in frustration. "Goddam cowards! If they do that this whole line collapses. The regiment can't hold out on its own."

The heat of battle was on him and he was not in a forgiving mood. If Mac had a weakness, it was his sometime failure to see another point of view. To him, there was the right thing and there was everything else. His life had few shades of gray.

By then my patience was worn as thin as my nerves. I didn't need to be lectured about our situation by him or anyone else.

"You infernal idiot, what are they supposed to do?" I snarled. "Throw rocks and make faces?"

His shock left him slack jawed. We disagreed many times before, but it was always in reasonable tones. I think how I said it more than what I said snapped some sense into him.

"All right, Danny," he agreed, suddenly calm again. "Tell them to reform a line as soon as they resupply. We'll cover their retreat as long as we can. Tell them not to go too far or we'll never make it back."

The 2nd Connecticut held for another forty-five minutes, finally falling back before it was overwhelmed.

Mac had another horse shot out from under him, this one with a bullet through the head, and took a slight wound in his heel.

Almost out of ammunition, we raced back and joined the new line a half mile to the rear. Grabbing handfuls of cartridges from the ammunition buckets, the tired men threw themselves on the ground and prepared to receive another charge.

Charge the Rebs did, no doubt assuming that they'd have us running for our lives.

When we fell back Mac captured a horse galloping rider-less across the field. He was only mounted for a moment when he was blown out of the saddle when something – he was never sure what – struck him square in the chest. Either the impact or the fall paralyzed both of his arms. They hung limply at his sides like a marionette with the strings cut.

He ordered Callahan to hoist him back on the horse, hoping that he'd regain feeling in his arms before too long. Until then the sergeant led the horse like Mac was a child taking a turn around the park.

I have never been in such a fight. I might as well try to describe hell. We heard that every other senior officer on the front was either killed or wounded, which left Mac in charge, though in charge of what we didn't know.

With constant pressure from the Rebs, and one withdrawal after another to new positions, there wasn't time to do anything but fight like the devil to keep the swarming enemy off our backs. We could only see for a few yards, our vision obscured by the thick smoke from discharged weapons. Our senses were battered by hammering volleys from both sides, the roar of artillery, drums beating, trumpets blaring, and screams from the wounded and dying. I stopped shouting orders when I realized that it didn't matter. The men knew what to do. They couldn't hear me anyway.

How does a man do what he must when he is surrounded by smoke, blood, noise, and flame that robs him of sense and reason? The answer is training and discipline. This moment is what all those hours of hard work were for. When terror claws at your belly, the enemy seems unstoppable, and every instinct screams run, discipline and pride find a way. What was left of the Army of the Shenandoah fought without coordination or thought. There was no notion of winning, only survival.

When it looked like one more push would break our wavering line, there was an unexpected lull in the fighting. I figured that the Rebs were gathering themselves for the final effort. The silence was eerie. I could even hear birds twitter.

In the distance, a rumble seemed to be moving our way. It was faint at first, then closer and closer. A voice cried, "It's little Phil!" It became a chant and then a roar: "Little Phil! Little Phil! Little Phil!"

He galloped toward us on Rienzi, looking as cool as if he were out for a leisurely ride.

He jerked back the reins to bring the huge black horse to a sliding halt.

"Who's in charge here?"

"I suppose I am, sir," Mac stood at my side with his mount's reins in one hand. His face was black with gunpowder but at least he'd regained the use of his arms. "Colonel Ranald MacKenzie."

Sheridan sized us up. "I know you, MacKenzie. You, too, Stone. I'm told you did grand work today. Probably saved the whole fuckin' army. Now I need you to do it again. Early's attack has stalled. Almost winning disorganized that son of a bitch even more than almost losing disorganized us. Reb prisoners say so many of his men fell out to pillage for food that he can't continue the attack. I doubt that he can even organize a decent defense. This is our chance!"

Taking a deep breath, Sheridan took in the terrible scene around him, the dead, the wounded, and the exhausted or battle shocked men, many of them on their hands and knees retching into the ground.

"I'm reinforcing the line with some of the men who ran away. They're eager to redeem themselves and damn well I intend to let them. We are going to counterattack and finish this once and for all. I have had enough of Jubal fuckin' Early!"

I think that might have been the best day of Phil Sheridan's life. He was more than ten miles away in Winchester when he heard the sounds of artillery where there shouldn't be any. Without hesitating, he mounted Rienzi and galloped back to the army he never should have left, his staff trailing along behind like puppies following a mastiff. The sight of the little man on the big horse put the fighting heart back into his men.

By the time the day was over, Jubal Early and his army were destroyed as an effective fighting force. After the worst possible start that morning, by sunset our victory was total.

Chapter Fourteen

That night, Mac shook me out of sleep, his face twisted in fear.

"Danny, have you seen Callahan or Gomez?"

He was desperate for me to say yes, but I hadn't seen either man since the battle.

"That's what I get from everybody," he whispered. "Everybody saw them sometime, but nobody knows where they are now."

Exhausted as I was, I jumped to my feet, cold fear tearing at my heart. Could they be wounded? Or even dead? Not Callahan and Gomez! They were indestructible.

Weren't they?

After sending a private back to search where the thousands of wounded were treated, we each grabbed a lantern, split up and began walking the melancholy battlefield in the dark. The dead would not be taken away until the next day, if then. The army needed time to reorganize and tend to the wounded. The dead were in no hurry.

Bodies from both sides lay scattered across the battlefield, a grotesque sight in the light from our lanterns. Foes still clutched at each other, fighting until they could fight no more. Others lay peacefully where they were cut down, their wounds invisible, as if they were only sleeping. Body parts from men blown apart by artillery were scattered over many acres.

We found them at the regiment's first position, where most of the men fell back and we stayed behind to give them time. They were lying with the bodies of a dozen Rebs around them. Callahan was on top of a Reb captain, his bayonet all the way through the man's chest, pinning him to the ground with a mighty dying thrust. The Reb still clutched the pistol he used to shoot Callahan in the heart. A defiant snarl on his face, Gomez was a few feet away. Wounded in a dozen places, his bloody knife was clutched in his fist.

"When there was nothing left to shoot with, they fought hand to hand," I said.

"Probably covering for somebody," Mac said.

"Yes," I said, lowering my head, "they would do that."

I heard a sound from Mac. He was weeping. I realized that I was, too, tears streaming down my filthy face.

We carried their bodies to the rear and cleaned them ourselves. There would be no common graves for these men. We dressed them in new uniforms and saw to it that they were properly buried like the heroes they were.

A supercilious staff officer with a clean uniform shouted at us for giving special treatment to "a couple of sergeants", Mac knocked him down and I had to pull him away before he killed the man.

Then I went back and knocked the fool down again.

* * *

Sheridan received a personal letter of thanks from Presi-dent Lincoln, along with a promotion to major general, meaning that only Grant, Sherman and Meade outranked him. Ordering a hundred-gun salute to celebrate the victory at Cedar Creek, Grant wrote Secretary of War Stanton: "Turning what bid fair to be a disaster into glorious victory stamps Sheridan what I have always thought of him, one of the ablest of generals."

Not long afterward, a poet named Thomas Buchanan Read wrote "Sheridan's Ride", a ghastly creation that exaggerated everything about the day, as if exaggeration was needed. I suppose that is what poets do. Despite, or perhaps because of, all the nonsense, the poem became astonishingly popular. Sheridan even changed Rienzi's name to Winchester.

I am surprised that the horse didn't bite him.

Despite his status as a hero that lingers to this day, as you have probably figured out, I am not a member of the Little Phil Admiration Society. Yes, he was good. There is no denying it. But others were better. Then and later, too often he let his vanity get in the way. He assumed that he was right because, well, he was Phil Sheridan. How could he be wrong?

Everyone talks about "Sheridan's Ride", but no one mentions that he never should have left in the first place. Outnumbered and outgunned, Jubal Early surprised and nearly defeated him.

There's a story that one of Napoleon's generals was up for promotion to marshal. After listening to the candidate's supporters sing the man's praises, Napoleon asked one question: "Is he lucky?"

To my mind, Phil Sheridan was lucky. He would never have a day like that again. Most men don't get one like that at all.

Chapter Fifteen

In my memory, the six months after Cedar Creek to the end of the war pass in a flash, but that is just an old man's recollection of events from long ago.

Shortly after Cedar Creek, Mac and I were transferred to the cavalry, which we both wanted. I had my fill of fighting on my feet and not being able to see anything. Even when we were mounted, serving with infantry around us just made us better targets, as Mac discovered all too often.

With his preference for bold and rapid movement, a growing tactical and strategic sense, and the decisiveness that command demands, Mac was a natural cavalryman. It is to our superiors' credit that they recognized it. It helped that after Cedar Creek we could do no wrong in Sheridan's eyes. If we wanted something, we usually got it.

With our transfer came promotion. Mac was promoted to the giddy heights of general. I made colonel and was happy with it. By then, I knew my strengths and weaknesses. I was a good number two – I didn't know a better one – but my nature was not suited for ultimate command. The responsibility weighed too heavily on me. Mac said that I felt too much.

In the spring, Grant broke through Lee's thin line at Petersburg and he finally was forced to abandon Richmond. I heard that Lee's messenger bearing the bad news interrupted Jefferson Davis at church service. By then even the stubborn Davis had to know that all the prayers in the world couldn't save his precious Confederacy.

Sheridan made sure that his cavalry was "in on the death", as he put it. Any time there was glory on the table Sheridan wanted in. As Lee's skeletal army staggered west, hoping for a miracle, our cavalry hounded it like a pack of hunting dogs.

Our worst fear was that Lee would disband the Army of Northern Virginia and the men scatter into the mountains to fight a guerilla war that might last for years. We learned later that a few cowards high up in the Confederate government wanted exactly that, including Davis himself.

Fortunately, Robert E. Lee was too honorable to approve such a thing. If Lee refused, then it didn't matter what anyone else wanted.

Despite what the history books say, the end came at Sayler's Creek, when we captured a fifth of Lee's army in one day, what was left of it. We didn't capture most of them as much as they collapsed by the side of the road without the strength to take another step.

How can I describe the surrender at Appomattox? From the somber dignity of Lee to the rough graciousness of Grant, I was there and saw it all, including the weeping men on both sides, who couldn't believe their war was over.

Of the Rebs, I can only say that I have never seen braver men fight for a worse cause.

After Appomattox, events moved so rapidly it was like being caught in a whirlwind, as if the long war pushed the nation into a final maelstrom of madness.

* In Texas, rather than surrender, hundreds of General Jo Shelby's Confederates crossed the Rio Grande into Mexico. I don't think anyone really cared as long as the fighting stopped.

* In the Carolinas, Joe Johnston finally surrendered to Sherman, though Secretary of War Stanton thought Sherman's terms too lenient and ordered that they be rewritten, an embarrassment to a great general at the hands of a pompous blowhard.

* Lincoln was murdered by a deranged actor, the worst thing ever to happen to this country. Secretary of State Seward was nearly butchered, too, slashed by a knife-wielding assassin in his own bed.

* After a massive manhunt, the assassin, John Wilkes Booth, was killed in a Virginia tobacco barn by a crazed Union sergeant who once castrated himself in a fit of religious fervor.

Strange as it seems, Mac and I didn't talk about the war's end until the night before Appomattox. I think we were afraid we might jinx ourselves, as if giving voice to it might bring us bad luck and, like so many others, we wouldn't live to see the end.

Is there anything more futile than the last man to die in a war?

It was after midnight and we were both too exhausted to eat. We were lying on the ground trying to get some sleep but too keyed up for sleep to come, knowing that we'd rise up again in four hours for what might be the last day of the war. We had tents but we were too tired to bother with them and slept wherever we happened to be after tending to our mounts. I used my saddle as a pillow while Mac preferred a rolled-up blanket.

The Virginia night sky was so clear that it seemed to show all the stars that ever existed, one of those sights when a man can't help but marvel at his own insignificance.

Out of nowhere I asked, "Mac, what will you do when it's over?"

At first, we didn't look at each other as we talked, caught in the rapture of the sky.

"I'll go where they send me, I guess," he replied. "After what we've been through it's hard to imagine."

"So, you'll stay in the army?"

My question surprised him, and he rolled over to face me, his head propped up on one hand.

"Of course. Are you saying you won't?"

"I don't know," I admitted. "I've seen fighting and blood and death until I'm sick of it. The truth is I want my life back."

"And what might that life be?"

"That's the problem, I don't know," I admitted. "Who knows? Maybe a wife and family?"

"Danny, have you been keeping secrets? Do you have someone in mind?"

"No, I'm afraid I don't," I admitted.

Except for the occasional whore and a few conversations with officers' wives I hadn't spent any time with a woman for almost two years.

"Young officers shouldn't marry anyhow," Mac sniffed.

"What idiot said that?"

"This idiot," he joked. "Who else?"

I chuckled into the night. "That's the dumbest thing I've ever heard."

"Well, think about it," he insisted, stubbornly refusing to give up an indefensible position. "There's no money, at least not much, and no security either."

"When the war ends, promotion will come as slow as it did before. We'll be posted God knows where to do God knows what and then we'll be transferred somewhere else probably just as bad or worse if we're not killed. And it'll be repeated over and over for twenty or thirty years. What kind of life is that for a married man? What about his wife and children? How will they live? *Where* will they live? It's not like we work at a bank and come home every night."

I understood his point, of course. Our shiny new rank looked and sounded good. We were proud of it because we earned it. But Mac was a brevet general just like I was a brevet colonel, a temporary rank, in other words.

Civilians still don't understand how it worked. Why should they? With the war, the army grew to thirty times its pre-war size. By the end of the fighting the north had some six hundred thousand men under arms. More men naturally meant more officers. For Mac and me, as with others, promotion came fast and often while the army grew ever larger and more officers were needed, especially experienced officers.

With the end of the fighting, the army probably would shrink to something close to its pre-war size of twenty thousand while we reverted to our permanent rank, which meant captain for me and major for Mac. As a matter of courtesy, we would always be referred to by our brevet rank. That's why today Custer is sometimes called General Custer and sometimes Colonel Custer, but even that's not accurate. On the day he died he was a lieutenant colonel.

But even if Mac had a point, which I still doubted, I didn't want to hear it.

"So, what happens if you meet the right woman and fall in love someday?" I asked. "Are you telling me you'll just shrug and walk away?"

"How would I know? I've never been in love. Never really had a chance."

He held up his mangled hand with its missing fingers and scars like old rope.

"Can you imagine a woman panting to be caressed by this talon?"

"I've never had a chance either, but I'd like to try one of these days," I declared. "I won't run away from it just because the great Ranald MacKenzie says so. Where do you get these ideas?"

The truth is that Mac would never love anything or anyone as much as he loved war. Rarely outgoing and awkward socially, in war he discovered the camaraderie he couldn't find anywhere else, even if most of it was with me, and relished what the rest of us hated. Up at 2 a.m. for a meal of hardtack and gruesome coffee before a fifty-mile ride into danger? Mac was your man.

He loved the heady rush of battle and the problems that demanded instant solutions. I think he even loved the danger, the great dark unknown that might do you in before you even know it's there.

I've known a few such men. War heightens their senses and makes them feel alive in a way nothing else does. There are clear winners and losers in war, too, clarity that's almost impossible to find anywhere else in life.

Mac loved matching wits against a capable opponent, especially one that he respected. He lusted for command and was eager to take on responsibility. He enjoyed the unpredictability, too, the way that no day was like any other day. He was good at it, knew it, and had no intention of doing anything else.

Even so, with the war's end he didn't know where he might go or what he might do. None of us did. Our world had disappeared, replaced by a world we did not know.

Me? I couldn't wait to get away.

Chapter Sixteen

"Colonel Stone, how would you like to be an observer?"

"Sir, I suppose it depends on what I'd be observing," I replied, not very helpfully.

I was in Washington, which is not my favorite place, where I was being interviewed by General Henry Halleck, who was not my favorite person.

The man Lincoln derided as "little more than a first-class clerk" was Grant's chief of staff, but that was in name only. They were always civil to each other, but Grant never had much use for Halleck. By this time, neither did anyone else.

When the war began, Henry Halleck was one of the most highly regarded officers in the army, an intellectual soldier and expert in military studies, whatever that meant. Unfortunately, the man's shortcomings became obvious once the fighting started. Everything was theoretical to Halleck. Battlefield reality – and its unpleasant surprises – was an inconvenience. He couldn't really *do* anything, at least not well, other than look important, shuffle papers, organize logistics, and play politics to his own advantage.

Earlier in the war, he was Grant's superior officer. Most of us felt that Grant's triumphant rise in the west came despite of the too-cautious Halleck, who had no faith in his subordinate's aggressiveness. It probably frightened him.

Now that the roles were reversed and Grant was his superior, Halleck's duties consisted of overseeing the supply of Grant's enormous army, which was easy enough given the abundance of the north. Halleck did get a promotion out of it, but that was nothing more than the time-honored military tradition of recommending a man everybody dislikes for a promotion that gets him out of the way.

As inept as Halleck was in the field, he might have been worse when he served as the Washington-based general in chief, where he had no eye for talent or strategy. His eccentric personality alienated almost everyone who came into contact with him. There was no doubt that eventually he would be shuffled to some position where he couldn't do any harm until retirement took him away.

For now, he was attending to the kind of mind-dulling detail that any competent government clerk might capably handle, which is how I came to be sitting in his office.

Halleck's high forehead was a ponderous dome as he pointed his goggle-eyed gaze in my direction. He hemmed and hawed and hesitated until I despaired of his saying anything at all. I couldn't tell if he was giving my comment deep thought or desperately trying to summon it. He had a disconcerting habit of folding his arms across his chest and rubbing his elbows as if he were trying to give them a nice shine. His nickname was "Old Brains". I assumed the irony was intended.

Just when I began to suspect that he must have perfected the art of sleeping with his eyes open, he sprang to life.

"You would be observing...foreign affairs from a...military point of view."

We stared at each other. I didn't know what he was talking about and had the strange feeling that he didn't either.

"You are...familiar with...the foreign military observers who were here...during the war?" he asked.

He finished just in time. I was in danger of losing interest before he came to the end of his sentence.

But at last, I understood. It was common practice for nations to send representatives from their army or navy to observe military activity in other nations. It was a good way of keeping up with new military and scientific developments and perhaps even do a little helpful spying at the same time. Nothing too overt, you understand, but information is always useful.

As a young officer, Halleck spent a year in France studying fortifications. It was a common practice. Both North and South saw plenty of foreign observers during the war, too, usually from Britain, Germany, and France, which had the largest armies in Europe and were so mutually antagonistic that they couldn't help but declare war on each other from time to time.

I knew what this really was; an attempt to keep me in the army and yet get me away from a life of which I was thoroughly sick in hopes that I would eventually return.

The idea started with Mac, I was sure, then moved up to Sheridan, to Grant, and eventually landed on Halleck's spotless desk. I suppose all the high-level attention was flattering, but I didn't much care.

"You are...highly...recommended," Halleck said.

"Thank...you," I replied.

Was Halleck aware that I was mocking him? It seemed doubtful. Besides, everyone mocked him. The toothless lion probably didn't recognize it for what it was anymore.

What he proposed was not a bad idea. Since I didn't know what I wanted to do next, much less where I wanted to do it, a posting as military observer in some distant but pleasurable country might be just the thing until I figured it out. How hard could observation be?

"How would you feel about Europe?" he asked.

"All of it?"

"Well...yes, I suppose. It is very...compact...you know."

No wonder they called him Old Brains.

After a few more excruciating minutes with that great fool, my new assignment became clear. By the time I left Halleck's office I was the military attaché at large to our embassies in Europe, which I had on good authority was very compact. The position apparently was created just for me, one that gave me leave to travel everywhere and do almost anything.

Other than filing an occasional report back to Washington, which I was certain no one would read, I would be more or less on my own, with no particular orders to follow and no enemy to kill or trying to kill me.

The papers still had to be properly shuffled and signed, which, this being Washington, could take months. But I was ready for my new life.

Chapter Seventeen

To paraphrase English novelist Charles Dickens, who wrote a fine novel with a title I can't remember and at this time in my life probably never will, the next few years were the best of times and the worst of times.

In my capacity as military attaché at large I merrily toured the capitals of Europe, meeting so many kings, queens, princes, princesses, prime ministers and eminent politicians that soon I ceased to be impressed.

One of my favorites was Queen Victoria. She was getting dumpy by then and still in mourning for her beloved husband, Prince Albert, who died five years earlier. Even so, I sensed a scamp lurking beneath the ritual and formality that encased her. Unfortunately, as far as I know, the scamp was never unleashed.

I also got to know many of the men who went on to become national leaders and even legends; men like Otto Von Bismarck and Charles Gordon. As ruthless a human being as I have ever known. Bismarck forged a united Germany and lived to a ripe old age. Almost twenty years after I met him in London, Gordon, a religious fanatic who regarded heaven and the British Empire as generally the same thing, was slaughtered and beheaded after a bloody siege at Khartoum in the Sudan, a place where he didn't have to be, in a conflict that served no purpose.

It surprises people when I say that the most impressive of them all was Giuseppe Garibaldi, leader of the fabled Red Shirts who did so much to create the nation of Italy but who is mostly forgotten today. I even rode with him for a few weeks, a natural commander who led thousands of men or a small band of guerillas with equal skill. I never met Abraham Lincoln, but Garibaldi possessed the same ability they say Lincoln had: He made you want to be a better man.

I almost fought one duel, too. My foe was the pompous son of the Duke of something or other who accused me of cheating at cards at his stuffy club. The fool was such a terrible gambler that cheating would have been a waste of time.

The day before we were to meet, a nervous young man representing my opponent showed up at my London hotel and proposed that we both fire in the air. That way honor would be satisfied and, more important, no one would get shot. I countered by demanding that the cheating accusation be publicly withdrawn so we wouldn't have to meet at all. To my surprise, he quickly agreed, and the duel was canceled. Afterward, I was reprimanded by the American ambassador in London for allowing myself to be dragged into such idiocy.

As usual, I paid little attention.

I indulged in many affairs, too, all of them brief because I was constantly on the move and liked it that way. While eluding the occasional outraged husband, I found the time to file several lengthy reports to Washington where, for all I know, they still sit in a pile waiting to be read.

I only casually kept up with the news from home. I was aware that Lincoln's boozy successor, Andrew Johnson, was nearly run out of office, saved by only one vote in Congress. To my surprise, three years after the war ended, Grant was elected president. I was not surprised that he was elected. Grant was easily the most popular man in the country. The surprise was that he wanted the job. It shows how adulation can warp a man.

From time to time, political, military and social nabobs from the United States came to Europe for what in those days was called a grand tour. My presence was often requested but I almost always arranged to be somewhere else. I even missed General Sheridan, despite an official communication from Washington requesting my presence.

So sorry, General, I begged off. Duty calls...pressing business... the natural intcrest...I'm sure you understand...maybe next time.

I composed that note in Vienna while lounging with my head in the lap of an Austrian countess.

Don't tell me I didn't have pressing business.

The general's reply was pure Sheridan: "I heard about the duel. You should have gone ahead with it and shot the son of a bitch."

Out of the other side of his mouth, he probably told our London embassy that I should be drawn and quartered in Piccadilly Circus for getting myself in such a mess. Anyone who claims that you can't have it both ways never met Phil Sheridan.

As you can tell, my duties were light, and I worked hard at enjoying myself. It was ridiculously indulgent, and I was surprised that the army let me get away with it. I suspected that I was all but forgotten back home, at least for the time being, which was fine with me. It couldn't last forever, but I was determined to make it last as long as possible.

And then I fell in love.

Chapter Eighteen

Her name was Anna Maria Macgregor, though I called her Amy. She was half Scot and half Italian. As I was to learn, it's a combustible blend.

With flawless skin lightly dusted with olive, jet-black hair, and dark expressive eyes that pleased and mocked like light on water, in many ways Amy resembled her Italian mother, Sophia. Supposedly a rare beauty when she was young, in middle age Sophia was a formidable dragon who detested me with every fiber of her considerable being.

Fortunately, Amy was small like her elfin father, Lachlan, with the same sense of twinkling mischief, so beautiful that I often caught myself holding my breath as I gaped at her.

For all his cheerful nature and fondness for "a wee dram", Lachlan Macgregor was well-known throughout Europe as a merchant prince who built a business empire from nothing, a valued friend and sometime business associate of the fabled Rothschild family.

From the second I saw Amy across the room in the golden

glow from the gas lights at a ball hosted by the American consulate in Livorno, I wanted to hold her in my arms for the rest of my life. I immediately began a determined campaign that rivaled Grant's siege of Richmond. It almost took that long, too. My sudden change dumbfounded most of my friends, who at first assumed I was taking the long route to another seduction.

With a deep breath, I marched across the crowded dance floor, dodging all the finely-dressed young men and the swirling skirts of their partners, and approached a clutch of chattering young women.

Arriving just as the music stopped, I asked the vision that was Anna Marie Macgregor for the next dance.

Regarding me like I was a fly in her soup, she responded with a steely refusal that cut like a stiletto, turned away, and left me staring at her delectable bare shoulder.

I should have been discouraged, perhaps even humiliated, but I was confident that it was only a temporary setback. Before the next dance I asked again only to be refused again. I doggedly kept trying until she finally said yes, "But only if you promise to stop being such a pest."

It was all the opening I needed. One way or another, I made sure that she didn't dance with another man for the rest of the night. It didn't occur to me that she was my co-conspirator that night.

Weeks later, after we confessed how we felt about each other, I asked why she refused me with such zest. Was I *that* awful?

"Oh, Daniel, you were much too sure of yourself," she replied with a laugh. "I just *had* to put you in your place. I wasn't going to be as easy as all the others."

"Others?" I spread my hand across my chest, trying to appear the innocent victim, which was never my best performance. "I am besmirched! Besides, that night I was anything but sure of myself. You saw to that easy enough."

"Yes, *others*, lots of them, and don't deny it," she sniffed. "I knew all about you. You are many things, Daniel Stone, but besmirched is not one of them."

"But what if I came to the ball with someone else?" I asked. "Or what if I didn't ask you to dance, or stopped asking when you refused me? We might never have met."

Amy smiled and it put the sun to shame.

"Poor boy, you were trapped and didn't even know it. I had my eye on you for *ages*."

We were sitting on an uncomfortable wrought-iron love seat in the over-manicured garden of her family's home in Livorno. I felt the ever-vigilant Sophia watching through a widow, ready to pounce. Fortunately, she couldn't see our legs touching from hip to ankle.

I seized Amy's hand, a move guaranteed to bring the dragon thundering out of her lair, reputed to be the largest private home in the wealthy city, one of Europe's major trade centers.

"You did put me in my place," I declared. "And that's right here beside you."

Squeezing my hand, Amy rose to fend off her mother with a flurry of Italian that involved much waving of hands and stamping of feet. Educated in Paris, Amy spoke Italian, French and English, and sometimes used all three in the same sentence.

I remember the moment so well because we were married six months from that day, altogether it was a too-long courtship and engagement that caused Sophia no end of grief, which caused *me* no end of grief.

It was late at night in Lachlan's home office that I asked the little Scotsman for his daughter's hand, a tasty morsel she had already given me, plus a great deal more. Although I am sure he knew what was coming, he answered with a mighty whoop, a

AND HELL FOLLOWED WITH HIM

hug that lifted me off my feet despite our difference in size, and a lot of thumping slaps on my back.

At least *he* liked me.

Settling down, as he struggled to open a bottle of champagne Lachlan gave me the bad news: I'd have to win Sophia over, too, or at least convince her not to object. I was not fool enough to expect an endorsement, but perhaps I could get her to at least tolerate me?

"Laddie, it's not that she doesn't like you...it's just that...well, all right, she doesn't like you," Lachlan admitted.

We'd finished the bottle and moved on to harder stuff. I was the worse for wear and I was almost twice Lachlan's size. With drink, his accent grew more pronounced until there were times, I could barely understand him.

"Anna Marie is a bonnie lass, though she was a wee sconner as a bairn," he declared.

I seem to recall there was a lot of declaring that night.

"She's our one and only and in her mother's eyes, there tisn't a man under heaven ta wash her little feet. As soon as she saw you ta gettin' serious, she didn't like it. You just need ta keep the haid 'n' wait 'til you war her down."

What I think he said was that Amy was beauty, which was obvious to anyone with decent eyesight. Though she was a strong-willed nuisance both as a child and a young woman, Sophia still didn't think any man was good enough for her daughter and only child, especially me. His advice was to be patient and hope Sophia eventually came around, though I didn't think it likely.

"Damn it, Lachlan! How long do I have to wait?" I cried, thumping the flat of my hand on the arm of the leather chair.

Sitting across from me with his feet up and shoes off to savor the warm fire in the huge stone fireplace, Lachlan only shrugged. "I dinna ken, lad. Sometimes my Sophie's a bewilderment."

Despite their differences in size and personality, Lachlan and Sophia were devoted to each other. He admitted that he never understood what a beautiful young woman from a well-to-do family saw in "a wee gnome like me, poor as a bleedin' church mouse". All he had in those days was enough ambition for ten men and a willingness to work hard and do whatever was necessary.

"But thoughts of what might someday be, made thin porridge," he admitted. "Many a night we went to bed hungry."

Lachlan never explained the stroke that led to his early success, although I had the feeling that it wasn't entirely legal. But once he got that break the man never looked back.

I suppose that did not really blame Sophia for her hostility. I was a foreigner and worse, a barbaric American. My future was uncertain, and I came to her daughter with a notorious reputation.

If I had a daughter, I would not have wanted her to marry me.

It did not help that Sophia and I could not talk to each other. I had no Italian, she had no English, and, judging by her reaction when I used either Amy or Lachlan as a go-between, everything I said was either lost in translation or Sophia didn't want to hear it.

But my girl knew what she wanted and didn't give her mother much choice in the matter. Never patient at the best of times, Amy decided to move things along. On a day that saw the sky filled to bursting with dark clouds and the sea madly churning, Lachlan and I anxiously waited outside of a closed door in their home while mother and daughter had it out in the dining room.

Lachlan looked stricken when we heard expensive china and crystal shatter against the walls, like the devil himself was hammering at his Scottish soul.

"Are you all right?" I asked, escorting the wobbly little man to a nearby chair.

"Lad, the breakin' two or three is fine enough. It's expected. But more than that's *extravagant!*"

The violence was followed by several minutes of weeping and wailing at such volume it could only have come from Sophia. Apparently all the physical and emotional weapons available to a pair of strong-willed women were in use inside that room.

Lachlan and I were happy to be on the other side of the door.

Finally, that door opened, and Amy walked out, her hair disheveled but her chin held high.

"I am pleased to announce that Mother has graciously agreed to our marriage," she said.

Judging by the flurry of angry Italian from inside, that is not exactly what Sophia said.

Mostly, I think, she realized that I genuinely loved her daughter and wanted the best for her as long as it was with me. That, and there wasn't anything she could do about it.

I much preferred a small wedding. It would have been fine with me if we simply eloped and avoided the fuss that comes with an extravaganza. But Amy wanted a big wedding, and a big wedding is what we had. It seemed to me that everyone she had ever met, corresponded with, and passed on the street was in attendance.

I was not the first to learn that on his wedding day no one is as superfluous as the groom.

It was during that time I discovered that I possessed a good head for business. Before meeting Amy, during my long frolic across Europe, I received a sizeable inheritance from my grandmother's brother, a Philadelphia relative I never knew existed. He left it to me because he had no one else to leave it to. Since my expenses were paid for by the government I was supposed to be representing, not knowing what else to do with the windfall I got some good advice, began investing, and discovered that I liked it.

I wasn't rich, or close to it, but Lachlan saw that my instincts were sound. Impressed by what I'd accomplished in a short time, he offered to set me up in the family business, or, more accurately, businesses. He'd started in shipping and moved on from there, with offices in all the major European capitals, plus another recently opened in New York City. If there was profit to be had across most of two continents, chances are that Lachlan Macgregor, or one of his companies, was nearby.

I thought seriously about accepting his offer. My stint as military attaché would end sooner or later, and I didn't know what I would do when it did.

Life was good, for a while.

Chapter Nineteen

I am not sure if I believe in God, but I certainly don't believe in fate. If there is a plan to our lives it is a poor one, badly executed, too. If there is a God, I see no reason to worship or make my peace with such a careless clod.

Is that blasphemy? Am I doomed to spend eternity in the fires of hell?

I will find out soon enough.

Amy and I rented a small chalet in the Italian Alps for a month. She loved winter sports, was a graceful skater and even better skier. She liked winter clothes, too, and looked adorable in them. I could neither skate nor ski but enjoyed watching her. At night, we would sometimes go out with friends, but most of all we liked to lay before a roaring fire in our little house, talk and make love.

We rented the chalet because I had to go to France for a short time, perhaps my last action as a military attaché. By then I'd all but decided to accept Lachlan's offer. The French army was engaged in winter maneuvers near Chamonix, and I was invited to observe, which I agreed to several months earlier.

We'd only been married for a few weeks and I didn't really want to go, although it seemed simple enough. A short trip through the mountains by train, a week or so of observation, and back again, followed by a dull report on the winter capabilities of the French army, as if the United States might someday go to war with France over an alp.

In other circumstances, Amy might have come with me, but I would be out in the field the entire time and there was no place for her. I explained that I wouldn't be gone long, a week or ten days at most. Nothing to it.

I was transported by sleigh to the train station and then a few hours across the border to Chamonix. As I left, I turned to see Amy blow me a kiss as she stood in the doorway of our little chalet, the sun reflecting off the Alps towering in the background.

That was the last time I saw her.

There hadn't had an avalanche in decades, so long ago no one could remember the last one.

My beautiful girl died there, and nothing would ever be the same.

Chapter Twenty

I don't remember much about what happened for a long time after that.

I do remember Amy's heartbroken parents. After the funeral, with tears flowing down his lined cheeks Lachlan took me aside to assure me that his offer to join him remained open. He knew how much I loved his daughter and promised that whatever I decided, if there was anything he could do for me he would do it, now and for the rest of his life.

Except from a distance at the funeral, I never saw Sophia again. It was as if she couldn't stand to be in the same room with me.

I should have been grateful to Lachlan for his generosity at such a terrible time, but I couldn't summon any feeling at all, not about his offer, not about anything. It was as if I was a shadow that did not exist in the real world. I am afraid that I treated that good man badly by not treating him at all.

As time passed, the little work I did in my official capacity went to hell, though it probably was a while before anyone noticed. If I filed any reports, I don't remember them, and if I did, they must have been gibberish. I don't think that I took to drink, at least no more than I did before, but I don't remember that either. In my limited memory of that time, good or bad, nothing seemed to touch me because nothing mattered.

My friends wanted to help, but there wasn't anything they could do. Various diplomats, politicians, businessmen, and military officers from many countries pitched in with advice.

Snap out of it, they declared, as if it were that easy. Stay busy. Distract yourself. Work is the answer.

Others went out of their way to introduce me to available women as a distraction from my misery. I pushed them away.

Too soon, I said. The way I felt it would always be too soon.

A few recommended medical miracle workers they were sure could help me. I tried a few. They didn't. Sometimes these physicians recommended unusual medications and potions that were certain to ease me through the crisis. I didn't bother.

I vaguely remember attending a séance. Maybe more than one. Yes, I was that desperate.

After a while, how long I cannot say, I did begin to feel something: guilt, massive, heart-breaking, soul-crushing guilt. I told myself that I should never have left Amy alone. I never should have gone blundering around in the snow to watch some silly *faux* war that meant nothing. If I'd only been there, I could have saved her. And even if I couldn't, I should have died with her, the way it should be.

Instead, my beloved wife died alone, and it was my fault. I might as well have killed her myself.

And so, I shambled through life in a thick fog of my own making. There was no sense of continuity or the passing of time. I couldn't remember what I did yesterday or what I was supposed to do tomorrow. I know now that I was wallowing in cowardly self-pity because it was easier than getting on with life.

Amy would have been ashamed of me.

Chapter Twenty-One

It was morning, late morning, judging by the sunlight blasting through the window.

Where the hell was I? Marseilles? Maybe. But I vaguely remembered leaving France, so that couldn't be right. Or did I leave Spain and come into France?

For all I knew, I was somewhere in the Sandwich Islands.

Without opening my eyes, I concluded that I was in a hotel room. I don't know how I knew, but I did. It was a cheap hotel, too. Even with my eyes closed, I intuitively felt the coarse nature of the place. I still had my clothes on, including my shoes. Not a good sign. I had no memory of the night before, or even the day before. I was getting used to that. Why bother to remember what doesn't matter?

I wasn't hung over. I just didn't give a damn.

My eyes were so gummy it was hard to get them open. I settled for one eye. It took a while, but it opened.

Lying down, I saw the world sideways through blurry vision. I blinked and blinked again. Both eyes were open now. Shocked into movement, I raised myself on one elbow and rubbed my eyes clear with my free hand. He was sitting on a chair at the side of the bed.

"Mac, is that you?"

* * *

He told the story while I cleaned myself up as best I could with a pitcher of yesterday's water, a cracked bowl, and a towel so thin you could see through it.

"Danny, you're a hard man to find," he said. "I've been chasing you for two weeks. Everywhere I went, it seemed like you just left."

"Why?" I asked, still befuddled from sleep despite my quick wash. I still couldn't believe that my oldest friend was sitting just a few feet away. It turned out that I *was* in Marseilles, although I still wasn't sure why or how I got there.

Mac stared at me for what seemed like an eternity.

"It's time for you to come home."

* * *

They say that the army is harsh and unforgiving. I said that plenty of times myself.

It's easy to forget that the army is more than an institution or an instrument of war. At its best, the army is a kind of brotherhood. Sometimes that brotherhood reaches out in defiance of all the rules that bind it.

It seems selfish, but I wasn't surprised that Mac crossed the Atlantic and searched Europe to find me. If positions were reversed, I would have done the same for him. I'm sure he knew it. There came a time when I did, or something like it. But I *was* surprised that the army let him do it.

It took a long time for news of Amy's death and my collapse to travel across thousands of miles and get back home, but eventually everyone who knew me enough to care heard about it.

Although I did not care, I was always aware that there was a great deal of envy among my peers regarding my assignment to travel Europe at army expense. Even my friends shook their heads and marveled at how I'd drawn a royal flush. When Amy died and I tumbled into my downward spiral, there was just as much smug satisfaction from the same people who envied my earlier good luck as they eagerly passed around the gossip, usually a smidgeon of truth embroidered with lies and exaggeration. The Germans have a word for it: *shadenfraude*, taking pleasure in the misfortunes of others.

When Mac heard what happened, he took it upon himself to investigate, not an easy thing to do at long distance. I didn't know it and wouldn't have cared if I did, but I was about to face a court-martial, though I probably would have been allowed to resign. Given my state of mind, there is a good chance that I would have wound up dying in a gutter somewhere in Europe, alone and forgotten.

Mac called in every favor he could, which led to his chasing me around the continent before finding me in a seedy Marseilles hotel.

He was right. It was time to go home. I needed purpose in my life and Mac knew just where to find it.

Chapter Twenty-Two

We traveled by train from Marseilles to Paris, where we stayed three days, plenty of time for me to submit my resignation as military attaché and recover some personal belongings I stored there.

No one seemed to regret my leaving.

From Paris, we boarded a train to Le Havre, where we secured passage on the ship Thomas Jefferson bound for New York City. The North Atlantic was rough and gray as usual, but Mac and I enjoyed the voyage while most of the passengers turned various shades of green. After drifting ever since Amy's death, it felt good to be moving toward something.

After a long time apart, it was only natural that both of us had changed. Mac added weight, all muscle from the look of it. He still had his side whiskers, but they'd filled out so that he no longer resembled a young man trying to appear older than he was. He'd added a decent mustache, too.

But the real change ran deeper. He carried himself with an air of authority that had nothing to do with rank. He still could be too intense and pigheaded. That would never change. But my old friend now was the kind of man other men defer to.

I changed, too, but not for the better. Unlike Mac, I lost weight, which came from not eating properly. While still a big man, I was badly out of condition, though I didn't look it. When we left Marseilles, I grimly began a serious twice-a-day exercise routine on the ship.

I saw the biggest change in my eyes every time I looked in the mirror. It would be a long time before I learned to fully enjoy life again, but thanks to Mac now I knew that one day I would. Sometimes I could even forget about the pain that clutched at my heart with cold fingers.

In bits and pieces during the voyage, Mac filled me in on his life since we last saw each other.

Grappling with the uncertainty we all felt with the end of the war, for a while he was content to float from one assignment to another while the army struggled to reorganize and reduce itself to a goal of twenty to twenty-five thousand men. He was kept on the move by serving on a series of regional boards to assess which officers were fit to continue to serve, duty he dismissed as "damned boring". I am also sure that he hated having to decide the fate of a fellow officer who might also be his friend.

After making his unhappiness known to his superiors, he took a month's leave to visit his family in New York before joining the Corps of Engineers in Portsmouth, New Hampshire, to rebuild the crumbling old fort that guarded the harbor, duty that didn't satisfy him either.

Longing for activity he considered meaningful, Mac decided that a posting in the West best suited his skills and inclinations. It was the only assignment that offered field command, and leading troops in battle is what we were trained for. Promotion came faster there, too, with more opportunities for an officer to distinguish himself.

Sitting backwards in a chair with his arms crossed along the back, he watched as I huffed and puffed my way through my exercise routine while the burley North Atlantic buffeted the old ship from bow to stern.

"Building new walls in old forts is not for me, you know that better than anyone," he explained. "There are plenty of officers who can do it better than I can. Who am I to deprive them of the pleasure?"

I snorted my derision. "You are too generous, as always."

Although many other competent young officers wanted the same thing he did, with his stellar record Mac was among the select few permitted to make their case in an interview with General Grant. To strengthen his position, he promised to accept any appointment Grant assigned him.

He didn't know it, but that was the opening Grant needed to solve a vexing problem. He was told to come back in two days and the general would have something for him.

"I felt sorry for Grant," he said. "I know that sounds ridiculous, but he was besieged by what seemed like everyone under the sun wanting everything under the sun. His waiting room was so crowded it was practically shoulder to shoulder – civilians, junior officers, senior officers, politicians, old friends, and strangers. I never expected to see the man so frazzled."

"And that was *before* he was elected," I wheezed, whirling two weighted Indian clubs around my head. I hated regular exercise in all off its torturous forms and now I remembered why. "I wonder how he likes being president?"

As Grant promised, two days later Mac had his assignment, along with a promotion; the colonelcy of the 41st, one of the four colored regiments mandated by Congress after the war. Although three officers had already turned it down, characteristically Mac saw it as an opportunity.

"It seems so obvious." He shook his head at the folly of his fellow officers. "If you can succeed where everyone else was afraid to even try, how can you *not* look good?"

"*If* brother, *if*, it's an important word." Breathing heavily, I settled the Indian clubs on a rack against the bulkhead. "You should let it run free through your addled brain more often."

I didn't want to belabor the point, but sometimes there is a good reason for reasonable reluctance, perhaps even a little fear. But trying to explain such a thing to Ranald MacKenzie would have been like preaching a sermon to one of the ship's boilers.

Still, being stubborn myself, I gave it a try as we left the tiny gymnasium and passed through the hatch on the way to breakfast. After the exercise I was ravenous.

"Another way to look at is that if you fail in a situation that everyone else had the good sense to avoid, how can you not look like, well, a failure, someone with more ambition than sense?" I said.

This time it was his turn to snort derision. We must have sounded like a barnyard full of pigs.

Mac joined his new command in the fetid climes of Baton Rouge, Louisiana.

"How was it?" I asked. "What was it like? What are *they* like?"

I knew nothing about coloreds or what kind of soldiers they made. I didn't know any growing up and didn't serve with any during the war. While there were a handful of colored regiments, especially late in the war, I heard that at first, they weren't even paid the same as white soldiers. For all I knew, they never were.

Nobody said so publicly but commanding a regiment of colored troops was regarded as a potential career killer. The assignment usually went to eager young officers like Mac who would take anything or disillusioned veterans who were close to retirement and didn't care. There was a half-hearted attempt to introduce colored cadets into the academy after the war, but it was met by hostility from both the cadet corps and the faculty.

We were shown to a table next to the bulkhead in the dining room. A porthole displayed the world of gray outside. Only the whitecaps made it possible to distinguish between sky and ocean.

"It was pretty rough in the beginning," Mac admitted. "Most of the men got shoveled into the army because nobody knew what else to do with 'em and they had no idea what to do with themselves. How could they? Most of 'em were field hands all their lives. Everything they knew, their whole world, disappeared overnight."

The quality of men improved when Mac announced that he would not accept recruits who couldn't read and write, a bold action from a young officer because it considerably thinned the numbers available to fill out his regiment. The truth is that half the white recruits couldn't read or write either.

"I can make a soldier out of any man, but to make a *good* soldier requires better raw material than we were getting," he explained. "Once we improved on that, those boys took to it. Pride in the regiment came fast. For most of 'em, the uniforms were the best clothes they ever owned. They haven't been bloodied in a fight yet, but they'll do grand service when they get in action. I'm sure of it."

"Of course," I said archly, "Ranald Mackenzie trained them, after all."

When he nodded in agreement, I realized that irony was wasted on my companion.

"We had one general in the regiment, too."

I gave him a long look. "Say that again."

"He goes by the name of Smith; Private John Smith," he explained. "Not terribly original, is it?"

"His real name is Cardiff, George Andrew Cardiff. He was a brigadier general with the Rebs, Bedford Forrest's cavalry. He's so much older than everybody else the men call him 'Pops'. Among the officers, his real identity is an open secret. I think he was assigned to a colored regiment just to humiliate him, though if he had a problem with it, he hid it well. His two sons were killed in the war and his wife died long before, maybe in childbirth. With his home burned to ashes along with most of the rest of Atlanta, and with no family left and no place in the world, he enlisted as a private under a false name. No duty was too menial that he wouldn't volunteer for it. It was as if he felt the need to debase himself. Anyway, I couldn't let all that experience go to waste and made him a corporal within a week."

I was familiar with a man's need to debase himself, but instead of falling into self-pity I wolfed down my breakfast of steak and eggs. Mac contented himself with a boiled egg and black coffee, which was all he'd eat until dinner. I never understood how a man with so much energy consumed so little fuel.

Motioning to the waiter for a refill of the ship's potent coffee, Mac continued with his story. After several weeks of training in Baton Rouge, the regiment was transferred to Brownsville, Texas, on the Rio Grande at the point where Texas cuts deepest into Mexico. As commander of the Military District of the Southwest, Phil Sheridan specifically asked for Mac.

"Officially, we were an army of occupation assigned to pacify people who were in rebellion against us not long before," he said. "But most of those folks were glad the war was over and gave us no trouble at all."

A worse problem was French intervention across the border in Mexico – forty thousand French soldiers propping up the puppet regime of the Austrian Archduke Maximilian. Under the pretext of long overdue loans and in defiance of the Monroe

Doctrine, while we were busy fighting each other France moved in on Mexico, which it had eyed for decades. By placing an Austrian on the newly created Mexican throne, France gave itself diplomatic cover, even if every nation on earth saw through it.

"Washington supported Benito Juarez and his government, of course, but most of the trouble along the border had nothing to do with any of that," Mac said. "It was banditry, pure and simple, vermin out to take advantage of the chaos. They pretended to be loyal to one side or the other when their only loyalty was to themselves."

With Sheridan ordering increased patrols, Mac's regiment was assigned to a hundred-mile span along the Rio Grande, where he set up pickets at the major fords. Smuggling was so profitable that it was impossible for either side to resist. Even the United States government played the game, occasionally "losing" an arms cache along the border so that Juarez's troops could find it.

As often happens, the Mexico problem eventually solved itself. When Juarez's popular support became too strong, France abruptly abandoned Maximilian, leaving him alone to face the wolves. The unfortunate "emperor" was captured by the Juaristas and executed by firing squad. Although Juarez claimed to like Maximilian personally an example needed to be made, the bloodier the better, and Maximilian was that example.

I remembered hearing news of the execution in Europe, talk of the continent for a while.

Aside from the border problems, like the rest of the South Texas remained under martial law. Mac was expected to see that the freed men and women of color received fair treatment, former rebels behaved themselves, rowdy frontiersmen obeyed the law, and his own troops refrain from causing problems, all of this to be accomplished with colored troops that rubbed up against the white population in sometimes unpopular ways while enforcing the law. Mac was careful to frequently rotate his troops so there wouldn't be enough time for incidents to develop between his men and the locals.

The temptations were extraordinary. The price of cotton shot to unheard of heights after the war. It was stored in great quantities all over Texas because it was virtually impossible to get it out during the last one or two years of the war. Speculators offered Mac huge sums – twenty thousand dollars in one case – to show a little favoritism so they could get their cotton out and sell it in New Orleans, where it was shipped to the northern states or off to Europe. Simply by ignoring a few unpopular regulations Mac could have become a wealthy man in a short time.

After making his usual success of a difficult assignment, Mac was transferred again, this time to Fort Clark. But with the army's typically bewildering behavior, a few days later he was ordered to San Antonio for courts-martial duty, where he languished for eight long months.

I expected to hear him grouse about the forced inactivity, but he hesitated as if he wasn't sure of his ground.

"What is it?"

I downed the last of my coffee as I contemplated another helping of eggs. One unexpected result of exercise was that I ate enough for two men.

"I really shouldn't say any more...it's...I... Oh, hell!"

I understood. I don't know how but I did.

"You met someone, didn't you?"

When he didn't reply, I plunged ahead. It never occurred to me that I was humiliating my best friend.

"You rascal! Who is she? *Where* is she? Tell me all about it! Every detail."

I shouldn't have pressed him. It was cruel. For most of Mac's life, women were a bewildering mystery he never solved.

Usually so sure of himself, he turned into a stammering, blushing boy when confronted by a woman, any woman, in almost any situation.

"Yes, I suppose I did...meet someone, I mean...but...you see...it didn't..."

I continued my assault.

"You *suppose* you did? You either did or you didn't. Get hold of yourself, man!"

My unfeeling stupidity was merciless.

"It didn't work out, that's all!"

Staring out of the porthole at the churning Atlantic, he began to tell the story.

Before he got too far, I realized my blunder. I reached across the table, put my hand on his forearm and apologized.

"I shouldn't have said anything. I'm sorry I pried. You don't have to say any more."

I didn't mean it, of course. I wanted to *know*.

I finally got it out of him, but it was like trying to pull a badger out of its hole by the tail. I can be an oaf sometimes, possibly more than sometimes.

Her name was Florida Tunstall. Her father, Warrick Tunstall, owned the boarding house where Mac lived during his eight months in San Antonio. According to Mac, there was nothing between them at first and they barely noticed each other. Then and now, I doubt that very much. Beneath his hard shell, my friend was a man of deep feelings he constantly fought to control, as if he were afraid of what might happen if he let them out to prowl. It seems more likely that he was smitten from the moment he laid eyes on her and didn't know what to do about it. He probably stumbled over the furniture in her presence.

At some point the nothing between them became something. She was eighteen, he was twenty-seven, and he was in love for the first time in his life. Like me, it hit him with the force of a blacksmith's hammer. I can only imagine how difficult it was for my awkward friend to express his feelings to the young Miss Tunstall.

Once the ice was shattered, they spent virtually all of their free time together. Unfortunately, the blissful months came to a calamitous end when an army doctor named Redford Sharpe returned to San Antonio from temporary assignment in Washington.

It turned out that Florida Tunstall and Sharpe, who was at least twenty years her senior, were seeing each other before he left for Washington. His assignment completed early, when Sharpe unexpectedly returned to San Antonio, instead of the confrontation everyone expected, the rivals for the hand of the tantalizing Miss Tunstall sat down for a civilized talk, like two nations negotiating a treaty.

I could not believe it. If I were in Mac's place, the only thing Sharpe would have heard from me is, "Go away!" followed by my size twelve boot on his backside. When Mac said that they agreed to work it out like gentlemen, I wanted to grab him by the lapels and shake some sense into him, even if it was too late.

Sharpe left for Washington believing that he had a commitment from Miss Tunstall, one she did not feel that she gave. Flirtatious she undoubtedly was, but she denied deliberately leading Sharpe on.

Of that, I am not sure. I wasn't there, but she certainly didn't discourage him. Perhaps she really did see it as simple flirtation.

Whatever the reason, Sharpe made certain assumptions, the most important being that she would wait for him so they could marry when he returned from Washington.

The young lady claimed to be shattered when Mac broke off their relationship without explanation. My stubborn friend refused to see her again, or even reply to her tearful entreaties. The naïve fool mistakenly believed that he caused a rift between two committed lovers.

In his eyes, *he* was the guilty party, the twit.

Florida's was heart was broken, at least that is what she said. I was doubtful, but maybe I was too cynical. To me, she seemed like a coquette who got in over her head. I *knew* that Mac's heart was broken. His decision to search for me in Europe gave him an excuse to escape the misery of the hopeless love triangle.

After our ship-board conversation that morning, he made it clear that we were never to speak of it again.

It was not a request.

Chapter Twenty-Three

We were headed to Fort Concho in Texas, Mac's new posting and where I was to be his second in command.

I protested, while hoping that he would ignore me. I was grateful for another chance but afraid that I might let him down.

It was years since I'd seen regular service, I said. I had never been west and didn't know a thing about it, I said. He was taking a big chance, I said. A lot had happened since we last served together, I said. What if I didn't have it in me anymore?

To all these questions, Mac had only one answer but voiced it repeatedly: "Oh, shut up!"

I couldn't find Fort Concho on the only map available on the ship, not surprising since the map was twenty years out of date. From Mac's description I concluded that it was not only near nothing I'd ever heard of. It was a long way from nothing I'd ever heard of.

Mac revealed that Corporal Smith was coming with us, too, once another promotion was arranged. A leap from corporal to sergeant major might cause some grumbling in the ranks, but

Mac didn't care.

"He's the best I've got," he said. "You know how I feel about a good sergeant. At the rate that man's going, he might make general all over again."

After disembarking in New York City, we traveled by train to Washington, where we received official orders confirming what had already been confirmed. The army does love redundancy.

From there it was a short train trip to Baltimore, then by ship down the southern coast, around Florida and north through the Gulf of Mexico to New Orleans, where we waited for most of a week before the next stage of our journey, by steamboat ninety miles north to Baton Rouge. We linked up with a massive wagon train of officers, men, and supplies intended to reinforce and resupply the dozen or more forts scattered across Texas from Fort Sill in the north to Fort Brown on the Rio Grande, and from Austin to El Paso.

Progress was slow but steady as we entered the steaming greenery of east Texas, which looked very much like the steaming greenery of Louisiana. It took three days to get the wagon train across the Sabine River, but most of the time we moved along at a steady average of fifteen miles a day.

The further west we traveled, the more gruesome my impressions. I often asked myself: We're fighting over *this*?

"Mac, why not let the Indians keep it?" I was not entirely joking as I waved one arm to take in the dreary landscape. "What could we possibly want with this miserable country?"

Riding side by side as we led a twisting line of mounted and marching men and creaking wagons that stretched for more than two miles, Mac only shrugged.

"Don't worry, Danny," he said. "You'll get used to it."

What a despicable thing to say!

Having never been west of the Shenandoah Valley, and after

years in the abundant greenery of Europe, I felt as if I landed on the moon. Several times the temperature plummeted from boiling hot to freezing cold in a matter of minutes, depending on the intensity and duration of what the locals colorfully called a "norther", a word that I learned to dread. Eventually I would learn to fear two words – "blue norther" – even more. They make me shiver even now.

Some wise man once said that if he owned Texas and hell, he would rent out Texas and live in hell. I understood completely, at least as it applied to the parts I saw, every rolling, brown, dry, rattlesnake infested inch of it as we slowly made our way west, stopping at the occasional dismal fort.

As the years passed, I actually grew to like it, well, some of it. But at first sight, I was convinced that if the Comanche, Kiowa and other hostiles we were supposed to subdue really wanted this miserable country enough to fight for it, we should offer our congratulations and hand it over.

It would serve them right.

Chapter Twenty-Four

"Gentlemen, the frontier is an open wound! It's disgraceful that a few stone-age savages have rolled back civilization until there are fewer people on our border than there were twenty years ago. Whole sections of the country are emptying out! People are running for their lives!"

General William Tecumseh Sherman was in a fine lather as he paced back and forth in his temporary office at the U.S. Army Department of Texas headquarters in San Antonio, his long legs gobbling up the floor as he waved an impatient hand toward Colonel Randolph Baxter, who accompanied Sherman to the conference.

"Baxter, what was the name of that county? We talked about it yesterday."

Like a good subordinate, Baxter had the answer.

"Wise County, sir."

Still pacing, Sherman snapped his fingers. "Yes, that's the one. In eighteen sixty, Wise County had a population of three thousand one hundred and sixty. Do any of you know what it was ten years later?"

The officers looked at each other. None of us knew the answer. I doubt that anyone would have replied anyway. Why interrupt such a fine performance?

"One thousand, four hundred and fifty!" For the mathematically impaired, Sherman added, "In other words, less than half of what it was ten years earlier! In some places the line of settlements has been driven back a hundred miles! A hundred miles!"

To Sherman, this was no mere recitation of numbers. It was personal, and that requires an explanation.

I can only imagine how Phil Sheridan's guts must have churned when Sherman telegraphed Sheridan's headquarters in Chicago to say that he intended to tour the Texas frontier and gather first-hand information from settlers who for years complained about their lack of protection against the Indians. Sherman was skeptical and wanted to see for himself.

Sheridan was the army's second highest-ranking officer, but Sherman was the commanding general, succeeding Grant when Grant became President. Despite what must have been a multitude of misgivings, there was nothing Little Phil could do to stop his superior from making the dangerous four-hundred-and-sixty-mile journey from San Antonio north to Fort Sill, a route that cut through the heart of Kiowa country.

Typical of Sherman, who detested pomp as much as he detested Washington, the general struck out with only a handful of soldiers as an escort.

They were about to become the luckiest men in Texas.

As his party approached the Trinity River, Sherman unknowingly rode through a carefully laid ambush set by more than a hundred Kiowa. The general spotted a few braves watching from a distance, but when nothing happened, he assumed that it was just a hunting party.

It wasn't until later that Sherman learned how close he came to disaster. The Kiowa consulted a shaman whose vision gave them instructions for their ambush. Ignore the first party, he said, even though it will be small and weak in appearance. They must not attack it. Instead, they must wait for the second, which turned out to be a wagon supply train laden with corn and fodder and driven by a dozen unlucky teamsters.

Seven men were killed in what became known as the Salt Creek Massacre, but that did not tell the whole story. The victims were stripped and mutilated. Some were beheaded and their brains scooped out. Their fingers, toes and privates were cut off and stuffed in their mouths. Others were tortured by live coals placed on their stomachs. One poor creature was tied between two wagon wheels and the wagon set on fire so that he was slowly roasted to death.

Not long after Sherman's party arrived at Fort Richardson, the five survivors, all of them wounded, staggered into the fort and told their terrible story, dragging along a wounded Kiowa brave. Before he died, the Kiowa told his version of events and the general realized that if it hadn't been for the shaman's counsel it could have been him roasted between wagon wheels.

Reaching Fort Sill, the angry general invited the Kiowa chief Satanta to parley. Meeting on the headquarters' veranda, Satanta not only admitted the raid, he took considerable pride in a job well done.

Rising to his feet, Sherman dramatically announced that Satanta was under arrest and would be tried for murder. When Satanta reached for his rifle, the building's shutters flew open to reveal a dozen soldiers with their weapons aimed at the burley chief.

Sherman's near miss convinced him that the settlers' complaints were true. If it could happen to him, it could happen to anyone.

William Tecumseh Sherman was mad as hell.

Chapter Twenty-Five

"I have called you here because I want your thoughts."
Sherman stopped his restless movement and faced us, hands on his hips. "I have my own ideas, but you are the officers in the field, and I want to hear what you have to say."

There were nothing but brave souls in that room, but no one wanted to be the first to speak up. I could see it in the averted eyes and nervous shuffling. Wesley Merritt, Nelson Miles, Jim Forsyth, Ben Grierson, Mac, myself – all of us high-ranking officers with excellent records and still we answered Sherman's appeal with silence.

Some of those present I liked and some I didn't, but there were no slackers among them. I knew what they were thinking. An ambitious officer could look very good at a gathering like this, or very bad. Don't commit yourself. See how things go first.

All but one.

"Sir, do you remember Frederick the Great?"

I was not surprised when Mac broke the silence. Someone had to.

Anticipating what Sherman might want, the night before, Mac and I came up with a rough proposal. We didn't know if we'd get a chance to present it, or if it would survive criticism from Sherman and the others, but we had the chance we wanted.

Sherman responded with such a withering look I was surprised Mac didn't turn to stone.

"I am not that old, MacKenzie. If you are asking me if I know *of* Frederick the Great, the answer is yes, of course. I attended the academy, just as you did. I probably had many of the same ancient instructors who taught the same boring classes in the same boring way. Now if you will be kind enough to make your point instead of asking nonsensical questions about a man who lived in the last century on another continent, we can get on with it."

Sarcasm was one of Sherman's ways of testing a man. He liked it when you showed spirit, although it was wise not to go too far. Everyone knew that it hid a large soft spot. During the war, Sherman's men were so fond of him that they called him "Uncle Billy". No one, not even Grant himself, had a better record.

"He who defends everywhere defends nowhere," Mac said, quoting the great Prussian general.

"He who defends..." Sherman's eyes took on a knowing cast, although with his back to the others only Mac and I saw it. If I interpreted it correctly, the general understood, just as we hoped. He offered Mac a curt nod that might mean anything before turning to address the rest of the officers.

"Since the rest of you seem to be struck mute, why don't we take a break of one hour while you consider what I want," he said. "And, gentlemen, I can only hope that you think faster in the field than you seem to be thinking right now."

We rose to leave with a shuffling of chairs and feet.

"Not you, MacKenzie. Remain here," Sherman said. "You,

too, Stone."

The look on the faces of the other officers was easy to interpret. They figured Mac and I were about to get a reaming over Mac's nonsensical comments.

On his way out of the room, the black-bearded Ben Grierson, one of the best cavalrymen in the army and a good friend to both of us, comically lifted one eyebrow and whispered, "Frederick the Great?"

When the door closed, Sherman turned on us.

"All right, start talking. Sheridan gave me an earache rattling on about you two. If you're as smart as he thinks you are then you probably conjured up something as soon as you heard I was coming. And I give you credit, MacKenzie, at least you didn't wait to see which way the wind blew before speaking up."

Mac glanced at me and I nodded. As my superior officer, it was up to him to start.

"It's just as I was trying to say, sir. Against the Comanche in particular, we try to defend everywhere and consequently defend nothing. The hostiles always have the initiative. We react to them and we're almost always too late to accomplish anything significant. Our few successes have more to do with luck than design. Sir, the enemy doesn't fear us. It laughs at us."

"Not being entirely dim, I am aware of that," Sherman said. "What I'm looking for is a way to break the pattern. Tell me something I don't know."

It was my turn. "It comes back to something General Grant, I mean, President Grant, once said."

The strong friendship between Grant and Sherman was well known and I figured it would do no harm to bring the president into the conversation.

"Not long after he assumed command during the war, one of his generals expressed concern about what Lee might do," I said. "General, I mean, President Grant, didn't like that. He said that it was about time Robert E. Lee started worrying about what *we* might do."

"He'll always be General Grant to me, too, Stone," Sherman said. "Running for president was the worst mistake he ever made. It will be his ruination. Now, as to your point?"

"We need to take the fight to the hostiles, sir, and make them worry about us for a change," Mac said. "Invade their territory, attack their villages and kill their horse herds. That's something we haven't tried much, and I never understood why. We should make an effort to capture their women and children, too, so that they *must* negotiate with us if they want to see them again. Not kill, capture. We need to act with less blood lust and more intelligence.

"Surprise, pursue and bring them to battle in ways that favor us. The army has been ordered to seize control of an entire native population that has a huge advantage in mobility, *except* when they settle in for the winter or when they are convinced of their safety in some remote camp. It is at then they are the most vulnerable. The Comanche must understand that there is no refuge no matter where they hide. If we do that, I believe that while success will not come overnight, it will come.

"If it continues to be a war of hit and run at their initiative, they will always have the advantage. They are tougher than we are and better at living off the land. Their grass-fed mounts are smaller and faster than our grain fed animals, too. They know every trail, waterhole, canyon and bluff. Riding flat out, a Comanche warrior can fire off a half dozen arrows with accuracy while one of our troopers might get off a shot or two."

It was one of the longest speeches I ever heard from Mac.

Chewing on his thumbnail, Sherman nodded. "All right, MacKenzie, keep talking, but keep in mind that it's not *their* territory. It's our territory. All of it, every square inch, is *our* country."

"First, leave the infantry behind to garrison the forts," Mac said. "I mean no disrespect but responding to a well mounted enemy with infantry is absurd."

"Take the war to the enemy," I said. "Surprise them for a change. Do it over and over and never stop."

I was redundant, but I couldn't just sit there and say nothing.

"You'll be interested to know that General Sheridan agrees with you," Sherman said. "On the northern plains, he intends to strike their villages, their food supplies, and their families whenever he can."

Sherman started pacing, back and forth across the small room.

"It's similar to what Custer did when he attacked that Cheyenne village on the Washita in the dead of winter, though it was considerably less than the great victory that infernal idiot bragged about. It's astonishing to me that the newspapers believe his bombast. It is not generally known, and you will say nothing about it, but while there were warriors present, the village was mostly women and children. A resounding victory over mostly noncombatants."

The general stopped pacing and turned on us.

"MacKenzie, how do you propose that we do something like that when we don't know the country? It's the damndest thing I've ever seen. The Comanche strike and then disappear into that area, what's it called, the ..."

"*Llano Estacado*, sir," I said.

"No white man knows it," Sherman continued as if I hadn't spoken. "It's almost as big as all of New England and might as well be the dark side of the moon. We don't know the trails, if there are any, or where the water is when there is any water. We're so likely to get lost that the hostiles don't have to do anything except watch us make fools of ourselves."

Sherman started pacing again, faster and faster as if to match his rapid speech.

"And the *Llano* is only part of it. The Comanche roam over the Southern Plains virtually unchallenged. The *Comancheria,* the Mexicans call it. I've had reports of our patrols riding in circles and didn't know it until they cut across their own trail. The Comanche probably ruptured themselves laughing. The few times we engaged in close pursuit we were chewed up until all that was left was a collection of broken-down horses and men who barely had the strength to stumble back to where they started. They steal our horses at night, wear us down on a futile chase, and send us packing."

One of the things I admired about Sherman was how he used the words "we" and "us" in good times and bad. Most generals are happy to do that with victory, but with defeat or hard times it becomes "you" did this or "you" didn't do that. In Sherman's mind, we were in it together and everyone who served with him loved him for it.

"There *are* a few white men who know something of the *Llano,*" Mac said. "We just haven't been systematic about gathering information. If we interview every scout, guide and buffalo hunter we find and work with them to create maps, we can come up with a decent perspective and add to it as operations commence."

"It's like making a quilt, sir," I said. "A square here, a square there, and eventually you have the whole thing."

"A strangely peaceful comparison, Stone, considering the subject, but I take your point," Sherman said.

"I can even arrange a meeting with Jim Bridger," Mac said. "I understand he's with a party that's headed this way."

Sherman smiled, his usually stern face changing into all sorts of unusual angles.

"Bridger? Good God! Now there's an interesting character.

I met him years ago in northern California before the war. He seemed old then. I'm surprised the old boy's still around. This far south we're out of his usual country, but it'd still be worth hearing what he has to say."

"There's something else to consider, sir," Mac said. "The Comanche and Kiowa draw most of our attention, but the Kickapoo and Apache cause almost as much trouble. From their villages in Mexico, they cross the Rio Grande to raid and escape back across the border where we can't pursue them. If we are to stop those raids, in my opinion we must destroy their villages in Mexico. We could be back across the border before the Mexicans knew we were there. Even if they knew it, they'd still have to prove it."

Sherman tugged at his chin. The man seemed always in motion; tugging at his chin, chewing a nail, ruffling his beard, juggling one leg as he sat, pacing back and forth. I have never seen anyone so restless.

"Quite the aggressive character, aren't you, MacKenzie, wanting to push into the *Llano and* into Mexico?" he said. "What's next? An amphibious operation against Greenland?"

Sherman pulled up a chair, sat down, put his elbows on his knees and stared hard at both of us, his eyes feverishly bright.

"You are not the first to raise such an idea," he said. "The problem is that we could never *officially* approve the invasion of another country, not without first informing the president, who would have to get consent from Congress, which would blather on and on until we died of old age.

"I'm sure you gentlemen are smart enough to understand what I'm saying. Even if what you propose is the right thing, no matter how much I like the idea I can't approve it. Any such action, however laudable, would be unauthorized."

The message was clear. Our superiors could never authorize an illegal campaign. There would be no orders, just carefully phrased encouragement that could be denied later, that certainly *would* be denied later, if necessary. If such an expedition into Mexico ever took place, there would be much looking the other way from the president on down.

If whoever led the invasion was discovered by the Mexican government, or drawn into conflict with the Mexican army, they might be killed or spend years in a Mexican jail. If they were lucky and got home, they'd likely be court-martialed for leading an illegal and unauthorized invasion.

I didn't like it and it wasn't just the danger that disturbed me. There was something artificial about all of this, at least on Sherman's part. It was as if he came prepared and, knowing Mac's aggressive nature, led Mac where he wanted him to go.

I thought it was craven and foolishly said so.

"Under those circumstances, sir, why would anyone make such a raid?" I asked. "What you're saying is that if anyone crosses the border and something goes wrong, they would get no support from the superiors who informally urged them to do it. Frankly, sir, it seems cowardly to urge someone else to do the dirty work at no risk to yourself."

I had gone too far. Sherman's face flamed crimson red while Mac's took on a sudden pallor.

"Cowardly? By God, I'll..." Sherman was on his feet and sputtering, his anger briefly rendering him incapable of speech.

"Major Stone!" Mac interrupted with a bellow. "You are dismissed!

Get out or I will have you escorted out! Until otherwise notified you are confined to quarters."

I was about to respond with hard words when I saw something in Mac's eyes. Unless I misread it, he was pleading for me to clear out and keep from making a bad situation worse.

Mac was playing a subtle game as he tried to save me from myself.

Was I right? I wasn't sure. Maybe I was only seeing what I wanted to see.

With the fuming Sherman looking on, I snapped to attention, gave a crisp salute, pivoted on my heel and marched out the door.

Chapter Twenty-Six

I stewed about it all night. Thanks to my big mouth, I alienated my best friend, offended the army's top general, and ended my career all at the same time.

I was stubborn and vowed never to apologize no matter what happened. Whatever the next move might be Mac would have to be the one to make it. The message I thought I saw in his eyes probably was never there at all. In the darkness of a sleepless night, I convinced myself that I only imagined it. He wouldn't be the first officer to pick career over friendship. I grumbled that if Sherman suggested that Mac fly off to a distant planet, he'd start building wings.

My words to Sherman were intemperate. "Stupid" might be a better word. I was right but sometimes being right did not matter.

Mac showed up at my quarters late the next morning, long after I despaired of his coming.

I heard the knock and knew it was him. I told him to enter, rose to my feet and saluted.

"Oh, Danny, will you stop that nonsense?" I could hear the

weariness in his voice. "I'm supposed to be the stiff-necked one, not you."

With a sigh, he sank into the only chair in the small room. Following his lead, I gingerly sat on my cot.

"Well, aren't you curious?" he asked.

"About what?"

"Good God, man! What do you think? I had to get you away from Sherman yesterday before you dug yourself an even deeper hole."

I let out a blast of air and tension that I'd held inside since yesterday. No matter what happened now, all was right between us.

"What happened after you threw me out?"

"Sherman was in a rage. I doubt that anyone has ever called William Tecumseh Sherman a coward before, even if that's not exactly what you meant. I promised to have you drawn and quartered on the parade square. You know, the usual. Then he started to laugh like he would never stop. The man had tears running down his face. It was a sight to behold."

Most generals are baffling to subordinates but Sherman was more baffling than most.

"Once he stopped laughing, and it took a while, he praised your – how did he put it? – 'unusual gift of eloquence'. He said no one talked to him like that in years. Refreshing, he called it."

Seeing my perplexed look, Mac repeated himself. "Yes, believe it or not, 'refreshing' was the word he used.

"He admitted that he agreed with you. Illegally invading another country is not a good idea, and he would prefer to find another way. The problem is that there may not be one. We wound up talking for a long time. He left this morning, just a few minutes ago. That's why I'm so late getting to you."

"What happens now?"

"My guess is nothing at all," he said. "You're lucky it was Sherman. If you'd spoken to most generals like that, you'd be in the guardhouse right now and out of the army in six weeks with a court-martial on your record."

I thought that might be better for both me *and* the army but didn't say it.

"I meant about going into Mexico. Where does that stand?"

Mac ran the back of his gnarled hand across his forehead as if he were trying to wipe away cobwebs.

"I think we'll have to go down there sooner or later. With the proper authority or without it, doesn't really matter if there's no other way."

"Mac, it's a bad idea...a *terrible* idea," I said.

"Maybe." He shrugged. "But sometimes a bad idea is better than no idea at all."

I disagreed. Sometimes a bad idea is just a bad idea.

But all that was far in the future if it was there for us at all.

First, the Comanche.

Chapter Twenty-Seven

"This here's my last chance to see some country, though I reckon there ain't much of anythin' new left to see. Problem is I'm breakin' down. Just too damn old, I guess. I need to get out and about one more time before I pack it in."

I heard of Jim Bridger all my life and could hardly believe this ragged old coot was the legendary mountain man, trapper, scout, explorer and guide. Friend to Kit Carson and John Fremont and founder of the Rocky Mountain Fur Company, stories of his legendary adventures could fill a library. Though his active days were pretty much over, they say he still could assess any wagon train, group, or individual, and once he found out where they were headed give expert advice covering any trail, destination and circumstance.

I do not remember exactly where Mac and I met Bridger, except that it was somewhere in north Texas, and he asked that we come out to his camp within sight of the fort. He was traveling with a dozen rough companions, six or seven spare horses, and at least three mongrel dogs.

"I like it better out in the open, always have," he explained. "'Preciate you comin' out here. Bein' cooped up inside too long gives me a bad case of the squirms."

Like Sherman, I was surprised to learn that Bridger was still alive. It turned out that he was quietly living out his days on his Missouri farm. As he said, his aging body was breaking down, the result of a hard adventuring life, much of it in circumstances that would have killed an ordinary man.

Suffering from rheumatism, arthritis, and failing vision, the old mountain man was still slim, though hunched at the shoulders. His hips constantly hurt – he admitted that most days he had to be helped onto his horse – and he moved slower than the tide. Wearing a broad-brimmed hat that looked too big for his narrow head, he was more leathery than old boots, and appeared to be about nine hundred years old.

If someone told me that Jim Bridger was present at the creation, I might have believed him.

Bridger sat on the ground with the small of his back against a worn saddle while Mac and I faced him, sitting cross legged. Every so often he leaned back so that his shoulders almost touched the ground on the other side of the saddle, a stretching maneuver that was always accompanied by a satisfied, "Aaahh!"

While he filled an old briar pipe with tobacco and fired it up, unleashing such an evil stench that I was happy to be outdoors, we explained the plans for our campaign against the Comanche and how we needed to acquire more knowledge of the *Llano Estacado* along with the surrounding territory.

It turned out that Bridger was hard of hearing, too, and we had to repeat ourselves several times and practically shout most of what we said. So much for secrecy.

"I do know the *Llano* some, but truth of it is I spent most of my time further north, though I 'spect you know that," he said, picking a speck of tobacco off the tip of his tongue with a crooked index finger that resembled an old stick.

"You know, my old pard Jed Smith got himself killed by the Comanche. The way I heard it he got caught too far ahead of his party lookin' for water. Young Jed was foolish sometimes. Always took too many chances."

Bridger shook his head. "Some forty years or more ago, that was. Don't seem near that long. The years just get away from a man."

Now that I'm probably twenty-five years older than Bridger was then, I know exactly what he meant. Forty years doesn't seem that long, barely a blink of time's eye.

"The Comanche near did in ol' Kit Carson, too," Bridger said. "Back in '64, I think it was. He led three companies out of Santa Fe and went after a Comanche band over near Adobe Walls. Kit and his boys sure 'nuff lived to tell about it, but just barely."

Bridger paused for a moment, a look of sorrow crossing his aged face.

"Now Kit's gone, too, just like most of my old pards. Time surely ain't no friend, is it? Just another damn thief, seems to me, only it steals your life."

Shaking himself out of his reverie, Bridger gave us a long skeptical look.

"I never faced the Comanche much and I'm damn glad of it. Everything they do they do better'n anybody else. Their tough ol' buffalo hide shields can stop bullets sometimes. Them lances must run to twelve or fourteen feet and they know how to use 'em better'n even Mexican lancers. Their bows and arrows can put the fear of the almighty in a man, too. I once saw a brave gallopin' on horseback fire off five or six arrows so fast that the last one was in the air before the first one hit the target, and they all hit the target. Any poor soul within thirty or forty yards or so is gonna get hisself stuck good."

Bridger took a draw on his briar pipe and thoughtfully watched the smoke waft away.

"You boys *sure* you want to go out there after that bunch? I'd say best you think about it some."

Although he claimed to not know that much about the *Llano*, once Bridger started talking it was clear that he knew more than anyone we'd met so far. Whether it was from personal experience or information he gleaned from others, it didn't matter. We believed him and, as it turned out, with good reason.

As he described it, the vast area of the *Llano Estacado* seemed every bit as forbidding as its reputation made it out to be, although he added that it was accessible if you knew what you were doing, which excluded most whites. He did not like the idea of a winter campaign and warned us against it.

"You can't hunt Indians on the plains in winter, for blizzards don't respect man or beast," he said. "'course summer's not much better; hotter'n blazes most times. What people forget about the L*lano* is that it's purty high, even if it don't seem like it when you're out there. Five thousand feet or more some places, they say. Altitude makes thirst and sun worse, and you don't even know it's happenin'. Sneaks up so a man's in a bad way long 'afor he even gets a notion of it. All they'll find is his bones where he dropped."

Some of what he told us we already knew, although it was good to have it confirmed by someone like Bridger, as if there was anyone like him. The *Llano Estacado* was bounded by the Canadian River on the north. To the east, the Caprock Escarpment, a vicious-looking cliff ranging up to three hundred feet in height, separated it from the red plains of Texas. On the west, the Mescalero Escarpment imposed the same kind of unforgiving border. The boundary isn't as distinct on the south, though most agree on the Johnson Creek branch of the Colorado River, mostly because it has to end somewhere.

Altogether the *Llano* stretches some two hundred and fifty miles north to south and almost two hundred miles east to west, or almost fifty thousand square miles altogether. Summers are long and hot, and winters are bitterly cold, with wind "that blows right through yer damn soul", Bridger said. Some years it's dotted with a few small lakes that may not be there next year, so you can't count on water being where you saw it last. Even when you find it, there's never much of it.

"Reckon it's no different than a lot of places that way," Bridger said, puffing away at his pipe. "Many's the time I've strained dirt through my teeth to get a little water. A man gets thirsty enough and he'll do anythin'. I've heard tell the Comanche kill their horses and drink the blood if they have to."

While this vast empty area is sometimes called the Staked Plains, the accurate interpretation of *Llano Estacado* is "stockaded" or "palisaded" plains, which is how the edge of it looks when it's seen from below the cap rock, a high rock wall that says come in at your peril.

Years later, writing a report about the *Llano* for Washington – another of my literary creations that I'm sure no one read – I came across a description by Francisco Coronado, the conquistador who wandered through the area and then all the way to Kansas in the 16th century, as lost and desperate as a man could be:

"I reached some plains so vast that I did not find their limit anywhere I went, although I traveled over them for more than three hundred leagues ...with no more landmarks than if we had been swallowed up by the sea... there was not a stone, nor a bit of rising ground, nor a tree, nor a shrub, nor anything to go by."

An American expedition in the 1850s made the same observation, describing the *Llano* as "a treeless desolate waste of uninhabitable solitude which always has been and must continue uninhabited forever".

We didn't know it then, but while the description was accurate the conclusion was wrong. Within a little more than a generation the *Llano* would be settled as the frontier disappeared altogether, which no one would have believed possible.

The land almost killed Coronado and his men, and it did kill many others. No one knows how many. The area was littered with the bones of its victims, most of them either done in by the Comanche or by the *Llano* itself. While it was only a part of what was known as the Comancheria, the empire where the Comanche roamed at will, let me tell you, it was the most dangerous part.

We talked with Bridger for more than two hours. He agreed to put the word out that we were looking for men to help us gain knowledge of the *Llano.* Such was the respect everyone felt for the living legend that a score of men did contact us, all of them with good information.

After a while we talked of things that had nothing to do with our mission. Bridger was an entertaining old boy, and it was a pleasure to listen, like conversing with a national monument.

Like most mountain men, he loved to tell tall tales and spin wild yarns. He was so well known for it that sometimes when he told the truth – the remarkable geysers he discovered at Yellowstone are a good example – no one believed him until someone else confirmed it.

"Did I ever tell you boys about the time I was chased by a hunnert Cheyenne?"

Since we just met him, we assured him that he'd never told us the story.

With great relish and many dramatic gestures, Bridger said that the Cheyenne chased him for miles.

"I used every trick I knew of and couldn't shake 'em a'tall."

Finally, he was trapped at the end of a box canyon, where they thundered down on him "with bad intentions in their hearts and death in their eyes".

We knew a cue when we heard one and dutifully asked, "What happened then?"

"Damned if they didn't kill me!"

Bridger laughed like he'd never heard his own joke before. We happily joined in if a bit less enthusiastically.

We parted ways from the old boy a few minutes later. We later heard that he finished his western trek and returned to Missouri, never to leave it again.

Before we left, Mac and I presented him with a gift, a beautiful pistol of blue steel we had specially made at army expense with Sherman's permission. The name Jim Bridger was spun in gold script across the pearl handle, and it was presented in a handsome walnut box that was polished until it gleamed, along with fifty rounds of ammunition.

Tears came into the old man's eyes as he fondled the weapon.

"Well, don't that just shine," he whispered, which I later learned was a mountain man expression meaning that he liked it. "Ain't never had better. Ain't never *seen* better. Come in handy, too. Can't see good enough anymore to use a long gun."

He looked up from the beautiful weapon, his eyes glistening. "Wish I could come with you boys. Wish I could do a lot of things. Wish I could undo some others, too, but that ain't the way it works, is it?"

We said our goodbyes, mounted our horses and rode the short distance back to the fort.

As we neared the fort, Mac stopped, turned in the saddle, and looked back with a final wave. Bridger was sitting where we left him, the old pipe in his teeth and the walnut box in his lap. He took off his old hat and waved it in the air.

"Danny, how often do you think he's told that old stretcher?" Mac asked. "Do you think he was chased by *any* Cheyenne?"

"I'd guess that at one time or another Jim Bridger's chased or been chased by just about everything there is, man or beast," I replied. "I bet he's told the story at least a hundred times and enjoyed every one."

Mac thought for a bit as we rode across the fort's parade ground.

"On the day that man dies, I will mourn."

Chapter Twenty-Eight

Some things I do remember, and I remember October 3, 1871, so clearly it might as well be yesterday.

There were six hundred and forty of us, including twenty-five Tonkawa scouts, bivouacked at a bend of the Clear Fork of the Brazos, a hundred and fifty miles west of Fort Worth. Dust swirled in thick clouds while bugles shattered the air. With the dust, the bugles, orders from leather-lunged officers, cursing sergeants, the jingle of tack and creaking of saddles, horses snorting and mules braying it hardly seemed like a carefully organized start of a major campaign.

To my eyes, the surrounding countryside was as uninviting as ever, a vast rolling prairie of brown grass dotted by scrub oak, sage, and chaparral. Even today, I think of it as a dry brown country. I know very well that it isn't, not always, but that image is frozen in my memory and it will never change.

The order snapped down the long line of men and animals and we slowly began to move out.

Few campaigns ever started with more uncertainty. We were

the largest force to ever enter the *Llano Estacado*. Despite all the information we gathered we still weren't sure what we'd find.

As uncertain and disorganized as it seems now, we were the last best hope for one simple reason: nothing else worked. The most recent failure was President Grant's attempt at a peace policy run by a collection of well-meaning Quaker appointees who managed to turn everything inside out. They unwittingly rewarded Indian aggression while penalizing attempts at genuine peace.

It didn't take the Indians long to figure out how to play the Quakers for fools. It was the same story from the Canadian border to the Rio Grande. Hostile Indians who spent the warm months killing and stealing at will accepted government bribes to come to the reservations in the fall. After spending the winter fed and sheltered at government expense, come spring they broke out to do whatever they pleased until the next fall, when they accepted more bribes to return to the reservation. The following spring the whole cycle started all over again.

Even the most violent outbreaks usually ended in some kind of agreement, accompanied by government gifts and tokens of friendship. In the meantime, those Indians who stayed on the reservation, behaved peacefully and made no trouble got nothing.

Actually, that's not true. They got punished.

When their fellow Comanche continued to raid, several times the promised annuities to the reservation Indians were forfeited to pay depredation claims, penalized for something everyone knew they didn't do, idiocy that made no sense anywhere but in Washington.

It was no wonder so few of them trusted us. Even Lawrie Tatum, the Quaker agent in charge of the Comanche reservation, where the permanent population consisted mostly of old men, women and children, admitted that the so-called peace policy failed so badly that brute force was the only solution.

I have always believed that most of the Indians could have been bought off and everything worked out more or less peacefully if the government hadn't been so parsimonious, and fraud so common. At the best of times, less than half of what was supposed to benefit the reservation Indians ever got to them and it wasn't that much in the first place. Trying to make peace on the cheap never works.

The government couldn't even keep its promises of reservation land. White settlers – miners, too, if there were rumors of gold – invaded the reservations virtually everywhere. Official Washington, perhaps the greatest collection of liars and scoundrels ever assembled in one place, only shrugged in response.

Instead of solving problems, the peace policy created more. As usual, the army was called on to clean up the mess.

Sherman went to Washington and spoke to President Grant in the blunt way that only he could, given their close friendship. Policy changed, on the southern plains Colonel Ranald Slidell MacKenzie was to be the primary instrument of that change, and I was his second in command.

At our final meeting with Sherman, the general explained exactly what he wanted.

"MacKenzie, you are moody, difficult, and implacable, a lone wolf without a diplomatic bone in your body. You seem to regard the chain of command as an inconvenience. You scare the hell out of your own men and there are times when you verge on insubordinate."

When Mac opened his mouth to protest, Sherman snapped, "I am not finished," and glared at us until I had the urge to squirm like a schoolboy.

"To me, many of these things seem like points in your favor, though people do say that I am peculiar. I need a hard thing done,

I need a hard man to do it, and I believe that man is you."

We were in San Antonio again. Phil Sheridan should have handled the briefing, but Sherman wanted no misunderstanding about what he wanted and traveled all the way from St. Louis to make sure. Sheridan was in Chicago, supervising a campaign on the northern plains.

"You will lead the largest force ever to encounter the hostiles anywhere in the West," Sherman said. "My orders are simple. I want you to kill Comanche. I want you to track them, find them, and fight them wherever they are. Into them you will put the fear of God and the U.S. Army. Gather as much information as possible, so it will be a little easier the next time. Return when you feel that the campaign has run its course. The timing is at your discretion. The only sure thing is that you will make mistakes, but I believe that you are smart enough to learn from those mistakes."

Sherman raised one arm and dramatically pointed at me, like an Old Testament prophet calling down the wrath of God.

"Heed that man's counsel!" Lowering his arm, the general added, "I am not telling you to always do what he says. In my opinion, he is too soft hearted. But I want you to listen to him.

"You are a stubborn man, MacKenzie. Sometimes you need to listen to a voice other than your own. Good or bad, I expect you to learn from experience. If something doesn't work, don't do it again. We have too many damn fool officers who think the answer to everything from butchered civilians to bad weather is to charge with flags flying and trumpets blaring."

The general held up one hand in a peace-making gesture.

"I will back you no matter what happens. It is an old story. If we succeed, we are butchers who slaughter the poor defenseless Indians. If we fail, we are imbeciles who could not protect a litter of kittens.

"It will be years before we win but win, we will. You aren't the only piece in this puzzle. Your fellow officers in this department all have parts to play. I will shortly issue orders coordinating the overall campaign. But your mission is the most important, something neither of you will repeat. We have too much rivalry as it is. If it works as I hope it does, your campaign could be the beginning of the end."

With that out of the way, Sherman seemed to relax. He walked to a window, moved aside a lace curtain gone yellow with sun and age, and looked outside at the empty parade ground and the barracks beyond. I doubt that he saw any of it.

"People think that I am a bloodthirsty bastard. Maybe they're right, but I don't know another way to win a war," he said. "We represent civilization and bring irresistible progress with us. We have settled our differences at home and for now we are unchallenged by any foreign power. We are on the cusp of a great new age and yet a handful of stone-age savages stand in our way. They don't just impede progress, they have all but stopped it. What they have achieved is remarkable, but I do not give a damn. They are the enemy, and they will be treated as such. There can be no other way."

Sherman turned from the window, his expressive face calm and thoughtful.

"Many people question why we need all this land. They consider the enormous emptiness of it and say that it couldn't possibly be settled in a hundred years or more. In my opinion they couldn't be more wrong. I believe that within two generations at most the frontier as we know it will cease to exist. I probably won't live to see it, but you and your generation will."

Sherman returned to his desk and sat on the edge. He was as relaxed as I ever saw him, but even then, one foot jiggled, the heel tapping lightly on the floor.

"With all these grand plans of ours, do you know what's really going to win the Indian wars?"

Sherman loved rhetorical questions, especially when he asked them.

"The buffalo," he said. "We're killing all the buffalo."

That made no sense to me.

"Sir, I'm afraid that I don't understand," I said.

"That's because you haven't been out there to see it all as I have," Sherman explained. "Be aware of the bigger picture, Stone, not just what directly engages you. To the Plains Indian, the buffalo is everything. He gets food from the meat and lodging from the hides. He eagerly devours the parts that we scorn. Buffalo chips provide fuel for his fires, tools come from bone, tack from hide, ropes from twisted buffalo hair, and clothing from hides and fur. His bowstrings come from buffalo sinews and he turns the hooves into war clubs."

"I *have* been out here long enough to understand that, sir." I never liked being lectured. "The part I *don't* understand is what you said about killing all the buffalo."

I pointed my chin at Mac. "Two weeks ago, we ran across a herd that was so immense we couldn't wait for it to pass. So, we rode around it, two whole days of us moving one way and the buffalo another. There were hundreds of thousands of the beasts, and it was only one herd. And you say we somehow will kill them all? Sir, with all respect, that's simply impossible."

"Stone, it's happening even as we speak," Sherman said. "Thousands of buffalo are slaughtered every day. Last year alone, Dodge City shipped over four hundred thousand hides east and that's just a fraction of the slaughter. It's hard to grasp the scope of it. As the railroads advance, buffalo are killed to feed the thousands of laborers. Hunters kill for the hides to be sold back east and leave the carcasses to rot on the plains. Did you know they only get twenty-five cents for a good hide and a nickel for a poor one? It's such a miserable way of life I'm surprised anyone wants it. Yet, many do. Someone recently discovered that buffalo bones make good fertilizer, which means the slaughter will only increase. The army kills buffalo to feed itself. Buffalo are killed for sport, too, though the beasts are so damn stupid I don't see much sport in it.

"Just recently General Sheridan provided an escort for some relative of the Russian czar who came west to hunt. Sheridan arranged for that young scout – what's his name, Cody, the one who calls himself Buffalo Bill? – to guide the party. With the rest of his group, the archduke, or whatever he was, killed more than five hundred buffalo in a week. Most of the time the mighty hunters didn't even get off the train. They sat on top of the cars and blasted away as the train slowly pushed through a herd, stopping from time to time to take a few heads for trophies on walls somewhere in Moscow, I suppose, leaving the rest for the buzzards. It was killing for the sake of killing.

"Grotesque as it is, I encourage such behavior. The kind of war we are waging is unique. There are no cities to attack, no fortresses to besiege, no lines of defense, and no opposing army as we traditionally think of it. When we are fortunate enough to find a village, the Indians rarely fight to hold ground because it doesn't mean anything to them. They simply melt away. We can't negotiate properly because nobody speaks for any particular tribe or nation, although Washington likes to pretend otherwise.

"That's one reason why our Indian policy is such a shambles. We work out a treaty with a chief who claims to have authority while the people he's supposed to be negotiating for don't even know that the treaty exists and probably would not care if they knew."

I now understood Sherman's point, though it still seemed absurd. Kill all the buffalo? Impossible. I did not know that in only a few years that is exactly what would happen. The slaughter was immeasurable. There has never been anything like it. Yes, a few buffalo survived, but only a few, like zoo specimens.

The world was changing faster than any of us could imagine.

Our meeting was coming to an end, but Mac, silent so far, had something more to say.

"General, you should know that we have gained a great deal of information since we last met," he said. "When we enter the *Llano* it looks like we will in pursuit of one band of the Comanche, specifically, the Quahadis, although there are at least five such bands and maybe as many as ten or twelve, each independent of the other. They plant nothing. They don't weave, make pottery or build. They hunt, they raid, and they make war."

Mac paused to get the rest of his thoughts in order. He wanted Sherman to fully understand what we faced.

"The Quahadis are the most dangerous of the lot. We don't know much about them because they always avoided contact. When they bother to trade, they prefer to deal with the Mexicans out of Santa Fe – the *Comancheros*.

"Even other Comanche fear the Quahadis. No one can out-ride or outshoot them on horseback, and they use those horses in ways hard for us to imagine. To them a horse is a commissary on four feet. When water runs low, a desperate Comanche kills his horse and drinks the contents of its stomach. If chased, a Co-manche rides his horse 'til it drops then cuts it open to remove the intestines. He wraps the intestines around his neck, mounts a fresh horse from the herd, and eats the intestines later. Strangely, a Comanche won't eat birds or fish unless he's starving, and he *never* eats the heart of a buffalo.

"They are nomads, but we do have a sense of their movements. While they hunt in the *Llano*, they sometimes camp in Palo Duro Canyon, a canyon so vast they are hard to find even when we know they are in there. They also camp near where the Pease River and McClellan's Creek meet, too. Blanco Canyon is another favorite spot.

"The leader of the Quahadis is named Quanah, a mysterious character who seems to have risen out of nowhere, and too young for us to know much about him. However, there *are* interesting rumors. If possible, we will find out more."

Sherman nodded. "I know what you're talking about, MacKenzie. I have heard bits and pieces myself. Despite what I said about killing the Comanche, any prisoners you take will be welcome as long as there aren't so many that they burden your movement. One way or another, we can get information out of 'em once you get back."

It was impossible to know how much of what we heard about Quanah was true. He'd already become a legend and as with all legends, facts were hard to come by.

In the most popular version of the story, Quanah was the half-breed son of a Comanche leader named Peta Nocona and Cynthia Anne Parker, a white woman famously kidnapped by the Comanche at Parker's Fort, about ninety miles south of Dallas, in 1836, when she was just nine years old. I remembered hearing about her when I was a cadet. Every attempt to find her failed. There were wisps of rumors but nothing that could be confirmed. No one even knew if she was still alive. Eventually so much time passed it was as if she never existed.

And then she was discovered in the smoking ruins of a small village of mostly women and children that was attacked by a combined force of army, civilians and Texas Rangers.

Standing alone in the midst of calamity and holding a baby daughter in her arms she looked like any other Comanche until one Ranger took a closer look and was startled to see blue eyes. When she responded to the first English she'd heard since she was captured, the Ranger suspected that he'd stumbled onto the long-lost Cynthia Ann Parker. Her husband was killed in the fight, but a young son named Quanah either wasn't there or got away.

By then, Cynthia Ann Parker was more Comanche than white. Although she lived several more years it was a tragic story, never adjusting to white society just as white society never adjusted to her. When her daughter, Prairie Flower, died she seemed to lose interest in living and virtually starved herself to death.

At least that was one version. No one knew the truth. Was Quanah really her son? It seemed like too much of a coincidence. As far as anyone knew, no half breed ever rose so high with the Comanche.

We didn't know it then, but we would hear the name Quanah until we were sick of it. His fearsome reputation alone probably was the equivalent of five hundred warriors.

In his abrupt way, Sherman brought the conversation back to his original path.

"But none of that really matters, does it? No matter who leads the Comanche, the point that Stone was impatiently waiting for me to make during my long-winded lecture about the buffalo is that we must destroy the hostiles' ability to make war, destroy their ability to feed, clothe and arm themselves, just as we did with the Rebels. Without the buffalo, which we are slaughtering at a remarkable rate, they can do none of those things. Until that day comes, we will keep the pressure on so that they are always looking over their shoulders. One way or another, we will defeat them."

I offered more feeble skepticism. "Sir, it still seems unimaginable that we could do that much killing of the buffalo in such a short time that it makes any difference."

Sherman smiled. "Stone, all it takes is bullets, and God knows we have plenty of those. If the war taught us anything, it taught us that we know how to kill."

The general was finished with us, having said all he intended to say and a great deal more. We were dismissed without even a "Godspeed" or "good luck". In Sherman's eyes, however much he may have liked us we were the best tools available to get the job done and you don't wish good luck to a hammer.

Walking across the parade ground to our quarters, I said to Mac, "Until the end, you were awfully quiet in there."

"Mostly Sherman didn't say anything I didn't already know," Mac said. "We met briefly this morning and he did most of the talking then, too. I barely get a word in. Seeing as how I'm supposed to pay strict attention to every little thing you say, he wanted to see to both of us."

I knew he was joking, but I still was piqued.

"Then why didn't you say something before instead of letting me make a fool of myself and take a schoolboy lecture like that?" I grumbled.

Mac shrugged. "A simple division of labor. I lead the troop. You take the lectures."

I was about to retort when a spasm of pain flashed across his face. He staggered and awkwardly reached back as if to grab at something between his shoulder blades.

I held his arm to steady him. "Mac, what's wrong?"

His face was pale, and he couldn't say anything, his breath coming in short gasps. It was a telling sign that he didn't jerk away. He needed my support. With a supreme effort, he pulled himself erect and took a hesitant step before stopping again, still unable to continue.

"What is it? What can I do?"

"It's nothing," Mac lowered his head and put his hands on his knees, partially muffling his voice. "Don't worry about it."

"Don't tell me that was nothing!"

After a moment to catch his breath, he admitted, "Sometimes my old wounds give me a little reminder, that's all. Most of the time it's my back. If I wait a few minutes, it always passes."

"Mac, what I saw was a lot more than a *little* reminder," I said. "How long has this been going on?"

"A while, I guess. When it hits, I feel like an old man stricken by a seizure."

That was the most alarming thing he could have said. Ranald MacKenzie did not like to admit to human weakness.

"Exactly what do you mean by 'a while'?"

He tentatively straightened up, as if testing his own body. The relief in his face was like a man given a reprieve from a firing squad.

"I don't know...a while...years, I suppose. Forget it, Danny. It's nothing."

As we walked back to our quarters, out of the corner of my eye I took a long look at him in a way that I never had.

For the first time, I saw gray in Mac's hair.

He was only thirty-one.

***

I recently had a conversation with a young doctor here at the facility. He said that the sniper's bullet that gave Mac his first wound might have creased his spine and the damage was undiagnosed, probably because Mac didn't feel unusual pain. Getting shot is supposed to hurt.

Knowing him as I did, I think it's more likely that he knew something was wrong but ignored it because he didn't want to be kept away from the field. The attending physicians, assuming there were any, didn't linger over one patient because so many others waited for attention.

"Over time your body changes." The young doctor pushed his glasses higher on his nose, obviously grateful to get a chance to talk about something other than the ailments of the aged. "That's possibly when it began to affect your friend, though it's also possible that he suffered from the beginning. Turn one way or the other, roll over in bed, or even do nothing at all. It could strike anytime. From what you tell me – particularly his comment about 'most' of the pain being in his back – his other wounds must have troubled him, too. I'm guessing, of course, but if I'm right I don't see how he kept it up."

Chapter Twenty-Nine

If we were supposed to learn from our mistakes, by the time the campaign ended we must have been the smartest men west of the Mississippi.

Every day our Tonkawa scouts fanned out ahead of the troop, as eager as hunting dogs on the scent. It was their job to look for sign, lead us to water, and find trails of the Comanche.

The Tonks were nearly exterminated by the Comanche years ago, and the few that were left lusted for revenge. But that did not mean we trusted them. At least I didn't. Until early in the century the Tonks were cannibals, much feared by Texas' settlers. I didn't know how much truth there was to the wild tales, although old-timers swore they were true, but I did not intend to put my trust in anyone whose grandfather might have been tempted to eat me for dinner.

It turned out that I was right to be wary. I just had the wrong reason.

The Tonks were supervised by two white scouts. One, Marcus Potts, was a veteran of more than twenty years on the plains.

As a young man, he lost most of his left arm to a poisoned arrow. The stump never properly healed, and he fashioned a cover for protection that had a long eagle feather dangling off it. The other scout was a quiet young man named Hogan, whose dark hair fell to his shoulders in the fashion preferred by many scouts in those days.

Although Hogan seemed to be Potts' protégé, we knew little about him. When Potts said that he wouldn't go with us without Hogan coming, too, that was enough for us. Both men proved their value every day of the campaign.

Our ambitious expedition could have ended in disaster on the first night.

Without consulting Potts or Hogan, who were riding with most of the rest of the scouts far ahead of the main body, we called a halt near a buffalo wallow because it offered a source of water. The water was stagnant, warm, smelly, and covered with green slime that had to be pushed aside, but at least it was wet. The men didn't much like it, but the horses and mules didn't care.

A howling windstorm moved in during the night, a common occurrence on the plains, where the weather seems to change every ten minutes.

Sometime after midnight, I was jolted awake by the tramping, snorting and bellowing of a buffalo herd at full stampede. We made the blunder of pitching camp between a large herd of buffalo and its water source. The windstorm kept us from hearing the buffalo thundering our way until it was almost too late.

The ground was shaking under our feet as the men burst out of their tents, fear bulging out of their eyes. The wind and the darkness made a desperate situation even worse because it was hard to tell where the sound was coming from.

Once we figured it out, Mac and I, aided by the steady hand of

Sergeant-Major Smith, got the men yelling and waving blankets in a desperate effort to turn the stampede, which by now seemed louder than an artillery barrage.

At Smith's suggestion, the firebrands we scrambled to light probably helped save us more than anything else we did that night. Like all animals, buffalo fear fire and will do anything to avoid it.

At the last moment, the stampede veered to our left, just enough to miss the camp. Even so, the buffalo flushed the edge of our terrified horse herd. Luckily, there were no casualties among the men.

We avoided catastrophe, but by slimmest margin.

We spent the rest of the night rounding up stray horses and calming the rest of the herd. Although we lost a half-dozen mounts either trampled or run off, we could have lost the entire herd, a calamity that would have ended the campaign that night, leaving us to walk back to the post with our tails between our legs almost before we started.

It was agreed that from then on, either Potts or Hogan would always travel with the main troop.

"It's my fault, I reckon," Potts generously admitted the next morning as we assessed the damage in the daylight. "Either me or Hogan should'a been with you boys. Fact is I didn't know how much you don't know. We'll be keepin' a better sight on things from now on and maybe try to educate you some as we go, though nobody can predict what a Comanche might do next."

"What do the Comanche have to do with it?" I asked.

"It was Comanche started that stampede," Potts said. "Figured they'd get buffalo to do their work for 'em. If it didn't work out, nuthin' lost. Buffalo might have milled around some when they found you between them and a good drink, but they wouldn't have run like that on their own."

I don't know if that made me feel better, but at least I didn't feel quite so stupid.

Something else bothered Potts, though he seemed reluctant to express it, and we urged him to speak up. As usual, Hogan hovered silently in the background, taking in every word but saying nothing.

The scout nestled his rifle in the crook of his good arm while he thought it over. Instead of using a Sharps as most scouts did, a weapon famous for its long range and accuracy, he preferred a Spencer, which had a short barrel, a necessity for a one-armed man.

He taught himself to fire the weapon by balancing the barrel on the stump. It looked awkward, but he was as accurate as anyone in the troop. Like me, for close work he kept a sawed-off shotgun in a horse scabbard.

Potts waved his stump toward the Tonkawa scouts who waited for orders to move out.

"I don't know who made the choice, but I wish we had somethin' other than Tonks with us. They been fightin' the Comanche for near a hunnert years and ain't never won a damn thing. They ain't bad men, but everythin' the Tonks do, the Comanche do better. It's my fear that the Tonks'll see only what the Comanche want 'em to see. We'll have to take their word on a lot of it 'cause me'n Hogan can't be everywhere."

Mac responded the only way he could.

"Marcus, it's too late to do anything about it now," he said. "We have to make do with the tools we have."

Potts took Mac's decision in stride, the way he took almost everything.

"I reckon you're right, Bad Hand. I'll go..."

"What did you call me?"

Mac didn't seem angry, just curious. Neither one of us heard that name before.

Looking surprised himself, Potts asked, "You sayin' you don't know?"

When Mac shook his head, the scout nodded at the waiting Tonks. "Bad Hand, that's what they all call you. The Comanche, too, I hear."

"How would the Comanche know to call me anything?" Mac asked. "Except for old men, women and children on the reservation we haven't even seen one yet."

He raised his mangled hand. "I know they may be watching us, and I believe you when you say they caused the stampede, but they can't possibly be close enough to see...this."

"You been known by that name for months," Potts said. "Word spread a while ago. They had you pegged as somebody to keep an eye on. They can tell from how a man carries himself and how other men act when they're around him. Anyone can see it, if they're payin' attention. It's an honor, if you think about it. They ain't happy you're the one leadin' this outfit.

"And beggin' your pardon again, sirs, but I figure it's time for your first tutorin'. There's a couple of Comanche close enough right now to count what's left of your fingers."

My body tingled and it felt like my hair was standing straight up. I looked around as if my head was on a swivel. I didn't spot anything out of the ordinary and didn't expect to, but there was no reason to doubt Potts' word. It's not a good feeling to know that the enemy can see you, but you can't see them, especially if that enemy is a Comanche.

"They been with us ever since we left," Potts said. "I got a notion where they are but there's no point runnin' 'em off. More'd just take their place and it'd take Hogan'n me a while to sight 'em again. Anyhow, if they keep to that same position when we move out, knowin' where they are might be useful if we want to fox 'em later on."

Tucking his rifle under his stump, Potts vaulted into the saddle, ready to lead the Tonks ahead of the troop. He'd also mastered the art of mounting a horse with one arm. As promised, Hogan stayed behind.

His mount dancing with high spirits, Potts jerked on the reins to keep him steady while he looked down on us and grinned.

"Surely is somethin' to think about, ain't it, Bad Hand?"

Chapter Thirty

While the Comanche were nomads, we did have a general idea of their range, along with some of their favorite hunting grounds and camps. If we kept looking, we'd find sign of their passing.

On the third day, the Tonks found a trail worth following.

As the hours passed, they assured us that we were gaining ground, especially one Tonk who seemed particularly sure of himself. As the sun set, instead of making camp Mac ordered a night march, hoping to catch the Comanche by surprise. With Potts, Hogan and the Tonks using torches to follow the trail, it was hard going as we struggled through the dense brush, steep ravines and arroyos in the darkness, cursing and fuming right into the dead end of a box canyon.

We had followed a trail to nowhere, deliberately set by the Comanche, masters of deception who must have laughed themselves silly at our bumbling.

Angry and humiliated, we waited until daybreak to find our way out of the canyon. Instead of following another trail that might lead nowhere, we headed toward a fork of the Brazos River in Blanco Canyon, a thirty-mile- crease in the earth that averaged only a quarter of a mile wide and was cut by several side canyons. We knew it was a favorite Comanche camp and as we drew closer, sign was everywhere. Even I could see it and I am no tracker.

We were followed by a group of four Comanche who stayed near enough to tantalize us but too far away to catch. Even so, eager to make up for the box canyon fiasco, some of the Tonks gave chase. We saw exactly what Potts meant when he said that whatever Tonks do the Comanche do better. It was almost comical to see the Comanche toy with their pursuers before vanishing as if the earth swallowed them up.

The men were so discouraged that night we allowed them the luxury of campfires and warm food. It was my idea and a bad one. Men with their bellies stuffed full of warm food after an exhausting day sleep hard.

My good intentions nearly did us in.

I was slammed out of sleep by a series of banshee screeches, followed by shots and more screeching. The Comanche war cries were even worse than the Rebel yell I heard so often during the war.

Seizing my Colt, I jumped to my feet, threw open the flap of my tent and was greeted by Comanche riders racing through camp and firing their weapons into the air.

As I stood with pistol in hand shouting orders – I have no idea what I said – what seemed like every one of our horses and pack animals raced through camp, too, tearing down tents as they reared, jumped, and ran at full speed. Everywhere I looked, men scrambled out of the way to avoid being trampled by our own mounts.

The iron picket pins we used to secure the horses at night became deadly weapons as they flew through the air like airborne knives. I saw one trooper sliced open from forehead to chin when a pin smashed him in the face. Several brave men tried to grab the pins as they whirled though the air. The few who managed to catch one were dragged along the ground for their trouble.

I was nearly trampled when I stepped in the way of a Comanche racing at full gallop. For some reason, he made an instant decision not to run me down and his extraordinary horsemanship probably saved my life.

His horse reared, so close that I could have touched its belly. As he towered above me, the mount clawing the air with his hooves, and the rider firing his pistol in the air, it was as if time stopped. I saw a powerfully built warrior on a coal black horse. His long hair hung in two thick braids over his chest. He had large brass hoops in his ears and was naked to the waist, wearing only leggings, moccasins and a breechclout. A string of bear claws hung around his neck. His face was smeared with war paint, which should have given him a demonic look except that he was smiling.

No, that isn't right. He was laughing, a man born for moments such as this.

A skeptic might groan that it was impossible to see so much detail at night in the midst of chaos. I can only tell you what I saw. Yes, the moon was half full and offered some light, but I believe there was more to it than that. Was it fate? Luck? Did the gods conspire to put all the pieces in place for the first time?

I didn't know the answer then and I don't know it now. But I believe that on that night I was destined to come face to face with the most capable foe we ever knew.

Quanah, war chief of the Comanche.

Chapter Thirty-One

Once again, we were lucky. The Comanche got away with so many of our horses we couldn't make an accurate count until daylight. It was a damaging blow, and we certainly didn't feel lucky, but we could have lost the whole herd.

Early that morning, Mac called a meeting that included me, Potts, Hogan and Sergeant-Major "Pops" Smith, the Confederate general turned trooper. When I informed Mac that two or three of the young officers grumbled about Smith's inclusion, meaning that they were unhappy with their exclusion, Mac swiped at the air like he was slapping them away.

"I don't care what some shave tail lieutenant thinks," he said. "I need him."

Mac and Smith had become close in the short time they'd known each other. I liked and admired Smith, too. Almost everyone did, although there was some hostility, usually from men who didn't serve in the war, blowhards who were out to show what patriots they were now that the war was over.

I think Mac enjoyed learning from him. Although he never

talked about it, Smith graduated from the academy twenty-five years before we did and had more experience than both of us put together. I think Smith enjoyed his role as Mac's mentor, too. It could have been awkward, but Smith never overstepped his bounds and seemed to appreciate the chance to pass on his knowledge to someone he respected.

Smith was the last to arrive, puffing on a curved Meerschaum pipe turned golden brown with age. Potts and Hogan sat on the ground Indian-style. I sat, too, using my saddle as an improvised desk, taking notes so that when we made our campaign report, we'd have something to help us remember details. Mac paced back and forth, his frustration and nervous energy too much to contain.

"Marcus, I thought you said we had enough pickets, most of them your Tonks," he said. "How the hell did the Comanche get through last night?"

The scout was not at all disturbed by Mac's temper.

"Beggin' your pardon, but if you'll remember what I said a while back, they ain't my Tonks by a long shot," he said. "We found four pickets this mornin' with their throats cut. Poor souls never knew what hit 'em. Comanche got in through the gap."

Mac sighed long and hard, releasing his anger like a tea kettle on high boil and raising a hand in apology.

"Sorry, Marcus," he said. "I didn't mean to take it out on you."

"I don't like 'em much, but I wouldn't be too hard on them Tonks, if I was you," Potts said. "The Comanche been at it so long they made stealin' horses a dang art. A Comanche can slip into a bivouac where a dozen men might be sleepin', every man with a horse tied to his wrist. He'll cut a rope within six feet of the sleeper and get away with the horse without wakin' a soul. I've seen it happen."

"We'll just have to be more vigilant," Mac said. "Double the number of pickets, too."

To Smith he asked, "What's the damage?"

"As Mistah Potts said, we have four dead; three Tonks and trooper Allen, all pickets," Smith replied in his soft southern accent. "Five troopers injured. Three of the injuries are light and the men'll be fine in a day or two. One man's face was slashed open by one of the picket pins. We stitched him up as best we could, but he'll have an ugly scar for the rest of his days. He won't be fit for a good while. The worst injured man is trooper McAllister. His skull's split open so you can see his brains. Probably got run down in the stampede or hit by a war club. He's unconscious and may not live another hour. Between the buffalo stampede and the raid last night, we're down seventy-six mounts."

Mac kept pacing, smacking his hat against his thigh with every step.

"If the trooper dies, we'll bury him out here in an unmarked grave, so the Comanche don't find him and dig him up," he said. "We'll be out too long to take the body with us. Bury him deep. We don't want the animals to get at him either."

"Bad way for a man to go," I said.

"'Fraid I don't know many good ways," Potts said.

Ignoring our chatter, Mac asked, "Sergeant-Major Smith, despite the losses of so many animals is there any possibility of all our men remaining mounted so that nobody walks? I don't want to double up either. It'll slow us down too much and exhaust the horses."

Smith blew away a cloud of sweet-smelling pipe smoke before answering. With his experience, he anticipated the question and had an answer ready.

"Yes, sah, I believe we can. As y'all know, we had some extra mounts anyhow, 'bout thirty. We can use the horses that belonged to the dead men, too. Even if there's a miracle and McAllister lives, he won't be ridin' anywhere, so that's five more. Ah can redistribute the supplies and ammunition packs and get rid of a few things. If each pack animal carries a heavier load it'll free up a few mules. Some of the boys may not like ridin' a mule, but if it comes to a choice between a mule and shanks' mare they'll take the mule right enough."

Smith raised one hand in caution. "Sir, understand that'll leave us no spares a'tall. From here on if any mount comes up lame or hurt, somebody's walkin'."

Mac's mood brightened at Smith's ready solution. "Sergeant-Major, you are a miracle worker. I want to move out as soon as possible. Get started and let me know when you're ready."

As Smith left to make his preparations, Mac turned to Potts. "Marcus, what are the Comanche up to? They seem more interested in our horses than us."

"Horses are more useful to 'em. It's the same as always. They want to wear you down, steal horses when they can, and get you so beat up without losin' any of their own that you'll give up and go back to where you came from. They're more aggressive about this time 'cause there's so many of us. They want to make sure you don't ever come back with these kinds of numbers. Seems to me they might even be a little scared."

"Why do they think we'll give up?"

"'Cause far as I know that's what everybody did who came before you," he said. "The Comanche won't fight unless they have a clear advantage, or they're forced into it. They don't like to take casualties and most of the time they don't have to, least not many. You high-educated folks are a different breed. You been taught to set a goal and figure in your mind the number of dead that's worth it. What's it called?"

"Acceptable casualties?" I said.

AND HELL FOLLOWED WITH HIM

"That's it," Potts nodded. "To a Comanche such a notion is crazy as hell. They don't necessarily want you dead, though they wouldn't mind that at all. They want you gone."

"They better get used to disappointment," Mac said. "I want my horses back. We'll move out as soon as Sergeant-Major Smith says he's ready."

As I got to my feet, tucking my notes away, Potts said, "Just one more thing, Bad Hand, if you don't mind."

"What is it?"

"While we're here I think we should have a word with that man."

Potts pointed at a Tonk, who was lounging on the ground about thirty yards away. Like most of the Tonks, he wore a scruffy mix of white and Indian clothing – fringed leggings, an old blue army jacket with the insignia cut off, no shirt beneath the jacket, and a sweat-stained slouch hat missing part of the brim.

The instant Potts pointed, the Tonk jumped to his feet and took off like the hounds of hell were on his tail, covering the ground in great leaps.

Fast as he was, he never had a chance. In less time than it takes to tell it, Hogan ran to his horse, used two hands on the mounts' haunch to vault into the saddle, and raced after the fleeing Tonk, his tough little mare eating up the distance.

Riding hard, Hogan shook out a lariat hanging from his pommel. Getting closer to his prey, he twirled it around his head three times and let it go. Like magic, the loop closed neatly around the Tonk's ankles. Hogan dallied his end of the lariat around his saddle horn, the line snapped tight and the Tonk was snapped off his feet.

Hogan wheeled his horse and trotted back to our group, dragging the helpless captive in the dirt behind him.

"All right, Marcus, explain," Mac said. "What was that all about?"

"We got ourselves a spy," Potts said. "If you'll remember, he's the one who was so persuasive about followin' the trail that led us into the box canyon. After that mess I started watchin' him close, though I wasn't positive 'til he ran just now. I wanted to put a scare into him and see what he did. Probably been signalin' or leavin' sign. He looks like a Tonk, but I'd bet a dollar to a dance hall girl he's at least part Comanche."

While Potts explained, the sullen Tonk, or whatever he was, slowly rose to his feet, his coat shredded from being dragged along the ground behind Hogan. When the captive heard Potts say "Comanche", he pulled a knife from a leather sheath hanging from around his neck beneath his blue coat. Before any of us could stop him, he took a deep breath and using both hands drove the blade into his chest just below the breastbone.

With a moan, he sank to his knees. Still using both hands, he cut himself open all the way down to his navel before toppling to one side, his guts spilling out of his body and glistening in the sun.

"Good God!"

The voice seemed to come from far away, but I recognized it as my own.

Potts walked to the body and kicked it with one foot to make sure the spy was dead. He removed the dead hands from the knife hilt, pulled the blade out of his body and wiped the gore on the dead man's ragged coat. He examined the knife, decided that it wasn't worth keeping, and tossed it aside.

"Why, Marcus?" Mac asked.

"Probably figured he'd be tortured 'til he told us everything he knew 'cause that's what the Comanche would surely do," Potts said. "The only sure way he knew to keep from it was to do what he did."

I think we were all shocked, even Potts. I could not imagine what it would take to defeat such courage.

"My God, what kind of people are they?" I asked, almost in a whisper.

"'Bout like anybody else," Potts said. "Only more so."

Chapter Thirty-Two

As Smith predicted, Private Ian McAllister, the trooper with the head injury, died within the hour.

Before we buried him deep in an unmarked grave, Potts and Hogan made a thorough patrol to make sure than there were no Comanche watching, who might come back after we left and dig up the poor man. Once he was buried, I ordered horses ridden back and forth over the gravesite to further conceal it. Digging the grave, the patrol, the burial ceremony and concealing the site delayed us by almost three hours but morale would have suffered if we hadn't taken the time.

I led the column while Mac rode down the line on one side and back up on the other to make sure everything was in order, something he did several times a day. He trusted his officers and made sure they knew it, but he always wanted to see for himself.

Inspection complete, he reined in at my side.

"Danny, I've had something on my mind for a while," he said. "What would you think about the idea of forming a special group, call it a flying squad?"

"Purpose?"

"We need a faster response," he said "We're still too cumbersome. From what Marcus says, the Comanche can tear down a whole village and be on their way in the same time it takes us to saddle our horses. What I see is fifty men, or thereabouts, some of our best horsemen. All of 'em good shots, too. Men with steady nerves who don't rattle. They'd move light and fast, carrying everything they need for independent operation. No pack animals to slow 'em down. Hit and run when it's called for but capable of full engagement if it comes to that. I want 'em fast moving and eager. They'd ride with the troop most of the time but be capable of independent operation at the spur of the moment. Does that make sense?"

"I suppose it could work," I agreed. "It probably depends on who commands."

"Who do you suggest?"

"Me, who else?"

Mac reached across the space between us and slapped me on the shoulder.

"I thought you'd say that. It's yours if you want it. Don't do anything about it yet. And don't tell anybody. I don't want the troop to be distracted by talk about who's in it and who isn't. Just think about who you'd want in such a squad, including a second in command, and a good sergeant. We'll talk when we get back and refine it."

On subsequent campaigns, we did form such a flying squad and it turned out to be as useful as we hoped.

But that was far in the future. We did not know that we were about to embark on a long and deadly chase along the cruel knife edge of the *Llano*, the like of which none of us had ever experienced, or ever would.

Chapter Thirty-Three

It was just after noon as the heat simmered across the bar-ren land. I led a detachment of two Tonks and twelve troopers following the fresh trail of a band of Comanche leading at least twenty-five that were almost certainly ours.

Mac had four other detachments searching in and around Blanco Canyon. If we cast our net wide enough, maybe we'd catch something.

Rounding a rock outcropping that blocked our sight we almost rode right into twenty or so Comanche with our stolen mounts. They had stopped while one dismounted rider checked his horse's hoof.

For once we acted first and charged on my order, rapidly gaining ground on the fleeing Comanche, who were encumbered by the stolen horses.

I should have known better. It was too easy.

Realizing their dilemma, the Comanche abandoned our horses and made a run for it, crossing a shallow ravine followed by a long open stretch before scrambling up to the higher ground of a butte that looked like it rose almost to the top of the canyon wall.

I assumed they were following a path that would lead out of the canyon. Once we were on the prairie, they could outride us. Our cavalry mounts were stronger but heavier. Their horses were lighter and faster.

I should have called off the chase. My assignment was to find and if possible, recapture stolen horses, not engage the enemy.

But the chase was hot, and my blood was up. After all we suffered, I couldn't ignore a chance to hit back. I yelled for two men to break off, gather the abandoned horses, and get them back to the troop while the rest of us pursued the Comanche.

We spurred our mounts over the top of the butte only to find that the Comanche had turned on us, along with fifty or sixty more waiting in ambush on the high ground where they couldn't be seen from below.

Tricked again! It felt like the breath was punched out of my body by a hard blow to the guts.

The flat top of the butte swarmed with Comanche racing at us with blood-curdling shrieks, conspicuously led by the same warrior who almost ran me down the night of the horse raid, a pistol in one hand and his reins in the other.

There was no way our winded horses could outrun them. Our only chance was a fighting retreat to the ravine where we could make a stand, if we lived that long.

There was just enough time. Maybe.

I ordered the men to dismount, relying on our Tonks to hold the horses. With every instinct screaming "run", fortunately the discipline that Mac and I worked so hard to instill came through when we needed it most.

The men yanked their weapons out of their scabbards, and I pulled my Colt. With the Comanche screaming their war cries as they charged, I cautioned the men to fire low. There is a nervous

tendency in combat to fire too high. I was counting on the fact
that the Comanche never faced anything as fast and accurate as
the Springfield carbine fired by men who knew how to use it,
few though we were.

And if we died here, I swore that the Comanche would remember this day.

We fired three volleys at close range. Riders and horses fell in
a wild tangle, fouling the charge just as I hoped.

When the Comanche pulled back to regroup, on my order we
jumped onto our saddles and used the precious seconds to ride
hard down the butte. Slipping and sliding in the loose dirt, it was
all any of us could do to stay in the saddle.

A glance showed that we'd taken casualties, too. One man was
wounded by an arrow that partially passed through his hand and
stuck out of both sides. A trooper riding next to me was hit in
the leg near the groin. Blood pulsed from the wound as he clung
to his saddle horn, doubled over in pain.

Down on flat land, the lip of the ravine was in sight before the
Comanche came at us again. This charge was even more furious
than the one before. We had to try to buy a little more time to
get to the ravine and set up a defense.

We dismounted again. With some men kneeling and some
standing, including the wounded men, we blasted three more
volleys that brought down more men and horses and gave us the
precious seconds we needed. All that time we forced the troop
to spend on marksmanship paid off.

We remounted, raced a few more yards, slid down into
the ravine and jumped off our horses again. To my horror I
saw that we left one trooper behind, a popular private named
Seander Gregg. His horse had two arrows buried deep in its
haunch. Driven mad by pain, apparently it threw its rider as
it violently danced on three legs, head and body jerking back

and forth in agony so that Gregg couldn't grab the reins or the saddle horn to remount.

The trooper's left arm hung awkwardly at his side, either wounded or injured in the fall. Realizing that he couldn't remount, using his good arm he gave up on the reins and frantically tried to pull his Springfield from its scabbard, his mount still dancing in a circle so that the desperate private couldn't get his hand on the weapon.

"Cover him!" I shouted.

Firing independently, we knocked down several more Comanche and drove the rest back, all but one, the man I recognized as Quanah. Casually riding toward his prey as if he had all the time in the world, he zig-zagged his horse so that he kept Gregg and his pain-crazed mount in our line of fire, turning the trooper into a human shield so that we could not shoot without hitting our own man. Several of the men tried anyway, but it was no good.

All we could do was helplessly watch as Quanah moved in and fired one shot into the trooper's head from close range.

Then came one of the most extraordinary sights I have ever seen. His human shield fallen, Quanah did not ride hard for safety as we expected. As he did the night of the horse raid, he reared his mount, fired his pistol in the air and cried his defiant war cry before racing away.

As soon as Gregg went down with a bullet in his brain, every one of us fired at the triumphant Comanche leader, some more than once. Bullets kicked up dirt on the ground around him and I am certain that others must have whistled past his ears and even creased his leggings. But not one of our shots found its target, man or horse. It was as if Quanah possessed some kind of magic that made him invulnerable.

Our small detachment was in trouble and every man knew it. There would be another charge, probably combined with a flank attack that was forming already. Maybe both flanks at once.

Despite the deadly Springfields, there were not enough of us to hold if we were assaulted from two or three directions. We dug in on the slope of the ravine, determined to kill as many of the enemy as we could before they butchered us all.

Then came a miracle. I can think of no other word for it.

We watched in astonishment as the Comanche turned and galloped away. Still screaming their war cries, they stopped to collect their dead and wounded so that nothing remained on the field except pools of blood. We never knew how many we killed that day.

Dumbfounded at our sudden deliverance, I didn't understand the reason until I looked over my shoulder and saw the most beautiful sight I've ever seen: an advance guard of troopers riding to our rescue with Mac at the lead.

Luckily, the troop was already moving in our direction when Mac heard the firing in the far distance, knew from the volume that we were in trouble, and rode to our relief.

Two years later, I was awarded the Congressional Medal of Honor for "gallantry and cool leadership in the face of almost certain death" and was credited with saving the lives of my men.

The medal was Mac's idea, endorsed by Sheridan and Sherman. I have never been proud of it and wore it only when ceremony demanded. I was badly fooled that day and trooper Gregg died because of it, although the two wounded men recovered.

What saved us was the Springfield rifle, with some guts behind it, Mac's quick response, and all the good luck anyone could possibly want.

I will take those things over a medal any time.

Chapter Thirty-Four

"You gents understand what's happenin', don't you?" Potts asked, confident that we did not.

"We are on the trail of a whole damn village, close to three hundred lodges, I'd say, fightin' men, women and children, old folks, provisions, probably more than a thousand horses and mules, a whole bunch of dogs, and even a few cattle."

In his excitement, Potts flapped what remained of his arm like a crippled bird wing. It was as if he was trying to point but forgot that he didn't have a full arm with which to do it.

"No white outfit I know of has ever been this close to a big Comanche village on the move, not in open country like this. If we stay on 'em and don't let 'em get too much distance on us there's no way they can hide. For once, they can't move that much faster than us, not a whole damn village. I know I'm 'sposed to be the expert but I confess still don't rightly know how it happened. I think mostly we got lucky. The army sendin' this many men and then your not givin' up the way everybody did who came before probably surprised the hell out of 'em. If you'll pardon my sayin' so, Bad Hand, they never figured on just how damn stubborn you are."

After following the trail for several days, we were more than seventy-five miles from the supply camp we established before the long pursuit began. For us, it was unknown and dangerous territory untouched by white civilization. For the Comanche, it was home.

The trail was so clear even I could have followed it. Most of the time it skirted below the cap rock that made up the hard edge of the *Llano,* and resembled the wall of a gigantic fortress towering above the long line of troopers.

Getting here, we passed several small buffalo herds and rode through the middle of a huge prairie dog village where a careless step could break a horse's leg, a deliberate move by the Comanche to slow us down. We also came upon an occasional grass and mud hut the Comanche used to tend their horse herds. We tore those down as we passed. Anything to strike at the enemy.

We discovered an abandoned village earlier that afternoon. Every sign indicated that the Comanche left in a hurry. Eager as he was to continue the pursuit, Mac agreed to linger for a few minutes so Potts and Hogan could take a closer look. That is when Potts informed us that we were pursuing an entire village, not just a fraction that split off from the main body.

Even more surprising, we weren't far behind.

"We sure 'nuff got lucky," Potts concluded, mounting his horse to lead the advance party. "After all we been through, I say we're deservin' of a little luck."

Our rising confidence gave us new energy and we spurred the troop forward, with Potts and the Tonks far in the lead. After a few miles the trail divided, then divided again as the Comanche seemed to split off in several directions without purpose or reason. The random trails crossed and re-crossed each other so often that it was impossible for the scouts to read anything significant from what they saw. It was simple but effective concealment. Follow the wrong trail and it might be hours before we recovered from our mistake.

No longer sure which way to go, we halted the troop. The scouts fanned out only to return an hour later with the discouraging conclusion that the trails came together far ahead, when the Comanche doubled back the way they came, making a long loop out of our sight.

So, we doubled back, too, and spent the night in the abandoned village, having accomplished nothing but exhausted ourselves.

The next day was worse. The Comanche achieved what seemed to be impossible by climbing up and over the top of the cap rock.

When we followed, the meager path turned out to be not as sheer and vertical as it appeared from below. We still had to dismount and lead our horses and pack animals up the barely visible trail, a hard struggle up the steep ascent, muscles straining and lungs heaving as our mounts fought against gravity's dangerous grip, and men and animals scrambled to keep their footing.

Once we were over the crest, Mac demanded to know how a whole village, complete with a large horse herd and many other animals, could make such a climb.

Potts only shrugged. "Hell, Bad Hand, they're Comanche," he said. "They can do damn near anythin'."

Everything changed when we entered the *Llano*. The world was flat for as far as the eye could see, covered only by short buffalo grass. Even using field glasses there seemed no end to it. Not a tree, not a rock, not the smallest hill or the tiniest ravine broke the awesome flat expanse of the high plains.

As we moved on, the countryside's eerie appearance and forbidding stillness weighed on us all. It seemed eternal, as if it always was and always would be, an unnerving place where the puny efforts of man mattered not at all.

Mac and I, along with Potts and Hogan, rode up and down the line encouraging the men. Though more formally, I often repeated what I heard Potts say: "If all this high lonesome starts to work on your mind, look down for a bit, not out. I swear you'll get used to it after a while, at least most do."

Once again, the Tonks ranged far ahead, with the Comanche trail more or less following the edge of the cap rock. To our dismay, the scouts reported that the trail went back down the wall. The skeptical Potts rode out to see for himself and confirmed the bad news.

So down we went, sliding and cursing, only to encounter another maze of confusing trails, including what appeared to be the main trail several miles ahead that climbed back up the wall.

Once again, we turned to Potts for an explanation.

"Seems clear enough," he said. "They're tryin' to confuse us, slow us down, discourage us and buy all the time they can. Figure if they get enough of a lead at least they can get the women, children and old folks out of harm's way if it comes to a fight."

The only choice was to push ourselves beyond anything we thought possible to close the distance. The strain was mental as well as physical, and by now the men were exhausted.

Mac rode up and down the line offering encouragement. "If they can do it," he said, "we can do it."

Even if that was true, that didn't make it any easier.

We spent days wandering in circles and crude figure eights as we followed the main trail. Time and again, we'd go off on the wrong trail only to be called back by Potts or Hogan when they found the right path miles away. Several times we crossed our own tracks. Despite the flat land and lack of cover the Comanche managed to stay out of sight, although we had the feeling that we were getting closer.

Looking back, despite all that we suffered I can honestly say that what I mostly felt was admiration. What the Comanche did seemed impossible, and yet they did it over and over, all of it to protect the weakest among them and to try to defeat us without risking the fight we so eagerly wanted. If Quanah truly was their leader, he was one of the greatest I ever encountered.

On the fourth day a norther hit us with savage force. By then I was so tired and muddled I was convinced that the Comanche led us into the storm, and possibly even created it. I wasn't the only one who was half-convinced that they possessed almost supernatural skill.

Potts was right. They could do anything, even call on the weather as an ally.

Within a few minutes, the blue sky we were used to turned dark and ominous. A frigid wind slashed through our worn uniforms while thunder and lightning cracked open the heavens. Given the heat when we started the chase, foolishly most of the men either did not bring gloves and coats or they were discarded along the way.

At those dramatic moments when lightning illuminated the dark world around us, we caught tantalizing visions of Comanche riders in the distance, silhouetted against the horizon. It was never more than a glimpse, too brief to know if they were part of the fleeing village or outriders watching our progress. In such country it seemed impossible to hide for so long, even for the Comanche.

More riders appeared on our flanks. In groups of three or four, they'd gallop out of the darkness, close in on our line, fire a few arrows and then gallop away, hoping to tempt us into pursuit. Once again, Mac patiently rode up and down the line, this time encouraging the men to remain in place. No one was hit by the

Comanche arrows, but, as Mac and I knew from the war, it is a hard thing to be fired on and not reply.

Encouraged by the debris we passed, everything from lodge poles to stone tools, we pressed even harder, pushing ourselves until nothing more was left to give. The Comanche were getting rid of anything that might slow them down. There were even abandoned puppies scattered among the debris. Several times I saw a man dismount, pick up a puppy, remount and hold it in his lap as he rode, or, if it was small enough, cradle it in his saddle bag, a touching and very human sight in the middle of war.

I should have ordered the men not to bother. What would they do with the puppies if we got the fight we wanted? But I couldn't do it. Neither could Mac, who didn't say a word. Some of those puppies grew into dogs that stayed with us for years.

By now we were so close to our prey that the Tonks began chanting their war songs and painting themselves for battle. Mac ordered the line to close up into a column of fours while a separate detail was assigned to guard the pack mules.

Without warning, the sky exploded in a thunderous fury that made what came before seem puny. I experienced a norther many times, but I was never assaulted so viciously by what Texans called a "blue norther", snow, rain, sleet, and hail all jumbled wildly together, driven by a vicious bitter wind strong enough to knock a man off balance and freeze him at the same time.

Worse, night was coming fast. What little light there was in the storm would soon disappear and we truly would be blind.

The moment had come. Every man knew it. Only Mac could decide what to do. We could charge ahead without knowing how far we'd have to go, driving our mounts though the teeth of the blue norther and hope to engage the enemy while we could still see to fight. Or we could break off and hope to pick up the trail the next day.

He called it off.

I can only imagine what it cost that proud man, but it was the right decision.

Our horses were exhausted and staggering. I am not sure we could have charged at all. Our mounts might have collapsed before we were close enough to engage. With their herd, the Comanche always had fresh mounts while we had none.

Without an accurate idea about how many warriors were with the village, we faced a fight in the dark in country we did not know against a desperate enemy of unknown numbers that knew it all too well.

After all we suffered, I am sure that many of the officers and men disagreed with the order, but they were too weary to protest.

Just as we stopped, the storm hit us even harder. Nature's raw power was astonishing as the wind seemed to blow the freezing rain sideways. Within minutes, most of the men and horses were coated with ice. Huge hailstones began to fall, battering man and beast alike.

We settled in for the most miserable night I have ever experienced. Blue northers usually move through quickly, but this one tortured us like an evil spirit. Without wood, we couldn't light fires for warmth or cook warm food. Mac gave his overcoat to a sick trooper and suffered until Sergeant-Major Smith found an abandoned rag of a buffalo robe discarded by the Comanche and tenderly draped it over his shoulders.

The next morning, we discovered that the Comanche did not stop that night, determined to gain as much distance as possible. I can only imagine how they suffered.

A grim tally in the gray dawn revealed that fourteen men became ill during that night, three of them critically. If we pushed on, they would die. Three horses and two pack mules froze to death. Six more suffocated when the moisture in their nostrils froze and they couldn't breathe.

Mac sent out Hogan with a patrol to find the Comanche trail, but by the time the scout returned it was obvious that we were in no shape to continue. Our supplies were almost gone, our mounts were in terrible shape, and we didn't have enough of them. The men not much better.

By then, I don't think there was a man among us to disagree: It was time to go home. The campaign was over.

Chapter Thirty-Five

We weren't quite through yet.

Climbing down the cap rock from the *Llano* two of our weakened mounts lost their footing and broke legs in the fall. Both were shot as they squealed in pain. With the horses we already lost, several men were riding double.

One trooper, a private named Sweeney, was injured when his mule went down, and the trooper took its full weight on his leg. The mule was fine, but Sweeney's leg was broken so badly you could see the jagged edge of the bone sticking out from his shin.

Using a rifle barrel for a makeshift splint, Sergeant-Major Smith reset the break as best he could. As he wrapped the barrel tight against Sweeney's leg, Smith joked, "At least we won't be shootin' you like we did the horses, not unless old Bad Hand's in a nasty mood."

Slight though it was, Smith's joke was the right medicine at the right time. Even Sweeney laughed through his pain. It lightened the troop's mood when we needed it most.

Riding in front of the column, Mac shook his head.

"Danny, I'm not *that* bad, am I?"

"Well, I don't know..." I said.

Sometimes jabbing at Mac was irresistible.

On the second day after leaving the *Llano*, riding ahead of the main body, Hogan and two Tonks spotted two Comanche hiding in a shallow brush-covered ravine. Hogan sent one of the Tonks to inform Mac while he and the remaining Tonk kept watch, ready to pin down the Comanche with rifle fire if they tried to get away.

Potts said the Comanche probably were positioned to report on our movements. Quanah wanted to be sure we didn't double back. Remembering Sherman's instructions, Mac wanted captives and decided to lead a small party into the ravine to capture the Comanche.

Sitting on our horses a half mile away assessing the position through field glasses, I argued against it.

"You shouldn't do this, and you know it," I said. "Once those Comanche realize that they can't get away all they'll want is to kill as many as they can. We can't afford to lose you to a lucky arrow or shot."

I wasn't getting anywhere, but I kept trying.

"Let me lead. Hell, let any other officer lead, maybe one of the lieutenants. I'm sure any of those young fire eaters would be happy to get the opportunity. Probably hope for a field promotion."

Not long ago, Mac and I were the young fire eaters. Like Potts and "Pops" Smith, most of the troop called Mac "Bad Hand" or "old Bad Hand" when they thought he couldn't hear them. Thanks to my size and black heard they called me "Griz", short for grizzly. I have been called worse.

If Mac and I had transformed into officers all hoary with experience, then why did I feel so young and bumbling? While I sometimes felt like an imposter, I learned early that acting like you were sure of yourself was as important as actually being sure of yourself.

In despair? Don't show it. So frightened you feel your guts quiver? Never let the men see it. Racked by doubt? Keep it to yourself.

It was impossible to imagine Grant or Sherman wrestling with such demons, but I know now that they probably did. Maybe they were better at hiding it than mere mortals?

Sherman often told the story about the moment he realized Grant was special. The first day of Shiloh was a catastrophe for Grant's army, surprised by the Rebel attack in the morning and perilously close to annihilation by nightfall.

Late that night, Sherman and Grant met for the first time that day. Sherman was frantic, exhausted, and had no idea how to get out of the terrible mess.

"Well, Grant, we had a devil of a day," he said.

Grant looked up from the map he was reading, cigar in the corner of his mouth.

"Whip 'em tomorrow though," he said.

Was Grant posing? Maybe. But it worked. To me, the subject of high command behavior was a puzzle I never solved, one reason why Mac was a better leader. If there were doubts, he never showed them. When I had doubts, too often I voiced them.

He was also the most stubborn of men. What he was about to do was arrogant, as if only Ranald MacKenzie could see the thing done properly. I made my case loud and clear. But I was pissing into the wind. Mac was angry and frustrated, ashamed that a campaign that began with such high hopes ended with Quanah making a fool out of him.

True, we did not lose, not by any traditional definition, but we didn't win either. Leading a squad to capture two Comanche lookouts was Mac's way of making up for what he thought was a failure and release some of his anger at the same time.

Following orders, I remained behind with the main body while he led the squad forward. I watched through my field glasses, but with the ravine so heavily covered in brush I couldn't see anything.

After several anxious minutes, I heard firing, perhaps a dozen shots, along with war cries from the Comanche.

Twenty minutes later, the detachment returned to the troop, the sullen prisoners trotting on foot with their wrists bound behind them.

It wasn't until they got closer that I saw something unnatural in the way Mac was riding. He was at the rear with the prisoners, and I couldn't get a clear look.

When he needed help to dismount, I saw what happened. Leading the men, as usual, he took an arrow in the thigh, down to the bone two or three inches above his knee.

The arrow's iron tip was barbed and had to be cut out of his leg. There was no easy way to do it, though at least the tip wasn't poisoned. The field surgery was painful and bloody business that Mac suffered without complaint.

We didn't know it then, but he would walk with a slight limp for the rest of his life.

Chapter Thirty-Six

Writing about our campaign against the Comanche ex-hausts me. I intended to work a short day today with an afternoon walk to clear my head.

But I did neither of those things, not after I learned that Libby Custer had died.

It shouldn't have surprised me. I hadn't thought about her in years. I didn't even know that she was still alive.

But surprise me it did. It was as if another part of my own life died. I should be used to that by now. Perhaps I feel this way because she represents one of the last pieces of what I used to be, maybe *the* last piece.

As far as I know, I am all that's left. I thought that before but now I am sure of it.

For some reason, I find it burdensome. At least I will not have to carry the burden much longer.

I came upon it by accident, on the front page of the New York Tribune. The newspaper was folded in half on a chair in what the facility calls "the recreation room". Given the age and condition of the residents, there is precious little recreation, unless you call a rousing game of dominoes or checkers recreation.

I don't know why I noticed the newspaper. I don't usually bother with such things anymore. Since I have become so immersed in the past, I rarely pay attention to the present. We are isolated from the world in this place. At least I am. I don't know if I like it, though many here seem to, but I accept it.

I suppose the headline "Custer Widow" caught my eye, though I was not aware of it. Something compelled me to stop and pick up the newspaper. It was then that I saw the rest of the headline: "Custer Widow/Dies at 90."

The strength went out of my legs and I sank into the same chair where I found the newspaper. Later, I did the arithmetic. Elizabeth Bacon Custer outlived her famous husband by almost fifty-seven years.

Feeling light-headed, I grabbed the newspaper with a trembling hand and crammed it in my ancient valise with the pages of my scribbling and went outside to a pleasant spot where an Adirondack chair nestled under the trees, for once ignoring my usual place at the table by the river. Such chairs with their radical angles are no longer easy to get into or out of, but for some reason I enjoy them. My old bones settle nicely.

I did not want to work. I did not want to think either.

I wanted to give in and let sadness wash over me. I wanted to remember.

* * *

They were such a famous couple that everyone knew the story. It was part of the myth.

Elizabeth Bacon Custer came from a good family. Her father was a prosperous judge in Michigan, and the widower had high hopes for his only surviving child. He made sure that she was well educated and a little spoiled. Like all fathers, Judge Bacon wanted his daughter to make a fine marriage to a man of means who was at least her equal in social status.

Instead, she married Custer.

The Custers were poor, rambunctious, and there were a lot of them. Libby was beautiful and bright. By the time she was sixteen she had too many suitors to count. It is no exaggeration to say that almost every man who knew her was a little in love with her.

Libby's beloved "Autie" – Custer's ridiculous childhood nickname that she adopted as an endearment – was, I thought, rather homely, though you wouldn't dare say that to Libby. She might have clawed your eyes out.

Custer was not the blockhead some have made him out to be. He was a year ahead of Mac and me at the academy, and while he was no scholar and finished last in his class it was mostly demerits that put him there. He was a cadet of high spirits who was constantly in trouble and never really grew up.

Though he was no military genius, at the end mostly Custer had bad luck. Yes, he was headstrong and rash, but that's not what killed him. He did some stupid things and counted too much on what became known as "Custer's Luck", but that did not make him a stupid man.

Sometimes things don't work out the way you think they will.

They married late in the war, in 1864, I think. By then Custer was a brevet general and the newspapers and magazines all gushed about "the dashing young cavalier" and his daring exploits. Despite almost two years of steady opposition from her father, Libby refused to give him up. Once Custer became a national hero, Judge Bacon decided that he wasn't so bad after all.

Libby didn't know it and it wouldn't have mattered if she did, but she was in for a hard life. It only seemed glamorous from the outside. As much as possible, she went where her husband was posted, no matter how remote, which made her unusual in the army. If possible, I am sure she would have accompanied him on that last campaign and happily died by his side at the Little Big Horn.

The life aged her. Though only thirty-four she was going prematurely gray by the time of his death.

There is no doubt that they loved each other just as there is no doubt that they both were tremendous flirts. It was a formidable weapon that she used on her husband's behalf in Washington during the war. From senators to cabinet members, no one seemed immune to her charm. Unlike Custer, Libby knew how to go right up to the line but never cross it, at least not that I ever knew.

I saw her in camp many times. When Custer wasn't around, Libby was often surrounded by eager young officers desperate for feminine companionship, if only for a precious few minutes. They practically fell over their own feet in her company.

She was aware of her effect, and I am sure she enjoyed it. Of course, at five feet, four inches, with chestnut hair, glistening gray eyes and a smile that could melt iron she was worth gaping at.

I didn't formally meet her until after the war. It was in the late eighteen sixties at Fort Riley, I think, a cotillion where she was one of only perhaps ten women among eight or ten times that number of men. Her husband was back east somewhere, for reasons I can't remember.

So many men flocked around her that most of the time she couldn't even be seen in the mob. She danced every dance, each one with a different partner, and made sure to speak with almost everyone present, male or female. She must have been exhausted by the end of the night, although she never showed it.

I am, or was, an excellent dancer and I remember enjoying

myself that night. But after a couple of hours, I had enough of the hot and crowded room, I stepped out into the cool night, with the intent of having a cigar before retiring.

Before I could light up, I felt a hand on my arm. I turned and it was Libby Custer.

Surprised, I bowed and said, "Mrs. Custer."

She surprised me even more when she asked, "Major, have I offended you in some way?"

"Ma'am, how would that be possible?" I said. "We have never met."

That sounded a little cold, so I smiled in what I hoped was gallant fashion and added a play on words. If not exactly clever it was the best I could come up with at the time.

"I'm sure I would not forget meeting someone as unforget-table as you."

Her laugh reminded me of Amy's. It was no coquette's breath-less titter. When something amused Libby Custer, she showed it with hearty laughter.

Over her shoulder, I saw two lieutenants moving in our direc-tion. I glared them away.

"Practically every moment inside I was surrounded by so many men there were times when I felt that I couldn't breathe," she said. "But you seemed to go out of your way to avoid me."

I made a slight bow again. "I do apologize if I offended you, but..."

"But?" she said.

"As you said, you didn't lack for company."

She cocked her head, a gesture she probably used to bowl men over like tenpins.

"And you don't like being part of a crowd."

I shrugged, my unlit cigar still in one hand.

"I never liked running with the herd. I don't care for fawning, either, especially if I do it."

She laughed again. Her face was flushed from the heat in-
doors and she began to fan herself. Her gown wasn't daring
but somehow seemed like it, her graceful shoulders exposed in
the night air.

"This may surprise you, but I don't care for it either, at least
not when I receive so much of it."

There was an awkward silence while she looked at me quizzi-
cally. I had no idea what she wanted and didn't know what to say.

"Major Stone..."

"You know my name."

"Yes," she said. "Why not? You know mine."

She took a deep breath. "Major Stone, would you be my
friend? I know that must seem a strange request, but I find that
I am in need of one at a time when it's difficult for me to make
friends. There's my husband, and our position, and...well, the
other women don't..."

"I think I understand." I suddenly wanted to help her. "But
why me?"

"You're not like the others. You showed that tonight. That's
the best I can explain it. And because everything I hear about you
is good. They say you are an honorable man."

"All good reasons," I said. "Flattering, too, though perhaps
they don't know me that well. Have you been making inquiries?"

"Not really," she said. "People talk and they like to talk about
other people. I must say, you are a popular man, too. Most everyone seems to like you."

"Only most," I said as if offended, wanting to hear her
laugh again.

It was a peculiar conversation, and we were getting strange
looks as people passed by, but I thought that I understood. Her
husband's fame, her beauty, their obvious ambition, his long

absences, and their many contacts among the powerful put her in an unusual and sometimes uncomfortable position.

At that time of her life, Libby Custer had hundreds, probably thousands, of acquaintances but precious few friends. I felt much the same way.

"Mrs. Custer, I would be delighted to be your friend."

I bowed again. She offered her hand. I took it.

"Then you must call me Libby."

"And you must call me Danny."

"Except in public," she said.

"Except in public."

And so, we became friends. In case you are wondering, that's all we ever were.

We didn't see each other that often. Custer and I were never posted in the same place. But in those days the army was small enough that we ran into each other from time to time.

I thought that Custer was something of a bore. He inevitably turned conversation toward the subject of George Armstrong Custer. When he was away, Libby seemed to relax, and we enjoyed our time together. Mostly she would talk, and I would listen, although I did tell her about my own life.

This may seem absurd, but Custer's death at the Little Big Horn may have been the best thing that could have happened to him. I think Libby might have agreed, though it's not something she could admit.

By the time of his death, Custer was no longer the high-spirited boy of old. He was thirty-six, life in the saddle meant that he probably felt every year, and his famous long hair was receding.

With forty not far away, he was getting too old to play the dashing young cavalier much longer. I heard that he considered resigning from the army and probably hoped for a last glorious campaign against the Sioux to propel him into civilian life.

Resign and do what? That was the problem. The army was the only thing he knew. The future was a worrisome mystery.

Although Custer believed otherwise – the man never lacked confidence – Libby confided that he had no head for business. He lost most of her inheritance in various failed ventures that found him floundering out of his depth. Before his death, he was thinking about politics and convinced himself that he could go far.

But Libby thought him too naïve and trusting. "People take advantage of Autie, they always have," she said. "He'd probably be caught up in some terrible scandal and it would just kill him."

When word came back to Fort Abraham Lincoln about the death of Custer and his men on that hot summer day in 1876, Libby showed that she was made of stern stuff. As the widow of the highest-ranking officer killed that day, she was informed first. After a few minutes of private grief, she pulled herself together and visited every new widow at the fort to tell them what happened and to offer what comfort she could. In some ways, she had more courage than all of us.

She spent the rest of her long life in ferocious defense of her beloved husband. He needed it. The army wanted a scapegoat for what may have been the worst disaster in its history and who better than the man who wasn't there to defend himself?

When President Grant publicly blamed Custer for what happened, practically alone Libby rose to defend him and fought at that bastion for the rest of her life. Her long campaign produced no less than three books – "Following the Guidon" is the best – and too many magazine articles and speeches to count.

That Custer today is regarded as a steely-eyed hero who died fighting overwhelming savage hordes has everything to do with the tenacity and devotion of Libby Custer. His mistakes are rarely mentioned. I think people became convinced that any man who can attract the love and devotion of such a woman must be the stuff of heroes.

It is not generally known, but her husband's death left Libby in virtual poverty. Her military pension was only thirty dollars a month. The value of his five-thousand-dollar life insurance policy was cut by the insurance company after his death because, it said, he was in a dangerous line of work, as if that was a secret.

Many years ago, I saw Libby in New York City. Our meeting was entirely by accident. I was sixty years old and while she was not far behind, she was still a beautiful woman, one of those people who when they walk into a room you don't see anyone else.

I told her how I tried to reach her after her husband's death, but time and distance made the connection more difficult than it should have been. Afterward, I didn't know where she'd gone. Although I'd hear or read about her from time to time we never did connect. I had my life and she had hers.

Standing on a busy street corner in New York City, I awkwardly explained that I was a wealthy man. Hoping not to offend her, choosing my words carefully I asked if she needed financial assistance.

With a warm smile, she graciously thanked me for the offer and revealed that through her books, magazine articles, speeches (every word about her husband) and canny investments, she worked her way out of the financial pit until the value of her estate approached one hundred thousand dollars, a fortune in 1900 and a considerable sum today.

Our conversation was too brief. I think we both wanted it to last longer but didn't know how. Too many years had passed.

She tugged off one glove and reached up to touch my cheek.

"Goodbye, Danny. I am so glad we met that night long ago."

I took her hand and gently kissed it. It was our only intimate contact.

"Goodbye, Libby."

We never saw each other again. She never remarried, which was no surprise to anyone who knew her. The newspaper said that she will be buried beside her husband at West Point.

That seems about right.

Chapter Thirty-Seven

To our surprise, we were greeted as if the campaign was a rousing success.

We were in San Antonio for another meeting of senior officers and where Mac would deliver his campaign report to Sheridan. I had already read it and like all his reports, it was dismal. His low opinion of what we'd accomplished was obvious in phrases like "keenest regret" and "disappointment".

In those days, a well-written report was a valuable tool when it came to praising your men and enhancing your career. It was important to strike the right tone. Some officers had the knack. They made saddling a horse sound like it was full of daring but never crossed the line into lurid braggadocio that earned scorn from their peers and superiors.

Unfortunately, Mac made his campaigns sound *less* daring than saddling his horse. Part of it was that he detested braggarts. He believed that deeds should speak for themselves, but he went too far. In his hands, a dangerous situation that saw us fighting for our lives turned into a "brisk engagement".

But at the same time, he hungered for recognition and the promotion that came with it. He never admitted it but he resented seeing officers he considered less capable move ahead in the endless contest for advancement.

It seems ridiculous now, but Mac also was embarrassed by his penmanship. Never a man to admit weakness, he foolishly never learned to write with his left hand. But writing with his mangled right hand was excruciating. He laboriously rewrote even the simplest sentence to make it look like more than a child's scrawl. It was all he could do to get words down in readable fashion and impossible to come up with the kind of crackling phrases and descriptive detail that capture events in a memorable way but don't overplay the writer's hand.

Bookkeeping ledgers made better reading that most of Mac's reports. Passing along my own campaign notes, I offered to help but he always turned me down.

It was his pride, I know, his damned stubborn pride.

As I have said before, Ranald MacKenzie was a complicated man.

Fortunately, that day Sheridan drew him out so that there emerged a fairly accurate picture of our campaign. When Mac finished, Sheridan praised what we accomplished as "the beginning of the end". Most of the officers seemed to agree.

There would be another campaign and Mac and I would play an important part, but not right away. Our exhausted men needed time to recover, and our equipment needed an overhaul. Some of the horses would never recover, weapons were ruined, and uniforms were little more than rags. Saddles and tack were threadbare.

Knowing we had time, I requested leave. I was leaving Mac alone to deal with thousands of details, but he reveled in that atmosphere. I needed to sleep on soft white sheets with pliable companions in an atmosphere that didn't resemble anything remotely military.

Selfish? Of course. Did it bother me? Not at all. I would be better for it. Fortunately, Fort Worth was not far.

It was two days before I could get away and when I got to Fort Worth my pleasure was delayed even more by Nelson Miles.

As an officer I was required to report to the army post and leave word where I could be reached in case of emergency. To my surprise, a note from Miles waited for me there. I had forgotten that he was temporarily stationed in Fort Worth. The note was mysteriously worded, a "social invitation" whatever that meant. I was too curious to turn it down.

Meeting in a room off the lobby of the only decent hotel in town, Miles was so affable I was immediately on my guard. After I declined an offer of whiskey and a cigar, he got down to business.

"Stone, I want you on my team," he announced.

Responding to my baffled look, he explained. "I consider you to be the best number two man in the army, but you are wasted with MacKenzie. You won't be wasted with me."

When I didn't reply, he kept the pressure on in his unique way. He could make a compliment seem like a slap in the face.

"You are content being second. That would never satisfy me, of course, but I like a man who knows his place. With you, I won't be constantly looking over my shoulder. You will rise as I rise and there's no doubt I will become the army's commanding general one day. Grant was there. Now sit's Sherman's time. Sheridan will be next, of course, but after that..."

He pushed himself to the edge of his chair, his intensity growing as he caressed his own ambition.

"Everyone knows that you and MacKenzie are close. But such things shouldn't matter to a man with the intelligence to look into the future and the ability to do something about it.

MacKenzie's not someone to follow, not for your own good. The man is too limited. He's adequate in the field, but away from it he's a worthless relic of the past. Times are changing and the army is changing with the times. Being a competent officer isn't enough anymore. We have to be diplomats and politicians, too, learn who matters and who doesn't, how to acquire power and how to use it."

Miles paused to savor what he obviously thought was a persuasive offer while I simmered over the word "worthless" to describe my lifelong friend.

"Politicians, even presidents, come and go. It is men like us who remain. As we rise, we hold the true power, not the MacKenzies of the world. Once he's served his purpose he will be discarded. It's as simple as that. Come the time, where will you be without your precious...what do you call him, your precious *Mac*?"

The scorn Miles put into that word pushed me over the edge.

"Permission to speak freely, sir?" I asked.

"Of course. There's nothing official here. No one even knows we *are* here."

I rose to my feet.

"It's only now that I understand what I dislike most about you. It's your belief that everyone is as contemptable as you are."

As far as I was concerned, the conversation was over. I turned toward the door.

"Stone!"

I faced him. It was the first and last time we were alone.

"I overestimated you," he said. "You aren't the man I hoped you were."

"And you are exactly the man I thought *you* were."

Chapter Thirty-Eight

Finally, I was free to do what I wanted.

The most popular destination for what I had in mind was famous, or infamous, as Hell's Half Acre. On the south end of town not far from the train depot, Hell's Half Acre seethed with debauchery, a wild mix of saloons, dance halls, gambling emporiums ranging from palatial to little more than a plank on two sawhorses, bawdy houses and shabby cribs that never shut down.

Cribs were rickety shacks or lean-tos where a desperate drover (they weren't called cowboys until later) fresh from weeks of eating dust and contemplating the south end of a thousand northbound cows could satiate his lust for as little as twenty-five cents a go. The act took about as long as you might expect for that amount of money in an atmosphere that ranged from disgusting to putrid. The diseases in such places were horrible to contemplate, but there still were long lines to get in. That's what happens when the price is low, and the men are desperate.

The women who worked the cribs always made me sad. Thanks to opium, alcohol, physical abuse and disease, most of them were dead before they reached thirty and by then looked twice their age. I wondered what gruesome turns their lives took to put them there. The cribs had to be the bottom. I couldn't think of anything worse.

No, that was not for me. I could never be that desperate.

Nor did I care for the saloons and bawdy houses with a line of tiny "hot bed" rooms on the second floor, where the walls were so thin, they might as well have been paper. They were called hot beds because they were never empty long enough to cool off. I preferred a more congenial atmosphere where I wouldn't catch anything I didn't want, and the beds didn't reek of the previous customer.

Fortunately, I knew exactly where to go.

It was owned by a formidable woman named Mina Rogers, although no one knew if that was her real name. Somewhere north of fifty, she still had dark good looks but confined her activities to ownership and management.

According to the most widely told version of her story, as a young woman she worked her way up in the brutal trade of organized prostitution in Kansas and Missouri until she saved enough money to acquire a small but popular bawdy house in St. Louis. After a few years, she sold it to set up a bigger operation in Hell's Half Acre, which was just starting to boom. To attract what she called "the quality" and avoid guilt by location, after a short time she found a place on the other side of town, where she intended to cater to high-class clientele by offering a refined setting.

Mina rigorously interviewed every young lady she employed. Most were not beauties, but by the time she finished polishing they seemed like it, especially compared to the competition. I was told that nine out of ten young women who applied to work for her were rejected.

The establishment was named Knight's Rest, which passed as a clever play on words in that world, with far too many jests about the lengths of Knights' lances. It was a three-story red-brick house with two parlors plus a dining room to entertain gentlemen downstairs, and ten bedrooms to entertain gentlemen upstairs. Musicians, usually a string trio, played softly in the background. No out of tune piano for Knight's Rest!

To get past the starchy hostess at the door, who in case of trouble summoned a duo of bruisers with the snap of her fingers, a letter of introduction from a known client was required for the initial visit, plus a one-time "membership" fee of five hundred dollars, which guaranteed that the clients were men of substance. The fee for a night's "residence" started at fifty dollars and went up from there. A week cost several hundred dollars. Special requests were accommodated for an additional fee, although there were limits to what Mina Rogers asked of her girls. If a client transgressed the house rules, he could not return. If he tried, the bruisers went into action.

The furnishings of Knight's Rest resembled what might happen if someone with no taste tried but had a lot of money to imitate someone who had excellent taste but never really got the hang of it. Parisian wallpaper contrasted with Italian furniture. The eye of a first-time visitor was overwhelmed by crystal chandeliers that made the light dance until it was almost blinding on a sunny day. Plush crimson velvet covered everything from settees to heavy drapes. Alluring portraits of the women who worked there were scattered among the landscapes that adorned the walls.

Upstairs, the rooms were furnished with everything from delicate perfume boxes to ornate hand-painted screens for tasteful dressing and, more important, undressing. The feather beds were comfortable. The food was excellent, and the cigars expensive. Champagne flowed like a river. Mina drank pink champagne, I think mostly because she thought it fit her image. In private, she preferred a shot of whiskey. Three bathrooms with running water were a special luxury. The staff kept the liquor cabinet full and the spittoons empty. Bookcases were lined with volumes, though no one read them. On one visit, I was surprised to discover the book about Spain written by Mac's father. Mina graciously let me keep it as a present for Mac.

As you have probably concluded, I was a member. I liked it because there were no consequences. I could afford it because after I left Europe, my father-in-law, Lachlan, assumed control of my investments and used his wizardry on my behalf. I did not know it until I received a telegram from Lachlan's agent in New York City asking what I wanted him to do with the considerable money I'd made from investments I didn't know I had. I was content to leave it in his capable hands.

I have never had a problem spending money and spent it lavishly at Knight's Rest. My favorite among the young ladies was named Betsy and I believe that I was her favorite client. And if I wasn't, the illusion was enough.

One rule of the house was that no last names were exchanged. Although Betsy and I got to know each other well, she never broke that rule. Betsy probably wasn't her real name anyway. There was something about the small scar on her lower lip from what she said was a childhood accident that endeared her to me. I was not alone, I am sure.

Mina encouraged her girls to pursue their dreams. Even in the best circumstances the working life of a prostitute is short, and it paid for the girls to save their money and have an escape plan. I know that Mina helped several of them financially, another reason why so many wanted to work for her. As far as I know, everyone paid her back.

Mina Rogers was a tough customer who would have laughed

at the foolish notion of the whore with a heart of gold. She was all business all the time. She took care of her girls and they repaid it with their loyalty.

One night while we lay in bed, Betsy told me that her dream was to return to her hometown of Cincinnati and open a hat shop for ladies. She intended to design the hats herself and proudly displayed several designs. I "oohed" and "aahhd" without having the slightest notion what I was seeing.

"I will be a *milliner*," she declared, as if everything she ever yearned for in life could be found in that word.

With a location already in mind, she was saving for the day and was already more than halfway there. No one in Cincinnati knew of her occupation. She left home as a girl and intended to return as a successful businesswoman.

Was I being played like a trout on the end of a line? I didn't care. I told Betsy that I would make up the rest of the money. It wasn't that much, although it seemed like a fortune to her. I wrote a bank draft, and she added her real name later so I wouldn't see it. The money safe in a Cincinnati bank, she left Knight's Rest a few months later.

For me, it was a bittersweet goodbye. I was the reason she left but I hated to see her go.

I only had one bad experience at Knight's Rest, and it was my fault, haunted by my past.

They didn't particularly resemble each other. For one thing, Betsy was blonde. But Betsy and my beloved wife Amy were physically similar. They were about the same height, with roughly the same figure.

Is that what attracted me to Betsy in the first place. Who can say?

One night we were sleeping like spoons, with my arms wrapped around her as she curled against me. She must have felt so much like Amy that I dreamed I was with her. It was as if Amy's death never happened, and the future would always be the perfect contentment I felt at that moment.

As consciousness slowly returned, I fought against it. I wanted to stay in the dream, no matter the cost.

And then it was over. I began to quietly weep. Betsy turned to hold me in her arms. I told her about Amy long before and she may have sensed what I was feeling. She probably was used to strange behavior from her clients.

Later that morning, sitting on the side of the bed as I pulled on my boots, I apologized, simmering in self-pity.

If I expected to be comforted again, I was disappointed.

"Jesus Christ! Do you think you're the only one who hurts?"

Stark naked, she stood with one hand on her hip and sneered at my weakness while I sat there with my mouth hanging open.

"Every woman in this place has been through things that would turn your blood to piss. Your wife died. All right, I'm sorry. But people die and the living move on. But not you. Oh, hell no! You have more than most people dream of, but all you can think about is what you lost. You shouldn't enjoy misery quite so much. It doesn't look as good on you as you think it does."

She was right, of course, but the lash stung, probably because she *was* right.

Chances are Betsy is dead now, but I hope that she opened her hat shop.

I hope she became a milliner.

Chapter Thirty-Nine

A knock on the door followed by a female voice out in the hall told me that I had a visitor waiting in the parlor.

I reluctantly rolled out of comfortable bed, splashed water on my face, and ran my fingers through my hair. I threw my clothes on and went downstairs to find Sergeant-Major "Pops" Smith happily surrounded by three or four of the Knight's Rest girls, all of them captivated by his courtly ways.

Seeing me on the stairs, Smith disengaged from his admirers, stepped forward, snapped off a salute, and handed me a note when I reached the bottom.

It was from Mac, telling me that the time had come for my return.

Just as I hoped, my stay at Knight's Rest cleaned me out and cleaned me up. Fool that I was, I was eager to get back in action.

"He could have sent a telegram or asked the post here to find me and save you a lot of trouble," I said.

"You know how the colonel thinks everything out," Smith said. "He didn't want the local army boys marchin' around town and findin' you where maybe you didn't want to be found. And without knowin' exactly where you were, he figured it might not be the kind of place where you'd be sure to get a telegram."

That was Mac. He cared more for my reputation than I did.

Smith took an amused look around the ornate parlor, stroking his gray goatee with one hand.

"But I see there's not a thing wrong here. It's as right as the mail."

He bowed toward the girls who watched him with a mix of lust and admiration. Despite all the time we spent together, I only then realized that despite his years Smith was quite a handsome man.

"Ladies, ah am afraid ah cannot tarry," he announced with a courtly bow. "Perhaps we can renew our acquaintance at more appropriate time."

I went back upstairs to gather the few things I'd brought with me. I said a quick, but not too quick, goodbye to Betsy, left a generous gratuity, and we were off.

Later, sitting together on the train on the way out of town, I couldn't resist the temptation to ask Smith a personal question. I phrased it so that he could avoid answering without giving offense.

"You seem more light-hearted lately," I said. "I don't know what changed and maybe it's none of my business, but I'm glad to see it. We all are."

I didn't think he would answer as he gazed out the window at the passing scenery.

But after a minute or two he did.

"A man can't mourn lost causes and lost loves forever," he said. "It's not fair to the dead or to the livin'. Life goes on. It has to."

In her blunt way, that's what Betsy was trying to tell me.

Chapter Forty

As I knew he would, Mac had everything well in hand. Having enough work to keep him maniacally busy was his idea of a fine old time.

I noticed the new drill right away. It was hard to miss.

The army separated shooting and riding as different disciplines, which, of course, they are. But hard experience taught us that the two had to be combined. Effective Indian warfare is warfare on horseback. There was little advantage in fighting the Comanche dismounted unless there was no other choice, such as our narrow escape that wound up winning me that ridiculous Medal of Honor.

The drill involved two six-foot-high posts spaced forty yards apart. In addition to his Springfield, each trooper was armed with a Colt. The men individually rode toward the posts at full speed, firing their rifles at one before turning back in the other direction to fire their pistols at the other. I am sure that Washington was scandalized by the extravagant waste of ammunition.

After going at it twice a day for weeks, at full gallop with

Springfield or Colt, every man could hit a target on the post
the size of a man's head. They also learned how to quickly
reload on horseback, which required even more dexterity.
It made them better riders, too, since they controlled their
mounts with only their legs.

We needed the men to be better trained than they were for our
first campaign because we were taking a smaller force. The more
than six hundred men we had last time, with all the support that
entailed, were too many. We learned the hard way that a force
that size couldn't move fast enough or react quickly enough.

There would be nothing but cold camps, too. There would
be no fires to give away our position and thus little in the way
of hot food. A light marching order meant that we moved faster
and with greater stealth, like the Comanche themselves, although
we'd never be that good. With the mounts equipped with specially designed packs, the men carried most of what they needed.
In addition to weapons and ammunition, each man carried a
change of underclothing, two canteens, a knife (I preferred a
Bowie knife, though most troopers liked something smaller and
lighter), fork, spoon, tin cup and tin plate. We packed a few
tents for the sick and wounded and scythes to cut grass for the
horses and the few pack mules we brought along. Where grass
was plentiful, we cut as much as we could carry. Along with food
and extra ammunition, the mules also carried as much water as
possible. In the *Llano,* water was more precious than gold.

"As of now, I have it down to two hundred and twenty-two
officers and men, plus nine Tonk scouts," Mac said. "I convinced
Marcus Potts to join us again."

When I asked about Hogan, the quiet scout whose rope work
I remembered so well, Mac said he disappeared. No one knew
if he was dead or gone elsewhere, not an unusual occurrence in
those days. Not even Potts knew where he'd gone.

As far as I know, neither one of us ever saw Hogan again. Years later, I read about a "lariat wizard" named Sam Hogan touring with one of the Wild West shows.

I assumed that Mac changed his mind about his promise of a flying squad, but he surprised me by saying that it was an important element of the campaign.

"The men I've picked for this campaign are the best the regiment has," he said. "I want you to take your time and pick fifty men from this group. That's your flying squad, the best of the best. The only man you can't have is 'Pops' Smith. Most of the time you will ride with the main body, but you'll have plenty of opportunity for independent command."

Ten days after my return and a week before we were scheduled to move out, Mac and I watched the men drill as they thundered back and forth between the posts, weapons blazing. I was pleased by how good they were, crack shots every one of them.

"You and I know that last time we were fooled by an enemy that knows more about this kind of warfare than we'll ever learn," Mac said. "They had us stumbling around in dead-end arroyos and box canyons, and practically stampeded our horses out from under us. Then an entire Comanche village led us on a chase that nearly killed us while they got away.

"Danny, I promise you that's *not* going to happen again!"

Standing beside his horse as we watched the drill, Mac pounded the side of his fist on the saddle for emphasis. His mount turned his head to look at Mac reproachfully, no doubt wondering what it did to deserve that kind of treatment.

I knew that he wasn't promising me as much as he was making a vow to himself. Contrarian that I am, I decided to argue.

"Mac, our campaign was not the disaster you think it was," I said. "The fact that you're the only who thinks so should tell you something."

I was mounted, Mac wasn't, and it was easier to make my argument looking down.

"The Comanche know their homeland is no longer safe," I said. "They know that we intend not just to protect, but to destroy. Thanks to our so-called *failed* campaign, we know how to do it and in you we have the man who can lead us to do it. Sheridan was right. What we did was the beginning of the end, even if the end is a long time coming. Until that blue norther, we had that village on the run. Yes, some of what happened was our fault, but the rest was just bad luck."

A half-smile crossed Mac's face as he stroked his horse along its neck to make up for his earlier outburst.

"You must have done some thinking in that Fort Worth whorehouse you favor," he said. "I'm surprised you found the time."

I fell back on an air of mock offense. "It's not a whorehouse, it's a gentleman's club, and yes, I did do a lot of thinking...when I wasn't, ah, busy."

Mac slapped me on the leg.

"I'm glad you're back, Danny. It wouldn't be the same without you."

Chapter Forty-One

I don't want to give the impression that the Comanche waited for us to come to them.

The mounted marauders plagued the frontier settlements as if they were invincible and nothing would ever change. It was the worst time in more than forty years for Indian raids, a reign of terror that grew even more brazen.

A district judge from southwest of Fort Worth took the desperate action of writing to President Grant, who passed the letter down the chain of command without comment. The judge complained about "scores" of robberies, rapes and murders, including entire families butchered. A good friend of the judge, a local justice of the peace, had his ears and nose cut off *before* he was scalped and killed.

There was even talk of more congressional hearings, as if gab out of Washington would solve the problem.

We needed a little luck.

And then it walked right into our hands.

* * *

The Rangers captured a *Comanchero* **named Ortiz who**
was found on foot and delirious at the base of the cap rock
marking the boundary of the *Llano*. His horse walked into a
rattlesnake den and was bitten so many times it died frothing
at the mouth. By the time the Rangers found him, Ortiz was
almost dead from thirst.

The *Comancheros* mostly worked out of northern and central
New Mexico territory, and were detested as Comanche collabo-
rators. The Rangers, who generally obeyed no law but their own,
treated Ortiz well, but only so that he would recover and be fully
aware when they hanged him.

With his hands tied behind his back and the noose tightening
around his neck, Ortiz saved his life by babbling about the ex-
istence of something many of us suspected but were never able
to prove – a route with reliable water cutting through the heart
of the *Llano*. Some claimed that it was as broad as a wagon road.
Others said it was no more than a trace and only someone familiar
with it could find it.

Whatever its size, it was down this mysterious path that the
Comanche moved stolen cattle and horses from Texas deep into
New Mexico. Keeping a few horses to add to their herds, working
with the *Comancheros* they traded the rest for guns, ammunition, flour, tools and anything else they needed.

We got word of Ortiz's revelation when the Rangers reluctantly postponed his hanging, figuring he'd say anything to save his
life. But even if he was lying it needed looking into. We arranged
to "borrow" him from the Rangers, with the private promise
that we wouldn't give him back if he helped us. If we found the
fabled route through the *Llano*, we'd not only disrupt the trade
in stolen cattle and horses, eventually we'd find the Comanche

where they least expected it.

Explaining Ortiz's new situation though the bars of a dank El Paso *calabozo* that looked as bad as it smelled, Mac made his offer to the battered *Comanchero*, who was not treated kindly once his captors learned that they had to give him up. Even in the poor light, his shiner and swollen nose was easy to see. Judging by the stiff way he moved, other damage wasn't so obvious.

"Come with us and the Comanche might kill you," Mac admitted. "But if we leave you here the Rangers *will* kill you. Count on it."

It took Ortiz a heartbeat to decide. We had our man.

There was one caveat, which Mac explained after Ortiz was released, jamming him against the *calabozo's* stone wall with one hand around his throat.

"If you made up this yarn to save your miserable life, I'll leave you out where the Rangers found you," he warned. "When I shoot you in the leg so you can only crawl, I figure it'll take three or four days at most before you become food for the buzzards."

Once Mac turned Ortiz loose to be outfitted, confident that he wouldn't run, I congratulated my friend on his remarkable power of persuasion.

"You even scared the hell out of me, and I knew you were bluffing," I said.

Mac gave me a dead-eyed look.

"What makes you think I was bluffing? If it turns out that he's lying, I may kill him myself and save the buzzards the trouble."

Chapter Forty-Two

I came to like Polonio Ortiz. Almost everyone did.

He was a small man, barely over five feet and a hundred pounds, an excellent tracker, a good shot, and one of the best horsemen I have ever seen. He was more comfortable on a horse than most people are in a rocking chair.

Ortiz was always cheerful and took life as he found it. As he said, "A man has to act as if everybody is his friend, or nobody is his friend."

He saw nothing wrong with his history as a *Comanchero* and did not apologize for it. The way he figured it, we stole this part of the country from Mexico with the treaty of Guadeloupe Hidalgo that ended the war with Mexico, a war that we probably started despite what I was taught at the academy.

Why shouldn't he trade with anyone he pleased? What did the Anglos ever do for him?

Our conversations also touched on something else that had bothered me for a while. I decided to raise the issue with Mac.

Late the night before we were to start the campaign, we were smoking cigars on the veranda of the two-room cottage where Mac lived on the post. I had a whiskey going, too. All that we could do had been done but we were too jacked up to sleep.

I brought up the subject to see what he had to say. Maybe he could relax my mind about it?

"Mac, have you ever wondered if we're doing the right thing?" I asked.

At first, he didn't understand my meaning.

"Have I missed something?" he asked, rising up straight in his chair. "It's not too late if you see a problem."

I took an easy sip of my whisky, intending to make it last.

"It's nothing like that." I waved my cigar to take in the darkness beyond the veranda, which was lit by a single oil lamp. "All of this is Indian country, or at least it was; the Comanche, the Kickapoo, probably some Apache, even the Tonks. Change the names of the tribes and you can say that about every acre west of the Mississippi. Hell, you can say that about the whole country. Our people crossed the Atlantic and we took it and we're still taking it because we can. But that doesn't make it right, does it? Sometimes I wonder about what we're doing. How will history look back on us?"

It was awkwardly expressed but maybe expressing it at all made it awkward? Ask most people how history might look back on them and they'll probably think you've lost your mind. While Mac was not much given to looking within himself, I hoped that he would understand.

He stared out at the night as he answered, the words slightly muffled by the cigar.

"Danny, I've heard other people ask the same thing and I figured you'd get around to it eventually. You can't help it. It's just the way you are."

When I started to protest, he held up a hand to stop me.

"I'm not saying that's bad. Mostly I admire you for it. You're the best man I know but sometimes those things that make you that man get in your way. There aren't always two sides to every question, or three sides, or ten sides. Sometimes there's no answer either, at least not a good one. I've seen you chew on something until you truly don't know what to think. It's like watching a man paralyze himself."

I took another sip of whiskey, half regretting that I said anything at all.

"Thanks, I think. But that didn't answer the question."

Mac shrugged. "Like I said, sometimes there is no answer. Maybe it all depends on what side you came into the world?"

Unhappy with how he put it, before he crafted a better response, he said something that I'd never heard, at least not from him.

"Stay with me on this, Danny. I've never tried to put it in words before."

A deep breath. "I see history like a great wheel that rolls slow but powerful. Sometimes a person, a people, even whole nations are crushed by that wheel, but it rolls on because it must. Maybe what is right and what is wrong depends on your point of view, on a lot of things you can't control.

"When William the Conqueror defeated the Saxons, do you think he was racked by doubt? They didn't call him William the Doubtful, or William I Can't Make Up My Mind. When Caesar conquered the Gauls he probably didn't lie awake at night wondering if he should have left the Gauls alone because what did they ever do to him and after all wasn't it their country in the first place.

"There are examples all through history: Alexander the Great, the Romans, Cortez. How much of what they did would we change if we could? What would happen if we did? The Indians were fighting each other hundreds of years before we came along so I'm not sure our being here really changed anything. Am I supposed to feel bad about what we're doing when I come along some poor settler who had his stomach cut open and watched his guts spill out while he was still alive to see it?"

Mac flipped the butt of his cigar into the night where I could see it glowing on the ground.

"You talked about it starting when people crossed the Atlantic from Europe. Are you saying they shouldn't have come? If I was born a Comanche, I'd be fighting people like us, right up 'til my last breath. But I wasn't. If we weren't here, there'd just be somebody else in our place."

The wood creaked as Mac pushed himself up from the chair. It was late and we had to try to sleep even though we probably wouldn't.

"I probably didn't answer your question," he admitted. "Maybe you're right, Danny. History will decide. It always decides."

"Or maybe history doesn't give a damn."

Chapter Forty-Three

After setting up base camp at a fork of the Brazos River in Blanco Canyon, we moved north along the cap rock, looking for sign. With Potts and Ortiz riding ahead of the main body and Tonks on either side, we crossed the southern fork of the Red River and entered the jagged beauty of the canyon lands.

Today there are towns and cities along our route, but at the time it was the most extraordinary wilderness I have ever seen. We were tiny figures against the gigantic landscape, like ants defying the immensity of the land.

Despite the heat, it had been a wet winter and wildlife was abundant. Sand Hill Cranes rose by the noisy thousands as we passed lakes that weren't there last year and might not be there next year. On two occasions, we waited for hours as buffalo herds passed, blocking our way.

I thought of what Sherman said about killing all the buffalo. I still couldn't believe it. How wrong I was!

We encountered thunderstorms that rattled our senses and gigantic ant colonies that could sting animal or man into madness. Twice we ran from raging wildfires. Some of the men were convinced that the Comanche started the fires. Others blamed lightning strikes, which seemed more likely to me.

We found no Comanche and precious little sign, but we were gaining knowledge of the country that would serve us and others later.

Through it all, Mac was a man obsessed, as usual driving himself harder than he drove the men. He neglected his health for the sake of the mission, getting by on four or five hours of sleep and often less than that, the last to sleep and the first to rise.

Knowing how his wounds pained him, I saw how the pain never really stopped. His body betrayed him, and he ignored it. If he was hard on everyone around him, he was hardest on himself.

We drilled the troops whenever possible so that come a fight, they wouldn't have to think about what to do. Although we were few in number, this was the finest fighting unit with which I was ever associated. Better still, we knew just how good we were, and our *esprit* soared.

Over several weeks, we crossed the *Llano* twice, a remarkable achievement at a time when only a handful of whites crossed it even once and many others died trying.

On our second trip across, thanks to Ortiz we made the discovery that changed everything. It was a trail, maybe *the* trail, one that we could tell was much used for many years.

Trying not to get our hopes too high, following the trail we discovered that it offered access to permanent water fit for both animal and man, exactly as Ortiz promised. Although each water source was no more than thirty miles from the next, a man could stand less than fifty yards away from most of them and not see anything at all. You had to know it was there.

Maybe the knowledge we accumulated would pay off during this campaign and maybe it wouldn't, but now that we knew where the Comanche moved so easily through the *Llano* it was just a matter of time.

Chapter Forty-Four

Mac halted the troop and allowed the men to dismount and rest the horses, while a weary Potts, who we had not seen in two days, rode in to report.

Throwing one leg over his saddle horn, he cut a hunk off a twist of tobacco and stuffed it in his mouth, chewing until it softened and rested comfortably in his jaw.

"Me'n Ortiz ran into a band of *Comancheros*," he said. "I kept my mouth shut for once and let him do all the talkin', which anyhow seems to come natural to that man."

The *Comancheros* knew Ortiz but didn't know that he was working for the U.S. Army. They assumed that since Potts was riding with Ortiz, he was one of them and they could speak freely.

"There were ten, armed like they expected a war," Potts said. "If they knew what we were up to we'd be as dead as Abraham Lincoln."

"They weren't curious about what you were doing out here on your own?" I asked.

"Sure, but none of them boys are on the side of the angels."

Potts spit a glob of tobacco juice to one side and wiped the back of his hand across his mouth. "That sort don't like to be asked too many questions and generally don't ask many themselves."

"Anyhow, they told us about runnin' into a band of Comanche camped up on the North Fork of the Red River. It's a fair size band, two or three hunnert teepees. Gave every appearance of stayin' a while, so they must be feelin' safe."

A vague description from men we did not know relayed to us second hand was all we needed. The only disappointment was that the Comanche were not Quanah's band. According to the *Comancheros*, they were led by a chief named Shaking Hand.

We moved cautiously, with Potts and Ortiz riding farther ahead than usual to make sure that we didn't stumble onto the Comanche by accident in case they went on the move. A large tipi could house eight to ten people, including fighting men, so we assumed that we were outnumbered by two or three to one. Our confidence was so high that we thought nothing of it. To a man, we were eager for a fight.

The scouts found the village right where it was supposed to be, along with a horse herd numbering in the thousands. The Comanche had no lookouts or scouts out. As far as they knew, there were no soldiers within two hundred miles.

Mac passed the word to the officers who passed it on to the men: We were to kill no women and children and there would be no mutilations or scalping. For a commanding officer in the west, I am ashamed to say that such an order was unusual. To be fair, when a Comanche rushes at you with a weapon raised to bash in your brains, there is no time to ponder whether it's a man or a woman.

We divided into four columns and maneuvered as close to the village as we could without giving ourselves away. With my squad in the lead, we attacked at four in the afternoon, when the stupefying heat was at its worst and even the Comanche were likely to have their guard down.

Our charge blew through the village like a hurricane, before most of the Comanche could get to their weapons, much less use them. At least a score of the enemy died in the first two or three minutes, plus many others wounded.

A band of perhaps a hundred survivors scrambled to take cover in a ravine set away from the rest of the village. Trying to dig them out would have cost time and casualties, so we let them come to us. We formed a line and they charged twice. It was suicide and they knew it, but they were fighting to give the rest of their people a chance to escape. Some of them weren't even armed.

They were brave men. The Comanche always were.

Another band took cover in a pool created by a brook that ran through the middle of the camp, concealed in the overhanging trees and tall grass that surrounded it. By battle's end, there were so many wounded and dying Comanche that the water turned pink. A few escaped into the brush of the river bottom and crawled away.

The battle, if that's what it was, was over in less than thirty minutes. We lost four troopers and one Tonk, which I will get to later.

I know that I killed that day, but I have no idea how many. Leading my squad, I raced through the camp, blasting away with my Colt before taking command of the line that slaughtered the Comanche charging from the ravine. Where Mac, Ortiz, Potts and "Pops" Smith were, I had no idea. As usual in battle, I lost track of everything except what was right in front of me.

We burned all the lodges and destroyed everything else so that nothing was left for the enemy to use. We took one hundred and twenty-four prisoners, most of them women and children.

It was a remarkable achievement; one we didn't fully appreciate at the time. Such a thing had never happened to the Comanche. We attacked and destroyed a village that was thought to be safe haven in the midst of their traditional stronghold. Our surprise was complete and the result devastating.

The Comanche did that to others. No one ever did that to them.

We also captured almost three thousand horses, which meant that almost all of those who got away were on foot without food or shelter. We never knew how many escaped because we didn't know how many were in the village in the first place.

Following Mac's orders, the men restrained themselves admirably in the heat of the fighting. The discipline we worked so hard to instill had bonds of iron.

The Tonks were another matter. I saw "Pops" Smith stop two Tonks from raping a Comanche woman, firing a shot at their feet as a warning.

But they did plenty of damage when no one was looking. Late in the fighting, with my shotgun ready I cautiously entered a tipi to find a young warrior butchered and scalped. At his side I saw a girl that I took to be his daughter. His arms were wrapped around her to offer what futile protection he could, but she was mutilated along with her father. I doubt that she was even ten years old.

Enraged, I stormed through the camp, cold, focused and looking for anyone else who disobeyed orders. I found one and blasted him to hell at close range. His bloody scalping knife was still in his hand and his victim, an old woman, at his feet.

After the battle, as we tended to our few wounded, Mac approached.

"We lost one of the Tonks," he said,

"Four troopers, too," I said. "Pretty light, I'd say."

"The Tonk was a strange case. His friends aren't happy, and Potts says they're making some wild charges."

"How so," I asked, pretending that I gave a damn.

"A shotgun nearly blew him in half. It was inside one of the tents," Mac said, waving his arm to indicate the direction. "It's rare for a Comanche to use a shotgun. Ammunition's too hard to find."

"Probably took it off of a dead teamster somewhere or traded with a *Comanchero*," I said.

Mac gave me a long look. "Yes, that's probably it."

He never said another word about it. He wanted me to know that he knew and there was nothing to worry about.

We placed the captives in the middle of our camp in a well-guarded circle. They were a mix of Comanche bands, including *Quahadis, Koytsotekas, Yamparikas, Nokonis,* and *Penetekas.* We were told, but never found out for sure, that two of the captured women were Quanah's wives. Apparently, he had several.

Mac ordered the captured horse herd moved a mile away from the ruined and smoking village, guarded by the remaining Tonks with one of our lieutenants overseeing.

History repeated itself that night. Coming in on foot, the Comanche eluded the guards and stampeded the horses. They not only got their horses back, they captured the Tonks' mounts, too. The next morning, they sheepishly returned to the main camp leading a small burro, the only animal that the Comanche didn't get.

It became known as the Battle of the North Fork of the Red River, which does not flow easily off the tongue. It was later shortened to the Battle of McClellan Creek. Few people know of it today, but it was one of the pivotal battles of the Indian Wars.

Potts described it better than anyone: "The Comanche know

we ain't gonna let up. If they're busy defendin' their own homes, they sure as hell won't be attackin' ours."

It wasn't that simple, but it was close enough.

For the proud Comanche, McClellan Creek was a humiliating experience. Nothing like it ever happened before and the depth of their grief was extraordinary.

Even the reservation Comanche were not immune. For weeks afterward, you could hear their wails in the night as they mourned for the dead. They rubbed ash on their faces, sawed their hair off with knives, and cut themselves on their faces, arms and chests. I think the worst of it was that they felt so powerless, forced to depend on the kindness of whites to get the captives back.

But even then, they were wily adversaries.

Bull Bear, a Comanche chief who never signed a treaty or reported to an agency, brought his band to Fort Sill to beg for the release of the captives. He said that he would prove his sincerity by putting his children in the white school and himself become a farmer.

Maybe Bull Bear meant it at the time, but only a fool believed it would ever happen. There were plenty of fools to go around.

All the Comanche we captured were brought to Fort Sill and given their freedom. As soon as they were safely away, Bull Bear and his band disappeared from the reservation.

Much later we found out another reason why the Comanche thought themselves safe in the village. Shaking Hand wasn't with his people. He was on a train to Washington to discuss peace with President Grant.

Chapter Forty-Five

Despite our victory, we returned more in sorrow than in triumph.

We were two days' ride after the battle when a trooper galloped to the front of the column.

"Sirs! Sirs! You've got to come..."

He was little more than a boy, perhaps sixteen, and fear crawled all over his unlined face.

With a glance at Mac, I raised my hand in a "slow down" sign.

"Calm down, trooper. Take your time and give us your message."

The youngster took a deep sobbing breath. "It's Pops Smith, sir. I... he's...he's..."

Mac and I yanked our mounts around and rode hard to Smith's position in the middle of the column.

We saw a cluster of dismounted troopers and instinctively headed for it. Our horses skidded to a stop and we threw ourselves out of the saddle.

Smith was on the ground, his gray head cushioned by a folded blanket placed beneath it. Falling to our knees beside his body, I remember Mac's soft moan: "No...no."

I looked up at the grief-stricken faces.

"What happened?"

A corporal stepped forward. I can't remember his name, just what he said.

"I saw Pops kind of slumped over with his chin on his chest, though he still had that big pipe of his clenched in his teeth."

Chin quivering, the trooper struggled to keep his emotions in check. I think we all did.

"Go on," Mac said, his voice gentle.

"I thought he was asleep in the saddle, though I'd never seen Pops do it. I was going to josh him a little. I rode up beside and gave him a poke in the ribs. He started to fall over but I managed to catch hold of him."

The trooper made a backward motion with his head. "A couple of the boys helped me get him on the ground. He never made a sound, not that I heard. I hollered for somebody to run up and get you, sirs. And, well, that's all."

The trooper ran his sleeve across his nose, stifling a sniffle. I didn't want to sniffle. I wanted to howl at the sky, beat my head against the ground and scream at the unfairness of it.

Suddenly Smith erupted with a great shuddering gasp that made everyone jump out of their skin.

We had no physician and didn't know what to do, although I don't think it mattered. My guess is that it was his heart. All we could do is make him comfortable as his breathing grew more and more shallow and the hard-bitten men gathered in misery.

He became delirious toward the end, fighting the war all over again.

"We will hold until Forrest comes up, no matter how many they send at us...uncase the colors and let 'em see who we are."

It was too hot to take his body with us. He had to be put in the ground as soon as possible. We buried him with as much ceremony as we could muster. There was no wood for a proper coffin, so we stitched saddle blankets together to make a burial shroud.

I remember the black grief of the men as they stood at attention to honor their comrade.

And I remember Mac's words, some of them:

"...George Andrew Cardiff, Brigadier General, Confederate States of America, known to all of us as Sergeant-Major John Smith...rest well, gallant friend."

Decades later, I came back in a chauffeur-driven motor car to find the spot where we buried the great man who I will always think of as Pops Smith.

I couldn't find it. Too much progress.

Chapter Forty-Six

"Sheridan wants to see you."

I barely passed through the door into Mac's tiny office when he made the announcement, summoned on the usual blazing hot West Texas afternoon.

I stopped in mid-stride.

"Where?"

"San Antonio."

"When do we leave?"

"*We* don't," Mac replied. "He wants you. You are to report immediately."

"Why? What does he want?"

"I don't know." Mac leaned back in his chair and planting his boots on the battered old desk. "I haven't heard a thing. You'll find out soon enough. I have some correspondence, mostly reports and such that I'd like you to deliver. It'll save sending a courier. I'm sure some of the men will have letters, too. The Kickapoo are up from Mexico and making mischief, so you'd better pick a dozen men from your flying squad as an escort."

My first thought was that this had something to do with the
Tonk I'd blown to hell, but I dismissed that immediately. Mac
and I would have heard any such rumbles from high up.

He was right. I'd find out soon enough.

* * *

"Stone, you are just the man we need."

I didn't like the sound of that. The phrase "you are just the
man we need" is never followed by good news.

Sheridan seemed even shorter and rounder than the last time we
met. There was more gray on his bullet-shaped head, too, though
he tried to hide it by cutting his hair down to stubble. I already
delivered Mac's official correspondence, most of it to Sheridan's
coven of book-keeping jackanapes who always found so much to
complain about, though Sheridan never seemed bothered.

"I am just the man you need for what, sir?" I asked.

Sunlight poured in through the office windows. He offered
coffee, which I didn't want, and water, which I did. Facing the
unknown always gave me dry mouth.

He came around and sat beside me in one of the two chairs
facing his desk. That was followed by the offer of a cigar. I didn't
want that either. He took one from a box on his desk, bit the end
off and stoked up. It smelled expensive.

I recognized the tactic. It was obvious: Strike a friendly tone
as a prelude to persuade or order me to do something I wouldn't
like. It was unusual for Sheridan, who usually issued orders without much care for what subordinates thought.

Perhaps sensing that I saw through the façade, the general
jumped to his feet as if lifted by invisible springs.

"Stone, let's go for a ride," he announced around the cigar
in his mouth. "I can use the exercise and the day is too pleasant

to be stuck inside."

Before I could reply, he ordered an aide waiting outside to ready his usual mount and find one for me.

"We can ride the Mission Trail," he said. "It's been a while since I was down that way."

He motioned me out the door, another concession since Sheridan usually marched ahead of everyone, his short legs pumping away. It was satisfying to note that while I had to duck, Sheridan passed through the doorway fully erect with room to spare. It was childish, but he always brought that out in me.

Ten minutes later, the mounted general impatiently waved away the escort that gathered to accompany us.

"Gentlemen, we will be perfectly safe." He gathered the reins in his stubby fingers while holding the cigar in his other hand. "Unless, of course, you think some fucking friar intends to kidnap us somewhere along the Mission Trail?"

In full sulk, the escort backed away as Sheridan shook his head.

"I'm so goddamned important, regulations say I'm supposed to have an escort everywhere I go, even to the latrine, it seems like. Just the two of us guarantees privacy. What I have to say is for no ears but your own."

We were off, headed south on a wide well-traveled road that passed a string of four old Spanish missions. Sheridan's mount was at least two hands taller than mine so that I would not tower over him as we rode.

We were a half mile down the broad trail before he spoke again.

"Stone, this army of ours is under siege," he said. "We are damned if we do, damned if we don't and damned from all sides."

Sheridan tossed the stub of his cigar to the side of the trail, touching the tip of his tongue with his finger to remove a bit of tobacco sticking to it before launching his tirade.

"We are supposed to enforce reconstruction policy across the South while protecting the settlers and miners who illegally occupy Indian land in the West, although why we protect law-breakers I do not know. We are expected to force free roaming Indians onto the reservations against their will while protecting thousands of legal settlers. We are ordered to protect mail and transportation routes and enforce the law in places where there is no civil law, and we are to accomplish all of this without having the men or the means to do it."

I'd seen Sheridan in action enough to know that he was just getting started, so I said nothing.

"The government awards contracts to thieves who overcharge us and then deliver cheap and shoddy goods to both the army and the reservation Indians and pocket the difference. Most of the enlisted men are deep in debt thanks to the overpriced goods sold by the commissaries that we cannot control because they are privately run. We struggle to repair worn out equipment, much less replace it with new. And when we get new it doesn't work. Have you heard about the rifles?"

I didn't know what he was talking about. It was a while since Mac and I received a new shipment of anything. We had become expert at improvising replacements. Some of our actions defied regulations and occasionally were even illegal. Dressed as *Comancheros*, twice we led small units to intercept a shipment of weapons meant for someone else. News was slow to reach us and garbled when it did.

"There's a flaw in the design or manufacture. I can't get a straight answer as to which and I suppose it doesn't matter. As usual, everyone blames someone else. The damn things overheat after two or three shots. When a trooper tries to eject the shell casing, the heat makes it so soft that instead of ejecting, the weapon jams. The trooper has to pry out the casing before he can reload while a hoard of savages rumbles down on him.

"We complained, of course. At first the supercilious shits claimed that the men weren't properly maintaining their weapons. When we shot that notion down, we were told there is no money for replacements, and we have to make do. Maybe next year, they said. It's always next year. I wouldn't bet my balls on it."

Happy as I was that the general's balls were safe, I didn't know what it had to do with me.

He twisted his stout body in the saddle to give me a long look.

"Stone, how long have we known each other? Since what, '63 or '64?"

I nodded. "That sounds about right, sir."

I didn't bother to point out that we didn't really know each other, we just ran into each other from time to time. Sheridan called up a familiarity we didn't have, comrades out for a leisurely ride.

Whatever he wanted, by now I was certain that it had no redeeming feature.

"Yes, you are perfect for what we need," he repeated.

Tired of the game, I pushed. "And what might my perfection actually *do*, sir?"

Sheridan laughed. "We – that is, myself and General Sherman – want you to go to Washington."

Probably noticing my sudden pallor, he quickly added, "Only temporarily, of course."

I could barely choke out the words.

"And do what, sir?"

"Stone, Washington is a den of snakes. I know you don't like the place. Why would you? A corkscrew isn't any more twisted than those people. Those who aren't crooked are simply stupid.

"Oh, not everyone. We have allies both in the press and in Congress, but not enough of them. It doesn't help that the Grant administration is rife with corruption, including the president's dim-witted brother and his personal secretary, Or-ville Babcock. Grant himself is an honest man, which makes him an exception in his own administration. He is far too trusting of the wrong people."

"Sherman and I have testified before Congress so often that no one listens to us anymore. They claim that we never have enough of anything and see conspiracies under every rock and behind every tree. We need a different voice, and we want that voice to be yours."

"Why me, sir?"

Calling out a friendly, "*Hola!*" Sheridan waved at a group of four vaqueros passing by in the opposite direction.

"False modesty doesn't become you, Stone. You are an im-pressive man, articulate and persuasive when you want to be. You are quite the chameleon, one of those people who seem comfortable in any situation. Your record is impeccable. Hell, man, you're a Medal of Honor winner! You have diplomatic experience, and you are adroit socially, which is where half of Washington's work gets done. You come directly from the field and speak from experience. It is well known that you are a man of means. You don't need the army. You are here because you want to be here. And any man who can give Sherman hell the way I heard you did won't be intimidated by a few mewling politicians.

"Stone, you are perfect!"

My mind whirling, I didn't know if I was complimented or insulted.

Sheridan obviously didn't know that most of my "extensive diplomatic experience" involved chasing women all over Europe.

The idea was appalling. Washington! Even the climate was repugnant.

"It won't be that long, Stone, a few months at most," Sheridan added, knocking down that objection before I could raise it. "You'll be so busy I'm sure it will pass quickly. You might even enjoy it. I can guarantee a promotion out of it, too. It's your choice, of course. I certainly don't want to order you to do it against your will."

The statement was so hypocritical it was breathtaking, but I let it pass.

"General Sherman approves?"

"Stone, it was Cump's idea. It's so good I wish I'd thought of it."

"What about Colonel MacKenzie? As my commanding officer, wouldn't he be the better choice?"

Sheridan sniffed. "MacKenzie's as diplomatic as a club to the forehead. In a bad mood he'd be as likely to shoot a congressman as to persuade him. He gets tongue-tied, too, as if his thoughts leap ahead of his speech."

For a moment, Sheridan seemed to give a damn about another human being, but it passed like a change in the weather.

"I know how close you are. A hell of a formidable pair in the field, too. And I know how you shade the rules to get what you want. I let it go because you get results. I don't condemn it. I admire it! That's all I want, *results!*

"You can trust me, Stone. I'll make it right with MacKenzie, and you'll be back before you know it. I know how it is – a fighting man like you wants to be there for the kill."

Sheridan didn't see it, but I winced at the word "kill". I'd seen too much of it.

The stumpy Irishman had me and he knew it. His claim that the decision was up to me was nonsense, although he did prefer that I go willingly.

An idea began to take shape. If I forced Sheridan to order me to go, I would lose what little influence I might have. It would not be a bad thing to have the army's two highest ranking officers in my debt. Sheridan might not recognize such a debt, but Sherman would.

Fool that I was, it appealed to my vanity, too. Maybe I could do some good? Stranger things have happened.

Although Sheridan had me, I still had a few moves.

"How independent would I be?" I asked. "I don't want to be closely supervised. My testimony wouldn't seem natural. The whole thing might take some, ah, *unusual* twists and turns we can't foresee. As you said, sometimes what goes on behind the scenes in Washington is what really matters."

Sheridan erupted in a barking laugh.

"Stone, I know about your reputation. If you have to seduce some congressman or cabinet member's wife for the sake of the cause, then have at it. Just don't get caught. I won't pay the price. You will."

That wasn't what I was thinking at all, but let it pass.

After assurances that I would be responsible to only himself and Sherman, and that I would be compensated for my expenses, of which I planned to have a great many, I'd made the best deal I could.

Insincerity being important to diplomacy, I bubbled with enthusiasm I didn't feel.

"Sir, I'm honored to do it," I announced.

With a broad smile, Sheridan reached out and shook my large hand with his small one.

"I knew I could count on you."

At that moment, we might have been the two greatest hypocrites on the continent.

Business concluded, he wheeled his horse around to go back the way we came.

"We need to get started," Sheridan yelled over his shoulder. "I want you in Washington as fast as I can get you there."

Chapter Forty-Seven

Sheridan's promised few months turned into almost two years. I knew that was likely from the beginning, which added to my growing sense I was a thumping great hypocrite.

I was supplied with a trunk full of information about all the scandals plaguing the Grant Administration. Despite Sheridan's comments, I tried to keep kept an open mind and told myself that everything that came out of his mouth was an exaggeration, including "hello" and "goodbye".

To my surprise, he may have understated it. While no one thought that the president was dishonest, as I waded through one sordid scandal after another, some not known to the public, I wondered if the man really was *that* naïve.

The answer, I concluded, was yes.

Politics was a dangerous world for Grant. In the army, the chain of command makes clear who is responsible for what. In Washington, it's as if no one is directly responsible for anything. Anonymous empire-building bureaucrats and venal manipulators working in the shadows hold most of the real power. The president's unbreakable loyalty was his worst weakness, a man of good heart incapable of supposing his friends to be dishonest, and fooled into trusting the wrong people.

My journey to the capital was mostly by water. Accompanied by an impressive twenty-man cavalry escort, I traveled by coach from San Antonio to Galveston where I caught a merchant ship – I was one of only four passengers – that stopped in New Orleans, Havana, Nassau, and Charleston, before reaching the end of my voyage in Baltimore.

It was a fortune-making endeavor for the ship's young captain, who also was the majority owner. He was an astute businessman and I watched closely as he profitably bought and sold at every stop, from cotton, hides, and spices to tobacco, indigo, and rum. When he returned to Boston, he intended to sell his share in the ship, combine that money with his impressive profit from the voyage, marry his sweetheart, and never put to sea again. I envied him.

The long days at sea gave me plenty of time to become familiar with the material Sheridan provided, including congressional testimony from Sheridan, Sherman and others, along with masses of background information. I felt like I was back at the academy.

I didn't want anyone to see what I was reading so some days I never left my cabin. I barely acknowledged the other passengers. The captain offered to set up a chair on deck, a setting more pleasant than my tiny cabin. It was a tempting offer, but I didn't want to call attention to myself and provoke the inevitable questions.

From Baltimore, it was a brief rail trip to the capital. On a short route the railroad didn't concern itself with passenger comfort. As a stout Maryland congressman grumbled, we were jammed "assholes to elbows", with some passengers forced to stand all the way. The engine belched so much smoke and cinder I was surprised that we didn't catch fire. Anyone with a window seat emerged with a soot-covered face.

With its wide and muddy boulevards, to my eyes Washington was as much of a festering swamp as ever. I am not referring to the fetid water. Some things don't change. The rancid culture of our capital is one of them. I know good people who love it and I do not understand. As usual, half the city seemed to be under construction, although both the Capitol dome and the Washington Monument were finally finished after years of delay.

Thanks to Sheridan's clout, I was comfortably put up at the Willard Hotel, where it is usually difficult to get a room. Ideally located on Pennsylvania Avenue a short walk from the President's Mansion, the hotel dates back to the republic's early days. It didn't take me long to learn that a great deal of unofficial business was done at the Willard's popular bar.

I was surprised by the number of military men roving Washington's streets, doing their best to look as if the fate of the nation was in their soft hands. Most were staff officers desperate to lap a few drops from the well of Washington's power.

Given my assignment, I wanted to stand out. I asked the Willard's concierge about the best tailor in Washington. I gave the unctuous little man a massive gratuity because a concierge is a prime source of gossip and I wanted to keep him favorably disposed, and I walked to the tailor's shop three blocks away. I was painstakingly measured and ordered six beautifully tailored uniforms, an expense I happily passed on to Sheridan.

The Grant Administration was the most corrupt in our history. The Harding Administration a few years ago might give it a run but I doubt that it was worse. Everything I know about the Harding scandals I read in the newspapers. The Grant scandals I knew intimately. Widespread corruption had been or was about to be uncovered in no less than seven federal departments: Navy, Justice, War, Treasury, Interior, State and the Post Office.

Yes, the Post Office. It couldn't even deliver an honest letter. There was a new word for it: Grantism. The President's Republican Party threatened to crack wide open, with the new progressive wing trumpeting that it intended to take over, throw the rascals out, and replace them with rascals of its own.

As Sheridan said, the president's private secretary was a major villain, an oily character named Orville Babcock who used his influence to control entire government departments. Appointments and contracts were sold to the highest bidder, with the money going into the secretary's capacious pockets.

Some government contracts provided no service at all. Dozens of mail routes in the West existed only on paper, although the government paid to run them. The routes were just lines on a map. Grant's hapless brother, Orville, received several lucrative surveying contracts for which he did, as far as I could tell, nothing. I doubt that he knew *how* to conduct a survey or knew anyone who did.

Anyone who expected me to be expert in the goings on at the Post Office or the Navy was a fool. I intended to concentrate on what I knew – issues and people directly affecting the Army and Indian policy. There was plenty to absorb my attention.

In my mind, Secretary of War William Belknap was the worst crook of all, with his snout buried so deep in the trough I am surprised he could breathe. Sherman had so little regard for Belknap that he refused to speak to him.

It pleases me to know that I might have had something to do with his downfall. Others testified against him, but I was regarded as more credible by certain nitwits. I could back up my charges and never said anything I couldn't prove. I detailed Belknap's evildoing during formal committee and sub-committee hearings and while standing with a drink in my hand in the homes of Washington's elite. I made myself available to the newspapers, too. My voice was heard everywhere. I made sure of it.

I received three substantial, but anonymous cash offers if only I would shut my mouth. Each offer was more than the one before it.

Belknap was the only cabinet secretary ever impeached. He escaped conviction when Grant, still believing the man's innocence, accepted his resignation only minutes before the House impeached him, like a man galloping out of town ahead of the lynch mob. Tried in the Senate, the necessary two-thirds to convict wasn't met because some senators didn't believe that they had the authority to put a private citizen on trial.

What made the disgusting ferret worse than the others?

Mostly he took bribes, or, to use a phrase popular during the Harding administration, kickbacks. So did a lot of people. The difference is that as Secretary of War he put thousands of lives in jeopardy.

Ironically, Belknap replaced John Rawlins, the man who so irritated me during my meeting with Grant during the war. When Rawlins died of tuberculosis after a year in office, Grant lost a loyal friend who might have kept him out of trouble.

Belknap's most ingenious maneuver was to finagle Congress into giving him authority to appoint and license "traderships", ownership of the lucrative sutlers' stores and trading posts. Under that arrangement, troopers could buy personal supplies only from the traderships. With soaring prices, easy credit and high interest rates, most enlisted men were always in debt to the traderships.

Indians bought there, too, usually trading hides and occasionally gold to acquire, among other items, the finest rifles available while our troops put up with government-issue weapons that didn't work.

Everyone Belknap named to run these posts paid for the privilege. His wife, Carrie, persuaded him to appoint a New Yorker named Caleb Marsh to the trading post at Fort Sill, although another man, John Evans, already had the position. Belknap arranged it so that Evans kept his job but paid Marsh twelve thousand dollars a year from the profits, which Marsh split with Carrie Belknap. When she died in childbirth the money went directly to Belknap, who had similar sources of illegal income all over the country.

What was a pleasure-loving man like me doing in the middle of this sordid mess? I often asked myself that question, especially after receiving an order disguised as an invitation to meet with the president.

Our meeting took place in a luxurious apartment on Fifth Avenue in New York City, owned by the infamous Jay Gould, the greatest financial manipulator of the time. Apparently, he was a friend of the president, too. Gould once cornered the gold market by bribing the secretary of the treasury for inside information until Gould and his partners owned sixty million dollars in gold. When the scheme was uncovered, a gold panic devastated the economy. Gould sold early and slithered away with a fantastic profit.

Officially, Grant was in New York to give a speech, while I was there to meet with Edward Verplank, the Swiss-born New York-based associate of my deceased father-in-law, Lachlan, and the man who handled my financial affairs. I was no Jay Gould, but I had become a rich man.

It was brutally hot that fall. Grant rose to greet me when I entered the suite. To my eyes, he seemed diminished. Was it seeing him out of uniform for the first time? Or had his worries worn him down? Had he changed, or had I? He was not the man I remembered, gray, bent and careworn.

With the ever-present cigar in the corner of his mouth, Grant motioned me to a chair and waved his escort of sycophants out of the room.

"There's no need for you gentlemen to stay," he announced. "This man is an old comrade."

I was as surprised as they probably were. We met exactly once. He was a general then and national hero. Now he was President of the United States.

Old comrade, indeed.

"Drink?" Grant asked, moving toward a side table crowded with liquor bottles.

The president as barkeep? I hoped that the danger signals vibrating through me didn't show. It was comforting to see that Grant's collar wilted in the heat just as badly as my own, which felt like a sponge soaked in warm water. A strange detail to notice under the circumstances, but it helped me relax.

"Just water, Mr. President."

"Of course." He used tongs to drop ice in a glass, followed by water from a crystal pitcher. Judging by the rich "ting" when the ice hit the bottom of the glass, the glass was crystal, too. I had no doubt that the tongs were silver. "If we don't use the ice in this heat it'll be gone in a few minutes."

Pouring water for himself, Grant handed me a glass and sat in a chair facing mine, crossing one short leg over the other.

I took a long drink of the cold water and said nothing. I wanted Grant to make the first move in whatever game we were playing.

He did, emphatically, too.

"Major Stone, why are you trying to fuck me?"

Grant rarely used profanity, while I probably heard that word every day of my life. The president's attempt to put me off balance, if that's what it was, missed its mark.

I replied in the only way I could.

"I don't know what you mean, sir?"

The president took a draw on his cigar and dropped it into the spittoon beside his chair. With the suite's lush décor, the spittoon probably was made of gold.

"Oh, I think you do, Major," he said. "You joined the crowd that claims I do nothing but lie, cheat and steal, me and my *cronies*. That's what the newspapers call us. Grant and his *cronies!*"

The president spat out the word like it was poison.

"I don't believe that, sir, although there are, as I think you will concede, certain, ah, problems, some of them dangerous both to you and to the country," I said.

It was a feeble reply. When the president asks why you are trying to fuck him, any civil reply seems feeble.

At least it was true. I did not believe that Grant's cronies did nothing but lie, cheat and steal. Nobody does that all the time. Even cronies have to sleep.

Grant scratched his graying beard, grown thicker than he used to wear it.

"I am glad to hear it, Major Stone, even if you don't mean it. I have always thought well of you and your friend MacKenzie, who you represented so ably when we met that day. It's quite a record you've made for yourselves. I envy the life of a fighting man. At least you know who your enemies are."

So, he did remember our meeting. Or maybe one of his lackeys reminded him?

If I understood the charade, we were two war comrades, good old Dan and good old Ulysses, swapping bullshit in an atmosphere of false intimacy. We might as well be down at the general store with our feet up on cracker barrels.

It was the same thing Sheridan tried in San Antonio but Grant being president upped the ante considerably.

And it still was a lot of rot.

"I am sure you know that I have launched official inquiries into the allegations, but despite what you seem to believe most of them are lies, innuendo and rumor designed to damage good men as a way of getting to me," he said. "When I find proof of wrong-doing I act on it. But so far there is precious little of that."

Having read a trunk full of it, I knew better. While I hid my skepticism, Grant reached into an inside coat pocket, removed a small leather case grown dark with age and withdrew another cigar. When I declined his offer of one for myself, he began the tiresome ritual of sniffing it, snipping off the end, rolling it in his fingers, and applying the flame just so.

If only he took as much care with his presidency as he did with his smokes.

"My administration is not perfect, I know that."

He spoke from behind the match's flame as if hiding from his own words.

"We have our share of problems and disappointments. Every administration has them. In my opinion, a lot of ambitious and unscrupulous men are looking ahead to the next election. They figure the best way to advance is to use me and my people as targets, with treachery as their weapon. The fact that they make all those insufferable accusations doesn't make them true."

Except when they are. It must have been obvious that I didn't believe him because the president ended his rant and attacked from a new direction.

"A man has to make do with the tools he has, even a president," he said. "Some of them aren't perfect, but I must use them, nonetheless. What else am I supposed to do?"

The answer seemed clear: Find new tools. But I didn't say that either.

Grant made a good point about the election. I agreed and said so.

Events proved us right, too. With Grant finishing his two terms, votes were bought and sold in the election of 1876 like haddock at a fish market. The results were held up for months while the nation held its breath and the crooks of one side tried to outdo the crooks of the other, all to elect a nonentity named Rutherford Hayes, a man better suited to life as a small-town bank teller.

But that didn't change the fact that Grant and his "cronies" were in trouble of their own making. Grant was naïve the way a child was naïve – when you see something frightening, avert your eyes and hope that it goes away.

I desperately wanted to be wrong. Then and now, I prefer a Machiavellian president to a blundering naïf. My hero – yes, he once was my hero – had lost something vital, some essence that made him the great man he used to be.

There is no doubt that Ulysses Grant was a great warrior. I wonder if that's *all* he was. He did well at the academy and brilliantly during the Mexican War, but come peace, his drinking forced him out of the army. As a civilian, he struggled in a life of failure and poverty. The old magic returned with the Civil War, but that was followed by tragic presidency. I did not know it at the time, but he would go bankrupt after he left office, done in by so-called friends and his own poor business sense before all those cigars killed him.

At that instant, although our conversation continued – to what end I did not understand – I knew that I didn't want to play the game anymore.

I might help harpoon one or two others, but it wouldn't change anything. I don't know why I ever thought that it would. I was fed up.

It was time to get out of Washington. It took a while before I could extricate myself, but I did.

Did I accomplish what I set out to do?

I don't know if I really accomplished anything at all.

Chapter Forty-Eight

"Danny, it's good to see you!"

Once his small adobe-walled office emptied of other officers, Mac seized me in a bear hug and pounded my back until I was sure I'd have bruises.

He stepped back and held me at arms' length, looking up and down at my tailored uniform and gleaming made-to-order boots.

"You know, if we took the time to properly display your magnificence, I think every hostile west of the Mississippi might throw down his arms and surrender."

I didn't bother to explain that a well-fit uniform was more comfortable in the saddle, which made a difference during a long campaign, and for all their expensive good looks the boots were built to last.

I didn't bother because there was something off about Mac's greeting. An openly emotional display wasn't like him. He resembled an actor who knows his lines, but the lines don't fit the character. As my friend Sam Clemens, the man the world knew as Mark Twain, once said about a writer finding the right word, it's the difference between the lightning and the lightning bug.

Mac looked tired, too, a weariness that went bone deep. I knew better than most that he lived a hard life, but the regiment hadn't been on any grueling campaigns that I knew about.

What was going on?

Later I found out that he was recovering from a violent attack of rheumatism that kept him out of action for most of a month. While he seemed too young for such an old man's infirmity, he never took proper care of himself, so anything was possible.

Mac dropped his arms from my shoulders. "I'm sorry but a courier leaves within the hour." He waved at a desk covered with paper. "I've got to finish *that* and get it to him before he goes. Let me take care of it and a few other things and we'll get together tonight and tell each other the usual lies. Being away so long I assume you have a batch of new ones."

Now he was too jocular. All this play acting was not like him. I decided to go along with it until I found out the reason.

I assumed a haughty air. "You know, some of us don't have to lie. "Our achievements speak for themselves."

Mac almost smiled and it almost seemed genuine.

"Ha! The first lie reveals itself," he said. "Give me some time and I'll find you."

Carrying my bag over my shoulder, I was led to my new quarters by Winfield Kartch, a lanky major whose lower face was mostly hidden by a huge brown mustache that drooped down to his chin. He was one of several officers who joined the regiment during my long absence in Washington. I remembered Kartch from the academy. He had my old role as second in command, which he assured me he was happy to give up.

"Thank God you're back!" he declared as we walked down a winding path of hard-packed dirt with big red rocks lining both sides. "I'm transferring out just as soon as I can. I'm all done in."

Kartch noted my quizzical look as we walked up the steps to a small veranda barely and through the door into my quarters. The spartan furnishings were all I needed: a rope bed, a small desk, an oil lantern, a wash basin, a chair, a dresser, and a cracked mirror on the wall.

"I know you're his best friend so please don't get me wrong," he said. "Colonel MacKenzie is a hard man but a brilliant leader. I've never served with anyone like him."

Kartch took off his hat and rubbed one hand over his thinning brown hair.

"The thing is, the Mexico campaign nearly killed me. A lot of us still haven't recovered. It almost did the colonel in, too, though most of the troop thinks he can walk through snow and not feel cold, or walk through fire and not be burned."

I did not like the sound of that.

"Mexico campaign? Kartch, what are you talking about?"

Leaning against the door frame so that I blocked the only way out of the room, I motioned for Kartch to take the chair. After a while, the words poured out, as if he wanted to talk about it but never found the right listener.

Chapter Forty-Nine

"You know how bad it's been with the Kickapoo, don't you?" Kartch asked.

"More than fifty million dollars in property destroyed, plus too many kidnappings and murders to count, the last I heard," I said.

I rummaged through my bag and pulled out a bottle of whiskey. I had a glass in the bag, too. I never liked drinking out of the bottle. There was another glass on the desk. Kartch picked it up, blew out the dust and I poured a healthy dram for us both. I wanted to loosen his tongue. I could hold my liquor. From what I remembered of Kartch, he couldn't.

With Kartch comfortably slouched in the only chair, I flopped down on the bed with my back against the wall and legs stretched in front.

"They'd cross the Rio Grande, hit ranches on our side of the border, then drive the stolen cattle, mules, horses, and captives back across the river where we couldn't chase 'em," he said. "Sometimes they'd ransom the captives, and sometimes they wouldn't and the poor souls just disappeared."

The raids concentrated on the upper Rio Grande border in West Texas. According to Kartch, Sheridan knew the area well. One of the general's assignments as a young officer was at Fort Duncan, between Laredo and Del Rio. He took the Kickapoo raids personally.

Sheridan knew he couldn't count on cooperation from Mexico, which didn't care what happened north of the border. But he wasn't concerned about international law either. In Mac, he had the perfect tool to fix the problem. Like Sheridan, Mac believed that the best strategy was to strike the Kickapoo in Mexico.

I knew that Sherman agreed that while such an incursion might work, it wasn't worth an international incident.

And I agreed with Sherman, but for a different reason. If anything went wrong, the leader of such a raid could wind up with his head on a pike. His superiors couldn't admit that they authorized an illegal invasion of a foreign country.

Sheridan and Secretary of War Belknap met secretly with Mac in Austin, keeping Sherman out of it. Mac was told to handle the situation "in your own way". The meaning was clear while the instructions were vague enough to mean anything.

Mac was so eager to get started that he didn't care what Sheridan said as long as it wasn't "no".

I would have tried to talk him out of it, something that Sheridan knew very well. I am not sure I would have succeeded, but I could have been a considerable nuisance, probably even protesting over Sheridan's head to General Sherman, which might have killed the whole thing.

But Sheridan was clever and endorsed Sherman's plan to send me to Washington where I was out of the way.

Did Sherman know what was going on? I don't think he did. Did Grant? I believe he knew from the beginning.

Perhaps I flatter myself, but I am convinced that at our meeting in New York, Grant tried to gauge the kind of man I was and how much trouble I would be if Mac was made a scapegoat. I think he also wanted to see if I had any inkling that the plan was in motion. If I did, I would have said so and he knew it. I can think of no other reason for a meeting that seemed so pointless.

A plot to cut out William Tecumseh Sherman seems preposterous, but that's exactly what happened. The president was informed because he had the best chance of keeping Sherman under control when he found out afterward, which he inevitably would.

Mac moved with his usual efficient energy to find the largest Kickapoo village within reasonable distance of the border. The plan was to destroy the village, capture women and children to pressure the Kickapoo to stop the raids, and get back across the border before the Mexicans knew they were there. Secrecy and speed were vital.

The village the scouts found was near the Mexican town of Remolino. They sent a rider back with a description, adding that most of the warriors were away on a long raid or hunt, leaving the place mostly undefended.

The raiders rendezvoused near the border at Las Moras Creek, where Mac revealed the mission and asked for volunteers.

"Every one of us volunteered," Kartch said.

"That's impossible," I said. "There had to be some who had doubts."

Kartch drained his whiskey, set the glass on the desk with a bang, and motioned for a refill.

"They trusted the colonel," he said.

I didn't believe him. As the silence grew, Kartch squirmed in the chair, looking down at his feet, at the ceiling, and out the open door, anywhere but at me.

"I suppose that's not the only reason."

"What else?"

"After it was over, one of the men asked what would have happened if he refused to volunteer. The colonel glared and said, 'I would have had you shot.' The men are more afraid of him than the devil himself."

That sounded like Mac, all right.

The raiders crossed the Rio Grande, heading southwest. "I remember the count because I made it," Kartch said. "We had three hundred and sixty men, seventeen officers, and fourteen civilians."

Following mule and cattle paths through the dense cane, after several miles they broke out into low chaparral desert, country so little known that it was marked as *"tereno desconocidio"*, or unknown land, on the map.

With the heat and heavy loads, after a few hours the pack mules couldn't keep up. Mac ordered a halt, distributed the supplies among the men and cut the mules loose, figuring they'd go back to the water of the Rio Grande, where they might be recovered later.

Making up for lost time, he set a killing pace. Reaching the San Rodrigo River near Remolino, using river brush for concealment, the raiders wound their way closer to the Kickapoo village until they were about a mile away.

The troop moved into attack position, a sequence of platoon charges. As each platoon completed its charge it wheeled out of the way for the next, reloaded and prepared to charge again.

"With most of the fighting men gone, the Kickapoo had no chance," Kartch said, holding his glass in both hands as he started down at his feet. "The old men and women defended themselves with anything they could get their hands on. The screams of the women and children...I'll never forget it."

Mac ordered the men to torch the reed and grass huts and

destroy the food and crops. The regiment took only three casualties. Kartch didn't know how many Kickapoo were killed or wounded. More than forty women and children were captured.

After mounting the prisoners on Kickapoo ponies, instead of going back the way they came, Mac led the raiders west several miles before turning north. After more than six hours in the blazing Mexican sun, the night was cooler but played on the nerves of men too long without sleep. Bristling with nervous energy, Mac rode up and down the line to keep the exhausted column together. As usual on campaign, he covered twice as much ground as any trooper.

"By then I was hallucinating," Kartch admitted. "We all were. One trooper shot the hell out of a barrel cactus."

"The prisoners began to fall off their ponies from exhaustion," Kartch said. "Colonel MacKenzie ordered the children lashed to the women and the women lashed to the ponies. The one thing we couldn't do was slow down."

By the time they crossed the border the men had covered more than two hundred miles. Most of the mounts were so broken down they were never used again.

In his report to the Secretary of War, which wasn't made public until much later, in a masterpiece of understatement Sheridan called the raid a "handsome chastisement given to the Indians by Colonel MacKenzie". Emboldened by success, Sheridan eventually came out of the shadows and supported Mac publicly.

"I have for a long time been satisfied that it is the only course to pursue and bring safety to...our side of the Rio Grande," he explained. "There should be no boundary when we are driven to the necessity of defending our lives and property against murderers and robbers."

I can imagine Sherman's anger at being kept in the dark, but he was a realist and backed his subordinates. Considering the result, there wasn't much else he could do. His real feelings were revealed years later when Miles wanted to attack the Sioux who crossed the border in Canada, citing the Remolino raid as a precedent.

Sherman slapped him down hard.

Just because Sheridan conspired "to act unlawfully in defiance of my authority...is no reason why I should imitate so bad an example". The raid did have a "certain salutary effect" but "pitting half of a regiment against a handful of women, old men and children can hardly be classed as a great feat of arms".

The Mexican government didn't react to the raid at all, at least not officially.

Afraid that the terrible Bad Hand might strike again, it was years before the Kickapoo dared raid north. Hundreds came back across the border to peacefully live on reservations.

When I confronted Mac after my talk with Kartch, he admitted everything and filled in many of the details. He expected me to throw a fit, which explained his earlier behavior.

The notion that Mac might be chary of me never crossed my mind.

Chapter Fifty

"With two thousand tame Comanches confined to the Kiowa-Comanche reservation in the Indian Nations, there can't be more than a thousand wild Comanches left, including perhaps three hundred fighting men. There also are about a thousand wild Southern Cheyenne, along with a comparable number of Kiowas. This means that over the *entire* Southern Plains we face about three thousand hostiles in all, or nine hundred to a thousand warriors at most."

"In short, gentlemen, thanks to your efforts we are winning at long last. Now it is time to apply the *coup de grace*, starting with the Comanche. General Sherman and I agree that it is time to bring the army's full might to hunt, engage, and destroy the most ruthless enemy we have ever faced."

Watching Sheridan's outsized personality on full display as he presided over another gathering of senior officers, he made it sound easy, but that was his specialty.

For one thing, I didn't trust the numbers. Most reported Indian agents reported what their superiors wanted to hear. The numbers were too conveniently round – a thousand of this and a thousand of that. It didn't take into account that hundreds of reservation Indians who weren't permanent residents. In the winter they accepted the government dole but with good weather they disappeared to join the other "wild" Indians.

The plan was simple. We would surround the remaining Comanche with five separate columns and drive them without mercy, using the tactics Mac honed to perfection. Their villages would burn, their children would cry from hunger and we would hound them until they dropped from exhaustion, surrendered, or had to fight.

With his hard-earned knowledge of the country and success against the Comanche and Kickapoo, Sheridan revealed that Mac would command three of the five columns. As I recall, our own 4th Cavalry moved north from Fort Concho, the 10th under Black Jack Davidson advanced west from Fort Sill, and the 11th under George Buell rode northwest between those two commands. Independent of Mac, Major William Rice's regiment moved east from Fort Bascom in New Mexico Territory while our old rival, Nelson Miles, rode south from Fort Dodge with the 6th.

The five columns totaled three thousand men, the most to take the field against Indians anywhere.

From what we learned from our scouts and *Comancheros*, the hostiles chose to make their stand outside in a rough section of the Texas Panhandle that seemed ideal for defense. With its deep gorges, rocky buttes, winding canyons and four major forks of the Red River, there was no better place to elude pursuit and grind the pursuers.

The worst of it was Palo Duro Canyon. More than a thousand feet deep in places, anywhere from a half mile to twenty miles wide and more than a hundred miles long, it was slashed through by arroyos and side canyons beyond count.

Looking at a map spread out across a table, Davidson did not exaggerate when he grumbled, "You could hide whole states in that country."

There were no secrets on either side. The Comanche knew what we were doing, and we knew how they would respond. They would avoid battle and try what worked so often before: Run us until our horses died, our spirit sagged, and the men collapsed. Despite our successes, they still were tougher than we were.

It is ironic that both sides had basically the same strategy – one in pursuit and the other in escape.

We did not know who we would face. There were rumors that Quanah was wounded at a fight with buffalo hunters at Adobe Walls in the upper Texas panhandle. The hunters' preferred weapon, the Sharps, had range the Comanche weapons couldn't match and it paid off. No one knew how bad Quanah's wound was or if he was wounded at all.

Part of me wanted to take him on again. As one of the few whites who saw him up close, I wanted another crack. At the same time, I knew that if he was out of action it was to our advantage because the Comanche had no other leader like him. I admired him and hated him, and he scared the hell out of me.

Whatever the truth about Quanah's wound, the defeat at Adobe Walls seemed to enrage the Comanche more than discourage them. Splitting into small groups, they launched a furious offensive from Southern Colorado to Texas. No wagon train, ranch or small settlement was safe. Stagecoaches were attacked, way stations burned, and women and children captured. Probably two hundred whites were killed, and many more wounded in the savage outbreak. Buffalo hunting stopped altogether as virtually everyone on the fringes of the frontier fled to the safety of the forts.

If we were winning, it didn't feel like it.

Chapter Fifty-One

We were in the field for more than five months.

During what is known today as the Red River War, the five columns crossed and re-crossed rivers, climbed up and down canyon walls, and followed trails that went everywhere and nowhere.

The hostiles knew they had no chance in open battle and did everything to avoid it. I have read that the Chinese have something called death of a thousand cuts, which is exactly how the campaign felt. The hostiles picked off small parties, ambushed scouts, and intercepted messengers. At night they tried to stampede our horses, a trick we knew all too well.

As the Indians cut and sliced us, we seized every opportunity to get at them:

* Miles drew first blood when he attacked a body of Cheyenne not far from Palo Duro Canyon. As usual, he exaggerated the numbers, claiming to face between four and six hundred warriors as he tracked a village of three thousand, which was absurd. In a running fight, his regiment killed twenty-five Indians, wounded more, and suffered only two casualties.

* Two weeks later, Rice encountered more than a hundred Comanche and Kiowa warriors who fought to screen the escape of their families before disappearing as if the earth swallowed them whole.

* After a long chase, Black Jack Davidson ran down sixty-nine warriors and more than two hundred and fifty women and children when the exhausted and starving Comanche finally could go no further and surrendered.

Our own regiment numbered five hundred and sixty enlisted men, forty-seven officers, and thirty-two scouts. With our experience and training, we were honed to a diamond-hard essence, the most seasoned force ever to fight the Plains Indians.

* * *

It rained hard that fall, downpours that made the buffalo grass flourish but turned the ground into mush.

Mac was irritable and impatient, growing characteristics as he got older. He developed the peculiar habit of snapping the stumps of his missing fingers. The faster and more frequent the snaps, the greater his impatience. He seemed to run hotter than other men, too, and felt warm to the touch, a restless smolder that never went out.

Walking most of the way to rest the horses in the mud, we covered twenty miles during a hard day heading toward Tule Canyon, which was cut by a creek that flowed north to Palo Duro Canyon. Close to sunset, a scout rode in with the news we'd spent weeks waiting for. A few miles ahead, among the maze of false trails the Comanche used to hide their real route was a big one, made by at least fifteen hundred horses.

It was almost a full moon that night and the trail was not hard to follow. Despite the moonlight, I couldn't shake the feeling that the Comanche were all around us, waiting to pounce.

After five miles Mac called a halt. We ordered the pickets doubled, the men to sleep with their boots on, and loaded weapons within reach.

At my suggestion, we not only hobbled the horses, they were cross-sidelined, with forefeet tied to opposite hind feet, and secured with ropes tied to fifteen-inch iron stakes driven deep into the ground, bigger than the picket pins that caused so much damage during our first campaign. In addition to the doubled pickets, three parties of a dozen men each were posted around the herd, ordered to constantly stay on the move.

As we knew they would, the Comanche came that night.

We had no warning until riders thundered through the camp perimeter, firing and screaming war cries as they tried to stampede our horses. When that didn't work, they began circling, probing for weakness. By this time, our horse guards had their range and blasted away. The firing kept the raiders at a distance until they gave up and rode away with a chorus of wild yelps.

We broke camp before dawn. Sunlight revealed a line of Comanche watching us from the high ground. Mac ordered a charge to see how they responded. When the Comanche retreated, a bugle call brought the men back. There was no point chasing what we couldn't catch.

The only casualty on either side came when a Tonk scout everyone called Henry shot the horse out from under a Comanche warrior who got too close. Henry was one of the worst marksmen in the regiment and it was a fantastically lucky shot.

Riding in for the kill, too late the fool realized that he forgot to reload his rifle. The Comanche dragged him from his horse. Having no firearm of his own and apparently no knife and no more arrows, he began to beat on Henry with his bow, carving great arcs in the air with every swing.

The men had a good laugh as Henry wailed and begged us to shoot the Comanche, who must have known he was a dead man as soon as his horse went down, and was determined to take Henry to hell with him.

Drawn by the laughter, Mac watched the one-sided fight for a moment, shaking his head. He called on three marksmen to shoot the Comanche, who probably was dead before he hit the ground.

Face covered with welts, the humiliated Henry staggered to his feet, drew a knife and scalped the dead Comanche with a few swipes of his blade. With a shout, he waved the bloody scalp in the air like the warrior he thought he was.

When the Tonk returned to our line, I knocked him on his backside with a punch to the face, jerked the scalp out of his hands and threw the bloody mess as far as I could. Blubbering for help, when he began to crawl away, I kicked him hard in the ass.

From astride his horse, Mac looked down as if he were sure that I'd lost my mind.

"Danny, why don't you save that for the Comanche?"

I snapped back. "As soon as we get close enough, I will, *sir*!"

Mac shook his head and rode away.

My answer made no sense, of course. I wasn't even aware of what I said until I was told about it later.

Why did I do it? What got into me?

I didn't like scalping, though many did it and I couldn't change that.

But there was more to it: Henry was a jackass. The better man lost.

Chapter Fifty-Two

Our good luck kept rolling when two scouts dragged in a ragged *Comanchero* they surprised while he was watering his horse at Tule Creek.

When he realized that he faced the fearsome Bad Hand he started chattering away, telling everything he heard about a big village in Palo Duro Canyon, a canyon so immense it could hide several villages.

Fortunately, the *Comanchero* gave us a good description of the location. Sending out every scout, our luck held when one scout spotted a trace of smoke from an early evening cooking fire and tracked it to its source before darkness concealed the smoke.

To fool any Comanche who might be watching, Mac ordered the regiment to move out in the opposite direction, taking our time so that we wouldn't have to backtrack too much. Once the sun went down, we turned around and pushed hard to the north, covering twenty-five miles overnight, a remarkable distance for more than six hundred men in the dark.

By dawn we were within two miles of the canyon edge. We

halted the troop for a well-earned rest while Mac and I rode ahead. We tethered our mounts a quarter mile from the cliff and cautiously edged forward, crawling the last fifty yards before peering out over a dizzying thousand-foot drop.

It was such a beautiful scene it was easy to forget that we were looking at the enemy camp. At some points, the canyon was so wide it was impossible to see the other side, although it was narrower here, just below the junction with the smaller Blanco Cita Canyon. At the canyon bottom, a winding stream was surrounded by greenery, including juniper, wild cherry, mesquite, cedar, and cottonwood.

With the abundance of water in a picturesque setting that couldn't be seen from above until right on the canyon edge, I understood why the hostiles set up their village here, probably a favorite spot for generations.

There were hundreds of lodges, plus a huge horse herd. Peering through our field glasses, we identified mostly Comanche, although there were Kiowa and a few Cheyenne, too.

Was Quanah among them? We had no idea. It was strange how I wanted him to be there and yet I didn't. I wanted to win but I didn't want him to lose. I did not say anything to Mac, who would not have understood. I didn't understand it myself.

Careful not to put ourselves in a position where we might be seen from below, we made our way along the canyon edge until we found a winding trail with many switchbacks leading down to the canyon floor. After several minutes lying on our bellies and peering through our field glasses, Mac asked, "See anything other than that trail that might help us get down? I sure as hell don't."

I nodded toward the narrow path. From our position, it looked like some sections were pitched at such an angle two legs could not stand on it, much less walk.

"It won't be easy," I said.

"It'll have to be on foot," Mac said. "Horses would never make it. Even if they could, they'd make too much noise. The trail won't take that many men either, not at the same time. They'd be scrambling and falling all over each other. It might take two hours for all of us to get top to bottom. I want to set up an advance guard down there in case the rest of the regiment is spotted on the way. It could get hot."

I didn't like the sound of that.

"Mac, you do know my flying squad can't really fly, don't you?"

Chapter Fifty-Three

We didn't know it, but several days earlier a medicine man assured the villagers they were in no danger. After the usual consultation with the spirits, he declared that the village was unknown to the white soldiers, and they were safe for as long as they wanted to stay.

No wonder I'm not a religious man.

A dawn attack was impossible. We'd fall all over each other trying to climb down in the darkness. Fortunately, the canyon's curve put the path out of sight of the village, although anyone who wandered more than a hundred yards in our direction couldn't miss us.

My squad's descent didn't take long but it felt like I held my breath the whole time. Strung out on a twisting line along the canyon wall, we felt alone and vulnerable, easy targets until we reached the bottom and outnumbered when we got there.

Secure in the promise of safety, the sleeping villagers didn't even post lookouts. Slipping and sliding, one by one my fifty men made it to the canyon floor. One unlucky trooper's feet went out from under him on the loose rock and he broke his arm in the fall, a brave man who chewed through most of his bottom lip rather than cry out.

Reaching the canyon floor, we established a crescent-shaped defensive position. Almost two hours later, we had most of the rest of the men either on the canyon floor or on the way down when someone in the village spotted the snaking line of troopers in the morning light and raised the alarm, a series of yipping cries that echoed through the canyon.

Hard experience taught us how Plains Indians fought when their villages were attacked. Their first action was a defensive effort to cover the escape of their women and children. There were only a few at first, then what seemed like hundreds of warriors firing rifles and arrows from behind rocks and trees to keep us at bay.

Mac was in the lead, as usual, waving the men into position as he ignored the fire. Fool that I am, I fought by his side. A wise man would have been anywhere that Mac wasn't.

The Indians abandoned their village and fell back into the narrower Blanca Cita Canyon. As we pursued, we passed through lodges crowded together on the canyon floor. The ground was littered with buffalo robes and thousands of pounds of dried buffalo meat abandoned in the escape, food that was supposed to see the Indians through the winter.

Reservation-bought goods were strewn everywhere, blankets, clothing, kettles and other cooking utensils, bolts of cloth, a few weapons, bags of sugar, and big sacks of flour. I saw what appeared to be a full set of china lying broken on the ground, taken from an ambushed wagon train or settler's home. The women tried to carry their treasures to safety but realized that it slowed them down and threw it all aside.

We couldn't get close enough to do any real damage. Both

sides took casualties, but not many. I had the uneasy feeling that we weren't forcing them as much as they were falling back with purpose.

I was right. As the canyon walls narrowed, the enemy lured us into a trap.

I saw two troopers go down before I realized that we were taking fire from above. Several warriors climbed up the canyon wall out of our sight, waited until we came in range and began shooting down at us, easy targets in the canyon bottom. Fortunately, it didn't look like more than twenty or so, at least for the time being.

A scrawny little bugler was struck in the cheek by a rock chip when a shot struck a boulder. The painful sting and blood flowing from the superficial wound scared the sense out of the youngster. He began wailing, "Help! Help! We're all goin' to die!"

Knowing that panic spreads like fire through even the most experienced men, I am embarrassed to admit that I did nothing. As arrows ploughed into the earth at my feet, bullets whizzed past my ears and the boy continued his nerve-rattling screams, I fell into a kind of strange paralysis, as if I were removed from everything around me, a spectator invisible to friend and enemy alike.

Fortunately, Mac kept his head. Another officer might have cuffed the terrified boy into silence, but Mac calmly put his hand on his shoulder.

"Don't worry, son," he said. "I got you in here and I'll get you out."

As if by magic, the little bugler stopped screeching as the men grimly went about their business like the professionals they were, taking their time and making sure they had a proper target before returning fire.

Mac moved to my side, his arm around the bugler's skinny shoulders. It was a strange sight, the dour Ranald MacKenzie holding a Colt with one hand and comforting a terrified boy with the other.

"Danny, how 'bout a charge up the wall?" pointing with the Colt as he shouted over the noise. "They won't be expecting that. If you do it now, we can drive 'em out before they're reinforced."

Shamed by my earlier inaction, I put on a face of bravado that I didn't feel and waved my faithful squad closer.

"Gentlemen, we are going to run those bastards out. Are you with me?"

The grins lighting up the dirty faces was all the answer I needed. Without proper assembly or even a plan we took off like demons, firing as we scrambled up the wall. The resistance evaporated within minutes. I killed one warrior who played dead and let me pass before leaping to his feet and trying to bash out my brains with a war club. I shot him in the chest with my Colt and then put one more in his head to be sure.

In their eagerness, the Comanche made their move too soon. Our charge up the canyon wall got to them before their numbers were too great for us to push them out.

We took one casualty, a sad one, too. The trooper who broke his arm on the way down from the rim ignored my order to stay out of the fight and joined us, his arm dangling at his side. Only a few strides up the wall, he took an arrow through the throat, blood pulsing out of his mouth.

Our work finished, Mac ordered the young bugler to sound retreat and we slid back down to the canyon floor, carrying the dead trooper with us, a brave man who deserved the burial with honors we later gave him.

Their resistance broken, the Indians' retreat turned into a rout. After sending a detachment ahead to keep them on the run, Mac issued orders to destroy the villages.

By now we excelled at destruction. It didn't take long to set fires and burn it all, every lodge, every buffalo robe, all the dried meat, every sack of flour and sugar, and every blanket. Everything that could burn was incinerated. By the time we finished, there was nothing left but smoldering ash and a rancid stink.

When the fighting moved into Blanca Cita Canyon, Mac left another detachment behind to guard the captured horse herd in case some of the Indians tried to double back and reclaim their mounts. A quick estimate showed it to be almost two thousand horses.

Even though the scouts found an easier way out of the canyon a few miles away, it took hours of hard labor to get that many horses up to the high plains. Once we got there, Mac came up with the ingenious idea of moving the horses along inside of a huge hollow square formed by the men, a kind of living corral.

In that slow-moving formation, we made our way back to Tule Canyon, arriving in the middle of the night. By then we'd been in the saddle or fighting for our lives for more than forty-eight hours. After posting a guard for the horse herd and threatening the men with all sorts of dire punishment if even a single horse was missing come morning, Mac let the rest of the exhausted men sleep. I heard him pacing all night as he moved around the camp, making sure everything was secure.

What happened the next day became legend, one that I am not proud of.

I find it strange that most people don't react that much when they hear of men being killed, but harm a few dumb animals and it becomes a tearful, wailing tragedy. I confess that I am the same way. There is no logic to it, and I have no explanation. I just know what I feel.

What we did lives in infamy. It had to be done, but that did not make it any less terrible. I know that I could never give such an order, which is one reason why I never wanted command.

The next morning, as a reward for their work Mac let the scouts pick a few of the best Indian horses for themselves and cut out a few more for pack animals.

He ordered the rest to be slaughtered.

Except for the din of our firearms, we carried out our duty in miserable silence. No one protested. There was no point. But no one was eager to obey either.

It was a sound military tactic. We destroyed enemy transport; the Plains Indians' means of survival. It also was a stunning symbol of defeat that every hostile on the plains would understand.

At first the horses were roped and led to the firing squads. As they were killed, the rest became harder to handle, driven mad by the smell of blood as they bucked and screamed and twisted. The men began firing without order or reason, eager to get it over. I am surprised we didn't shoot each other.

Not every shot was a killing shot. The more difficult the horses became, the harder it was to shoot them. Hundreds were only wounded with the first shot and had to be shot again and again. Other shots missed altogether.

Some of the men refused to aim while others fired over the horses' heads or into the ground. But that only prolonged the agony. Once all the horses were down, men circulated among the piles of carcasses to kill those that were still alive.

We fired more than five thousand rounds that day. As an officer I did not fire a shot, but I made sure that the men saw me among them. I did not want to isolate myself from their pain and wanted them to know it. I saw several men run from the slaughter, fall to their hands and knees and vomit.

We did not finish the grisly work until late in the afternoon. The plains were covered by heaps of dead horses for the vultures to feast on. Eventually the butchered horses became piles of bleached bones, a grotesque monument to the evil that men do, a macabre landmark that tourists sometimes went out of their way to visit.

I cannot imagine why.

Decades later, I heard that someone had the bones gathered, pulverized, or whatever the hell you do, and sold for fertilizer.

The Comanche never recovered.

Facing winter on foot, their shelter, food and mounts destroyed, defeated in the heart of their last stronghold, and with the buffalo herds already thinned out, one at a time or in small groups the survivors of Palo Duro Canyon came staggering into the reservation at Fort Sill, ragged and starving. It wasn't long before they were followed by the rest of the Kiowa and Southern Cheyenne.

The indomitable Quanah was not among them, although he and his band, by now no more than four hundred men, women and children, including perhaps seventy-five warriors, ceased to be a major threat. They raided when they could, but they would never again be a power in the land they once ruled.

In three campaigns covering thousands of square miles, Mac and others pursued the Comanche leader and his few followers with all the energy and vigilance they could summon, but it was like chasing a ghost. Mac never could bring his great foe down.

While Quanah's band refused to give up, it was all it could do to survive. Always on the move because it was too dangerous to spend more than one or two nights in the same place, the proud Comanche were reduced to a pitiful diet of nuts, grubs and rodents.

Eventually Quanah and his band came in, too, the last of the free Comanche.

I was told that Quanah and Mac became friends, which did not surprise me, and that Quanah was a good shepherd for his people in peacetime, which did not surprise me either.

By the time all of that happened, I was long gone.

Chapter Fifty-Four

I did not look forward to what I was about to do.

"Rather formal, aren't you, Danny?" Mac's roll-top desk was against the wall and he turned sideways to face me when I entered his office. "Why did you of all people 'request' a meeting? What's going on?"

I wanted formality because I needed something to prop me up.

"Mac, I'm getting out," I announced.

He misunderstood, or maybe he understood very well and didn't want to hear it.

He opened a desk drawer, pulled out a sheet of paper, scrawled his signature, which was virtually unreadable, as usual, and passed it to me.

"Here you are, signed and ready to go," he said "Just fill in how much leave you want. Going back to that, ah, *establishment* you favor in Fort Worth?"

"It's more than that this time," I said. "Mac...I'm resigning."

The words came in a torrent.

"I'm tired of the killing. I'm sick of not being sure that what we're doing is right, and of doing what we're ordered just because we're ordered to do it. I hate what it's doing to me. I've killed too many men and seen too many killed. There's another life out there and I want a chance at it before it's too late. It's... it's...everything!"

The words were out, and nothing could bring them back.

Mac looked as if he just learned the date and time of his own death.

Silence filled the room, a hateful thing. There was no ticking clock and no noise from outside, just the nothing between us, the loudest sound I ever heard.

"You're leaving me," he said.

Not "you're quitting", or "you're resigning", but "you're leaving me". Of all the words he might have used, those were the worst.

I had a document of my own. I held it out. He took it as if I handed him a viper.

"This is my letter of resignation," I explained. "It needs your signature as my commanding officer. Everything else is filled out and in order."

"You are very...thorough," he said.

He stared at the letter, although I am sure he didn't see a word on it.

"You're leaving me."

He laid my resignation on his desk and gently smoothed out the folds with his palm. He carefully picked up his ink well and held it in the palm of his hand like he was contemplating a ball.

Jumping out of the chair, he hurled the ink well past my head to shatter against the wall on the other side of the room. Ink sprayed across the wall like blood splatter.

"You're nothing but a coward!"

It was a sound I never heard from a human voice. It wasn't

a shout or a bellow. It was a piercing scream that came from a dark and ugly place.

"What we do is too *hard* so you're running away to the soft life all your goddamn money can buy. You've been coddled like no one else I know, but you're leaving me, you gutless..."

The next thing I knew we were fighting. I don't know how it started or who threw the first punch. What does it matter?

We tried to kill each other. There is no other way to say it. My vision was a narrow tunnel with Mac at the end of it. If I'd managed to get my hands around his throat, I would have squeezed the life out of my best friend. I felt the hatred radiating from him like poison in the air.

I don't know how many times I was hit or how many times I hit him, but I didn't feel a thing. Neither did he, I am sure, because I hit him harder than I have ever hit anyone.

Strong arms pulled us apart. We were grappling on the floor. I had no idea how we got there. There was a cut along Mac's eyebrow and the eye already was swollen shut. Blood poured out of my nose, leaving a copper taste as it flowed over my mouth.

"Get out of here, you goddamned coward!" he screamed, still trying to get at me. "Get out!"

As a young lieutenant and one enlisted man barely restrained Mac, two enlisted men hustled me out of the office, their wide eyes full of fear.

My resignation needed Sheridan's signature, too, but that was a formality. Sheridan typically signed such things without really looking at them. He believed that if a man wanted out it was best that he go as soon as possible.

I did not want to wait for the slow-moving army procedure to take care of it. I wanted it done quickly. For that I had to see to it myself. I left the fort along with a shipment of hides going to Galveston, with a stop in San Antonio on the way. I was not traveling in any official capacity. Until Sheridan signed off on my resignation I was in limbo.

Or in hell.

I did not see Mac again. I wanted to, but I was too proud to make the first move, and I knew that if one of us did it would have to be me.

We were fools.

As I rode out with the wagon train, I saw the curtain of his office window move.

There was no breeze that day. But the curtain moved. I know it.

Chapter Fifty-Five

"Stone, are you sure about this?" Sheridan asked.

"Sure as I've ever been of anything," I said.

Phil Sheridan hunched over his desk, put pen to paper and suddenly it was over. I was Daniel David Stone, private citizen.

What did that even mean?

"I'd say this calls for a drink." Sheridan went to a tall cabinet against one wall. He swung open both doors to reveal a well-stocked bar. He took out a bottle about three quarters full. "Join me?"

I was surprised and probably because I was surprised, I said, "Why not?"

What else did I have to do?

Sheridan filled two glasses with what he said was bourbon. We clinked glasses. Sheridan took a sip. I gulped, something I rarely do.

"You're one of the best I've ever served with," Sheridan said, relaxing into his chair. "I can't say that it's always been a pleasure, but it's sure as hell been interesting. I hate to see you go but I'm sure MacKenzie hates it a lot more. I remember the first time I saw you two. You were as green as grass. Of course, back then I wasn't exactly a graybeard myself."

Another sip of bourbon and the subject changed.

"I heard about your *confrontation*." He was careful to find just the right word. "I'm truly sorry. It's a hard way to end a friendship like yours. It always seemed to me that you were closer than brothers, two parts that added up to some greater whole."

His comment about Mac made me feel guilty, or guiltier. The rest of it didn't help either.

I took another gulp. Sheridan refilled my glass.

Easing back in his chair, Sheridan asked, "What will you do now?"

"I don't have any idea," I admitted.

Riding to San Antonio with a dozen wagons loaded with stinking hides, several pounds of army dispatches and private letters, and a ten-man cavalry escort, I thought of very little else. I didn't expect to receive an epiphany on the road to San Antonio like Saul on the road to Damascus. Mostly it was a way to keep my mind occupied.

As I considered possibilities, nothing seemed right. It probably would take a while before something did. Counting four years at the academy, I'd been in the army all my adult life, even *before* my adult life.

"For what it's worth, I understand," Sheridan said. "I've seen it more times than I can count. There comes a moment when a man has to get out. It's not just the army. It could be anything from peddling ladies' corsets to building barns. It hits like a thunderclap and there's not a damn thing you can do about it. You just know you've got to go and what comes next doesn't matter."

Sheridan smiled, one of the few times I'd seen that phenomenon when it seemed genuine. It made me uneasy, but then

Sheridan always did.

"You're a man of means," he said. "That'll make it easier. You don't have to do anything you don't want to do."

Unlike some officers, Sheridan didn't hold my money against me. For him, it was part of who I was, like the color of my eyes.

I was seeing a different side of the man. He didn't have any stake in me, nor I in him. I wasn't a subordinate who wanted something, and he wasn't trying to manipulate me and bend me to his will. I was a civilian now and there wasn't anything we could do for each other.

"General, what will become of Mac?" I asked.

The chair creaked as the stout little man crossed one stubby leg over the other. He seemed to give it serious thought as he swirled the bourbon in his glass.

"I don't have an answer," he admitted. "I worry about MacKenzie, same as you, but not for the same reasons. Despite what happened he's still your friend. If he wasn't, you wouldn't have asked the question. It speaks well of you. You're a good man, Stone. I've always known that.

"But my point of view is purely selfish. I *need* MacKenzie. Officers like him come along maybe once in a generation. I need him out there. The man is invaluable. But anyone as brittle as MacKenzie – any man who pushes himself as hard as he does – is bound to break. He's like a clenched fist every day of his life.

"But, hell, maybe he's not much different than the rest of us. Nobody gets out alive. Maybe all that matters is what we do until the time comes. Or maybe none of it matters. I'd hate to think that's true, but who can say? We can only do the task before us and hope there's meaning to it. With luck, maybe we can enjoy ourselves a bit along the way. I'm afraid that's something MacKenzie never figured out."

I'd had enough. The feeling was like a crashing wave. The

bourbon tasted sour, the room seemed oppressive, and I didn't want to spend another moment with Phil Sheridan, no matter how congenial he seemed.

It was time.

I read that when Ulysses returned from the Trojan War and all of his fantastic wandering, he had the urge to put an oar over his shoulder and walk inland and settle where no one knew what an oar was.

That's how I felt. I didn't know where I'd go or what I'd do. I just knew that it wouldn't be where I'd been or what I'd done.

I put the glass on the general's desk and got to my feet. It was strange how I followed Phil Sheridan off and on for so many years but never learned to like him.

"Sir, I'm afraid it's not much help," I said.

Sheridan rose from the chair to shake my hand like he meant it and walk me to the door with one hand on my shoulder.

"Stone, I'm sure you figured out by now that I'm not in the help business," he said.

Outside the door, I stopped in the bright sunlight, pivoted to face the general and snapped off a crisp salute. As a civilian, it wasn't necessary, but I wanted to do it. It was the last salute of my life and I wanted to make it a good one.

To my surprise, Sheridan returned the salute in equally sharp fashion.

A moment like that stays with you.

Chapter Fifty-Six

I didn't know it, but I was about to stumble into the hap-piest time of my life.

I decided to go to New York City to see if I was as well off as everyone seemed to think. Communicating by occasional letter and telegram, I'd kept only loose oversight of my financial situation. Given my circumstances with the army, anything else was impossible.

After a voyage that saw me in foul humor thanks to the uncertainty I faced, in New York I was gratified to learn that everything was in much better shape than I deserved considering my lack of attention.

Before my father-in-law, Lachlan, died he put a Swiss named Edward Verplank in charge of my affairs. Lachlan also left me an impressive sum in his will, which I didn't know until I had a long meeting with Verplank, who worked in New York, where Lachlan had an office. After Lachlan's death, in several letters that often took months to find me when they found me at all, the aging bachelor expressed his eagerness to retire and return to Switzerland.

Verplank was a dry old stick whose joy at my arrival was so complete that he almost smiled. He'd done so well on my behalf that I tried to persuade him to stay but nothing I could do or say changed his mind. He grumbled that he found America too "unruly" for a man of his age and temperament.

After gushing my thanks, along with a parting bonus, I saw him off at the docks after paying for the most luxurious trans-Atlantic voyage money could buy.

Two weeks later, I learned that poor man died of a massive heart attack only three days out of New York.

There was a lesson there: Do not postpone what you want because you may never get another chance. In my old age, the few regrets that I have are mostly things I *didn't* do.

Thanks to Lachlan and Verplank, I was a wealthy man, not that it matters anymore. All the money in the world can't scale away the years or bring the dead back to life.

While I was not in the same rarified atmosphere as a J. P. Morgan, I was wealthier than most but didn't care to live like it, at least not in some of the obvious ways. I enjoy quality and doing many of the things that money allows, but I was never the type for diamond stick pins or legions of servants.

One summer in Newport, after only a few minutes mingling with those smug, self-satisfied blowhards, I knew that if I had a choice between the Comanche and those ninnies, I would choose the Comanche.

I did enjoy the cut and thrust of business. My specialties became shipping, the acquisition and sale of land, large-project construction, in partnership with investors I liked and trusted, and the buying and selling of currency.

I did not want my life to be all about the acquisition of money. Fortunately, it wasn't necessary. Even when I lost interest much later in life, unless you are incredibly stupid or take too many risks it is not difficult for a large fortune to become self-sustaining.

And I had diversions, many of them.

For one thing, I fell in love again.

Her name was Dana. She was named after Richard Henry Dana, an old Massachusetts friend of her father's and the man who wrote the popular memoir "Two Years Before the Mast".

Although he came from a well-to-do family, as a young man seeking adventure Dana joined the Merchant Marine as a common sailor. "Two Years Before the Mast" was the story of his brutal voyage from Boston, around Cape Horn to Southern California and back again.

I used to tease Dana that it's a good thing he wasn't named Richard Henry Smoot.

It wasn't until months after Dana and I met that I found out how mutual friends "accidentally" brought us together at a dinner party in New York, thinking that we might enjoy each other's company.

And we did...for almost fifty years.

Aside from Dana being the most interesting person I ever met, I marveled that such an extraordinary woman would actually be in love with me, a feeling that stayed with me until the day she died in my arms. She was all I wanted and more than I deserved. We never stopped enjoying each other's company, never stopped laughing, and never ran out of things to talk about and do. She was a stimulating woman in all the ways there are.

Did we argue? Of course. I could never convince that stubborn creature that I am always right. How is that possible, she countered, when *she* is always right?

Did the mostly silly arguments matter? Not a bit.

We never had children, which didn't bother us because we had each other. If we had a choice, I might have wanted a daughter, a little Dana. But it was not to be, and we had no regrets.

The years passed happily and much too quickly. I found some small success as a writer, too, mostly magazine articles about my experiences in the West and our many travels that were eventually put together and published in book form. We *did* travel a great deal, including two world tours of more than a year each, which allowed me to renew old acquaintances in Europe. We kept homes in New York City, the Berkshires in western Massachusetts, and Charleston, South Carolina, where we went to escape the northern winters.

We had many good and joyful friends, too, including Sam Clemens, the man the world knows as Mark Twain. We saw a great deal of Sam and his family when he built the opulent home of his dreams in Hartford, Connecticut.

During the happy hours we played billiards there – Sam's only physical activity, as far as I knew – he liked to tease Dana about why she wasted her time with a "broken down old horse soldier" when there were so many better men to choose from.

With a laugh, she'd reply that I was a reclamation project that was taking longer to reclaim than she anticipated.

Bill Cody was another dear friend. After hearing about the famous scout for years, our friendship began when I became an investor in the first of his Wild West shows that went on to gain worldwide popularity. There was a time when "Buffalo Bill" Cody might have been the most famous man on the planet. I eventually pulled my money out with an excellent return when he was at his glorious peak and no longer needed my investment.

When anyone asks about Cody, and it's surprising how many still do, I tell them that he was the kind of man who made colors seem brighter, conversation more clever, men better looking, and women beautiful.

I never add that he was a terrible businessman, a colossal spendthrift and a soft touch. He eventually went broke and lost his show. His name still had value and he continued working for lesser men long after sickness riddled his body, and he should have retired with dignity. I tried to help, but he was too proud to take it. To him, all setbacks were temporary, and redemption was just around the corner.

He just ran out of time.

As best I could, I kept track of Mac through newspapers and bits of information through the military grapevine. We never spoke or communicated in any way. Such was our foolish pride that neither one of us was willing to take the first step.

Would it have changed what happened if we did? I do not know, but I doubt it.

As Sheridan predicted, Mac never stopped waging war. He was too good at it. There were at least two more incursions into Mexico. After the Custer debacle at the Little Big Horn in the summer of '76, he was called north to deal with the Northern Cheyenne and Sioux. There was a campaign against the Apache and another against the Utes.

I am sure there were more I didn't know about, but that was enough.

It seemed as if every time the army faced a crisis anywhere in the West, it called on Ranald MacKenzie. However difficult the situation and no matter the odds against him, he was expected to take care of it.

And he always did.

If a miracle worker can be taken for granted, I think that is what happened to Mac. The army treated him as if he were indestructible because he seemed like it.

He finally made general, this time as a permanent rank, but *after* Miles, who was much better at promoting his favorite cause – himself. How Mac must have hated that!

As the years passed, inevitably life began to take away almost as much as it gave.

Ulysses Grant died in '81, done in by all those cigars, although he managed to finish his tremendously popular memoir a few days before he died. Sam Clemens was his publisher. Aside from his own writing and lectures, it was Sam's greatest success.

Sheridan succeeded Sherman as General of the Army when Sherman retired in '83. Unfortunately, Sheridan's time didn't last long. He died five years later after a series of crippling heart attacks. By then the little man weighed well over two hundred pounds.

Sherman, who lived only a few blocks from Dana and me in New York City, died in 1891. Seven years earlier, the power brokers of the Republican Party tried to draft him into a run for the presidency. They didn't know their man. His reply was a classic still quoted today: "I will not accept if nominated and will not serve if elected."

He was held in such respect that when he died his old Confederate foe, General Joe Johnston, who contested Sherman for every mile from Tennessee down to Atlanta, and then later in the Carolinas, made the trip north to attend the funeral as an honorary pall bearer.

It was a wet and freezing February day and Johnston, who was in his eighties, stood at attention the entire time, removing his hat as a sign of respect for his old opponent.

I was standing nearby and was one of many who urged Johnston to sit down. If he wouldn't do that, at least he could put on a hat.

He refused, of course.

"If I were in Sherman's place and he in mine," Johnston declared, "he would not put on his hat."

The gallant old man came down with pneumonia and died a few weeks later.

Quanah, who took the name Quanah Parker to honor his mother, died in 1911 after leading his people as well in peace as he did in war. He was the greatest of all Comanche, and to my mind the greatest Indian of them all.

We never met. I wish we had.

Sam Clemens died in 1910. All the world mourned the death of the great Mark Twain.

Bill Cody died in 1917, the year we entered a so-called world war that accomplished nothing. His death truly marked the end of an era. I am not sure that what we have today is an improvement.

My beloved Dana passed ten years ago.

I miss her every day but take pleasure in the memories. Sometimes it is as if she still is alive. Occasionally one of the attendants here will see me smiling and ask what amuses me. Almost every time I am thinking of something Dana said or did.

But all of that was far in the future.

I did not suspect what was just over the horizon.

Chapter Fifty-Seven

The message from San Antonio was brief and bewildering, especially in the abbreviated language of the telegram.

"Ranald disappeared. He was not well. Army took him. Please help."

It was signed Florida Tunstall Sharpe.

Handing the young messenger a gratuity, I read the telegram while standing in the foyer of our New York brownstone. Then I read it again. It wasn't any clearer the second time.

"Who the hell is Florida Tunstall Sharpe?" I muttered.

Standing behind me, Dana read the telegram with her chin on my shoulder.

"She sends something like this, and you don't even know her?"

"I don't have any..."

Suddenly I remembered. It didn't come to me right away because she was only a name to me. Florida Tunstall was the woman Mac fell in love with years ago in Texas but who wound up marrying an older man named Sharpe.

What was this all about? Mac was ill? The army "took him"?

And why contact me, a man she didn't know, who hadn't seen Mac in years?

* * *

I replied to the telegram with one of my own, she replied to that and we made the wires hum all day. Although it's difficult to express anything complicated by telegraph, a picture began to form.

Florida Tunstall Sharpe and Mac reconnected after her husband's death. The relationship continued for years even though Mac was away for months at a time. He always came back, and he always came back to her. Eventually he proposed and she accepted, but they were not yet married.

Somewhere along the way he began having what she called "disturbances", a morsel of information that left me with more questions.

I assumed that she didn't know many details because he was away so much. Even when they were together, Mac wasn't a man to talk about his troubles.

Not long before they were to be married Mac mysteriously left town, at least that is what she was told.

He never came back.

What happened? Where did he go?

She couldn't get a straight answer from the army. After a while she didn't get any answer at all. Mac had disappeared.

Her desperation was clear, even in a telegram. I was her last hope.

"What will you do?" Dana asked that night as we lay in bed.

"I don't know," I admitted.

But I would do something. I had to.

Chapter Fifty-Eight

In my last telegram of the long day, I told Florida Tunstall Sharpe that I would find out what I could.

I said it to comfort her, but I didn't know where to start. For all I knew, Mac was perfectly safe. He could be anywhere from Texas to Montana or leading another mission into Mexico. Maybe he didn't tell his fiancée because he didn't want her to know? He wouldn't be the first to get cold feet on the verge of matrimony.

It was impossible to know what was true and what wasn't when everything I thought I knew was based on the word of a woman I never met, who lived more than a thousand miles away.

But why would she make up such a story? What she said about "disturbances" bothered me more than anything else.

"Danny, I think you should go to Texas," Dana said.

We were eating breakfast the next morning. I was a hearty eater no matter the circumstance or time of day – Sam Clemens called me "a gallant trencherman" – while Dana ate less than some birds.

I came to the same conclusion during a restless night but wasn't sure how to bring it up. Texas was a long way, and I had no idea how long I'd be gone.

"You rarely speak of it, but I have watched what happened between you and best friend eat at you for as long as we've known each other," she said. "I know this story coming out of nowhere seems strange, but how can you *not* go if only for your own peace of mind?"

"Will you come with me?"

She shook her head, breaking off a piece of scone that was barely more than a crumb and popping it into her mouth.

Echoing my own thoughts, she said, "I don't think I should. You don't know how long you'll be away or what you're taking on. You might need allies back here. In Texas I would be useless. Here we have friends and resources. I can help if you need it."

She was on the mark, as usual.

"All right," I said. "I can work at it from there and let you know what you can do, if you can do anything."

"What does your gut tell you?" she asked.

"There's something to it," I replied, pouring a final cup of coffee. "I can feel it and it doesn't feel good.

"It's hard to explain, but there's always been a sense of tragedy, or something like it, clinging to Mac, as there was a price to be paid for the way he is. The woman's story fits, somehow. I can see the army trying to quietly get him out of sight if something was wrong. Mac's a legend out there and legends can't be seen as vulnerable."

"That sounds awfully cruel," she said.

I drained my coffee in one long gulp.

"It is," I agreed, "and I sure as the devil hope I'm wrong."

We recently installed one of those new-fangled telephonic devices in our home, although I didn't know how to work the thing. I was even a little wary of it. That it actually did what it was supposed to do seemed like voodoo to me.

At my request, Dana did whatever maneuvers were necessary to connect to our shipping office down at the New York docks, where we had a similar device installed. In the shipping business, time is one way to gain an edge over the competition and these (to me) mysterious inventions gave us that edge, at least until everybody else got one.

After a minute or so, I was talking to my shipping manager, Gus Cartwright.

"Gus, do we have any idle ships in New York or Boston?" I asked, as usual marveling that I could hear a voice, however tinny, through this... thing.

"Idle! What kind of dim-witted oaf do you think I am?"

"Gus, this is serious," I said. "I need to get to Texas as quickly as possible, and that means by ship. Galveston or Houston, it doesn't matter which. No cargo and no putting in anywhere even for a few hours except to refuel. Just get me there."

Hearing the urgency in my voice, Gus stopped joshing. It was an unusual request, but in his job, Gus dealt with the unusual every day.

"Golden Cloud just put in from Halifax. It's supposed to load the day after tomorrow for Southampton, then probably on to Copenhagen if I can close a deal," he said.

"Can we lay off the cargo to another ship?" I asked.

"Not one of ours. Nothing's available. There's not a foot of cargo space. Business is *that* good."

"What about another line?"

"A competitor?"

There was silence on the line while Gus thought it over.

"The thought makes my balls shrivel but yes, any of 'em would love it, even at the last minute," he said. "This late it'll probably have to be spread across two or three ships, but it can be done. Losing on the cargo and turning the Golden Cloud into your private yacht will cost us plenty, though."

"It doesn't matter. How soon can Golden Cloud be ready?"

"The crew is on shore leave, though they'll be back by sunset. Most of 'em sober, too. They're a good lot. With no cargo, we'll have to load ballast so she won't ride too high. We wouldn't want the ship to capsize and sink with the big boss on it, unless I'm in your will in a big way. Is in the morning soon enough? Name the time and we'll be ready."

"An hour after sunrise then, so we don't have to try to get out of the harbor in the dark. Thanks, Gus. And don't worry, I'll only take part of our loss out of your bonus, nothing more than a hundred percent."

"Boss, I'm just *so* grateful."

I was lucky to have Gus Cartwright. He probably turned down two or three job offers a year. His annual bonus was a one percent share of the shipping company. He already owned eight percent and had nothing to worry about on the profit end. I'd make up the loss myself.

Chapter Fifty-Nine

The train from Houston to San Antonio had everything.
It was crowded, dirty, hot and slow.

Every window was wide open but the air in the passenger car
still was foul with too many unwashed bodies crowded together
and made worse by the stench of cheap tobacco belching from
pipes and cigars.

If that wasn't enough, our car was plagued by a loud, foul-
mouthed drunk in an expensive suit and bowler hat who tor-
mented the passengers with a voice like a braying jackass.

And I was traveling first-class. I never cared for train travel and
this was a good reminder why. Do I sound like I was spoiled by
the good life? Well, yes, I was. I *liked* being spoiled.

As the train swayed along, the drunk staggered down the
crowded aisle, carelessly shoving standing passengers aside as he
headed more or less in my direction, if he was headed anywhere.

Just as he reached my aisle seat the train rounded a curve. The
drunk lost his balance and fell, sprawling all over me, his foul
breath worse than most horses.

Instead of rising to his feet and apologizing for being a clumsy, drunken, swine, which may have been too much to expect, he stayed where he was, befuddled by finding himself stretched across a stranger's lap when he was perfectly upright just a second ago.

An idiot's grin on his florid face, he reached into his coat pocket, pulled out a half-empty pint bottle and waved it in front of my face.

"Shorry, fren'," he mumbled. "Here, have a li'l drinky on me. I got plenny more where that came from, too. Gotta keep fortified, y'know."

I grabbed his ear and gave it a twist, which elicited a satisfying yelp. I rose to my feet, forcing my new "fren'" to stand with me unless he wanted to lose his ear.

"Listen, stupid, I've been in a bad mood for a couple of weeks." I twisted the ear even harder and got another high-pitched cry for my effort. "If you don't get your ugly face out of my sight, I will throw your worthless ass off this train while it's still moving and keep your ear as a souvenir."

Several passengers applauded as I let go of the fool's ear, seized his shoulders, turned him toward the exit and gave him a shove that put him on his knees. With one hand cupped over his injured and, I hoped, permanently misshapen ear, on all fours he scrambled down the aisle toward the next car, at least as much as a drunk can scramble.

A few minutes later, a neatly-dressed, black-suited man of middling height and a lean outdoors look eased into the car from the same direction the drunk departed, moving easily through the passengers still buzzing over the confrontation. As crowded as the car was, there was something about the man that made a path open like Moses marching through the Red Sea.

He stopped at my side, tipped his flat-crowned hat back on

his head and leaned over, speaking softly so that only I could hear him.

"You wouldn't happen to be Daniel Stone, would you?"

I looked him in the eye and saw no bad intentions.

"Yes, I would," I said.

"Same man who rode with Ranald MacKenzie?"

I nodded, my curiosity rising.

"And you are?"

He motioned toward the empty seat facing me. Threatening to throw an obnoxious drunk off the train may have been popular with other passengers, but now no one wanted to get too close. That was fine with me. I enjoyed the space.

I gestured my approval and he sat. As his coat opened, I saw that he wore a shoulder holster. I couldn't tell what weapon he carried, only that it had a walnut grip.

The stranger offered his hand, and I shook it. He gave off an air of quiet competence, someone who was hard to surprise and even harder to impress.

"Thought I recognized you," he said. "I was at Palo Duro Canyon, though I was just a youngster and didn't do anything to make you remember me."

I gave him a long look while I searched my memory, which he didn't seem to mind. I figured that he would have been twenty or so at Palo Duro Canyon, where we defeated the Comanche and slaughtered their horse herd. Maybe even younger. I tried to take away the years, the obvious hard-earned experience, the air of competence and the thick black mustache.

"Silas...Silas...Penny," I said. "You were promoted to corporal at the end of the campaign. I remember standing beside you for a bit at the horse slaughter. Neither one of us was happy to be there."

Impressed, he raised one eyebrow. "That was good. You must have a memory like..."

"That's the man! That's the man I told you about! I want him arrested right now!"

The drunk was back and pointing at me in boozy indignation, the other hand still holding his swollen ear.

With a sigh, Penny rose out of his seat. He removed a small notebook from his inside coat pocket, produced a stub of a pencil and scribbled something. He ripped the page out of the notebook and stuffed it in the drunk's vest pocket.

"Sir, bar and dining are two cars up," he said, nodding his head to show the direction. "I will take care of this gentleman. Trust me, he will get what he deserves. Why don't you go on up and enjoy yourself? What I wrote on that paper gets you a fine meal with all the trimmings along with a drink or two, paid for by the railroad as a way to make up for all your, ah, suffering."

He put his arm around the drunk's shoulders and pulled him close just a little too forcefully.

"You would be doing me a favor if you took me up on my offer," he said.

There was just a touch of menace there. Unsure of Penny's true intentions, the drunk let himself be guided away so that he was halfway to the next car before he knew it. He looked over his shoulder, offered me a disdainful "Humph", and disappeared to irritate other passengers.

Penny returned to his seat and grinned, his teeth white and even beneath his mustache.

"That was nicely done," I said. "As soon as you figure out what I deserve let me know. I've often wondered myself. Are you some kind of law?"

He shook his head. "Not in the way you mean. I work some with the Pinkertons, which is what I'm doing here. I don't want to work for anybody fulltime, so they hire me when they need me. Though train robberies are pretty much dying out, this train's been robbed a couple of times in the last year by a collection of youngsters who think they're the James gang. The railroad wanted some extra protection. It contacted the Pinkertons and the Pinkertons contacted me."

"Has it been robbed since you started protecting?" I asked.

"One try," he said. "It didn't work out for 'em."

There was a story there, but I would learn that Silas Penny wasn't the kind of man to tell it, although we wound up talking all the way to San Antonio.

He explained that he left the army after two years. "Joined as a boy from southern Indiana wanting a little adventure but I saw right away there wasn't much future in it. Served my hitch and got out. Discovered I didn't like taking orders that much, let alone being yelled at. Rather work things out on my own."

The last few years Penny worked as a lawman here and there, doing what he called "piece work" for the Pinkertons, and taking on assignments from other employers that needed what I suspected was his considerable skill in investigation and enforcement.

Sometimes you get a feeling about people and I had that feeling about Silas Penny. I'd already decided I needed someone with his talents if I was going to find the truth about Mac in timely fashion. He appeared to be just the man.

I did not know it, but he would work for me for ten years and become a close friend. Penny was like an all-purpose tool that could do anything with quiet efficiency. He could be diplomatic, or he could be a hardcase, whichever worked.

Penny left me after ten years because he wanted to start his own business before he got too old. He never said anything, but I don't think he ever felt truly at home in the east, particularly New York. Knowing his capabilities, I loaned him money to help get started, which he paid back quickly and with interest. Calling himself a "consulting detective", he did well with a thriving firm until he was killed in the Great San Francisco earthquake back in...oh, whenever the hell it was.

As the stifling passenger car rocked along, I asked Penny about his prospects. He said that his current association with the Pinkertons ended when the train arrived at San Antonio. He had offers but none of them were that interesting. I told him I had something in mind that might interest him and invited him to dinner the next night to talk it over. I wanted to meet Florida Sharpe before making any offer to Penny. He was not a man to whom vague words would appeal, and vague words were all I had at the moment.

We agreed to meet it the restaurant at San Antonio's best hotel, the Menger, where I was staying. That would give me time to see the lady in the morning and figure things out.

At least I hoped so.

Chapter Sixty

She was tall for a woman, slender, too. Her light brown hair was pulled back from a long face with prominent cheekbones and a generous mouth that looked like it smiled often, though probably not lately.

Not at all beautiful in the way people usually mean it, I suppose the word handsome described her best. She had alert dark eyes and a sense of ready intelligence, someone who is used to looking after herself.

We met in the parlor of her San Antonio boarding house, an imposing two-story stone structure that was once her parents' home. Before the war, when he commanded the Department of Texas for the U.S. Army, Robert E. Lee was a frequent guest of the family. There was a picture of a young Lee – with a black mustache and without the gray beard – on the mantel. Although she had help running the boarding house, she did most of the work herself because she had high standards and liked to keep busy.

It was mid-morning, and the two boarders were out so we could use the parlor to talk in private. She offered tea or coffee.

I declined both, having had my fill of coffee during breakfast at the hotel and not wanting to interrupt our conversation with an undignified trip to the privy.

"Mister Stone, how much do you know about...us?" she asked, sitting prim and erect in the edge of a high-backed chair next to mine. The chairs were separated by a small round table with a marble top on which she placed a saucer and a cup of steaming tea she sipped from time to time, carefully bringing it to her mouth with both hands.

"Not much," I admitted. "I was in Europe when you met Mac, though he told me what happened, at least his version. He never talked about it again, not that I heard. Truth is we haven't talked in a long time."

I shook my head. "It was..."

"I know." She leaned forward to touch my hand, a comforting gesture from a woman who needed comfort herself. "Ranald told me about how you parted. He regretted it very much."

"So did I. We were a couple of damn fools."

I apologized for my language. She smiled and said that she'd heard worse and besides, it seemed to exactly describe the situation.

"So how can I help you, Mister Stone?" she asked. "Where do I start?"

"First, please call me Dan, or Daniel. I'm not sure of my ground so I want to know everything. Start at the beginning as you know it and I'll ask questions as you go. Anything, even if it seems without consequence, might help. I don't know what I'm looking for and the best I can do is hope to know something helpful when I hear it."

I prompted her, just to get started.

"I had no idea you two were back together. How and when did that happen?"

As I hoped, the question got things moving. Her husband, Dr. Redford Sharpe, died four years after they married. She was surprised when Mac sent a note of condolence. She wrote back to thank him for his kindness, and they began to correspond, not often at first, but more frequently as time passed. They even managed to see each other occasionally.

That was my first surprise. I thought I knew Mac better than anyone and yet I had no idea. The man knew how to keep a secret.

"I don't know when it became...something more," she said. "There was no spectacular moment full of flying arrows from Cupid's bow. It just happened over time. Eventually we had what I suppose you could call an understanding."

A tight little smile and another sip of tea. "To be honest, I pushed for more, but it was hard for Ranald to talk about personal things, even with me. After your quarrel he had no close friends at all. I offered a kind of oasis in his life and he would come to me whenever he could. I think that what we had was so comfortable for him that he was reluctant to change it with marriage. It was as if he thought that our finding each other again was such a delicate thing that even the slightest shift might damage it beyond repair. But it wasn't enough for me. I wanted to marry him. I know now that I always did, even when we were young, and I made a foolish choice."

She thought about what she said and apparently didn't like the way it came out.

"Please don't misunderstand," she said. "Redford was a good man but I knew right away that I didn't love him. Of course, by then it was too late."

As the years passed, one obstacle in their way was Mac's long-pending assignment as commander of the District of New Mexico in Santa Fe. In the structured ways of the army, the com-

AND HELL FOLLOWED WITH HIM 321

mand was a necessary prelude for advancement. When it finally came, the assignment lasted more than two years and as expected ended with his promotion to brigadier general and reassignment to command the Department of Texas in San Antonio.

She could have gone with him to Santa Fe, but said, "I did not wish to accompany Ranald as his concubine. He understood that. He also had a social position to consider so I doubt that I would have gone even if I wanted to."

That didn't ring true with me. I'd known too many high-ranking officers with unusual living arrangements. The real issue, I suspected, is that they were two stubborn people. She knew exactly what she wanted while Mac didn't know what he wanted, and the uncertainty disturbed him so much that he dug in his heels and did nothing at all.

"I know now that I should have gone with him because Ranald was a different man when he returned from New Mexico," she said. "It's hard to explain. Two years is a long time and people change, but it was much more than that. He was often morose, which wasn't like him. Quiet, yes, but never so dark. I believe that he might even have contemplated suicide, but I could never get him to talk about it. He resented it when I tried. It was the only time we argued.

"At other times he was wild with manic energy. I heard rumors of violent behavior but never saw it myself. He was never that way with me, but sometimes his emotions did overwhelm him. Two or three times I found him quietly weeping for no obvious reason. The first time, he was ashamed that I saw it and refused to talk about it, as if ignoring it would make it seem like it never happened. The other times I foolishly pretended that I didn't see it because I knew that's what he wanted.

"I hate to say it, but, as much as I loved Ranald, he could be a difficult man," she said.

"You are being tactful," I said. "Mac could be impossible."

Mac surprised her when he talked about retiring from the army, though she was pleased to hear it. They even bought land in the Texas Hill Country with retirement in mind. But at other times it was if he never considered it at all. He was full of plans for his future in the army, everything from new campaigns to reforms to be tackled, a long list that would carry deep into the future.

To her surprise, he proposed that they marry in late December. It being her second marriage, they planned it as a quiet affair. Not many people knew, no more than five or six and all of them her friends.

"As far as I know, Ranald didn't tell anyone," she said.

And then he disappeared.

"I didn't think anything of it at first," she said. "I know that sounds strange, but his duties made life unpredictable, and I was used to it. He traveled all over the state and often left without warning. We could go quite some time and not see each other for any number of reasons."

She seemed composed, but her hands twisting against each other in her lap revealed the turmoil she felt.

"When I tried to reach him in the usual way there was no response," she said. "I finally went to headquarters myself, but it did no good. At first, they put me off with vague talk about a special assignment, though no one explained what that meant or how long Ranald might be gone. After a while they refused to see me, at all, as if I'd become a nuisance or an embarrassment."

"I was desperate. I had to know what happened to him. Even if it was bad, at least I would know something. That's when I contacted you. I appreciate your coming all this distance more than I can say. There is no one else. You are my last hope."

We talked a while longer. I especially wanted to know about

the "rumors of violence" she mentioned, but she knew precious little, which was part of her anguish. Just so many whispers in the wind.

There was something out there, something ominous, she was sure of it. But it was nothing she could identify. It was almost as if Mac led a double life, with no connection of one to the other.

I left the boarding house convinced that Florida Tunstall Sharpe wasn't lying. She believed that something terrible happened to the strange man she loved, and the army knew what it was but refused to tell her.

But that didn't mean she was right.

I asked myself how a general, especially one with Mac's reputation, could just disappear. I also wondered if anyone on the post knew of their relationship, not that they were to be married, but that they were together at all.

If she wasn't family, and if no one on the post knew about them, then from the army's point of view she was a stranger demanding confidential information that wasn't any of her business.

From what she said, it was possible that Mac wasn't all that eager to marry. He seemed ambivalent. Did that have anything to do with his disappearance?

Whatever the truth, I told her that I would try to find it.

Chapter Sixty-One

As planned, I met Silas Penny for dinner in the Menger's ornate dining room. After his promise to keep it secret, I told him everything I knew and many other things I wasn't sure about but thought he should know.

I asked if he'd ever been to Santa Fe. He replied that several years ago he did some civilian scouting in Northern New Mexico and knew the area well.

Perfect. I told him that I wanted him to go to Santa Fe and find out everything he could about Mac's time there. Nothing official, I said, and nothing too obvious. According to Florida Sharpe, something happened to Mac while he was there, and I wanted to know what.

"Remember, this is delicate," I said. "It must be quietly done. I need a stiletto, not a shotgun."

Penny chuckled. "Interesting way to put it, but I understand. I probably still know some of the boys 'round there, some in the army, some not. Official Santa Fe won't even know I'm there. You can count on it."

Unless it was something I should know right away, he would hold off telling me what he found until he returned to San Antonio. I didn't want prying eyes reading anything they shouldn't in a telegram. Speed was important, I said, but he needed to be thorough and secretive at the same time.

I asked Penny about his rate, what the Pinkertons paid him and if he was happy with it. When he told me, and said he was, I doubled it.

He didn't say anything, but his raised eyebrows asked a question.

"Silas, when this is over, however it turns out, I'd like you to come work for me," I said. "The word troubleshooter more or less describes what I have in mind. I have a variety of business interests, all of them legal. You'd report directly to me. I can promise good money, loyalty, variety in the work and quite a bit of travel."

He agreed right away, echoing my own thoughts on the train.

"You get a feeling about people sometimes," he said. "It doesn't happen often. I have a good feeling about you."

I hoped that he would accept my offer, although there was no reason to think he would, and brought a considerable amount of money with me. Careful not to draw attention, in my lap I wrapped a thick wad of notes in a napkin and pushed it across the table.

"This should take care of expenses," I said.

"And plenty more," he said, hefting the napkin-wrapped money in his hand. "I'll give you a full accounting when I get back."

With that and a firm handshake I excused myself for the night. Although I was not yet fifty and still had no idea what old age really was, I sure as hell wasn't as young as I used to be either.

Chapter Sixty-Two

I decided to take a look at the land supposedly purchased by Mac and Florida Sharpe.

Was she telling the truth? I thought so. If she *were* telling the truth, I wanted to see where Mac intended to settle down, although I could not really imagine such a thing. Based on what she said about his changing thoughts and behavior, I was not sure Mac could either.

The land office was an easy walk from the hotel. I explained that I was in the market to buy and had a seller lined up. I wanted to independently verify the ownership, the size of the property, and the location, meaning that I wanted to see the records for myself. I wasn't asking anything unreasonable or suspicious. It was all public record.

The dusty old clerk quickly found what I needed. As I reviewed the documents, it was clear that the couple became substantial landowners at relatively modest cost.

In three transactions over eighteen months, they bought about three thousand nine hundred acres of prime land close to

Boerne and about twenty miles from San Antonio. They paid two thousand dollars for the first parcel of one thousand three hundred and forty acres, before picking up six hundred and forty acres at a land auction for only seven dollars and ninety-five cents.

I read it again to make sure: Seven dollars and ninety-five cents? A winning bid for such a ridiculous amount of money almost certainly meant that they were the only bidder, which seemed unlikely. Having participated in such things myself, I figured that the auction probably was rigged by an insider who made sure that the land never went to auction although the record showed that it did. Both Mac and Florida Sharpe had the contacts to pull off something like that, but my money was on her. From our conversation I could tell that she had good business sense while I doubted that Mac did, at least not the man I knew.

They ended their buying spree a few months later by purchasing one thousand nine hundred and twenty acres for one thousand four hundred and ninety-five dollars.

At those prices I would have bought the land, too. The way Texas was growing, given its location just hanging on to it for a while made it a good investment.

I thanked the aged clerk for his time, and he shuffled back to life among the files.

It still was early and the day pleasant. I walked a few blocks to a livery to hire a horse. The road to Boerne was easy and clearly marked. I could ride there today, spend the night, take a look at the property tomorrow, spend another night, and return to San Antonio.

By mid-morning the next day I was guiding my hired gelding through the couple's thirty-nine hundred acres on a beautiful day, with a few high clouds adding texture to the blue sky. As I learned at the land office, the property was consolidated in two sections not far apart. The couple probably planned to live on one and sell the other. The rolling countryside was thick with cedar, oak, and poplar trees, often growing in small groves. There was scattered cactus, too, mostly yucca. Picturesque streams and creeks abundant with fish wound through the property. In the west, water was always a concern, but it was not a problem here.

All of it was exactly as described by Florida Sharpe. She spoke the truth and I was glad to see it.

It was nearly dark by the time I got back to Boerne. I did not look forward to spending a second night there. After paying too much for the privilege, I was sharing a boarding house room with two beds and four men. It was a while since my roommates bathed and the beds were so old, they seemed to creak every time any of us took a breath.

If it grew even a little, Boerne could use a decent hotel. As an investor, I resolved to keep that in mind.

After an uncomfortable, smelly and mostly sleepless night, I rose early the next morning, ate a tortilla smeared with sour butter and drank two cups of coffee so vile it was even worse than the army version. After seeing my horse properly fed and watered, I saddled up. By the time I got back to San Antonio I was desperate for a bath, good meal and a feather bed. Years of prosperity made me soft.

My body stiff and aching in ways I hadn't felt in a long time, the next day I paid a call on army headquarters. I decided to present myself as an ex-officer who happened to be in the area indulging himself with a tour of his past. There was enough truth in it that I wouldn't have to remember anything complicated to bolster my deceit.

Such a visit did not make me unusual. Mac and I often experienced it from the other side when some old soldier suddenly appeared and expected a grand tour because he served in the army back when the world was young. We gave such men every courtesy, usually assigning the post's junior officer as a guide.

Now that *I* was the troublesome old coot, I hoped to receive the same treatment. It had been a long time since I left the army, but I'd served with thousands of officers and enlisted men. There was a fair chance I'd recognize someone at the post, or they'd recognize me. If so, I'd try to arrange a meeting later without giving the game away.

The recently appointed commander of the District of Texas was John Pope. He also commanded the Department of the Missouri. In what I interpreted as an admission by the army that Pope wasn't its brightest general and needed help, Lt. Col. Thomas Vincent assumed daily command in Texas, reporting to Pope until Mac's permanent successor was named.

That told me a couple of things. Whatever happened to Mac came on so fast that the Army was forced to make a stop-gap arrangement, that being the Pope-Vincent combination. It also revealed that Mac wasn't away on some temporary assignment. If it were only temporary, a subordinate could have taken over until Mac's return.

Wherever Mac was and whatever happened to him, he wasn't expected to return.

Lt. Col. Vincent wasn't in, which I already knew. I arranged my visit to coincide with his absence. Although I had to explain why I was poking around the post, I didn't want to go through a lot of official nonsense with the commanding officer.

When I identified myself to the young sergeant at the desk in Vincent's outer office, he jumped to his feet, snapped to attention and saluted.

Replying with a casual half-salute, I said, "That's hardly necessary, Sergeant. I've been a civilian for a long time."

"Beggin' your pardon, sir, but the name Daniel Stone is well known in these parts. I've heard all about old Griz, the medal of honor winner who rode with Bad Hand Ma..."

An uncertain look flared crossed the sergeant's florid face. He almost said a name he was not supposed to utter.

I wasn't that happy myself. I didn't like being remembered as *old* Griz.

"You were about to say MacKenzie, General Ranald MacKenzie?" I said. "It's true we were close once, but I haven't seen the man in years."

That seemed to relieve the sergeant. It also was the beginning of my real investigation.

I spend the next several days quietly wandering here and there. I talked to anyone who would talk to me without seeming like I was interested in anything in particular.

What I found was not good and it wasn't that hard to find.

A square-jawed Australian named Marsden said it best after drinking a half bottle of tequila in a popular San Antonio cantina one afternoon. By then I developed the skill of seeming to drink along with anyone but without consuming much at all. It helped that I never developed a taste for tequila, especially out of glasses that looked like they hadn't been washed since Texas belonged to Mexico.

"The whole thing's as simple as milk from a mother's breast," Marsden declared in the way only a half-drunk man can. "The old boy lost his cabbage."

The phrase was new to me, but my heart sank because the meaning was clear.

"How do you know?"

"Saw it m'self." Marsden poured another shot. "We all did."

Throwing his head back to down the tequila, Marsden, who worked off and on as a civilian teamster for the army for almost twenty years, glared at the glass as if it were a disappointment to find it empty.

"Y'see, I knew Bad Hand from before." Nodding at me, he added, "You, too. I mean, I'm not sayin' I *knew* either of ya, but I saw the kind of men you were."

He poured another shot, the tequila sloshing over the edge of the glass.

"Bad Hand wasn't the same this time. He seemed like two different people. One you couldn't rouse to action for love or money. He didn't take an interest in anything, a man lost in a private fog for days at a time. We all saw how the other officers covered for him. In my opinion it was a grand thing that speaks well of 'em all.

"Other times he was a different man, but that was even worse. He'd snap and snarl for no reason at all, like he had this rage boilin' up inside and couldn't keep it down. He didn't look the same either. You know how erect he was, shoulders back and proud like. Now he seemed like a man let himself go and grew old before his time. I never saw evidence of it, but I heard he took to drink, too. I do know he lost weight the way heavy drinkin' folk sometimes do."

The skinny teamster was not aware of the irony of his statement. By this point, thanks to the tequila he was not aware of most everything.

But Marsden was sober enough to confirm a story I'd heard about what might have been Mac's last spasm of madness before the army spirited him away. The details varied with each telling, but the gist was always the same.

"With his foul temper, they say Bad Hand got in a few scrapes with civilians and the last one he got walloped good. The way I heard it, he lit into three men all by himself for no reason at all. To keep him down they had to tie him up. It was right after that they took him away, a few days maybe. They told us he was indisposed. Maybe, that's true, but I can tell you he was indisposed a hell of a lot before then, too. They put him on a train headed east with a proper escort and we never saw him again."

None of that sounded like the man I knew, but it did seem like a more extreme version of Florida Sharpe's description. I hated myself for believing it, but I did.

After some searching, I found the men who "walloped" Mac, two bachelor brothers named Eric and Albert Dorfman who came to Texas from Pennsylvania about ten years ago, looking to make their fortune. Unlike most others, they actually did make their fortune, or at least got off to a good start. They owned a prosperous San Antonio mercantile with a nice corner location.

The details of what happened weren't generally known because nobody bothered to ask the brothers. As far as they knew, there was no official investigation, army or civilian. It was obvious that the army was happy to pretend that the confrontation never happened at all.

"Why would we enter into fisticuffs with a famous general unless there wasn't any other choice?" said Eric, who I took to be the older brother. "The way that man went on, he could have killed us both."

The brothers both had thick dark hair and dark eyes, with Eric bigger than Albert by three inches and thirty pounds. They lived above their mercantile, which sold everything from clothing and canned food to farm equipment and weapons.

They had closed for the day and the three of us were alone while they told the tale, both of them standing behind the counter while I faced it. The story was strange, but the details were so specific that any skepticism I felt disappeared like smoke on the wind.

Mac became obsessed with a watch on display in the storefront window. For some reason, he was convinced that it once belonged to his father and that the brothers must have stolen it, although they were born long after the Commodore died. Over a few weeks, he confronted them several times demanding that the watch be returned, each time more agitated than the last.

"That man might be a hero like they say, but he was crazy as all get out," Eric said.

As best I can recall, Albert didn't say anything at all, the most silent of partners.

"I don't know how much business he cost us, but it had to be a lot. People wouldn't come near the place when he was on the prowl, actin' crazy. To call him mad as a hatter just ain't fair to hatters, far as I'm concerned."

An outdoor stairway on the side of the brick building led to their upstairs residence. Mac showed up in the middle of the night, pounding on the door and demanding that they return the watch they'd "stolen" from his father.

He made so much noise that they reluctantly opened the door to try to calm him down, understandably not wanting everyone in town to hear General Ranald MacKenzie's charge that they dealt in stolen property.

As soon as the door opened a crack, Mac burst in and started swinging.

As Eric described it, it was like tangling with a whirling dervish.

"After a bit, we got in some shots of our own, enough to put down most men," he said, making a fist. "But that lunatic didn't even blink."

Despite the two-to-one odds in their favor, the brothers were getting the worst of it when the young Mexican they employed to unload delivery wagons and keep the mercantile stocked heard the commotion from where he was sleeping in a storage shed out back. Seizing one of the shovels he was supposed to transfer from the shed to the store the next day, he ran up the stairs, quickly sized up the situation, took a swing and clubbed Mac on the back of the head.

When Mac went down, "I don't mind tellin' you that we might have kicked and punched that fool more'n a few times. Our dander was up, and we owed him some."

When they cooled off, they were afraid that they might have killed him. Finding Mac still alive, not knowing what else to do in the middle of the night, they carried the unconscious general down the stairs, tied him to a display case in the mercantile in case he woke up, and contacted the fort early the next morning.

"Pretty quick, before we opened up and people could see him, some soldiers came with a wagon, laid him out and took him away," Eric said. "That's the last we saw of him. I say good riddance, too."

When I asked if I could see the watch that caused so much trouble, they looked at each other, their expressive faces making their thoughts as clear as if they'd said it aloud: "Oh, no! Not again!"

After assurances that I believed their story – which, unfortunately, I did – and only wanted to try to understand why Mac believed the watch once belonged to his father, they showed me to a display case in the window.

I was too young at the time to remember if the Commodore even carried a watch, though I assumed so since most well-to-do men did.

What I saw in the display case was a watch like any watch, silver with a chain attached, though the chain was sold separately. With intricate designs etched on the case it was over-decorated for my taste. Nothing about its appearance jogged my memory. It clearly was new – the brothers showed me the invoice to prove it – and I had no idea why Mac thought it belonged to his father. Did it resemble the Commodore's watch in some way? I did not know.

I offered to buy it, thinking that if I ever found Mac, seeing the watch in my possession might comfort him in some way. Fifty dollars was too much for a watch the like of which I could buy for less than half that amount almost anywhere, but the brothers knew that they had me, and I bought it on the spot.

I still have it, too, although I never took it out of the box. It didn't seem right to throw it away.

Chapter Sixty-Three

My investigation in San Antonio was at an end. No one I talked to knew where Mac was taken, only that he was accompanied by an escort and left in a specially reserved railroad car.

If there was an official investigation into his condition and behavior, then Washington was the most likely place, but that was only an educated guess.

Silas Penny returned from Santa Fe four days after my conversation with the Dorfman brothers. We met in my room at the Menger because I wanted the conversation to be private. I let Penny take the only chair while I sat on the bed. He didn't look like a man who just traveled hundreds of miles of hard country on horseback. The black mustache was neatly trimmed, his hair recently barbered, and his dark suit laundered and pressed.

When I commented on his appearance, he said, "I kept the suit here for when I got back. I don't like looking sloppy even when I'm on the trail. Besides, riding from Santa Fe to here isn't that hard these days, not like it was back in your time. Quite a few little towns and settlements sprung up 'tween here and there. If you plan it right, you can sleep in a bed most every night."

With my memories of dangerous and lonely desolation in that part of the country, I could not imagine what Penny described, but kept the thought to myself. I already felt ancient thanks to "back in your time". My time didn't seem that long ago. Between one comment and another, it was as if the trip to Texas added years to my life. I didn't feel older, at least not most of the time, but I suppose the proof was in the mirror.

I told Penny everything I found. When I finished, he digested it for a moment while smoothing his mustache with thumb and forefinger.

"Fits what I heard, I 'spose," he said. "I don't know if Bad Hand's problems started in Santa Fe, but that's when they became noticeable. It didn't seem to change how people felt about him. Despite it all, he was so respected there they hated to see him go."

In New Mexico Territory, Mac faced the usual problems that come with command, particularly with the Mescalero and Chiricahua Apache in the south, who mostly did what they pleased under leaders such as Naiche, Chatto, and Geronimo. His own government was no pleasure to deal with either, but he was used to the ignorance of the local situation and bungling of even simple details that comes out of Washington. He'd seen it all of his professional life.

"Some of the folks I talked to think it started to go wrong in a fight against the Cheyenne before he ever got to New Mexico," Penny said. "A good while after you left it seems that he found himself a pro...pro...what do you call it, a younger man you take under your wing?"

"A protégé?" I suggested.

Penny nodded, filing the word away. "When the protégé

got killed it brought him down low and some say he never came a way out of it."

The young officer's name was McKinney, a West Point graduate from Tennessee who gambled and drank too much. Mac must have thought he had promise because when he learned that McKinney had heavy gambling debts, he wrote a personal check for five hundred dollars to cover what was owed in exchange for McKinney's promise never to gamble again. They became good friends and as Penny described it protégé seemed exactly the right word.

In the battle with the Cheyenne when McKinney was killed, according to Penny, Mac took many more casualties than he normally did. It weighed on him, especially when the dead were buried in the usual way on campaign, out in the middle of nowhere with all traces of their graves obliterated as if they never existed.

Penny talked to a lieutenant who was wounded in the leg during the battle. The wound was too painful for sleep and the lieutenant remembered watching Mac pace back and forth all night, gesturing and muttering to himself. Such a thing did not surprise me. I saw the same sight many times.

Over the next few days, his officers were shocked to hear Mac publicly reproach himself for his failure as a commander, the first time they ever saw him lose confidence in his ability. From what Penny learned, he convinced himself that as he aged, his leadership degenerated until he'd become "a worthless old fool". His depression grew to the point where he even talked about killing himself.

"It's true that young McKinney's death hit him hard, but it seems to me that dark thinking like that it must have been building for a long time," Penny said. "But I'm no expert. Who can tell what's in another man's mind?"

When Penny finished his story, we were silent for a while. I didn't know what to say and Penny was too tactful to say anything.

We agreed to meet the next day. I did not sleep that night.

* * *

By now we had done all that we could in this part of the country. I wasn't sure about the next step except that I wanted to go home. I sent a telegram to Dana: "Coming home with new friend. RM taken east by blue men. Don't know where."

RM was Mac, of course. Blue men represented the army. As codes go, it was childish but served its purpose. I didn't want to put it in the open for anyone to gossip about.

Dana wired back: "Miss you and look forward to return. Sherman?"

My wife was brilliant. Of course! General Sherman! *He* was our next step.

Chapter Sixty-Four

I thought that Silas Penny might have trouble adapting to New York City, but I was wrong. He never had trouble adapting to anywhere. New York would never be a favorite, but he moved through it like a shark through the ocean.

As infuriating as the city could be, I still loved it. Its brawny vitality never failed to surprise, delight and sometimes dismay. The never-ending bustle, with thousands of noisy horse-drawn cabs, carriages and delivery wagons rattling over tons of fragrant horse droppings in the streets. The elegance of Delmonico's and the many other fine restaurants were a pleasure. Grand Central Station was already more than ten years old, but the architecture still seemed miraculous. The crowded harbor offered an endless parade of ships from all over the world, a few from my own fleet. It changed for the better over the years, but Five Points was still a dangerous place where gangs made their own law. The city's other delights, at least to me, included the high-walled reservoir to the north, and Central Park, which was anything but central in those days, always jammed with carriages and strolling couples on Sunday.

Crowded, noisy, crude, and much too sure of itself, New York possessed all the culture you could possibly want and all the pomposity that comes with it. With its mighty, and sometimes mighty crooked, financial institutions and eager questing spirit it was a seething cauldron of all that makes us human.

Sherman lived in an elegant brownstone a ten-minute walk from our own. I wrote a note asking permission to visit, citing an urgent and confidential matter. He immediately accepted and greeted the three of us at the door the next day.

The general struck me as older and ageless at the same time. He moved slower but his vitality was still formidable and his carriage erect. His hair and beard were gray, but his flashing eyes showed the old fire.

He gallantly kissed Dana's hand, informed me that I married above my station, and quickly took the measure of Silas Penny, apparently liking what he saw. He apologized for not being able to introduce his wife. She was "not feeling well" and confined to her room upstairs. According to gossip, she was an invalid who never left her room. No one but Sherman and her physician knew the truth of her condition.

He offered refreshments and we accepted coffee. I didn't particularly want it but sometimes saying yes to the offer relaxes everyone present. I still was not sure how to approach the subject.

On the spur of the moment, I decided the direct approach was best and told Sherman everything. If we wanted his help it was only fair that he know it all.

I did most of the talking, with Silas and Dana adding bits and pieces of fact and conjecture. When we finished, Sherman stared at us for an uncomfortable moment, back straight, long legs crossed, chin in hand, and deep in thought.

"Goddamn them! Goddamn them all!"

After the general's silence, the outburst was so unexpected that I practically jumped out of my chair. Keeping the direct approach in mind, I said what I was thinking.

"Sir, I don't know if that's a good sign or a bad sign."

That brought the grim smile I knew so well.

"Sometimes I'm not sure myself," he said. "In this case, let me assure you that it's a good sign. Delighted as I am to see you again, and to meet your beautiful wife and formidable friend, after what you told me I assume you came here to ask for my help."

Before I could reply, he added, "Well, you've got it. I'll do everything I can. My wrath was for Washington. Whatever his difficulties may be – and I have heard rumors, but nothing more – Ranald MacKenzie deserves better than to disappear as if he never existed."

We talked a bit more, with Sherman asking questions and the three of us doing our best to answer. He promised to contact "some people I know" in Washington to find out what he could. What that meant I did not know since he knew everyone.

I was comforted by his last words as he saw us to the door, placing his hand on my shoulder.

"We will find him," he said. "Trust me, Stone, whatever happened and wherever he is, we will find him."

As we walked back to our brownstone, Penny said, "It's not often you run into a legend who lives up to his reputation. I bet that old boy was a man to step aside from when he was young and limber."

"I wouldn't cross him even now," Dana added. "He could turn you inside out with a look."

Chapter Sixty-Five

I was summoned to see Sherman again. "Only you, for now," the note said.

It was a cool and rainy afternoon. The low-hanging clouds were oppressive and made it seem colder. I bundled myself in a heavy coat and had our coach and driver brought around for the short ride to Sherman's brownstone.

As he did before, the general answered the door. I shrugged off my wet coat and he hooked it on a rack in the foyer. He led me up the stairs to a small but comfortable second-floor office where he had a warm fire going. Hundreds of books lined the walls, but I saw not one memento of his extraordinary military career, which did not surprise me. Regarded as emotional to the point of instability when he was a young man, William Tecumseh Sherman was a sentimental man of deep feelings who taught himself not to seem like it, at least most of the time, hiding behind an irascible personality, a pose that did not fool anyone who knew him.

He closed the office door and sank into the big chair behind the desk, motioning for me to take a seat in a chair facing him on the other side.

He reached into a lower drawer, pulled out a thick folder held together by a red ribbon and pushed it across the desk.

"Here's the full report on MacKenzie, plus various notes and comments from some of the people involved, along with a few items I gathered myself," he said. "I'm afraid it's not good news, but I doubt that you expected good news."

He reached out and tapped a long finger on the folder. "One of the promises I made to get this is that it can't leave this room. However, who I share it with is up to me."

Sherman put his hands on the arms of his chair and pushed himself to his feet, his knees cracking like wood in a hot fire.

"I want you to have plenty of time to digest it all," he said. "This is not the time for rash decisions. I'll leave you alone while you read. Take as long as you want."

He motioned toward a sideboard. "There are cigars and brandy if you want them. Water, too. When you're finished, just open the door."

He left the office, quietly shutting the door behind him.

Still chilled from the dank weather, I moved my chair over to the warm fire, poured a glass of brandy, and settled in.

The papers, a collection of official reports, transcripts from military hearings, personal observations and newspaper clippings, were in chronological order.

As Silas Penny discovered, there were concerns about Mac's behavior as far back as his early days in New Mexico Territory, though there was no official action taken. I doubted that anyone wanted to deal with it. I didn't blame them.

That changed in San Antonio, where Mac was carefully watched from the beginning. The first army physician to examine him after his bloody fight with the Dorfman brothers was blunt: "I am convinced that his present deplorable condition has impaired his usefulness for a further exercise of command in this department."

As I suspected, Mac was quickly but quietly relieved of command. No one seemed to know what to do next. There were questions but no answers about his "future care and medical treatment". No one knew what was wrong with him, although another physician confidently declared that he suffered from "nervous prostration" and "violent delusions" and should be committed to an asylum for his own good "and the good of the army".

The words were so general it was clear that the physician knew nothing and protected himself with medical jargon.

The only certain thing was that the army wanted Mac out of the way. The hero had become an embarrassment.

Mac didn't help his case by first denying that anything was wrong and then becoming agitated at the suggestion that something *was* wrong.

Someone high up, I suspected Secretary of War Robert Lincoln, the late President's son, decided that Mac should be taken to either New York or Washington, where he could be examined by specialists. Given his "delicate" condition and penchant for violence, a ruse was deemed necessary to get him out of San Antonio without fuss. He was told that he was temporarily ordered to Washington to consult on the reorganization of the army, a subject had recently become an obsession.

A separate unsigned note, once again probably from Lincoln, said, "Prevent notice of departure from getting into the newspapers," proof that the whole thing was carried out in secrecy, which explained why no one I talked to knew where Mac was taken. From what I read, I doubted that more than a dozen people knew.

Accompanied by a medical officer and the officer's two aides, plus two brawny orderlies in case their patient turned violent – I couldn't imagine what lies they told Mac about their duties – the railroad provided a special car and the small group left San Antonio for St. Louis, the first leg of the trip.

In St. Louis, an argument about where Mac should go next brought the journey to a temporary halt. Some thought that he was so well known in Washington that it would be "disruptive" to take him there. I interpreted that to mean that the brass was worried that in the capital they couldn't keep Mac's condition and whereabouts secret.

To my surprise, it was agreed that Mac be taken to the Bloomingdale Asylum in New York City.

Was it possible that all this time he was only a few miles from where I lived?

The railroad provided another special coach on an express to New York City, where it ended its journey at Pennsylvania Station at 10:20 p.m. on December 29, met by a man identified only as "Doctor N".

It sent a chill down my spine to read that Mac was "helped" into the carriage taking him to the asylum.

If Mac thought he was going to Washington, how was he convinced to go to New York? One possibility is that he wasn't told. It would have been difficult, but not impossible, to keep the secret if he were secure in a special railroad car, or even drugged. Another possibility is that by then his condition deteriorated so much that he no longer knew where he was or where they were taking him.

After a series of examinations, including one by an alienist, who I learned was a physician specializing in the diagnosis and treatment of the insane, the conclusion was harsh: "There is no probability of General MacKenzie's recovery and his usefulness to the service is destroyed."

With that in hand, the army convened a retirement board "with a view of his (Mac's) retirement from service". In other words, the board knew its verdict even before it met. The inquiry was headed by Major General Winfield Hancock, a Civil war hero who once ran for president, and included Quartermaster General Samuel Holabird, two majors, who were also physicians, and a captain acting as the official recorder.

As I read the rest of it tears came to my eyes.

At first, Mac seemed lucid as he defended himself, but he finally met an enemy he couldn't outfight or outwit, a foe he couldn't see and didn't understand – the tragic deterioration of his own mind.

As before, at first, he denied that anything was wrong. When he sensed that argument wasn't working – I doubt he believed it himself – he shifted ground to claim that not only was his condition temporary, he had it under control, even though he obviously didn't know what "it" was and never explained how he was so sure he could control it.

The almost childish phrases in the transcript did not seem like they could have come from the man I knew, but perhaps that man no longer existed: "I think that I am not insane. I think that I have served as faithfully as anybody in the army. I would rather die than go on the retired list. The army is all that I have got to care for."

That was followed by a pathetic plea to be released from the asylum: "I don't want to stay here anymore."

Struggling to express even simple thoughts, he said, "You all know me and have known me for a great many years. I think it is very hard if I am left out of the army where my services have always been gallant, and honest, and faithful. For only a few months' sickness, I think it will be very hard if I am separated from the active list of the army."

It didn't take long for the board to reach its foregone conclusion: "Brigadier General Ranald MacKenzie is incapacitated for active service and the duties of his office, and in the judgment of the Board, said incapacity is due to 'General Paralysis of the Insane', and the Board further finds that the disability of Brigadier General Ranald MacKenzie was incurred from wounds received and exposure in the line of duty as an Officer of the Army."

As far as I could tell, he never left the asylum.

Sherman included several newspaper articles about the Bloomingdale asylum. It was an ugly picture.

Opened more than a hundred years ago on twenty-six acres of land in upper Manhattan, for years it was the only hospital in the state that cared for the mentally ill. Despite the original good intentions, the asylum's reputation was notorious. A few years ago, a journalist with the New York Tribune went undercover and had himself committed with the help of his editor and friends posing as family. His articles chronicled the abuse of inmates, who were sometimes beaten until they were bloody and unconscious. I found it telling that they were called inmates and not patients. Some were driven to suicide. The slop buckets in the cells – yes, "cells", not rooms – were so rarely emptied that they overflowed until there was no point in bothering to use them. The disgusting gruel that passed as food was offered once a day. The inmates got five minutes to eat before it was taken away and those who didn't eat were punished. No one bothered with medical care for patients considered beyond help. If there was any bedding it was filthy, and lice infested. Some inmates hadn't seen sunlight in years, chained to the wall or to their beds and never released.

The exposé led to a flurry of activity that passed quickly and accomplished nothing. I vaguely remembered the articles myself.

More than a dozen patients were released after it was determined that they should never have been there in the first place, but there was no record of any other meaningful change.

My guess was that if there were any improvements in the care and treatment of the "inmates" they were superficial, aimed at convincing authorities that conditions at the asylum were improving.

The truth is that no one spoke for the insane. Even today, I am not sure that has changed. Despite what we say, we want such people kept out of sight, so they don't intrude upon our comfort. Those who can't be cured must be hidden.

When I finished reading, I don't know how much time passed while I sat quietly in front of the dying fire, lost in my thoughts. As Sherman predicted, I needed time to absorb it all. I felt as if my heart was breaking.

I rose from my chair, poured another glass of brandy and downed it in two gulps.

All I could think of was Mac's plea: "I don't want to stay here anymore."

I returned the chair to its proper place, opened the door and a moment later the general walked in. He took one look at me and said, "I know. It affected me the same way."

"General, do you think he's still there?"

Sherman shrugged. "There's no record that he was moved so, yes, I'm afraid he is."

"We've got to get him out," I said. "We've got to find a way."

Sherman nodded. "I know."

I took a deep breath and extended my hand.

"Sir, I want to thank you for your help," I said. "I don't know what we would have done without you."

Sherman looked at me like I was the one who should be in an asylum.

"What are you talking about? I'm not through with this until you're through. As you said, *we* will get him out. I may be just another retired old soldier, but I think I've got one more campaign in me. That is, if you'll have me."

This time he extended his hand. I took it gratefully.

"It would be our pleasure, sir."

"Stone, I don't think pleasure describes what we're in for."

Chapter Sixty-Six

Working with his Pinkerton contacts, Silas Penny obtained a detailed plan of the asylum. Dana and I spread it out on the dining table in our brownstone, the room brightly lit by the wall gas lamps.

We were all there that night: Dana, myself, Penny and Sherman, who seemed energized by our mission. He even had a name for us: "Daniel Stone's Band of Immortals."

Penny looked around the table. "At least now I know what the word 'motley' means."

Sherman laughed and slapped Penny on the back. Despite their differences in age and virtually everything else, they developed an instant rapport.

"My young friend, we could do a lot worse," he said. "I would ride to hell with this group anytime."

"Let's hope that's not necessary," I said.

Through Dana's work with a charity group that paid the medical expenses of those who can't afford it, she learned that the asylum kept the sexes separated, and troublesome inmates were fed in their cells.

She pointed at one wing on the blueprint. "The men are there." She moved her finger to the left. "And the women here."

"That's still a lot of territory," Penny said.

"How many inmates are there?" Sherman asked.

"No one knew for sure, but it's probably in the low hundreds," Dana said.

"Lot of people, too," Penny said.

"Silas, are you always this cheerful?" Sherman asked. "You're positively inspiring."

That got a laugh out of Penny and helped brighten the mood that had grown somber when we realized what we faced.

"I've thought about it and I think the direct approach is best, especially if we go in late at night," I said.

"What do you mean by 'direct approach'?" Dana asked.

"We walk right up late at night when we're sure the people who run the place have gone for the day," I said. "We pound on the door and demand to be let in. Once the door opens, we rush in before whoever answers can stop us. The important thing is to get inside as quickly as possible."

"That's direct, all right," Dana said.

"Hope they're not armed," Penny said,

"Why would they be armed?" I said. "Who tries to break *into* an insane asylum?"

I leaned forward and put my fists on the table. "We've got one of the most famous men in the country with us: General William Tecumseh Sherman. Chances are that whoever opens the door will recognize him on sight and be shocked at what they see. Silas can reasonably identify himself as associated with the Pinkerton Agency. The Pinkerton's reputation might add a little fear and we can use that. I'll pose as the general's aide, or something like that. Dana's can say she's an associate of Clara

Barton, who's got the medical community shaking in its boots with all her clamoring for reform."

I looked at Dana. "You even know Clara Barton, isn't that right?"

"I know her well," she said. "I've even been to her home in New Jersey. If it's just a simple turnkey who answers the door – assuming anyone answers – I could even say that I *am* Clara Barton. She's older than I am but I doubt he'll know that. The name Clara Barton should resonate even with a dullard."

"It resonates like hell with me," Sherman said. "She's a formidable woman. This is just the kind of thing she'd do, too."

"So we go at night, hoping that somebody who's not too bright answers the door so we can bullshit our way in," Penny said. "We want 'em to see the general clear, but Miz Stone not so much. Then we start what'll likely be a room-by-room search and hope we find General MacKenzie before morning comes and somebody important shows up and starts asking a lot of questions we can't answer."

Penny nodded at Dana to apologize for his language, and she responded with a derisive "pfft" sound. My salty wife said worse than that every day.

When no one said anything, Penny asked, "What'll we do when we find him?"

"I've got a private suite ready not far from here," I said. "We don't know about his condition, so I've got a medical team ready, too."

There didn't seem to be anything else to add.

"I wouldn't worry too much." Sherman was enjoying himself. "Half the battles I fought had a worse plan than this."

Chapter Sixty-Seven

The attendant opened the door at our late-night battering,
took one look at Sherman and erupted with a bug-eyed, "Jesus
Christ!"

"Not this time," Sherman said. "But you're close enough."

For effect, despite several years of retirement Sherman dressed
in full uniform, and light from the lantern I held high glittered
off the gold braid. Before the attendant could react, the general
pushed the asylum's heavy door open and marched in like he
owned the place.

Still holding the lantern high, I followed Sherman like the
underling I was supposed to be. The lighting inside the asylum
entrance was dim, another break for our side.

Dana came in next, followed by Penny, who closed the door
and shoved the bar lock back into place so there would be no
surprise from outside.

And just like that we were in. I hoped that our exit went as well.

"I see that you know who I am," Sherman announced. "Good.
That will expedite matters. We have business here, important

business in the national interest."

"The gentleman with the lantern is my aide." Sherman nodded at Penny. "This gentleman is an associate of the Pinkerton agency. I'm sure you've heard of it."

"And finally, may I introduce Miss Clara Barton."

As Sherman made the last introduction, I lowered the lantern so that the shadow from my body obscured Dana's face. I doubted that my precautions were necessary. The attendant looked as if he had been struck by lightning.

We agreed that only Sherman's name would be used so that the rest of us could not be easily identified. For himself, he did not fear retaliation.

Raising the lamp again, I stepped up to the attendant. "We are looking for one of your patients, a man named Ranald MacKenzie. Where can we find him?"

An effort at defiance: "This is...well, it's plenty irregular is what it is," the attendant protested.

With his quicker than expected recovery from the astonishing appearance of General Sherman and Clara Barton, the man seemed anything but the dullard we hoped to find.

"I should contact..."

"No, you should not," Sherman barked. "The fewer people who know about this the better. As you can see by my presence, this is an operation planned and carried out at the highest level. You should be flattered that we took you into our confidence at all."

I thought the general was laying it on a little thick, but it seemed to be working. It gave me a chance to take a good look at the attendant. I was too distracted before but now I saw that he had only one leg and supported himself by a homemade crutch under one arm.

His clothes were worn and patched but he was neatly-dressed

and clean-shaven. Despite his obvious impoverished circumstances, I read him as a man in his mid-to-late forties who did
the best he could with limited resources and still took pride in
his appearance.

Sherman saw it, too. He placed his hand on the attendant's
broad shoulder, a familiar gesture. Like most men who rely on
crutches and wheelchairs, he had a powerful upper body.

His voice turned soothing, Sherman asked, "What's your
name, son? Where did you serve? How did you lose your leg?"

"My name's Michael Chapman and it was during the Peninsu-
la Campaign," he said. "I was a sergeant in the Michigan twelfth.
One morning we went on patrol. The Rebs were waiting for us in
force where we were told they wouldn't be. It turned into a dog
fight before we got out and a dozen of my boys died for nothing."

He looked down at his missing leg. "And I lost this."

Sherman nodded in sympathy. "McClellen was a fool. He got
close enough to Richmond to see the church spires, lost his nerve
and Lee drove him out of Virginia like a frightened puppy."

Thanks to Sherman's camaraderie, it looked like Chapman
now was on our side just as surely as if he walked into a recruiting
station and volunteered.

I repeated my question, "MacKenzie?"

"I don't know," Chapman admitted. "We, the staff, I mean,
aren't told names. They're all just numbers. The administration
knows their names I suppose but nobody ever uses 'em."

"So, for all you know he could be number ten or number
hundred and four."

He nodded glumly. He wanted to help and failed.

That left us with no alternative but a long search that might
take more time than we had.

And then my brilliant wife spoke up.

"The man we're looking for has a mangled hand that's missing two fingers," she said. "Does that help?"

Chapman brightened. "Yes, Ma'am. I've only seen him once or twice, but I think know I where he is." He nodded toward a door off the entrance. "All the keys are in there, labeled by number. He's thirty-four, I'm pretty sure."

He propelled himself toward the room. Despite his crutch he moved quickly, and I jerked my head at Penny to follow him. Even with Chapman's cooperative attitude, we didn't know who else was in the asylum and I didn't want to take the chance that he might warn someone, especially if the asylum had a telephonic device like my own.

While Chapman searched for the key, I whispered to Sherman, "How did you know he lost his leg in the war? It could have been anywhere."

"When you see a man about his age with a missing limb you can bet that's what happened," he said. "There are so many of 'em, too damn many."

After a minute or two, waving two keys attached to a black iron ring, Chapman hobbled out of the room with Penny at his side. Penny shook his head to signal there'd been no trouble.

"The man you're looking for is downstairs where they keep the troubled ones," he said, turning toward another heavy door at the far end of the entryway.

"I thought they were all troubled or they wouldn't be here," Dana said.

"You put it like that, and I suppose it's true," he said. "But some are worse than others, a lot worse."

"Wait!" I said. "Who else besides you and the patients are here?"

He pivoted on his crutch to face me. "Nobody. There's hardly ever more than one of us on duty overnight."

"Really?"

"What can happen?" he said. "All the inmates are secure, too secure if you ask me. It's a shame what goes on here. It wears on me so much I can't sleep sometimes."

He fumbled at the lock with the key, opened the door, found a lantern on a hook, struck a match, lit the lantern and led us down a long flight of stairs, stone or brick, by the feel.

The lower level was enormous. While the ground level where we entered seemed divided into smaller rooms, the underground level was like a huge cave. Although Chapman's light added to ours, when we reached the bottom of the stairs all we could see was a long line of doors with small openings about head high crossed with iron bars. The end of the line was invisible to us, somewhere in the darkness. Even the wall on the opposite side of the doors was too far away to be clearly illuminated. It felt as if we entered a medieval dungeon that was at least ten or fifteen degrees colder than upstairs.

There was a peculiar noise I couldn't identify until I realized that it was a chorus of moans and cries from the poor souls trapped in the bowels of this place, imprisoned behind the long line of locked doors.

"If you hate it so much why do you work here?" Dana asked, her nose crinkling at the smell.

"How much work do you think is for a cripple?" There was a lifetime of bitterness in his voice. "If I could find anything else, I'd take it. I truly hate this place."

I had an idea but put off doing anything about it until we found Mac.

Chapman counted the doors as we passed. He stopped at one that looked like any of the others, put the lantern on the floor, inserted the key into the lock and opened the door. I expected a ghostly creaking, but it opened quietly and smoothly, the hinges well oiled.

"Here," he said, holding his lantern high. "You'd best harden your hearts 'cause you won't like what's in there. I don't come down here much and I never get used to it."

I stepped into the room – cell is a better description – and nearly fell flat on my face. I didn't see the two steps from the door to the floor. The stench was vile. I have no words to describe it, so bad it made my eyes water.

My lantern revealed very little in the darkness of the cell. We heard the sound of rats scrabbling away from the light and saw a small pile of rotting straw against the wall opposite the door, probably what passed for a place to sleep.

Raising the lantern higher I turned in a full circle to examine the rest of the cell and saw nothing more except a slop bucket tilted on its side.

"Where is he?"

Chapman stepped to my side and pointed with his lantern. "There."

I missed it before in the shadows, a small pile of rags against the wall next to the straw. Not sure what Chapman meant, I walked to it and got down on one knee.

It was Mac.

Chapter Sixty-Eight

I looked hard to find the man I knew. He was dressed in rags that I wouldn't have used to rub down a horse, and I doubt that he weighed a hundred pounds. His hair and beard were long and tangled.

He looked up as I knelt beside him but there was nothing there, not even a brief flash of recognition.

Ignoring the lice crawling in his beard, I put my arms around him to lift him to his feet.

Chapman said, "Wait!" and got down on his knees at my side.

"He's probably chained around the waist," he said. "Most of them are down here."

He felt along what I now saw was an iron band around Mac's waist, attached to a thick chain that ran into the wall. He found what he was looking for, inserted another key and the band sprang open.

When I lifted Mac to his feet, I could feel the bones in his emaciated body. Penny moved to the other side and we each put one of Mac's arms across our shoulders so he wouldn't have to support himself. I am certain he would have collapsed if he tried.

With Dana and Chapman holding lanterns and leading the way, followed by me and Penny, with Mac between us, and Sherman last, we cautiously made our way up the uneven stairs. Mac groaned twice as his head lolled back. I didn't know if we were hurting him or it was the unaccustomed movement. Either way we could not stop. We had to get out of this place.

My coach waited outside where we left it. When we boosted Mac inside, he groaned again. I steeled myself to ignore it. Penny climbed up beside the driver, a trustworthy man who had been with me for years.

After Dana and Sherman got in the coach, I turned to Chapman.

"You have a choice to make," I said. "Come with us and I can promise you a better life. I don't have time to explain. You'll just have to trust me. But I give you my word that you will have honest work to do at a good wage with opportunity for advancement. What you make of yourself is up to you, but at least you'll have your pride again."

I put my hands on his shoulders and looked him in the eye. "We have no time for you to think about it. Decide now."

He didn't hesitate. "I'm with you." He motioned at the coach boot. "I can ride back here. I've been in worse." He lifted the leather cover, tossed his crutch into the boot, and nimbly followed it, lowering the cover behind him.

I climbed into the coach. Mac was lying across one seat, curled in the fetal position with Sherman and Dana facing him on the other seat. I squeezed in next to Dana, reached outside and smacked the roof with my palm, the signal for the driver to get moving.

As the coach lurched forward, I let out a sigh. Mac was free.

Chapter Sixty-Nine

Mac was in no condition to be left alone, even for just the night. Instead of taking him to the apartment I rented, I directed the driver to our home, dropping Sherman off on the way.

Standing on the dark street in front of Sherman's townhouse, I was overwhelmed with gratitude and seized the general's hand.

Anticipating what I was about to say, Sherman issued a warning: "Stone, don't be too grateful. We're not clear yet. When they find out they're missing a patient and an attendant, they'll start investigating. As far as we know, there was no one around to see what we did, but they might track down Chapman, who could lead them to us. We've got to keep the initiative and that means confronting the asylum director as soon as possible. We'll tell him what we did, why we did it and defy him to do anything about it. We'll put the fear of God in him and make sure he understands that if he doesn't keep his mouth shut, he'll be in so much trouble it will make hell look like a holiday.

"And one more thing: however this plays out, it's vital that we get a statement out of him saying that MacKenzie was released in your care. That should be enough to put us free of penalty and guarantee his safety if there's an investigation."

As it turned out, the general called it exactly. Faced with the threat of my wealth and the resources that come with it, along with Sherman's reputation as a merciless foe, plus our promise not to go public with what we saw and heard in the asylum, we got everything we wanted. Except for Mac we didn't see or hear that much, but the asylum's administration didn't know that.

Maybe I should have tried to do something for the poor souls still trapped there, but I did not. Getting Mac out and keeping him out was my only goal. To make that happen, I would have made a deal with the devil.

In a way, I suppose I did.

Entering our home, I noticed that while Chapman took in everything with wide eyes he was not as surprised as I thought he'd be.

"It didn't take long before I figured out you weren't really Sherman's aide," he explained. "I remember how it was in the army. You never looked to him for approval of what you said or did the way most aides would. Most of 'em wouldn't blow their noses without permission."

Turning to Dana, he added, "Once I figured that out, I began to wonder if you were really Clara Barton, especially once I got a good look at you in the lamplight downstairs by the cells."

So much for our clever ruse. At least it got us in.

"If you knew we were lying why did you help us?" Dana asked.

"You were my chance to get out that place," he said. "I knew I'd never have a better one, especially after you made that offer."

Chapman was exhausted, probably emotionally as much as physically. He leaned on his crutch so heavily that I told him to sit down before he collapsed. Falling onto a love seat in the parlor, he explained why he took the chance without knowing anything about us.

"It was the way you acted. You were trying to rescue somebody you cared for. I could tell that by the gentle way you treated him. I told myself you couldn't be that bad. And I was pretty sure you wouldn't leave me there to tell the constables what happened, even if Sherman was the only name I knew, and they'd probably never believe it anyway. Imagine my story: 'Clara Barton, General Sherman, his aide and a Pinkerton man drove up in a coach and pounded on the door until I let them in. They rushed right past me, kidnapped a sick man from his cell and took him away.' Once they heard that they'd probably throw *me* in a cell."

"Anyhow, what with the expensive coach and the way you were dressed I knew you were well off and had the resources to help me if I helped you. When you made the offer, I knew I'd guessed right. Besides, I didn't think for a minute that General Sherman would associate himself with a pack of scoundrels. As long as he was with you, I was never afraid."

Penny was impressed and said so. "That was pretty clear thinking under the circumstances. You're mostly right, I 'spose, though after tonight we'd probably qualify as scoundrels. Tell you the truth, I kind of like it."

I told Chapman he could spend the night with us. When I gave him one hundred and fifty dollars to get by until he started working again, in his exhausted condition his emotions almost overwhelmed him. He said it was twice his monthly wage at the asylum. When I inquired, he added that no one there knew or cared where he lived, and he was always paid in cash so it seemed unlikely that he could be traced.

Just to be sure, I instructed him to go back to where he lived in the morning, gather his belongings as quickly as possible and change residences. I gave him the address of a small but respectable hotel I knew would take him in for free because I was one of the owners. I told him to take his meals in his room and stay out of sight until he heard from me. Penny volunteered to go with him in case someone from the asylum, or worse, the law, was waiting at his residence, though from what Chapman said it didn't seem likely.

As I suspected, he turned out to be a hard-working man who never had the chance to show it, at least not since he lost his leg more than twenty-five years earlier. I suspect that in his Michigan regiment he was just the kind of sergeant Mac and I always wanted in our command. Over time, he became a valuable employee, married, and rose to become one of Cartwright's assistants in my shipping business.

When he returned, Penny volunteered to clean up Mac, which was no small task, given his filthy condition. Rather than risk lice infestation of our living quarters, we carried him down to the big tub in the basement where the staff washed our clothes.

Two hours later, Penny reported success, but not without a lot of hard work.

"I shaved his hair and beard and rubbed him all over with kerosene to kill the lice," Penny said. "After that I had to refill the tub three times to get all the filth off him. It was like bathing a baby, not that I've had much experience in that line. He let me do anything I wanted and never said a word. Never really looked at me. I tossed the rags he was wearing, in your furnace and lit 'em up."

Smoothing out his mustache with thumb and index finger, which by now I recognized as a prelude to addressing a difficult subject, he added, "I hate to bring it up, but you saw it, too. He's in a bad way. We can hope for the best and maybe all the expensive doctors you're planning to get can do something, but...

well, I just don't know."

I didn't say it, but those were my thoughts, too. We got Mac out of the asylum, but he still was locked in the prison of his own mind.

When the physician, William Bowers, who also was my personal physician, examined Mac the next day he found nothing wrong with his body that rest, care and decent food wouldn't fix. In his opinion, Mac hadn't been abused as much as neglected. As for his mental condition, he admitted that Mac's troubles were beyond his expertise and recommended that we call in a specialist.

Two days later, we moved him into the apartment, transferring him in an ambulance on a stretcher, careful to keep his face hidden in case anyone was watching. I arranged for male nurses to stay with him in shifts, so that he was never alone. I wanted strong men in case Mac became violent. I swore them to secrecy and promised a bonus if they kept their word.

Over the next two months, while Mac gained weight and looked healthier, nothing else changed. What seemed like an endless array of specialists examined, probed, and attempted to treat the patient, but none were successful.

I was usually allowed to remain in the room during the examinations, figuring that as his oldest friend my presence might be comforting, but it didn't make any difference. He never seemed to recognize me or Sherman, who stopped to see him several times.

A few times he tried to speak, or perhaps thought he was speaking, but it resembled a baby's gibberish more than human speech. After a while, he stopped even that.

He also was given to nightmares. Many times, his screams awakened anyone within hearing and he always remained agitated for the rest of the night.

Yet, he heard us when we talked to him because he usually responded to simple requests and commands, although not always. If he was asked to sit up, for example, he would, but his movements were slow, as if he was under water, and he never seemed fully engaged in anything or anyone. Several times we found him with tears running down his face. Whatever the reason, I am afraid it was not to be found in the world we knew.

He was trapped in a kind of living death. I did not know how to save him from it.

Chapter Seventy

Mac's physicians agreed that he might benefit from more
time outdoors, somewhere in the country with sunshine, fresh
air and quiet.

I know they suggested it because everything else failed, but it
still made sense to me. What did we have to lose?

My lawyer also warned me that continuing to keep Mac exclu-
sively in our care might put me on shaky legal ground, especially
upon Mac's or my own death. Despite the asylum turning him
over to me, and having the documents to prove it, I was not
family and did not have the rights of family. All they knew was
that he suddenly appeared in my care and I possessed the means
to provide for him in a way they could not. Although I am sure
they were relieved to let me take the responsibility, one day they
might justifiably claim to having been kept in the dark.

My lawyer was concerned that while the law was vague and the
circumstances unusual, there could be trouble later. If anything
happened to me, I didn't want Dana to be burdened with it.

Before making any changes, my brilliant wife came up with

an idea we had to try. I wanted to boot myself in the backside for not thinking of it earlier.

"I think we should have Florida Tunstall come here, especially now that you say he looks more like his old self," she said. "They were supposed to be in love, after all. He might respond to her a way he wouldn't respond to anyone else, even you."

And so we arranged for Mac's fiancée to come to New York. Eager and brave, she lived with us while spending virtually all her waking with Mac, holding his hand, reading to him, talking and sometimes just sitting quietly beside his bed. I saw her weeping a few times when she left his room at the end of a day. I didn't blame her. Sometimes I felt like it myself.

After six weeks nothing had changed except that she was haggard and exhausted, verging on a breakdown of her own.

Once again, Dana stepped up. "Danny, I know it was my idea, but it isn't working," she announced, holding my hand one night after we'd climbed into bed. She didn't have to say what "it's" was. "She can't go on like this much longer."

"I know, I just haven't been able to face it," I agreed. "I'll talk to her in the morning."

It wasn't a long conversation. "You need to get on with your life," I said. "It's not helping Mac and it's killing you."

She protested, at first, but didn't have the strength to put up much resistance and finally agreed. I took her to the train station three days later.

As her bags were loaded into her private compartment, she seized my hand, her eyes welling with tears.

"I can't tell you how grateful I am," she said. "You've done everything that could be done, more than I could even imagine. You even gave Ranald and me another chance, one I never thought we'd get."

A quick hug and she was off. I never saw her again.

Not long after, I agreed to a change in location for Mac. He had a brother, Morris, and sister, Harriet, still living. With their permission, I rented a house on the village square in Morristown, New Jersey, a country town where Mac's family lived for a time when he was a child before I joined the family. Harriet and I agreed that revisiting a childhood place might help, or at least make him more comfortable, and she agreed to join him there.

Despite our hopes, Mac's condition worsened to where he couldn't feed himself or take care of basic needs. He occasionally eluded Harriet and wandered off on his own, which terrified her. Several times he was found lost and agitated inside the large rambling house, and twice he was found in a similar state outdoors, once more than a mile away.

It was too much for Harriet to handle by herself. I agreed to move him again, this time to a cousin's house on the corner of Lafayette and Henderson Avenues in New Brighton, a village on the north shore of Staten Island, which added the sea and salt air to countryside and sunshine.

When Harriet again agreed to accompany her bother, to lighten her responsibility I hired two attendants to care for him. By then Mac's condition deteriorated so much I doubted that he was even aware of the move.

I visited Mac when I could but there seemed no point to it. My old friend never recognized me, and my visits became more and more infrequent.

On January 19, 1889, I received the news that I had long expected. The telegram was from his brother, Morris, and also was sent to the U.S. Army Adjutant General's Office in Washington. It was brutally brief. At this point there wasn't anything left to say: "General Ranald S. MacKenzie died this morning."

Perhaps it sounds cruel, but as much as I dreaded it Mac's death was a relief. I believe that Harriet and Morris felt the same way. The man we knew died a long time ago.

No one except me is alive to remember, but it is just possible that Mac committed suicide. Perhaps I should have been disturbed at the thought, but I was not. I never really tried to find out the truth. What did it matter?

I knew there was a weapon in the house, which was not unusual in those days. So many guns of all sorts were manufactured during the war that even a generation later it was common to have at least one around somewhere. This one was an old service revolver kept loaded and in good condition by Mac's brother. Everyone knew its place in an old *chiffonier* in the hallway, although no one thought much about it.

Only one of the attendants was on duty at the time of Mac's death. He was so docile for so long that vigilance slipped. I did not blame anyone.

When I paid off the attendant a week after Mac's death, having no more use for his services, I asked about the events of that day, assuring him that he was in no way responsible. He said that he was stretching his legs along the shoreline about fifty yards from the house when he heard what might have been a shot, although he wasn't sure. The sound was faint and could have come from anywhere. He'd forgotten about the old gun in the house and was not alarmed. By the time he returned to the house thirty minutes later, Morris and Harriet had already found Mac's body in his bedroom, just down the hall from where the revolver was kept in the *chiffonier*.

I have heard a lot of gunfire in my life and know that everything from water and trees to rolling countryside distorts sound and direction. Did it come from the house? Was it even a gun shot?

The attendant said that Morris and Harriet did not allow him to help with Mac's body, behavior I found peculiar, although people often did strange things when crushed by grief and stress. Perhaps they felt that caring for Mac themselves was the last tender service they could do for him?

Suicide had a stigma in those days. It still does. To avoid scandal, it would not have been difficult for Mac's brother and sister to convince a caring physician not to reveal that Mac took his own life.

He was buried at West Point in a closed-casket ceremony.

In his condition it is hard to imagine that Mac killed himself. But was there a moment, a sudden flash of awareness in the darkness of his damaged mind, when he took his last decisive action?

I do not know.

Chapter Seventy-One

What I most feared has happened.

I have run out of time.

They tell me I had a stroke that left me unconscious for more than twenty-four hours and paralyzed along the left side of my body.

I have no memory of the stroke, but I know that death is close. I feel it coming. A minute, an hour, a day, certainly no more than that.

I have failed by taking too long. I am too feeble to get out of bed or even feed myself, much less see that what I have written is somehow made public. My voice is such a weak croak that no one can understand me.

Writing these last few lines takes what little strength I have left. I don't know what will happen now. Will anyone see what I have written? Will anyone care to even look?

Mac, I am so sorry. I did the best I could.

A Look At: Sam Houston: The Historical Fiction Trilogy

Vividly evoking the triumphs and tragedies of Sam Houston's life.

A war hero, statesman, maker of marathon speeches, prodigious drinker, brawler, and leader of the Texas revolution, Sam Houston was also a peacemaker and diplomat. Robert Wisehart tells Sam Houston's story as a grand, coursing adventure of the early nineteenth century, placing the reader amid the swirling currents of the times.

He served as governor of Tennessee and Texas and as president of the independent Republic of Texas. His two contrasting father figures were a Cherokee chief, who had adopted him as a runaway teen, and President Andrew Jackson, who later assigned Lieutenant Houston with the task of moving the Cherokee off their cherished ancestral lands in the Southeast.

A gripping story of a crafty leader whose faults sometimes overwhelm his considerable virtues.

Sam Houston: The Historical Fiction Trilogy includes – Born For The Storm, The Rising and The Lion At Bay.

AVAILABLE NOW ON KINDLE

About the Author

The author of eight novels, Robert Wisehart was born in Indianapolis, Indiana, and now is fortunate enough to live in Santa Fe, New Mexico. He worked for many years as an award-winning reporter and columnist for newspapers in Florida, North Carolina, Louisiana and Northern and Southern California, plus occasional flirtations with radio and television as an on-air commentator.

Wisehart and his wife, Dana, have been married for a lifetime and intend to make it a very long lifetime indeed. Their two sons, Marc and Carl, live in New York City.